THE
DARLING DAHLIAS
AND THE
NAKED LADIES

THE
DARLING DAHLIAS
AND THE
NAKED LADIES

Susan Wittig Albert

BERKLEY PRIME CRIME, NEW YORK

S

THE BERKLEY PUBLISHING GROUP
Published by the Penguin Group
Penguin Group (USA) Inc.
375 Hudson Street, New York, New York 10014, USA
Penguin Group (Canada), 90 Eglinton Avenue East, Suite 700, Toronto, Ontario M4P 2Y3, Canada
(a division of Pearson Penguin Canada Inc.)
Penguin Books Ltd., 80 Strand, London WC2R 0RL, England
Penguin Group Ireland, 25 St. Stephen's Green, Dublin 2, Ireland (a division of Penguin Books Ltd.)
Penguin Group (Australia), 250 Camberwell Road, Camberwell, Victoria 3124, Australia
(a division of Pearson Australia Group Pty. Ltd.)
Penguin Books India Pvt. Ltd., 11 Community Centre, Panchsheel Park, New Delhi—110 017, India
Penguin Group (NZ), 67 Apollo Drive, Rosedale, Auckland 0632, New Zealand
(a division of Pearson New Zealand Ltd.)
Penguin Books (South Africa) (Pty.) Ltd., 24 Sturdee Avenue, Rosebank, Johannesburg 2196,
South Africa

Penguin Books Ltd., Registered Offices: 80 Strand, London WC2R 0RL, England

This book is an original publication of The Berkley Publishing Group.

This is a work of fiction. Names, characters, places, and incidents either are the product of the author's imagination or are used fictitiously, and any resemblance to actual persons, living or dead, business establishments, events, or locales is entirely coincidental. The publisher does not have any control over and does not assume any responsibility for author or third-party websites or their content.

PUBLISHER'S NOTE: The recipes contained in this book are to be followed exactly as written. The publisher is not responsible for your specific health or allergy needs that may require medical supervision. The publisher is not responsible for any adverse reaction to the recipes contained in this book.

Copyright © 2011 by Susan Wittig Albert.
Interior text design by Tiffany Estreicher.

FIRST EDITION: July 2011

Library of Congress Cataloging-in-Publication Data

Albert, Susan Wittig.
    The Darling Dahlias and the naked ladies / Susan Wittig Albert. – 1st ed.
      p. cm.
    ISBN 978-0-425-24128-8 (hardcover)
    1. Gardening—Societies, etc.—Fiction.   2. Women gardeners—Fiction.   3. Nineteen
thirties—Fiction.   4. Alabama—Fiction.   I. Title.
    PS3551.L2637D39 2011
813'.54—dc22   2011009395

PRINTED IN THE UNITED STATES OF AMERICA

10   9   8   7   6   5   4   3   2   1

To garden clubs everywhere,
with grateful thanks for
making your communities more beautiful.
The Darling Dahlias and I send you our love.

Author's Note

I love writing about real places. The little town that is the setting for this series is fictional, but it is located in a very real place: in southern Alabama, in the wooded hills west of Monroeville and east of the Alabama River, about seventy miles north of Mobile. You will find a map of Darling on the series website: www.darlingdahlias.com. You will also find other items of interest there, including: Depression-era recipes and household tips, some historical background of the 1930s (the period in which the series takes place), and information about Southern gardens. I'll be adding new material frequently, so please bookmark the site and visit often.

I also love language, and in this series, as in all my books, I've tried to use the language of the people and their times. This historical series includes language and social practices appropriate to the early 1930s in the rural South. For instance, the characters use the terms "colored," "colored folk," and "Negro" when they refer to African Americans, and the attitudes of white people toward their black fellow citizens reflect the conscious and unconscious racism of the times. To write truthfully about this time and place requires the use of language and ideas that may be offensive to some readers. Thank you for understanding that I intend no offense.

As I work on these books, I especially find myself loving the spirit of the times. The 1930s were terribly difficult years, because so many people were facing daunting challenges that resemble some of the economic challenges we face today. But people didn't lose hope. They had faith in themselves, in their families, and in their communities, and they did whatever they could to help themselves. I am touched by this spirit as I read the newspapers and books published in those years, and as I remember my mother and my aunts talking about the "tough times" they lived through in the decade before I was born. Ordinary people were tough and resilient enough to weather extraordinary challenge, and I hope to represent that spirit in these books.

Susan Wittig Albert

November 1, 1930
Darling, Alabama

Dear Reader,

When the author of The Darling Dahlias and the Cucumber Tree asked us if she could write a second book about us, we were thrilled. It's not every garden club that gets a book written about it, much less two books! But we agreed because we liked the way Mrs. Albert gave you all the ins and outs of what happened in The Darling Dahlias and the Cucumber Tree. Mr. Dickens naturally didn't print the full story in the Dispatch, so lots of people in town didn't know all the details and were very surprised when they found out. In fact, some people were so surprised that they tried to boycott the book when Mr. Mann put a stack of them out for sale in front of the Mercantile, and Mrs. Lima was heard to say that she didn't know how she was going to hold up her head in this community, now that everybody knew what had gone on in the back room at Lima's Drugs. We're sorry about that, but we do believe that Mr. Lima will toe the straight and narrow from here on out, and that Mrs. Lima won't have a thing to fret about. Everybody understands that people make mistakes. Live and learn, as the old folks say.

Anyway, when Mrs. Albert learned that we were in the middle of another mystery and asked us if she could look over our shoulders and write everything down as it happened, we thought it was a good idea. Several of us were especially wondering about the pair of ladies who had moved into Miss Hamer's house on Camellia Street, the one with all the naked *ladies in the front yard. And if you don't know what naked ladies are, well, you can read this book and find out. We won't tell you anything more about that, since we don't want to spoil the story for you.*

And it's true that we need stories these days, don't you think? Times have been hard since the Crash, people are out of work all over the country, and it seems like too many of us are scraping the bottom of the barrel. But stories—even when they include a few folks who don't measure up by the Golden Rule—help us to forget our troubles for a little while and learn something about people and the silly (and sometimes dangerous) things they do.

So we hope this story brightens your day a little. And speaking of bright, Aunt Hetty Little wants us to remind you of something we have said before but which bears saying again. We keep our faces to the sun so we can't see the shadows, which is why we plant sunflowers and marigolds and cosmos in amongst the collards and sweet potatoes and okra in our gardens.

We hope you will, too.

Sincerely,
Elizabeth Lacy, president, The Darling Dahlias
Ophelia Snow, vice president & secretary
Verna Tidwell, treasurer

The Darling Dahlias Club Roster, October 1930

Aunt Hetty Little, oldest member of the club, town matriarch, and lover of gladiolas.

Myra May Mosswell, owner of the Darling Diner and an operator in the Darling Telephone Exchange. Lives in the flat over the diner. Has a vegetable garden.

Lucy Murphy, the newest member of the club. Lucy is married to Ralph Murphy and lives on a small farm on Jericho Road. Just planted a peach orchard.

Miss Dorothy Rogers, Darling's librarian. Miss Rogers knows the Latin name of every plant and insists that everybody else does, too. Lives in Magnolia Manor.

Beulah Trivette, artistically talented owner/operator of Beulah's Beauty Bower, where small groups of Dahlias gather almost every day. Loves cabbage roses and other big, floppy flowers.

Alice Ann Walker, bank cashier. Her husband, Arnold, is disabled. Loves spring-flowering bulbs.

THE
DARLING DAHLIAS
AND THE
NAKED LADIES

ONE

The Naked Ladies

Elizabeth Lacy opened the small shed behind the Dahlias' clubhouse and stowed the rakes, hoes, and spades inside. She closed the door, took off her floppy-brimmed hat, and turned to Verna Tidwell.

"The garden looks really swell, don't you think?" she said, surveying the result of the afternoon's hard work.

"Well, it ought to," Verna retorted crisply, stripping off her green cotton gardening gloves. Her brown hair was short and combed straight back from her face in a characteristically no-fluff style. "We've poured a lot of time and sweat into this place over the past few months. How many Dahlias were out here this afternoon, slaving in the sunshine? I counted ten. That's a good turnout."

Lizzy stretched down and touched her toes, working out the kink in her back that came from kneeling in front of the phlox bed for two hours, pulling weeds. "Ten is right. Voleen Johnson said she had company, and Ophelia's boy was playing in the baseball tournament at the fairgrounds. Oh, and Myra

May had to work the switchboard because Violet is up in Memphis." She straightened up and stretched her hands over her head. "Her younger sister just had a baby and Violet's helping out. Myra May said the sister isn't doing too well."

Verna stuck her gloves in the pocket of her gardening skirt, wrinkling her nose distastefully. "Have you ever noticed that Voleen always manages to have out-of-town company on one of our work days? If you ask me, I think she invites them on purpose, so she doesn't have to come over here and risk breaking one of her fingernails, all pretty and polished up."

"You might be right," Lizzy said, in a noncommittal tone. She didn't like to criticize other people because you never knew when they might be criticizing you, and they might not be as nice about it as you were. But it was definitely true that Mrs. George E. Pickett Johnson rarely lent her perfectly manicured hands to the task when it came to the Dahlias' garden. Or her own beautiful garden, for that matter, since she had a colored man who did all the work for her. The George E. Picketts were among Darling's hereditary nobility and Mrs. Pickett's garden was a showplace, with never a leaf or a twig out of place.

"We managed all right without her," Lizzy added, looking around appreciatively. "The garden hasn't looked so pretty for quite a while. Mrs. Blackstone couldn't do much in her last years."

The small white frame house the garden club had inherited from Mrs. Dahlia Blackstone sat fairly close to Camellia Street. Behind the white picket fence out front, the yard was mostly hydrangeas and azaleas and roses. But behind the house, a large garden swept down toward a tall magnolia tree, a clump of woods, and a small, clear spring smothered in ferns, bog iris, and pitcher plants. This garden had once been so beautiful that it had been written up in newspapers all over the South, and as far away as New Orleans. But as Mrs.

Blackstone grew older and less able to care for it, the plants had become disheveled and shaggy, in the ragamuffin way of gardens when there's nobody to pull weeds or deadhead or prune the roses or dig and separate the perennials or even mow the grass regularly.

Then Mrs. Blackstone had died and left her house and the garden to the garden club she had founded, whose grateful members quickly renamed themselves the Dahlias in her honor. Then they (well, most of them, anyway) pulled on their garden gloves and picked up their rakes and hoes and trowels and clippers and set about restoring the garden to its former glory. They had yanked the smothering weeds—the dog fennel, henbit, ground ivy, and (the biggest garden bully of all!) the Johnson grass—out of the curving perennial borders, so that the phlox, larkspur, iris, asters, and Shasta daisies could take a deep breath. They had dug and divided and replanted Mrs. Blackstone's much-loved lilies: Easter lilies, spider lilies, oxblood lilies, and her favorite orange ditch lilies. They had untangled the cardinal climber and crossvine and honeysuckle on the fence and repaired the trellises so the mandevilla and confederate jasmine could stretch up and out. They gently disciplined the hibiscus and the dozens of roses, including the climbers, the teas, the ramblers, the shrubs, and a charming yellow Lady Banks. Yet to be done: the cleanup of the woodland and spring at the foot of the garden, where Miss Rogers thought they ought to put the bog garden. And every time a Dahlia set foot on the place, she saw something else that needed to be done, such as painting the shed, or repairing another trellis, or planting a ground cover over a bare spot. Gardens, of course, are a labor of love, and love—and its labor—is never-ending.

"It is gorgeous, Lizzy," Verna agreed. Even she (by nature a wary, critical person who always saw the flaws in a thing while everybody else was still admiring it) had to admit that the Dahlias were well on the way to restoring Mrs. Blackstone's garden to its former glory. And the only money they had spent on the project was the fifty cents they gave Old Zeke to cut the grass and trim along the flower beds every other week.

Which had been a very good thing (as Verna, the club's treasurer, knew very well), because when the Dahlias inherited the house, they were nearly broke. Mrs. Blackstone had left them enough to pay the property taxes for several years, relieving some of Verna's worry. But there was barely enough in the club kitty to keep the lights on, let alone fix the leaks in the roof and replace the plumbing in the bathroom.

And then, glory be and hallelujah! When they dug the holes to plant their Darling Dahlias sign in front of their new clubhouse, the Dahlias had struck silver. That is, they had uncovered the chest of sterling flatware that Mrs. Blackstone's mother (a Cartwright) had buried to keep it from falling into the greedy hands of pillaging Yankees as they stormed through Alabama near the end of the War Between the States. When the Dahlias began to look through the chest, they found, in addition to the sterling, a bracelet set with an old-fashioned square-cut emerald, a pair of pearl teardrop earrings, a diamond ring, and a velvet bag containing ten gold coins: twenty-dollar double eagles, still as perfect as the day they were new-minted.

But the discovery of this buried treasure had resulted in a hot debate about what to do with it. Some wanted to keep everything. After all, the silver, the coins, and the jewelry were heirlooms, and all of it was very beautiful. But Earlynne Biddle had pointed out that these were Cartwright heirlooms and every last Cartwright was dead and gone from this earth and in no position to care about heirlooms. Aunt Hetty Little had pointed out that if the Dahlias kept the silver, the Dahlias would have to polish it, since they couldn't afford a maid to do it for them. And Verna had added that the whole kit and caboodle must be worth a small fortune, and the club needed cash money a whole lot more than it needed heirlooms.

So the Dahlias voted (Mrs. Johnson being the lone dissenter) to sell. Verna and Lizzy took the silver, the gold, and the jewelry to Ettlinger's Jewelry store in Mobile, where it brought enough to fix the leaky roof and repair the plumbing, with some left over. The Dahlias could now face the autumn rains without fear of flooding, they could flush without fear of overflowing, and their savings account in the Darling Savings and Trust was, if not fat, nicely plump. They called it the "Treasure Fund."

"It's hard to believe we've accomplished so much in just five months," Lizzy replied, fanning herself with her hat as they walked around the house toward the front. She felt a justifiable sense of pride. After all, she was president of the club and she'd worked hard to organize the garden project.

"Hot months, too," Verna said. The Dahlias had held the first meeting in their new clubhouse in May, and the summer months in Alabama are not exactly the most comfortable months for outdoor work. But the Dahlias were not delicate Southern belles—most of them, anyway. When it came to gardening, they didn't wilt.

Lizzy pushed her brown hair out of her eyes, put her hat back on, and paused, looking at the large empty lot beside the house. The area had once been Mrs. Blackstone's vegetable garden, with a border of strawberries, two peach trees, and a fig tree in the back. Old Zeke had mowed the weeds for them, but the place still looked straggly and forlorn.

"I've been thinking about this area," she said. "What would you say to turning it back into a vegetable garden— not for just us Dahlias, but for everybody? There are lots of folks in this town who might be willing to trade some garden work for sweet potatoes, carrots, turnips, okra, collards—things that are sure to grow. I'm sure we could get Mr. Norris to bring Racer over and plow the ground early next year." The name of Mr. Norris' horse was a joke, because the old bay gelding was slow as blackstrap molasses in January. But he knew what to do when he was hitched to the business end of a plow, and he and Mr. Norris made a few dollars every spring by plowing gardens.

"Good idea," Verna agreed cautiously, "but what makes you think people will be willing to help? Everybody loves a handout, but when it comes with a rake or hoe attached—" She shrugged.

Lizzy clucked her tongue. "Verna, you are so cynical."

"Just realistic," Verna replied with a chuckle. "Comes from working in the county courthouse. Want to see people at their worst? Sit behind my desk for a day or two."

"Well, the folks who come into Mr. Moseley's law office don't win any happiness prizes," Lizzy retorted. "They only need a lawyer when they're in really bad trouble." Mr. Moseley was one of Darling's three lawyers, and as his secretary, receptionist, and legal assistant, Lizzy had an insider's view into people's problems. Unlike Verna, she had an innate sense of compassion and concern and always tried to put herself in the other person's shoes. "But just because I see the ones who are unhappy or in trouble doesn't mean that everybody in town is like that," she added.

"Maybe not," Verna said, "but at least half of them are. Times are tough. People are scared. They're hanging on for dear life to their jobs or their farms or whatever. If they don't have money, they'll do almost anything to get it. If they have it, they won't spend an extra nickel."

"Well, then," Lizzy said reasonably, "maybe they'll be willing to work for some fresh food—so they can save their nickels."

They had come around the front of the house now. Mrs.

Blackstone's prize azaleas, hydrangeas, and weigelas had finished blooming months before, but the Autumn Joy sedum was gorgeous, next to some red spider lilies that looked like a fireworks display. Lizzy smiled, thinking that while jobs and money and food were definitely important—you couldn't live without them—beauty was important, too. Vegetables could provide a feast for the table, but flowers were a feast for the soul.

"Aren't those lilies pretty?" Lizzy said admiringly. "Or *Lycoris radiata*, as Miss Rogers would say." Miss Rogers, the town librarian and its leading intellectual, always insisted on calling plants by their Latin names, an insistence that drove everybody crazy.

"Yes. But not half as pretty as those naked ladies in front of old Miss Hamer's house." Verna pointed across the street, where a two-story frame house, weathered gray with green shutters and in need of a coat of paint, was fronted by a few rosebushes and a mass of leggy lilies in a rainbow of colors: pumpkin orange, sunshine yellow, sizzling scarlet, as well as the quieter mauve, blush, and white. Verna chuckled and imitated Miss Rogers' high-pitched voice. "*Lycoris squamigera*, girls. 'Naked ladies' is not a respectable name for a plant."

"My mother calls them 'resurrection lilies,'" Lizzy said, and laughed a little. "When I was a girl, I always thought they were sort of magical, the way the leaves died in the summer and then the stalks poked up out of the ground, all of a sudden, and in the next day or two, here came the blooms—poof!" She waved her hand. "Maybe the new people will clean up the front yard a little," she added. "Those naked ladies deserve a place to show off. You can hardly see them for all that grass and weeds."

"The new people?" Verna asked, raising her eyebrows. "You mean, somebody has moved in with old Miss Hamer?"

Miss Julia Hamer had to be eighty if she was a day and

probably older, although nobody knew for sure, except possibly Bessie Bloodworth, the town's unofficial historian and genealogist, who knew everybody's family tree as well as she knew every branch of the flowering dogwood just outside her kitchen window. Bessie, who lived next door to the Dahlias' clubhouse, had written up Miss Hamer's family story in the collection of local histories she had gathered years before. Miss Hamer's father had been among Darling's early settlers, and the old woman had lived in the house on Camellia Street, across from Mrs. Blackstone and Bessie Bloodworth, since long before Lizzy was born.

There were other women in town who didn't go out much, but as a recluse, Miss Hamer without a doubt took the cake. She hadn't been to church for forty years, which was scandal enough to raise all the Darling eyebrows, and when the Presbyterian, Methodist, and Baptist preachers made their annual round of visits to inquire about the state of her eternal soul, the door was always shut in their faces, and not very politely, either. Miss Hamer's colored maid, DessaRae (an aunt of Lizzy's mother's maid, Sally-Lou), took the weekly grocery list to Hancock's Groceries, but the household's milk, eggs, and ice were of course delivered right to the door and the bills regularly paid by mail. Old Zeke was employed to mow and trim the yard twice a year, not often enough to keep it neat but just enough to keep the weeds from taking over. And if Miss Hamer sat outside on a warm summer evening, as most folks did in Darling, she sat in her daddy's old pine rocker on the back porch, where she couldn't be seen because the backyard was entirely enclosed by a holly hedge so dense that not even the neighborhood children could peek through it. Nobody except Bessie Bloodworth, Doc Roberts, and Dessa-Rae had so much as laid eyes on the old lady for a very long time, except as a pale shadow moving slowly behind the drawn window shades in the evening, after the kerosene lamps were lit.

And now she was no longer living alone.

"They moved in last Saturday," Lizzy replied, in answer to Verna's question. "Two ladies. Miss Hamer's niece and her friend, Miss Lake. Miss Jamison—that's the niece—is doing some legal business with Mr. Moseley. He's handling the sale of her house back in Illinois, and he's been corresponding with her. I met her when she came into the office right after she and her friend arrived, and she's been back a time or two." Lizzy wrinkled her nose. "She's kind of a cool customer."

"Two women, moving into Miss Hamer's house?" Verna said, shaking her head incredulously. "Don't you find that a little surprising, Liz? After all, she's lived by herself—with DessaRae to help out, of course—for decades."

Lizzy shrugged. "Miss Jamison told Mr. Moseley that her aunt invited them. Maybe Miss Hamer needs more help than she's getting from DessaRae, who has a bad back, Sally-Lou says. And Miss Jamison *is* family." Which of course explained it, Lizzy thought, since family usually pitched in to help when things got difficult.

"Well, I'm sure there's room," Verna said in a practical tone. "That house must have at least three bedrooms upstairs. So you've met them. What are they like?"

Lizzy raised her eyebrows. "Well, I haven't met Miss Lake, so I couldn't say about her. But when it comes to Miss Jamison, you'd really have to see her to believe—"

But just at that moment, the front door of the house opened and a woman came out onto the porch. She was dressed fit to kill in a stylish fire-engine red dress with a dropped waist and a pleated skirt that came just to the knee. A filmy red scarf was wrapped several times around her neck, the ends flowing loose. A chic red felt hat with a floppy red bow on one side perched on her platinum blond hair. She was wearing black gloves and red suede high-heeled shoes with four-inch French heels and narrow ankle straps, and carried a red-and-black pouch handbag big enough to stuff a live chicken into.

"That's her," Lizzy said. "Miss Jamison."

"Jeepers," Verna muttered, staring.

The woman came down the steps, looked up and saw them, and gave a little wave before she turned away. Even from a distance, it could be seen that Miss Jamison's face and eyes were heavily made up, that her mouth was painted bright red, and that she was generously endowed in the bosom department. Very generously.

But as Lizzy waved and smiled in return, she couldn't help thinking that, unless Darling's newest resident changed her style, she was going to find it difficult to fit into the local scene. For one thing, while one or two of the smartest ladies might wear a red dress and makeup to an evening party, particularly around the winter holidays, red was not considered an appropriate choice for afternoon shopping. And nobody—not even the younger women—wore that much makeup, ever. If Lizzy knew anything about the residents of Darling, she'd bet dollars to doughnuts that Miss Jamison would cause a titanic stir in Hancock's Groceries or Mann's Mercantile or Lima's Drugs, wherever she was going. In that red dress, she would be as noticeable as a big brown June bug in a plate of grits. Tongues would be wagging around Darling's supper tables tonight.

Verna's eyes were wide. "Jamison?" She turned to Lizzy. "Is that the name she's using?"

"Well, yes. Nona Jean Jamison. As I said, she's Miss Hamer's niece. She—"

"I heard what you said. But Nona Jean Jamison has another name, Liz. She is Lorelei LaMotte. *Lorelei LaMotte!* She's a Broadway star! A vaudeville dancer!"

Lizzy frowned doubtfully. "Are you sure? She didn't say a

word about a dancing career or being in vaudeville or any-thing like that. What Miss Jamison told Mr. Moseley was that her mother was Miss Hamer's younger sister and that she grew up over in Monroeville and visited here in Darling. But that was years and years ago. She said she'd never been back since she was a little girl. She came here from Chicago—one of the suburbs, actually."

"She didn't mention being Lorelei LaMotte?"

"Nope." Lizzy shook her head. "If you ask me, she's had a rough life, Verna. She's definitely well preserved and still very pretty, but up close, you can tell that she is definitely looking over her shoulder at forty. I'm not doubting your word, but if she's a dancer, she—"

"Doubt my word?" Verna was sputtering. "I am *right*, Liz, and I have a souvenir playbill to prove it. A photograph of Lorelei LaMotte, nearly naked, with her actual signature on it! I'd know that face and figure anywhere. She's the naughty half of the Naughty and Nice Sisters. They're dancers."

"Nearly naked dancers?" Lizzy's eyes got big, and she turned to look as the woman in red, hips swaying, walked down Camellia Street toward Rosemont. "Where was this, Verna? And when? And wouldn't you think she'd mention it to Mr. Moseley?"

"It was the Ziegfeld Frolic, back in 1920. Ten years ago, but it seems like yesterday. I remember every minute of it."

"The Ziegfeld Follies?" Now Lizzy's mouth fell open. "Seriously?"

"No, not the Follies, the Frolic. The Midnight Frolic. The Follies were designed for a more refined audience." Verna gave her a wicked grin. "The Frolic was naughtier. The girls were more . . . um, naked."

"More naked than the Follies?" Lizzy stared at her, remembering the scanty costumes she had seen in photographs. "But how in the world do you know about this, Verna?"

"Because I was *there*, you goose! Walter's cousin Gerald was living in Brooklyn at the time. He took Walter and me to see her do the shimmy." Walter was Verna's husband. He'd been killed when he walked out in front of a Greyhound bus on Route 12. "We rode the train to New York and Gerald showed us the sights. The Statue of Liberty, Coney Island, the Brooklyn Bridge, Times Square. And the New Amsterdam Theater, where Mr. Ziegfeld had his shows."

"I didn't know you'd been to New York." Lizzy was impressed. She had never been any farther than Atlanta. "And you're saying that Miss Jamison starred in the Frolic? She's the one you went to see?"

"And how!" Verna nodded vigorously. "Only her name was LaMotte, not Jamison. The show was in the rooftop theater at the New Amsterdam, on West Forty-second Street. Fanny Brice and W. C. Fields headlined, and the Naughty and Nice Sisters did this swell song-and-dance act." She rolled her eyes expressively. "Boy-o-boy, that woman could kick up her heels. And shimmy? You wouldn't believe it, Liz. She did this song called 'Shimmyshawobble.' " Verna held her arms out straight and shook the rest of herself. " 'I can't play no piano,' " she warbled, " 'I can't sing no blues, but I can shimmysha-wobble from my head down to my shoes.' "

"Oh, my stars," Lizzy said, wide-eyed at the sight of Verna doing . . . what Verna was doing. "Is *that* what the shimmy looks like?"

She had heard "Shimmyshawobble" on the radio, of course, but she'd had to use her imagination when it came to the shimmy itself, as well as the Turkey Trot, the Bunny Hug, the Texas Tommy, none of which she had ever seen. She *had* seen the Charleston, though. Vaudeville acts featuring singers, dancers, and comedians sometimes came to the Dance Barn, out on Briarwood Road. Last year, a pair of girls had danced the Charleston. It had caused quite a sensation. The Baptist preacher (who had dropped in to make sure that there were no "licentious acts" that might sully the souls of his flock) even called the sheriff. When Sheriff Burns got there, he asked the girls to give him a private performance, just so he could see what the preacher was complaining about. He declined to press charges.

Verna dropped her arms and stood still. "That's what the shimmy looks like—except that I'm not any good at it, compared to *her*. She shook everything, Liz. And I do mean *everything*, top to bottom and all parts in-between. Walter was bug-eyed. Gerald said he went to the Frolic whenever he could afford it, just to watch a hometown girl do the shimmy."

"But how did Gerald know that she was a hometown girl?" Lizzy asked reasonably.

"He said he went to school with her. He and Walter both grew up over in Monroeville, you know. Of course, I had no idea that Lorelei LaMotte had an aunt here in Darling, and I'm sure Gerald didn't, either. He just thought it was a really swell joke. He got a big kick out of seeing her up on stage, all made up and beautiful, shaking her chassis and belting out those songs. He said he'd never in the world have recognized her."

"Shaking her *chassis*?"

Verna laughed at Lizzy's shocked look. "Well, that's what she was doing. And you should have seen her costume—what there was of it! For all practical purposes, she was naked. After the show, we went backstage and she signed the playbill for me. 'For Verna,' she wrote, 'with all my love. Lorelei LaMotte.' This is the same person, Liz. Believe me."

"What about her sister?" Lizzy asked, by now completely convinced. "The 'nice' part of the act. Did she shimmy, too?"

"No, she mostly played the mandolin and sang—not very well, but I think her mistakes were on purpose—and made remarks about how naughty Lorelei LaMotte was and how it was going to get her into trouble if she didn't watch out. She was funny and everybody laughed. She wasn't really Lorelei's sister, though. That was just the way they were billed." She paused, frowning. "What's the name of Miss Jamison's friend? The one who's moved in with her and Miss Hamer?"

"Miss Lake. Lily Lake, I think she said."

"Of course!" Verna snapped her fingers. "That was her— Lily Lake! The 'nice' half of the Naughty and Nice Sisters. She was pretty, too—a brunette. But Lorelei LaMotte was the famous one, because of the shimmy."

"If she's so famous," Lizzy replied thoughtfully, "how come folks around here don't know who she is?" She frowned. "For instance, Mr. Moseley had no idea. I'm sure that if she'd told him that she was a Ziegfeld Girl, he would have mentioned it to me."

Verna shrugged. "If she hasn't been back to Darling since she was a girl, there's no reason for people around here to make the connection. Please forgive me for besmirching Benton Moseley, but I seriously doubt that he pays any attention to show business. In fact, he's probably never even heard of Mr. Ziegfeld."

"I suppose you're right," Lizzy conceded. For years, she had carried a secret torch for her boss, but even when she was so head-over-heels she couldn't see straight, she hadn't been blind to his limitations. Mr. Moseley was nice-looking and very smart, but he was not the most scintillating man in the world. He almost never went to the movies, and while he subscribed to newspapers like the Sunday *New York Times* (which came on the bus from Mobile every Thursday), he mostly read about national politics and international affairs, not the entertainment section. Mrs. Moseley said he was a "stuffy old stick-in-the-mud," and Lizzy suspected that this had something to do with her recent decision to get a divorce.

"Anyway," Verna went on, "the Naughty and Nice Sisters may have been a big hit back in 1920, but that was before

Prohibition. Lots of clubs folded, and I read that Mr. Ziegfeld himself hasn't been doing so hot lately. It's no surprise that nobody in Darling has ever heard of Lorelei LaMotte or the Naughty and Nice Sisters." She narrowed her eyes at Lizzy. "But I'll show you that playbill, and you can see for yourself who Nona Jean Jamison is. Who she *really* is, in the flesh, so to speak."

"Well," Lizzy replied with a little laugh, "I guess they'll hear about her now. In that red outfit and those high heels, she'll be the talk of the town." In Darling, gossip was everybody's favorite recreation.

"Oh, golly, Liz!" Verna snapped her fingers. "I have just got the most incredible idea!"

"Idea? What idea?" Lizzy asked cautiously. Verna was very intelligent and eminently practical, but she could be too smart for her own good. Sometimes she outfoxed herself.

"About the talent show." Sponsored and organized by the Dahlias, this annual event was held at the Darling Academy gymnasium in late October. It was always a mixture of the melodramatic (Mrs. Eiglehorn reciting "Curfew Must Not Ring Tonight") and the comic (Mr. Trubar clowning around with his shiny trombone and his dancing dog, Towser). It was the highlight of Darling's fall social season. Everybody in town looked forward to it with a great deal of anticipation.

"Uh-oh," Lizzy said. Mildred Kilgore was putting the talent show program together, and she was a very detail-oriented person who liked everything to turn out just the way she planned. Where Mildred was concerned, the only successful program was the one where even Reverend Trivette, the minister at the Four Corners Methodist Church, could go away saying what swell family entertainment it had been. The Naughty and Nice Sisters would give Mildred Kilgore heartburn.

"No, no," Verna protested. "It's a *good* idea, Liz! Let's ask Miss LaMotte and Miss Lake to do an act for the talent show.

I'll bet they'd really bring in a crowd. We could put up posters and advertise—"

"Verna! You know Mildred wouldn't think of inviting those ladies to perform. Why, the audience would be scandalized! Most of them would get up and walk out, and the ones who stayed would cause a riot."

"I wasn't thinking of asking them to do their Ziegfeld Frolic act," Verna replied hastily. "It would be different—something suitable for a Darling audience. If they're planning to be in Darling for any length of time, it would be a perfect way for them to get acquainted. I'll bet the Dahlias would be delighted to have their help with the show."

"I'm not so sure about that," Lizzy said, shaking her head warily. "From what you say, they sound like an intriguing pair, but they'd probably feel more at home out at the Dance Barn. You'd better talk it over with Mildred before you get all excited about the possibilities." She thought of something else. "Listen, Myra May and I are having supper at the diner tonight, and then we're going to see *The Saturday Night Kid*. Clara Bow is in it, and Jean Harlow. Want to come with us?"

"I'd love to," Verna said. "But what about Grady? How come you're not going out with him?" Grady Alexander, the county agricultural extension agent, was Lizzy's more-or-less steady boyfriend.

"He drove over to Auburn for an ag meeting. He'll be gone through the middle of next week." Lizzy sighed. "To tell the truth, Verna, I'm glad to get a little breathing space. I'm trying to put off—" She turned down her mouth. "Well, you know."

"Yes, I know," Verna said sympathetically. She grinned. "But it's a nice problem to have, in my opinion." The courthouse clock began to strike. It was several blocks away, but its booming note could be heard all over town. The people of Darling always said they didn't need watches. They had the courthouse clock, so there was never any excuse for being late.

Lizzy counted the strikes. "Mercy. Four o'clock already. I need to get home. Is six okay for supper? The movie starts at seven fifteen."

"Sure," Verna said. "Six o'clock, at the diner." She looked thoughtful. "I wonder if the Naughty and Nice Sisters have ever met Clara Bow."

TWO

Lizzy's Key

Lizzy said good-bye to Verna, turned, and walked east along Camellia. She crossed Robert E. Lee, went another block, and turned north on Jefferson Davis. This was a pretty part of town, and even though the houses weren't as big and fancy as the newer ones out near the country club, they were painted white or gray with blue or red shutters, and the front porches were furnished with a rocking chair or a porch swing and wreathed with honeysuckle. There were lawns, too, with grass that was green in the spring and turned brown in the dry, hot summer. It was early October and the lawns were brown now, but most of the houses had flower beds out front, and in the dusky evenings, people sat on their porches, knitting or reading the newspaper and watching the little girls jumping rope and the boys playing baseball or tag in the dusty street.

Glancing at the houses, a stranger might find it hard to tell that times were so tough and money was so hard to come by. But if he looked more closely, he'd see that half the shingles on Mrs. Weber's roof had been ripped off in a wind storm and hadn't been replaced yet. Mrs. Weber didn't live there anymore. She had lost the house to foreclosure and had gone to Mobile to live with her daughter. And three doors down, the house with the two broken windows in the front had been vacant for so long that the bank's faded For Sale sign was hidden in the withered grass. People who couldn't pay their rent or make their mortgage payments were moving in with family—with their children or their parents or their brothers or their sisters. They had to. They had no place else to go.

But Lizzy wasn't thinking about this. She was thinking about what Verna had told her. A pair of vaudeville stars had moved to Darling! And if Verna was right (Verna usually was), one of them had come a long, long way. To go from being plain-Jane Miss Nona Jean Jamison of Monroeville, Alabama, to Miss Lorelei LaMotte of the Great White Way must have been an incredible journey.

And then a wonderful idea suddenly popped into Lizzy's head. The Naughty and Nice Sisters act wasn't suitable for the Dahlias' talent show, but wouldn't Miss LaMotte make a splendid subject for a feature story in the Darling *Dispatch*? Wasn't this exactly the kind of article that Charlie Dickens, the newspaper's editor, would love to print?

Why, of course it was! It was one of those uplifting, heart-warming, hometown-girl-makes-good stories that everybody likes to read, especially in hard times. And while Darling wasn't Miss LaMotte's hometown, Monroeville was, and Monroeville was only fifteen miles away. Lizzy shivered a little, thinking of the exciting possibilities. She could do an interview with Miss LaMotte about her life, starting with her small-town girlhood as plain-Jane Nona Jean Jamison. And then her move to New York, where she had enjoyed a huge success in the glamorous and competitive world of vaudeville, catching the eye of Mr. Florenz Ziegfeld himself. Miss LaMotte had doubtless taken a few hard knocks along the way, which Lizzy could use to show how dedicated she was to becoming a dancer and how hard she'd worked to get to the top. The article could end with her decision to leave her big-city life and move to tiny Darling, Alabama, where she planned to care for her aging aunt and lead a life of quiet and peaceful retirement, far from the madding crowd. It would be a charming true-life story that everybody in town would read and talk about for weeks, maybe months.

And she—Elizabeth Lacy—was the perfect person to write it, wasn't she? For the past five years, she had written a garden column for the weekly *Dispatch*. Lizzy loved writing about plants and people's gardens and the passing of the seasons and the sweltering heats and sudden storms of their Alabama climate. She enjoyed doing research and corresponding with other Southern gardeners.

But in May, she had written a feature story about a young woman who had been shot in a green Pontiac roadster that belonged to a dentist and the car pushed into Pine Mill Creek. The story was based on her own investigation into the life and death of Eva Louise Scott, the girl in the car, and everybody told her what a great piece of reporting it was. It was a sad story, too, for Bunny—that was the girl's nickname—had been beautiful and gay and young. And even though she was a bit reckless and heedless and wanted jewelry and other pretty things more than was probably good for her, Bunny hadn't deserved to die, which of course was the main point of Lizzy's article.

After that successful debut as a feature writer, Mr. Dickens had told her that if she came up with another interesting story idea, he'd be glad to consider it. Lizzy had thought of several, but none seemed to be exciting enough. The summer had passed with its customary sedateness, with nothing more explosive than the fireworks blowing up at the Elks' Club

Fourth of July picnic or more tragic than the swimming hole drying up in the long August drought or more unexpected than the out-of-the-blue emergency landing of a Cessna Model A airplane on the grassy airstrip near the county fairgrounds—none of which put a match to Lizzy's creative fire.

But this was different, Lizzy thought excitedly. A story about Lorelei LaMotte, famous Broadway performer, would give her a chance to do some serious writing about a woman who surely had a fascinating personal history of success in a difficult profession, with a few intrigues and adventures here and there. It would definitely be a literary challenge, which was just what she had been looking for.

For years Lizzy had read everything—good, bad, and indifferent—that she could get her hands on. She kept a notebook, writing little stories about people she knew and places that captured her attention and events that took place here in town. And even though nothing very big or exciting ever happened in Darling, there were always lots of little things going on, surprising crises that poked up unexpectedly out of the serene surface of the day like . . . well, like those lilies, those naked ladies shooting suddenly up out of the grass when you had absolutely no idea they were there and dazzling you with their astonishing blooms. They weren't the kinds of stories you'd read in the newspaper, which was usually full of facts and figures, but Lizzy enjoyed writing them.

But while Lizzy was a small-town girl who knew she could comfortably write about Miss LaMotte's small-town beginnings, she couldn't even begin to imagine the life of a vaudeville performer. She would have to do a huge amount of research—talk to Miss LaMotte at length and maybe Miss Lake, and read entertainment magazines like *Variety* and *Billboard*—before she could even think of writing anything. She frowned. But if she couldn't imagine Miss LaMotte's life, maybe she'd never be able to write about it, no matter how much research she did. It's hard to write about something that is entirely foreign to you.

Occupied with these thoughts, Lizzy had crossed Dauphin and Franklin and reached her block of Jefferson Davis. She was home almost before she knew it, walking up the steps to the front porch, putting her key into the lock and turning it, with the special happiness that she felt every time she stepped through the green-painted front door and into the tiny front hall, which was just big enough for a single shelf, an oval wall-hung mirror, and a row of coat hooks, where she now hung her floppy-brimmed hat.

Home. The word had taken on a new and very special meaning a couple of years before. Until then, Lizzy had lived her whole life with her mother. Her father had died when she was a baby, leaving his widow a nice little cache of money, safely and prudently invested. It wasn't enough to allow her mother to live an extravagant life, but it was certainly enough to keep her from working or worrying her pretty head about anything of any consequence. This fiscal consideration had allowed Mrs. Lacy to focus every bit of her attention, energy, and concern on Elizabeth, her only child. She loved sewing and hat-making, and she dressed her daughter in her beautiful creations: ruffled and embroidered dresses and hats piled with ribbons and silk flowers.

Her mother's attentions had not bothered Lizzy so much when she was a little girl, but as she grew older, the fuss over what she wore and how she fixed her hair turned to a constant, quarrelsome nagging. It was "Elizabeth, if you keep on frowning, your forehead will be permanently wrinkled!" and "Elizabeth, stop chewing your nails this instant! Your hands are a scandal!" and "Elizabeth, I simply will not allow you to bob your hair!" And every time Lizzy turned around, her mother had made her another new hat—or redecorated an old one—and insisted that she wear it.

The only way she could escape was to close the door to her room and write in her journal or read, for Mrs. Lacy couldn't follow her into the pages of *The Railway Children* (who were blessed with a very agreeable mother) or *The Adventures of Huckleberry Finn* (Huck had no mother at all). The trouble with writing in her journal, of course, was that Lizzy was writing about the secret places of her own inner life, and she could never be sure that—no matter how carefully she hid her work—her mother hadn't found and read it. Lizzy was under no illusions. Her mother was that kind of mother.

Sometime during her last year of high school, Lizzy realized that she was never going to have a life of her own if she didn't find a way to escape. Unfortunately, there weren't that many options. The Lacys were well enough off to live comfortably in the house Mr. Lacy had left them, but not so well off (at least, that's what her mother said) that Lizzy could go away to college. There hadn't been any available jobs in town at the time, and the thought of leaving Darling for some unknown city was so daunting that Lizzy (more timid then than she was now) couldn't even think it.

So when Reggie Morris had proposed the day after her high school graduation, Lizzy had said "yes" without a second thought. Reggie's father was a building contractor and the Morrises were well enough off so that Lizzy and Reggie would have their own house. Against her mother's loudly expressed wishes, she took Reggie's modest diamond engagement ring and began dreaming about the joys of having her own home, where she could read and write to her heart's content and her mother would come only when she was invited.

But when the Alabama 167th came home from France in 1919, Reggie hadn't come home with them. It took a long time to get over the death of her dream. Lizzy (who by that time was older and somewhat braver) thought of moving to Mobile or Birmingham to find work and get away from her mother, which would have been the right thing to do. But she had already taken a secretarial job at Moseley & Moseley Law Office, where she found herself developing an extra-ordinary crush on Mr. Benton Moseley. He was just out of law school, handsome and bright, newly in practice with his father, a widely respected lawyer and former state senator. Mr. Benton Moseley had always been a complete gentleman, of course, although Lizzy (who by this time was reading a great many dime-novel romances in which beautiful and worthy but penniless young women met and married hand-some, worthy, and wealthy young gentlemen) found herself conjuring up endless fantasies about him.

When the senior Mr. Moseley died, the junior Mr. Mose-ley continued the practice, and Lizzy (who had finally put Reggie's diamond in a box in her dresser drawer) had gone to work every day happily cocooned in her romantic dreams. She continued to live at home, but her mother had somehow faded into the background—still bothersome, of course, but more like an annoying barking dog that lived in a house a block away, rather than on the other side of the fence. Lizzy, so fully focused on Mr. Moseley that she felt his presence shining on her like a warm spring sun, lived for the hours she spent at work. It had been rather like living in a dream that was so intense and so magically real that it usurped all other realities. It hadn't mattered that the object of her adulation didn't return her feelings—or even appear to notice them.

In fact, Lizzy had gone on glorying in her unrequited love even after Mr. Moseley had courted and married a blond deb-utante from a wealthy Birmingham family, built a big fancy house out near the country club, and fathered two girls. Then had come his election to the state legislature, and Lizzy had dutifully carried on, keeping the practice going while he fol-lowed his father's footsteps to the capitol in Montgomery.

That was probably what brought her to her senses. With

Mr. Moseley away for weeks at a time, Lizzy woke up from her dream and began to realize what an utter fool she was making of herself. She toted her dime-novel romances out to the backyard and burned them. She took the treasured snapshot of Mr. Moseley out of the secret place in her billfold and added it to the fire. Then she went back to writing in her journal—but she kept it with her, in her handbag, so that her mother could not find and read it.

Mrs. Lacy, of course, never suspected any of this. She had decided that her daughter (her heart broken by the death of her young fiancé) would be a lifelong spinster, quite naturally preferring to live with her mother for the rest of her life. And Lizzy, who had been putting away money out of every paycheck against the increasingly remote possibility that something would happen to change her circumstances, found herself beginning to share her mother's unassailable belief that the two of them would go on living together, forever and ever, world without end, amen.

And then something unexpectedly wonderful had happened.

Old Mr. Flagg died. He had lived across the street from the Lacys for nearly four decades, in a small frame bungalow with a postage-stamp parlor, a kitchen, two little upstairs bedrooms, a front porch with a swing, and a screened-in back porch. Mr. Flagg had been a gardener who lavished his time and attention on his large yard, where he grew sunflowers and a fig tree and pink roses on the trellis and a perennial border. There was also a small vegetable garden—just large enough for one person—only a step away from the back porch. Lizzy was suddenly seized by the idea that she had to have this house, and she had taken her improbable scheme to Mr. Moseley, who was in charge of settling the old man's estate.

But Mr. Moseley didn't think it was improbable at all. With his help, Lizzy secretly bought the house, commissioned the necessary repairs—including a bathroom, electricity, gas, and water—and furnished it. She didn't say a single word to her mother, who was in great suspense about the secret identity of the new across-the-street neighbor, until the work was done and her new home was ready to move into. The announcement had sent Mrs. Lacy into hysterics, of course, but Lizzy, for the first time in her life, had held her ground.

And even though her own house was not quite far enough away to qualify as an "escape" from her mother, it had made all the difference. For the first time ever, Lizzy held the key to her own life. She could step into her own place, close the door behind her, and be perfectly at home. She still felt a warm affection for Mr. Moseley, but the torch she had carried for so long was quite extinguished and there had been another man in her life—Grady Alexander—for more than a year. Lizzy wasn't sure exactly how she felt about Grady, who always seemed to want something from her, and she knew (uncomfortably) that she would have to make a decision about their relationship before very long. But for the moment, she felt she could handle the situation. She hoped things would stay that way.

And now, as she turned up the path that led from the street to her front porch and saw Daffodil, her orange tabby, sitting on the porch railing waiting for her, Lizzy felt once again the pleasure of coming home to a house that was completely, entirely, and remarkably hers.

Except that her mother had a key.

This was a new situation—it had just happened the week before—and Lizzy was still quietly fuming about it. Mrs. Lacy had apparently lifted Lizzy's spare key from its hook by the back door and taken it to Musgrove's Hardware, where she said that her daughter wanted her to have a copy. Lizzy knew about this bald-faced lie, because Mr. Musgrove had happened to mention it to her when she stopped in to get a new rubber plug for her bathtub. She hadn't yet decided whether to tell her mother to hand over the copied key or have Mr. Musgrove install new locks on the front and back doors. Either way, there was going to be a battle.

But Lizzy always tried to see things from both sides of the question and give the other person the benefit of the doubt. On balance, she felt that her mother probably wouldn't use the key very often, and she was determined *not* to let it disturb the pleasure she felt each time she put her very own key in the lock of her very own door and turned it.

"Come on, Daffy," she said, as the cat rubbed against her ankles, purring an enthusiastic welcome. "Let's get you some milk."

Stepping inside, Lizzy took a deep breath of the faint lemony fragrance she used to polish the furniture and savored the quiet that fell on her like a shawl every time she came in. On the left, a flight of stairs led up to two small bedrooms. On the right, a wide doorway opened into a little parlor, which she had furnished with a very nice Mission-style leather cushioned sofa, a chair she had reupholstered in dark brown corduroy, and a Tiffany-style lamp with a stained-glass shade. She had paid seven dollars and fifty cents for that lamp—far too much, she knew, but she had fallen in love with its amber-colored light, which gleamed richly against the refinished pine floors. Behind the parlor was the kitchen with a tiny dining nook, just big enough for two, looking out on the garden. At the end of the hall was a large storage room, part of which she had converted into a bathroom with a claw-footed tub, tiny sink, pull-chain toilet, and newly tiled floor. (Mr. Flagg had used the privy behind the garage.) It was the most perfect house in the world, she felt, and—after all the quarrelsome years she had lived with her mother—a perfectly private place, almost like a sanctuary.

She went down the hall to the kitchen, Daffy running

eagerly ahead of her, and stopped stock-still in the doorway. In the middle of the oilcloth-covered table was her last-year's blue felt cloche, newly decorated with exquisite peacock feathers and glass beads, all shades of blue—a gift from her mother, no doubt. Beside it was a folded note.

Her eyes narrowing, Lizzy picked it up. It was written in her mother's hand, telling her to look inside the refrigerator, where she found four thick slices of Sally-Lou's meat loaf (one of Lizzy's favorite dishes), a large bowl of potato salad, two ripe tomatoes, and two pieces of apple pie. The note said that since there was enough food for two people, Mrs. Lacy was planning to join Lizzy for supper at six o'clock.

Obviously, Lizzy's mother had used her key. And she wasn't making any secret of it.

Huffing out an aggravated breath, Lizzy poured milk into a saucer for Daffy. As he got down to business, she went to the phone that hung on the wall. She and her mother were on the same party line, so she didn't have to ring through to the telephone exchange. She cranked two shorts and a long.

In a moment, Sally-Lou answered with her pleasant, musical "Miz Lacy's residence."

"Sally-Lou, let me speak to Mama, please," Lizzy said. Then she thought of something else. "Oh, before you get her, I wonder—have you heard from your aunt DessaRae since Miss Hamer's niece and her friend have moved in?"

"Yes'm, Miss Lizzy, I has," Sally-Lou said, and paused, turning the silence into the unspoken question: *Why you askin' me 'bout this?*

Sally-Lou had been fourteen when Mrs. Lacy hired her to take care of two-year-old Lizzy. An orphan, she had been a long-limbed, gangly girl, as black as night, young enough to play games and sing songs with Lizzy but old enough and smart enough to make the little girl mind. Still, Lizzy had grown up thinking of her as a friend. In fact, when Mrs. Lacy had climbed up on her high horse about something or other, Sally-Lou became not only a friend but an ally and a staunch defender, adroitly helping Lizzy stay out of her mother's way and sometimes even standing between mother and daughter. She had never married—whether by choice or happenstance, Lizzy didn't know. But as she got older and became more sure of herself, Sally-Lou had made her own place in the household and become her own woman. If you didn't know her, she might seem so meek that butter wouldn't melt in her mouth and you might think you could push her around. But she was strong as a stick of cordwood when need be, and feisty as a banty rooster.

"I'm asking because . . . well, because I saw Miss LaMotte this afternoon," Lizzy replied, a little lamely. "I was just wondering how they were getting along." Actually, she was asking because it had occurred to her that maybe, via Sally-Lou and DessaRae, she could get an insider's view of Miss LaMotte.

Sally-Lou's reply was guarded. "It look like they done moved in to stay, is what Aunt Dessy say. Brung they clothes and suitcases an' such."

There wasn't much information in that, Lizzy thought, disappointed. She tried a different question. "Is Miss Hamer happy with the new arrangement?"

What Lizzy really wanted to know was whether Miss Hamer was aware that her niece had once been a vaudeville dancer, but she didn't think it wise to ask. Anything she said to Sally-Lou would reach DessaRae's ears, and in this case, that might not be a good idea. Not yet, anyway.

"Miz Hamer happy?" Sally-Lou chuckled wryly. "Well, now, I don' know 'bout that, Miss Lizzy. That ol' lady ain't happy wi' much of anythin' these days. Aunt Dessy just say the ladies are gettin' settled is all. She ain't seen nothin' of Miz Lake, though. She lay low in her bedroom, don't come out at all, even to eat her meals."

"Hmm," Lizzy said, thinking that this wasn't much help, either. "Well, keep your ears open for me, would you?"

The silence stretched out a little. "If you don' mind me askin', how come?" Sally-Lou asked, almost warily. "Somethin' bad goin' on over there?"

"Oh, no," Lizzy replied hastily. "I'm just curious, that's all." Before Sally-Lou could ask another question, she said, "Could I speak to Mother now?"

"Sho thing, Miss Lizzy," Sally-Lou said. "Hang on—I get her."

Lizzy took a deep breath. When her mother came on the line, she said, very firmly, "Thank you for fixing my hat, Mama, but tonight isn't a good night to have supper together."

"Oh, dear," Mrs. Lacy said, and heaved a pained sigh. "Whyever not, Elizabeth?" There was a brief pause, and then her usual question, tinged with hopefulness: "You and Mr. Alexander are goin' out for supper, I s'pose."

Grady Alexander had been Lizzy's boyfriend, more or less, for the past year or so. Mrs. Lacy, who had gotten used to having her unmarried daughter handy whenever she was needed, had opposed the relationship at first, finding all kinds of reasons why Grady wasn't right for Lizzy. But in the past couple of months, she seemed to have changed her mind about him and was now leaning the other way—and leaning on Lizzy about it, too.

"You're not gettin' any younger, you know, dear," she said, several times a week. "There aren't that many eligible men in Darling. And he is *such* a fine-lookin' gentleman."

This sudden change of heart was a mystery, since Grady was exactly the same person he had always been. But maybe the answer was as simple as a dependable paycheck. Grady had a job in the Alabama Agricultural Department and it looked like he was going to keep it. Or maybe it was a matter of status. As the county agricultural agent, he was respected in the community. Either money or status, in Mrs. Lacy's eyes, might have transformed him from Mr. Wrong to Mr. Right.

Lizzy took a deep breath. "No, Mama, I am not going out with Grady tonight. Myra May and Verna and I are going to the movie—just us girls. We're going to see *The Saturday Night Kid*. Clara Bow stars in it."

The minute the words were out of her mouth, though, she knew she had made a mistake. Her mother didn't approve of Clara Bow, the "It Girl." (Nobody knew what "It" was, exactly, but everybody suspected it was "Sex Appeal.") In fact, Mrs. Lacy had told Mr. Greer, the owner of the *Palace*, that he should not show any more movies starring Clara Bow, because she was nothing but pure trash.

Mrs. Lacy said testily, "I wish you wouldn't, Elizabeth. You know my opinion of Clara Bow."

"Yes, I know, Mama. But—"

"And don't you think we could have supper first?" Her voice tightened. "There's something we need to talk about, Elizabeth. Something important. Surely you can spare a little time for your mother, can't you?"

Lizzy straightened her shoulders. "Of course I can. But not tonight, Mama. Verna and Myra May and I are going to have supper together before the movie." She tried to put a smile into her voice. "How about if you come over here tomorrow after church?" Her mother was Presbyterian and never missed a service. "We can have Sally-Lou's meat loaf and potato salad for our dinner. Will that do instead?"

"I suppose it'll have to," her mother said reluctantly. She heaved a plaintive sigh. "I just wish you were goin' out with Mr. Alexander tonight, Elizabeth. He is such a fine, upstandin' Christian young man and comes from such a good family. His mother sits in the pew right behind mine every Sunday morning. You could do worse than marry him. And of course you don't want to live out your life as a tragic old maid."

"Yes, Mama," Lizzy said. She didn't point out that Grady never accompanied his mother to church, either, and that for a fine, upstanding Christian young man, he'd been awful hot and heavy-handed in the front seat of his blue Ford coupe the last time he'd taken her out. They'd gone to see Gary Cooper in *The Virginian*, and then driven out to watch the moon from the hill above the fairgrounds. Lizzy had finally had to get out of the car and take a cooling-off walk.

"Well, then, don't forget," her mother said. "Sunday school starts at nine. You can wear that nice new blue hat I made you."

Lizzy rolled her eyes. "Mama, we've been over this a hundred times. Sunday is the only day I get to sleep a little late. You just come on over here when you get home and we'll have a nice Sunday dinner together. I've got some fresh string beans I can cook up with onions and fatback, the way you like them." And when they were eating, she would tell her mother that it had been wrong to copy that key. She would have to give it back, or promise not to use it except in an emergency, or—

"I would go with you to the movies," her mother said petulantly, "if I was asked. And if you weren't goin' to see Clara Bow. You know how I feel about that immoral woman. I wouldn't go into a movie house that was showin' one of her films." Mary Pickford was the only movie actress Mrs. Lacy admired (*Pollyanna* was her favorite, along with *Rebecca of Sunnybrook Farm*), but even Miss Pickford's star had dimmed in Mrs. Lacy's eyes since the actress had bobbed her hair and married Douglas Fairbanks, who, as everybody knew, led a rake's life out there in Hollywood, where it was said that nobody paid any attention to Prohibition. Marriage to him could not be good for Miss Pickford's moral character.

"Yes, ma'am," Lizzy said, glad now that she had mentioned Clara Bow. "Well, then. Sunday dinner after church. All right?"

"All right," her mother said. "And don't forget, y'hear, Elizabeth? There is somethin' impo'tant that we need to talk about, and it can't be put off. It's got to be discussed now, before either of us gets a day older."

With a long sigh, Lizzy put the receiver back in its cradle. Once every few months, her mother came up with "something impo'tant" they needed to discuss and would pester her nonstop until they sat down and talked. The last time, it had been the green straw hat that her mother was making. She couldn't decide between big red silk rosettes and a red veil or small white silk daisies and a white veil, and needed Lizzy's advice.

What was it this time?

THREE

Verna Is Rebuffed

Verna watched Liz walk off down Camellia Street, heading for home. She hesitated a moment, then turned and went the other way, hurrying a little, so that by the time she got to the corner of Camellia and Rosemont and started north, toward the courthouse square, she could see Miss LaMotte. Except for the business section of town, there were no sidewalks in Darling, and Miss LaMotte was making very slow forward progress on those silly high heels, which were suitable for city sidewalks only. If Verna wanted to, she could have caught up.

But she didn't, exactly, at least not yet. Verna hadn't known that she was going to follow Miss LaMotte in the first place, and she wasn't exactly sure why she was doing it. Yes, there was the idea of asking her to appear in the talent show, although Verna knew that she really should talk to Mildred first. But the real truth was that Miss LaMotte's sudden appearance in Darling had been a shocking surprise. It had brought back such a flood of memories that Verna almost felt as if she were drowning.

Now, Verna Tidwell was not a sentimental person. In fact, she thought of herself as not having a single schmaltzy bone in her body, and she took serious pride in her reputation for a hard-headed, no-nonsense approach to life. Oh, she had loved Walter well enough, but she had never been "in love" with him, if by being in love you were thinking of that corny lose-your-head-and-your-heart nonsense that Rudy Vallée was always crooning about. She had agreed to marry Walter because it made pretty good sense at the time he asked her, and she had been truly sorry when he died, although not so sorry that she went around wearing a rusty black dress and black hat and gloves for years afterward, the way her mother had when Verna's father passed on.

Some of her acquaintances felt that her lack of sentiment was a character fault, but Verna did not agree. It was just part of her nature, along with her habit of wanting to know what was behind the appearances that other people put on when they went out the door in the morning, and suspecting their motivations, and questioning their intentions. "Why?" was one of Verna's favorite questions, along with "Who says?" and "What's that got to do with it?" Walter had always complained that she was suspicious, and Verna felt he was right. She was the sort of person who rarely took anything at face value, and she knew it.

Unfortunately, Verna's suspicious habits had been very hard on Walter during the three years of their marriage. He taught history and civics at Darling Academy and lived in a world that was studded with indisputable facts, the way an oak door is studded with nails. As far as he was concerned, all you had to do to get along happily was to learn the facts and repeat them in the right order when you were called on, and everything would be honky-dory. Verna's habit of asking questions that didn't have any clear-cut answers had made him very uncomfortable, and if he hadn't walked out in front of that Greyhound bus on Route 12 that rainy afternoon ten years ago,

Verna suspected that they probably would have gotten a divorce before very long. Instead, Walter had ended up under a sycamore tree in the southwest corner of the Darling Cemetery, out on Schoolhouse Road, and Verna had ended up a widow.

The month before the accident, however, they had gone on a trip to New York together. It was their first vacation and their last, so you might call it Walter's trip of a lifetime. His cousin Gerald had taken them on the new subway line from Manhattan all the way out to Coney Island to eat cotton candy and Nathan's Famous frankfurters and ride the new 150-foot-tall Wonder Wheel, so high it seemed to scrape the sky. And then they took the ferry to Liberty Island, where they climbed all 354 steps inside the Statue of Liberty so they could look out from the windows of the crown and marvel at the magical city across the blue, blue water.

And on their last night Gerald had taken them to see the Naughty and Nice Sisters in Mr. Ziegfeld's notorious Frolic, where Miss Lily Lake and Miss Lorelei LaMotte paraded onto the stage right over the heads of the gasping audience, on a runway made of see-through glass. In another act, scantily clad dancers strutted out into the audience, encouraging male customers to use the glowing tip-ends of their cigars to burst the balloons that covered essential parts of the girls' anatomy. Walter had been bug-eyed, and even Verna couldn't remember a more exciting evening.

So even though she swore she didn't have a sentimental bone in her body, Verna certainly had a few sentimental memories and this was the best of them. Walter had been happy and she had been happy and that happiness had followed them like a rosy cloud all the way back to Darling, Alabama, where Walter had stepped out in front of the Greyhound bus and Verna had become a widow.

And there, just a half block ahead of her, teetering along on her ridiculous red high heels, was the reason for that happiness. Miss Lorelei LaMotte, who had put on a performance that had made Walter's eyes bug and made Verna laugh out loud. Miss Lorelei LaMotte, who had given Verna and Walter something interesting and unusual to talk about on their long journey home. And Verna, who wouldn't ordinarily have bothered to do any such thing, felt suddenly compelled to tell Miss LaMotte just how happy her performance had made them. She picked up her pace.

But right when Verna had almost caught up, Miss LaMotte slowed, looked around as if to make sure where she was, then turned to go into Lima's Drugstore, which stood at the southwest corner of the courthouse square. At that same moment, a 1929 lemon yellow Cadillac Phaeton, the canvas top folded back, came down the street at a fast clip, trailing a thick cloud of dust. It was Mr. Bailey Beauchamp's Cadillac, driven by Mr. Beauchamp's colored man, Lightning, with Mr. Beauchamp himself, dressed in his usual white suit and wearing a white straw hat, sitting in the backseat, smoking a large cigar. As the Cadillac zipped past the drugstore corner, Verna saw Mr. Beauchamp's head swivel, like one of those funny wooden dolls with its head on a spring. He was staring at Miss LaMotte. He was still staring as Lightning drove into the next block.

Verna chuckled. Miss LaMotte was a head turner, all right. It was no surprise that she had attracted Bailey Beauchamp's attention. He was a gallant Southern gentleman, of course, and the owner of one of the largest plantations in the area. But he had been widowed three years before, and in the time since, had developed quite a reputation with the ladies. He was currently reputed to be pursuing Mrs. Sophia Hobart, a widow of substantial fortune and influence in Darling. Rumor had it that Mrs. Hobart was planning to go to Atlanta to shop for her trousseau, so the announcement of their engagement was expected soon.

Verna turned and followed Miss LaMotte inside Lima's

Drugstore. Owned and operated by Mr. Lester Lima, the shop had a glass display window that featured a variety of products. Today, it was a pyramid of men's Brylcreem ("For Head-First Brilliance"), Wildroot Hair Tonic ("For Dandruff and Falling Hair"), and an assortment of combs and hairbrushes, along with a large poster that featured a handsome man being rejected by a pretty girl, with the ominous warning, "You should have used Listerine—kills germs in 15 seconds!" The shop was long and narrow, with a soda fountain on the left, where Earlynne Biddle's son Benny was washing glasses, and a cosmetics department on the right, where Bunny Scott used to work. Mr. Lima himself presided over the pharmacy department at the back of the store.

Benny looked up. "C'n I help you?" he asked, shaking the suds off his hands. "Oh, hi, Miz Tidwell. C'n I make you a banana split? A malt, maybe?"

"Not today, thanks, Benny," Verna replied. "I'm just browsing."

"That's jake." Benny grinned and nodded toward the back of the store. "Real looker, ain't she?" He licked his lips hungrily. "Hotsy totsy."

"Your mother wouldn't approve of that language, Benny," Verna said sternly.

The boy looked down. "Sorry," he muttered. "Didn't mean nothin'."

Verna turned away to a display of boxes of Euthymol and Pepsodent toothpastes, glancing surreptitiously over her shoulder. She had expected to see Miss LaMotte, who was a cosmetics customer if she had ever seen one, browsing the lipstick and nail polish displays. But she wasn't. She had gone directly to the back of the store, to the pharmacy counter, where she was handing a piece of paper to Mr. Lima, a tall, thin man in a white coat and a pair of round gold glasses that rode low on his long, thin nose.

Mr. Lima examined the paper. Frowning, he handed it

back to Miss LaMotte. "I am sorry, madam," he said, "but I can't fill this prescription."

"And why not?" Miss LaMotte demanded. She jabbed her finger at the paper. "It's got the doctor's signature on it. Right there. Can't you see?" She spoke fast, in a high, clipped voice. She seemed to have lost any Alabama accent she might have once had. She sounded, Verna thought, like a Yankee. An impatient Yankee.

Verna stepped past the toothpaste, moving a little closer, not wanting to miss anything. She bent over, pretending to read the label of a bottle of Lydia Pinkham's Vegetable Compound. She couldn't see Miss LaMotte's face, but she could see the line of her jaw, which was a bit saggy. Still, the platinum blonde hair looked pretty much as it had ten years ago, and while the lady was wearing far more clothing than she had worn on Mr. Ziegfeld's stage, the line of her generous bust was very obviously the same. Verna turned and caught Benny staring at Miss LaMotte's figure. He colored, dropped his head, and went back to his soapsuds.

Mr. Lima cleared his throat. "I can't fill it, madam, because it's over a year old. I suggest that you visit Dr. Roberts. Show him this and tell him why you need it. I'm sure he'll be able to—"

"But Dr. Roberts is out of town!" Miss LaMotte shrilled. "He won't be back until Tuesday or Wednesday." She pushed the paper back across the counter. "I need this filled today. Right now! It's vitally important. It's a matter of life and death!"

Life and death? Verna pulled in her breath. Really, if Miss LaMotte's health was in danger, Mr. Lima ought to sell her enough of whatever it was to tide her over until she could get in to see Doc Roberts. Or maybe she needed the medicine for Miss Hamer. Either way—

"My dear lady," Mr. Lima said. "Veronal is a dangerous barbiturate. I cannot and will not fill a prescription for it unless the patient—I assume that is yourself—is under the care of a doctor. Preferably a Darling doctor." He looked down at the prescription. "Not a doctor in Illinois."

Veronal. Verna let her breath out. *Sleeping pills.* So it wasn't a matter of life and death, after all—although insomnia wasn't pleasant. Verna knew, because she sometimes suffered from it herself. Her favorite remedy was a glass of warm milk and a handful of soda crackers. The combination usually put her to sleep.

"It's not for me." Miss LaMotte tapped her foot impatiently. "But if you won't fill it, you won't. What can I buy instead? Something to make her sleep."

"It's for an adult?" Mr. Lima asked.

Miss LaMotte gave a short laugh. "When she's not acting like a spoiled child. But yes, she's an adult. What can I buy that will get her a good night's sleep?"

"Well, let's see." Mr. Lima turned, scanned the shelves behind him, and reached for a bottle. "I can suggest Dr. Miles' Nervine. It comes in either pill form or liquid. We sell a great deal of it here, particularly to the ladies." He held up the bottle and read the label aloud. "For sleeplessness, nervousness, irritability, nervous headache, and functional hysterical disturbances."

"'Functional hysterical disturbances.'" Miss LaMotte laughed bitterly. "That's rich." She opened her red handbag. "Well, if you say it'll work, I'll take it."

"Liquid or pills?"

She considered. "Liquid. Better give me two bottles. No, make it three. Just in case." *Three* bottles? In case of what, Verna wondered. Miss LaMotte added, grudgingly, "It might be a while before Dr. Roberts can see her."

"That will be three dollars," Mr. Lima said, and took the money she handed him. "I hope it helps—at least, until the doctor is available."

"I do, too," she said grimly. "This situation is driving me abso-lute-ly bonkers." The red bow on her hat jiggled.

Mr. Lima gave her back two dollar bills and put the bottles into a paper bag. Unbending a little, he said, "You're new in town, aren't you?"

"Yes. I'm Miss Hamer's niece. Nona Jean Jamison. I'm staying with her—helping out. She's ill, you know."

"I know that she has been under the weather for some time, yes." He gave her a thin smile. "Well, then, welcome to Darling, Miss Jamison. Your aunt has been a customer of ours for a good many years."

Miss LaMotte made a huffing sound. "Then I would've thought you could've helped me out with that prescription."

Mr. Lima looked humble. "I'm sorry. Is there anything else I can get for you this afternoon?"

"No, thank you," Miss LaMotte said, lifting her chin. She took the bag and turned to go.

By this time, Verna had decided on a course of action and a way to introduce herself. She followed the lady out of the store and caught up with her just as she turned onto Rosemont.

"Miss LaMotte," she said, "I couldn't help overhearing what you and Mr. Lima were talking about. I've had some experience with insomnia, and I would like to recommend warm milk and crackers." She smiled cordially. "It may sound simple, but it works for me every time."

Miss LaMotte had turned and was regarding her with some disdain. Verna was suddenly conscious that she was wearing her gardening clothes—a plaid cotton blouse and a green twill skirt, neither of them clean or pressed.

"You are speaking to me?" Miss LaMotte asked, frowning.

"Well, yes," Verna said, thinking that this was obvious. She held out her hand. "My name is Verna Tidwell. I had the privilege of seeing you perform ten years ago, at the New Amsterdam Theater, in New York City. You were *swell.*"

At that moment, Mr. Bailey Beauchamp's Cadillac came around the courthouse square on Dauphin and cruised down the block toward them, slowing so that Mr. Beauchamp could have another look. As Lightning turned onto Rosemont, to begin another circuit around the square, Mr. Beauchamp tipped his hat and gave Miss LaMotte a flirtatious smile.

Miss LaMotte turned away, pretending not to notice. She faced Verna, lifting her chin. "I am sorry," she said sharply, ignoring Verna's outthrust hand, "but you are mistaken. You are confusing me with someone else. My name is Nona Jean Jamison. I am staying with my aunt here in Darling."

"Yes, Miss Jamison," Verna said, feeling rebuffed. She put her hand (her nails really were a little grubby) into her skirt pocket. "I understand that you're Miss Hamer's niece, and that you grew up over in Monroeville. But my husband Walter—he's dead now—and I saw you at the New Amsterdam on West Forty-second Street with Walter's cousin Gerald. Gerald is from Monroeville, too. So he knew who you were—although he said he would never in the world have recognized you." She smiled reminiscently. "You and Miss Lake were the Naughty and Nice Sisters. You danced the shimmy, and Miss Lake sang and played the mandolin and made funny jokes. I just want you to know that my husband Walter enjoyed it so much. It was all he talked about on the train back to—"

Miss LaMotte stamped her foot. "I said," she cried shrilly, "that you are wrong! Wrong, do you hear? I have never been in the theater, and I don't know a thing about Mr. Ziegfeld's shows or dancing and singing! I should like to go on about my business now. And I'm sure you have something else to do besides accosting perfect strangers." Chin up, shoulders straight, clutching her handbag and the paper sack Mr. Lima had given her, she turned away.

But not before Verna saw the shadow of fear in her eyes.

FOUR

Saturday Night in Darling, or Life Is Just a Bowl of Cherries

Over the summer, Grady had taught Lizzy to drive his blue Ford coupe and encouraged her to practice whenever they went out. She was saving her money to buy a car, but that would take a while. In the meantime, she could ride her bicycle or walk anywhere she wanted to go in Darling and the surrounding countryside. Her house was only a couple of blocks from the courthouse square, around which most of the town's businesses were located, including the law office where Lizzy worked, upstairs over the newspaper office.

Directly opposite the *Dispatch* building, in the middle of the square, stood the Cypress County Courthouse, an imposing two-story red brick building with a bell tower and a white-painted dome with a clock that struck every hour. The courthouse, built in 1905, was surrounded by a ragged brown apron of scuffed grass bordered with bright summer annuals: marigolds, zinnias, nasturtiums, cosmos, and the like. The flowers were planted, watered, and weeded by the Darling Dahlias for everyone in town to see and enjoy. The Dahlias believed that when times were hard, a few flower seeds could go a long way toward making people feel better, and they put that belief into practice wherever they could. Times were definitely hard in Darling these days, although folks who had been up north or back east said it was a lot worse in the big cities, where people were mostly strangers to one another and had to rely on the Salvation Army soup kitchens for food and Red Cross shelters when they didn't have a place to sleep. "We'd rather be in Darling than anywhere else," those folks said when they got back home, "especially when things are bad."

Darlingians generally agreed. Of course, there were the usual complainers, who didn't like this or that or the other thing. But for the most part, people thought their little town was a fine place to live. It was located in the gently rolling hills seventy miles north of Mobile—a full half-day drive away, more, if the roads were muddy—and a hundred miles south of the state's capital, Montgomery. As Bessie Bloodworth related the story in her lectures on local history, the town had been established in the early 1800s by Joseph P. Darling, a Virginian who had come into the area with his wife, five children, two slaves, a team of oxen, two milk cows, and a horse. Surveying the rich timber and fertile soils, the nearby river and the fast-flowing creek, Mr. Darling thought that the little valley would be a good place to live—and besides, his wife was sick and tired of life on the road and insisted that they settle down. According to Bessie, she said, with extraordinary firmness, "I am not ridin' another mile in that blessed wagon, Mr. Darling. If you want your meals and your washin' done steady, this right here is where you'll find it."

So Mr. Darling (who liked to eat every day and wear a clean shirt on Sundays) built two log cabins (a big one for his family, a smaller one for his slaves) and a barn, and then (because he was of an entrepreneurial turn) a general store. The gently rolling hills were covered with loblolly and long-leaf pines, with sweet gum and tulip trees in the creek and river bottoms, and magnolia and sassafras and sycamore and pecan. Mr. Darling's cousin, who had followed him from Virginia, built a sawmill, so that all those fine trees could be turned into boards for building. A gristmill followed almost immediately, which meant that anybody who could put in an acre or two of corn could get it ground and make corn pone. A couple of churches came next, and a schoolhouse, and not long after, several cotton gins and a cottonseed oil mill, which processed the cotton grown on plantations around the town and along the Alabama River, a few miles to the west. The roads were indescribably bad when it rained (which was often), so the Alabama River carried most of the north-south traffic, with steamboats shuttling back and forth between Montgomery and Mobile, delivering people and supplies at plantation landings and picking up baled cotton and other products.

Darling's history didn't include very much in the way of historic events, except when some Union soldiers tore through the town at the end of the War (always spoken of in Darling with a capital W). Or when the railroad spur was finally finished, connecting Darling to the Louisville & Nashville Railroad just outside Monroeville and delivering a final blow to river travel, since trains and railroad tracks were more reliable and cheaper to operate than the old-fashioned paddle wheelers, which had a nasty habit of sinking when the steam engine blew up or the boat rammed a snag. Oh, and there was the 1907 tornado, which had done more damage than the damn Yankees, tearing the bell tower off the recently built courthouse and ripping the roofs off houses and killing a dozen people.

But after that, things quieted down. The bell tower was

rebuilt, the town grew a little bigger, and when the Great War came, the price of cotton went through the roof. Still, nothing much of note had happened since the boys of the 167th came home from France in 1919—or didn't, as in the case of Lizzy's fiancé, Reggie Morris. The Roaring Twenties had roared through Darling very quietly, since the local ladies weren't crazy about bobbed hair and skirts so short they couldn't sit down in them, and most of the people in town belonged to a church that turned thumbs-down on dancing. There wasn't supposed to be any drinking of alcoholic beverages after the Alabama legislature passed the Bone-Dry Act of 1915, five years before the rest of the country followed suit, but that didn't mean a whole lot, since Alabamans always talked dry and drank wet. Voters thought that prohibiting alcohol was the Christian thing to do, since it might help people whose spirits were willing but whose flesh was weak. But there were plenty of folks who were Christians on Sunday morning and dancers and drinkers on Saturday night, and if somebody wanted hooch, he (or she) knew right where to go to get it.

They knew where to get a good meal, too, although most people in Darling ate breakfast, dinner (the main meal of the day, at noon), and supper at home with their families. If you had a reason for eating away from home, you had several choices, depending on who you were. If you were a traveling gentleman staying at the Old Alabama Hotel or a husband who wanted to give his wife a treat by taking her out for an expensive meal, you could go to the hotel dining room and sit down at a table with a bowl of flowers in the middle of a white damask tablecloth, and a waiter would pour water into a crystal goblet and offer you a menu that featured (depending on the time of year) tomato frappe, asparagus vinaigrette, green peas and carrots, your choice of a thick filet mignon wrapped in bacon or a cold plate with chicken, and a maple nut sundae for dessert—for which you would pay seventy-five cents. While you dined, you could listen to Mrs. LeVaughn playing soft, elegant dinner music—Chopin and Debussy and Liszt—on the beautiful rosewood square grand piano, which was surrounded by potted palms in the Old Alabama lobby.

If you were a single man and wanted a hearty meal that would stick to your ribs (beef stew and dumplings, say, or baked ham and mashed potatoes), you could walk over to the Meeks' boardinghouse two blocks west of the rail yard where the railroad workers and some of the men from the sawmill boarded and see if Mrs. Meeks could make room at the table for one more, which she usually could, especially if you didn't mind waiting until the second shift sat down. For the main dish, plus corn bread and green apple pie and all the coffee you could drink, you would expect to pay thirty-five cents, but you had to eat fast, because there was usually a third shift waiting to sit down. There was no time to talk, or anybody to talk to, either, since all the diners had their heads down, shoveling in their food. Definitely no dinner music.

Or you could go to the Darling Diner. You wouldn't pay a fortune, you wouldn't have to rush through your meal, and you could talk all you wanted with your friends, since all your friends were likely to be there, too. As for dinner music, there was the Philco radio on the shelf behind the counter. It played whatever the customers wanted to listen to—mostly farm information, daily crop and livestock and milk prices, weather reports, and stock market information, which often produced hisses and boos from those listeners who felt that Wall Street was another word for the devil.

For thirty years, the diner, located between Musgrove's Hardware and the *Dispatch* building, was owned and operated by Mrs. Hepzibah Hooper, who lived in the apartment on the second floor. Mrs. Hooper had a large garden out in the back, where she grew some of the okra, green beans, Southern peas, collard greens, tomatoes, bell peppers, and sweet potatoes that she served to her customers. As time went on and her clientele expanded, she found she had to have help with the cooking and was lucky (or smart) enough to hire Euphoria Hoyt, a colored lady who specialized in fried chicken, meat loaf, and meringue pies. It wasn't long before Euphoria was acknowledged as the best cook in that part of Alabama, and business got even better.

But Mrs. Hooper was a heavy woman, and when her legs began to swell, she had trouble standing behind the counter for more than a couple of hours, so she decided to sell. By that time, she had bought a half-interest in the Darling Telephone Exchange, and Mr. Whitworth (who owned the other half-interest) installed the switchboard in the storage room at the back of the diner. The Exchange started out with just one operator working part-time, but before long, almost everybody in town was on the telephone, except for a few holdouts like Miss Hamer, who was hard of hearing, and Mr. Norris, who objected because the ringing jangled his nerves. This meant that the Exchange had to have an operator on the switchboard every hour of the day and night, which was more than Mrs. Hooper had bargained for, especially after her legs started to swell. So she began looking around for a buyer— for both the Exchange and the diner.

And that's where Myra May Mosswell and Violet Sims came into the picture.

Myra May had learned her kitchen savvy when she managed the kitchen and the dining room at the Old Alabama Hotel. Her daddy, a much-loved Darling physician, had died and left her a house, some cash money, and a 1920 Chevy touring car named Big Bertha. Myra May was still considering what to do with her inheritance when a young woman named Violet Sims got off the Greyhound and applied for a job at the hotel. Violet was brown-haired and petite and very pretty, in a feminine sort of way, although this didn't mean that she was any pushover, because she definitely had her own ideas about the way things ought to be done. And the fact that she liked to wear pretty cuffs and collars and jabots made of lace and silk georgette and smiled a lot and laughed in a soft, sweet voice didn't mean that she was soft on the inside, too. Inside and out and through and through, Violet was definitely her own woman.

Myra May, on the other hand, wasn't anybody's idea of feminine—or pretty, either, for that matter. She was the only woman in town who wore belted trousers every day of the week (including Sundays) and was trim enough to look good in them. She had a square jaw, a strong mouth, a long, horsey nose, and an intense, questioning look that made people wonder if their ties were crooked or they had spinach between their teeth. She was a serious, practical person with a reputation for saying exactly what she thought, regardless of how she thought you were going to feel about it, and for making up her mind without shilly-shallying around. She had a tendency to answer in short, brusque sentences, and any man who got up enough nerve to ask her out once usually didn't repeat the request.

After Myra May graduated from the University of Alabama with a major in Domestic Science and a minor in Education, she decided that she really didn't have the patience to be a teacher. She also decided that she probably didn't have the patience to be somebody's wife, either, and by the time she was thirty and had gone out with all the available men in Darling, she was sure of it. One of the charter members of the Darling Dahlias, she certainly had her share of friends and loyal supporters, but people who did not like strong, direct, no-nonsense women had a tendency to keep their distance.

So it came as something of a surprise to folks when Myra May and Violet became fast friends. Whether it was because Violet was looking for somebody who would steady her down, or Myra May was looking for somebody who would lighten her up, nobody could be sure. But it wasn't long before they moved in together and began to talk about starting a business of their own. When they heard that Mrs. Hooper was thinking of selling out, they got excited about the possibilities and began investigating right away.

The diner's location between the *Dispatch* building and Musgrove's Hardware, right across from the courthouse, made it especially handy for people who had courthouse business around the noon hour and wanted to catch a quick bite. The building needed some painting and fix-up, but the kitchen appliances and equipment were in good shape and the counters, stools, and tables were all fair-to-middling. But best of all was the diner's outstanding reputation for good food at reasonable prices.

The two women inspected the property and discussed the matter upside down and backward. In the end, they decided to buy both the diner and Mrs. Hooper's half-interest in the Exchange, which meant that they now owned half of the town's telephone system. They imposed only one condition: that Euphoria Hoyt (who was still known as the best chicken fryer in southern Alabama) would continue to cook and manage the kitchen. Myra May traded her house for her share of the business, and Violet put up all the cash she had and some she borrowed from her sister in Memphis, and the deal was done and everybody was happy—including Euphoria, who took a shine to both of her new bosses. And before long, the customers at the diner (who had been a little skeptical about the new management) were very happy, too, because Myra May kept the food moving efficiently from Euphoria's skillet to the customers' plates and Violet kept on smiling in her sweet and friendly way.

It was a good situation all the way around.

Before Lizzy went into the diner that evening, she paused to read the headline of the Mobile *Register* on the wire newspaper rack beside the gray-and-red-painted pay telephone booth that had recently been installed outside the diner.

HOOVER SET TO CREATE COMMITTEE FOR UNEMPLOYMENT RELIEF, the newspaper headline announced. Lizzy shook her head doubtfully. She was no fan of the president, who had come into office before the Crash and seemed to be stuck on the idea that any "relief" for the unemployed ought to come through volunteers and private charities. Would this committee be any different from the others that had tried to mobilize volunteer efforts? Lizzy had no problem where charity was concerned—everybody ought to pitch in and help out where they could. But it was high time that government stepped up and did its part, too. Happily, there was another headline, much more appealing, and she bent over to read it: SIXTH GAME SERIES WIN FOR PHILLY ATHLETICS OVER ST. LOUIS CARDINALS. That would make Grady smile. He was an Athletics' fan.

Myra May was behind the counter when Lizzy opened the door and went in. Since it was Saturday night, Euphoria was frying catfish instead of chicken, and the plates were heaped with mashed potatoes, cream gravy, and a choice of beans, cabbage slaw, or fried okra, along with hush puppies and sweet tea or coffee—all for thirty cents. A slice of pecan pie (the usual Saturday special) was another dime, but Euphoria cut her pie into sixths, rather than the usual eighths, so it was worth the extra money.

And since it was Saturday, you had dinner music at no extra charge, for the radio was tuned to the National Barn Dance, on WLS in Chicago (the initials stood for "World's Largest Store," because it was originally owned by Sears and Roebuck). Gene Autry—new to the Barn Dance—was singing a cowboy ballad, but the four men at the counter weren't listening. They were talking about the poor cotton yield due to the drought, the rising unemployment rates, and the latest exploits of Chicago's notorious gangster and mob boss, Al Capone, who ran the city's speakeasies, bookie joints, gambling houses, brothels, racetracks, and distilleries.

"Hey, Liz," Myra May called out from behind the counter. "We've got the table in the corner. I'll be with you and Verna in a minute. Fredda's taking over for me this evening." Fredda was the youngest Musgrove girl, capable but not always dependable—which probably accounted, Liz thought, for Myra May's frazzled look.

Lizzy waved to Myra May, then turned and threaded her way between the tables, stopping to say hello to Ophelia Snow, vice president of the Dahlias, and Ophelia's husband Jed, the conservative mayor of Darling. They were eating supper with Charlie Dickens, the editor of the progressive Darling *Dispatch*, and his sister Edna Fay. Seeing Mr. Dickens, Lizzy was tempted to stop and mention her idea for a human interest feature about Miss Jamison's Broadway career, but she thought it would be better to approach him in the office, where they could sit down and discuss the details.

Anyway, Jed and Mr. Dickens were having their regular Saturday night argument about politics and the economy, with Jed making his usual passionate defense of President Hoover's conservative "leave-it-alone" approach: the notion that the federal government should stand back and let individual communities deal with their own individual problems. It was Jed's belief that the Darling volunteers—its fine churches, the Ladies' Club, the Benevolent and Protective Order of Elks, and the Merchants' Association—could handle anything that came up, and it was ridiculous to think that the bureaucrats in Washington would have any better idea of what needed to be done than the folks right here at home. He wasn't in favor of the new committee for unemployment relief and thought that Mr. Hoover had gotten pushed into creating it because some in the Republican party were afraid that they would lose more Congressional seats in the upcoming midterm elections if the president wasn't seen as doing *something*.

Mr. Dickens, on the other hand, took a more liberal (but equally passionate) approach, arguing that Washington needed to do more to help out. The British government, for instance, had for some time funded an old-age pension, so its elderly citizens didn't have to go to the poorhouse when they could no longer work. And with unemployment growing every day, he argued, the federal government ought to provide some kind of relief. There were lots of jobs that needed doing. Government ought to be organizing the effort to pair jobless men to work. Between the drought of the last few years and the old sharecropping system that turned so many—black and white—into de facto slaves, Southern farmers were in dire need of help. Huey P. Long, governor of Louisiana, could clearly see the scope of the problem and was offering a whole bushel of solutions. Why couldn't President Hoover?

Lizzy generally agreed with Mr. Dickens, although she wasn't so sure about Governor Long, who had just been charged with kidnapping a pair of witnesses in a fraud investigation. People called him "the Dictator of Louisiana," and with good reason. But as she passed the table, she caught Ophelia's eye and gave her a sympathetic smile. Ophelia and Edna Fay were trying to have their own conversation, on the subject of Edna Fay's efforts to organize the Darling Quilting

Club, of which she was the president, to produce quilts for needy families. But they had to do it under the 'menfolks' loud discussion, which had already gotten to the table-pounding stage.

So Lizzy just said hello and headed for the table in the corner, which was covered with a red-checked cotton cloth. Verna Tidwell was already seated there, wearing a pretty brown and gold two-piece silk shantung dress and a brown felt hat. Lizzy's hat was blue (the one her mother had refurbished) and her blue crepe dress had a separate sleeveless jacket, a jabot tie and a belt, and a pleated and flared skirt. Women in Darling liked to dress up when they went out to supper and the movies, even if they weren't going on a "date."

As Lizzy pulled out a chair to sit down, Verna leaned forward, her brow furrowed. "I talked to Miss LaMotte after you went home," she said, without preamble. "I swear, Liz. Something about this situation is really fishy. She denies being who she is."

Lizzy blinked. "You mean, she isn't Nona Jean—"

"No, no, no, the other way around. She denies being Lorelei LaMotte. She swore up and down that she'd never been on Broadway, doesn't know Mr. Ziegfeld, and has never been a dancer."

"When did you talk to her?" Lizzy pulled off her blue gloves and folded them into her lap. "Where?"

"This afternoon, just outside the drugstore. She was trying to get a prescription for Veronal filled but Mr. Lima wouldn't do it because the prescription was out of date. She was really upset—said it was a matter of life and death. He sold her some Dr. Miles instead."

"That old snake oil medicine." Lizzy rolled her eyes. "My mother takes it. But how did you happen to be at the drugstore, Verna? The last time I saw you, you were headed for home."

"Well, I—That is, I—" Verna stopped, embarrassed. "To tell the truth, I followed her."

"Followed who?" Myra May asked, appearing at the table with a loaded tray. She had taken off her white bibbed apron and was wearing her usual beige linen trousers and a red button-front rayon short-sleeved blouse, with a loose paisley scarf. She began setting plates on the table. "No, no, hold on a minute. Whatever you're telling, wait until I get back with the iced tea. I don't want to miss any of it."

Which meant that Verna had to start all over again when Myra May came back with the pitcher, and Lizzy had to explain who Nona Jean Jamison was before she became Lorelei LaMotte. The story was a little confusing, but finally Myra May had it clear.

"So this woman is incognito," she said, buttering a piece of hot corn bread. "I guess that means she doesn't want anybody in town to know that she was in vaudeville."

"But why?" Verna asked, waving her fork. "I mean, for heaven's sake, Myra May. She's famous! Why wouldn't she want anybody to know?"

"Maybe she's trying to get away from the newspaper reporters and all that attention," Myra May replied. "Maybe she just wants some peace and quiet. People do, you know. And it probably isn't all that easy to earn a living as a performer these days. Since Prohibition, I mean. And since the Crash. People don't have as much money as they used to."

"Peace and quiet?" Verna laughed shortly. "If that's what she wants, she's going to have to hang that red dress in her closet and wash that makeup off her face. Putting a bag over her head wouldn't hurt, either. Bailey Beauchamp was about to jump right out of that fancy Cadillac of his and gobble her up right there in the middle of the street, like she was a piece of candy."

Myra May chuckled. "Don't let Mrs. Hobart hear about

that. She's the jealous type, you know. If Bailey Beauchamp hasn't put his misbehavin' behind him, she'll show him how."

Lizzy sighed. If it was true that all Miss Jamison wanted was peace and quiet, her newspaper article idea probably wasn't going to work. If Miss Hamer's niece wouldn't admit to Verna that she was a Broadway star, it wasn't likely that she would submit to an interview for a feature story in the *Dispatch*. But maybe Verna hadn't approached her right. Or maybe she had simply caught Miss Jamison at an awkward moment, when she was upset about not getting her prescription refilled. Lizzy frowned, wondering what that was all about. Veronal was a very strong sleeping medicine, from what she had read. It must be for Miss Hamer. Was the old lady having trouble sleeping? Was she very ill?

"Actually," Verna said, pursing her lips, "now that I think about it, I wonder why Miss Hamer's niece is here. Doesn't it seem odd to you? I mean, has she ever in her whole adult life visited her aunt? If she had, surely somebody would have noticed, wouldn't they?"

"That's true," Lizzy replied. Strangers in Darling were an irresistible source of gossip. And Miss Jamison was the sort of person that people would talk about. "Maybe she's here because she's down on her luck. Myra May is right. Money is tight everywhere—it can't be the best time in the world to be in show business." That would be another angle for her story, she mused. Small-town girl dances into the Big Apple limelight, then slips and falls back into shadowy obscurity. A spectacular rise; a tragic fall.

"And if she's never been here," Verna was going on, "why not? I mean, doesn't it seem a little strange that she's never once bothered to visit her aunt—and all of a sudden she's *living* here?" She frowned, pushing her mashed potatoes around with her fork. "Come to that, how do we know who this woman actually *is*? She's already lying about not being Lorelei LaMotte. Maybe she's lying about being Miss Hamer's niece, too."

Lizzy dug into her catfish, which was crispy brown on the outside, flaky and delicious inside. "For heaven's sake, Verna. Can't you ever just take people at face value?"

"Nope." Verna tossed her head. "Doesn't pay, Liz. Lots of people cheat. Others lie. And some will do anything to gain an advantage. I see it all the time in the probate office, you know."

Lizzy sighed. Verna was by nature a suspicious person. But she had become even more wary over the years she had managed the records in the Cypress County probate clerk's office, where she was responsible for recording election results, people's wills and estates, property transactions, and the like. Verna always said that if she stubbed her toe on a rock, she was compelled to look under it, to see what was hiding there.

"And something usually is," she would add. "Something we probably wouldn't go looking for, if we could avoid it."

Lizzy had to admit that Verna had a point. Some people cheated; others lied. She had recently read a news item about a family in Florida who had welcomed their long-lost son, kidnapped years before. Unfortunately, the man turned out to be an imposter angling for an inheritance. She supposed it wouldn't hurt to look a little more closely at Miss Lorelei LaMotte.

"Maybe we ought to have a talk with Bessie Bloodworth," she suggested. "Bessie has known Miss Hamer longer than the rest of us. If anybody knows anything about why Miss Jamison is here in Darling, it would be Bessie."

"Actually, now that you mention Bessie, I do remember something," Myra May said. "I'd forgotten about it until right this minute. But somebody—a woman—in Chicago telephoned Bessie a couple of weeks ago, asking about Miss Hamer. Since it was long distance, I stayed on the line long enough to make sure that the call went through okay. The woman said she was calling Bessie because her aunt doesn't have a telephone, and she needed to find out a few things."

"Find out what things?" Verna asked curiously. "What else did she want to know?"

"I have no idea. I got off the line." Myra May pointed at Verna with her fork. "And even if I hadn't, I couldn't tell you what I heard. I shouldn't have told you as much as I did."

"All you've said is that a woman was calling from Chicago, Myra May." Verna sounded cross. "Anyway, we're not asking for the combination to the bank vault. We're just trying to understand why a woman calling herself Miss Hamer's niece—"

"Forget it, Verna," Myra May said firmly, and applied her fork to her mashed potatoes. "You've worked on the switchboard yourself. You understand that the operators aren't supposed to listen to people's conversations. And if they do catch a bit of it, they're definitely not supposed to talk about what they hear."

Lizzy knew that this was true. Verna had worked part-time on the switchboard a few years back, when Mrs. Hooper was sick and needed the help.

"Violet can keep her mouth shut," Myra May was going on. "But Olive and Lenore are still just kids. If I told tales and they found out, they'd think it was all right for them to do it and then I'd have to fire 'em. I love you with all my heart, Verna dear, but don't ask me to tell you anything I might've heard on the switchboard. Okay?"

Verna rolled her eyes. "Myra May, you are a *hard* woman. I am sure glad I don't have to work for you."

Lizzy chuckled. The four switchboard operators had to be among the best-informed and most up-to-date people in Darling. All the news in town went through the Exchange—the price of cotton, how many kids had the measles, whose wife had left him, whose sister had miscarried. But Myra May made sure that her operators played by the rules. What comes into the Exchange, stays in the Exchange.

She changed the subject. "Speaking of Violet, what do you hear from her, Myra May? When is she coming home from Memphis?"

Not looking up, Myra May spread butter on her corn bread. "She called this morning." She spoke reluctantly, almost as if she didn't want to talk about it. "Her sister isn't doing so well, I'm sorry to say."

"It's her sister's first baby, isn't it?" Verna asked.

Myra May nodded. "A little girl named Dorothy. The baby's okay, apparently, but Violet is worried about her sister. The doctor is keeping her in the hospital, and of course there isn't much money. Violet is worried about how they're going to pay the bill. I'm afraid—" She stopped, as if she didn't want to say the words.

"Afraid of . . ." Lizzy prompted gently.

Myra May pressed her lips together. "Afraid she'll decide to stay in Memphis, I guess," she said slowly. "There's a heck-uva lot more exciting stuff going on up there than there is in Darling. Dunno why she would come back."

Lizzy was surprised. This was more than Myra May had ever said about her relationship to Violet—which was proba-bly a clue to just how troubled she was. "Violet left Memphis because she didn't like living in the city," Lizzy reminded her emphatically. "And she stays here because she likes living in Darling. And because of you," she added. "You know that."

"I guess." Myra May sighed. "I'll just be glad when she gets home, that's all. I miss her. And we could use her help. We've been pretty busy here at the diner, and Olive has a bad cold and missed her shift at the switchboard last night. She'll be out tonight, too. I've got to get back here right after the movie and fill in." She glanced at the Snow's Farm Supply clock on the back wall. "Speaking of which, looks like we'd better get going, don't you think? We can come back later and have our pie and coffee."

"Dessert after the show," Verna said with a grin. "Sounds swell."

As it turned out, the Snows and Mr. Dickens and his sister were going to the movie, too, so they all walked together down Franklin Street in a group, past the *Dispatch* building and Hancock's Groceries. The Palace was at the end of the block, its brightly lit marquee jutting out over the sidewalk. The owner, Mr. Don Greer, stood outside, welcoming the patrons.

As usual, there was a line at the glass-fronted ticket window, where the Greers' daughter Gladys sold tickets at twenty-five cents apiece, and at the candy counter, where Mrs. Greer did a land-office business selling candy, popcorn and hot roasted peanuts, as well as icy-cold bottles of Coca-Cola out of the cooler. Inside the theater, in the dimly lit haze of cigarette and cigar smoke that hung in the air, Mrs. LeVaughn was playing the piano. The movie was a talkie, so she wouldn't be playing during the film. But while the younger folks loved the talkies, many oldsters still preferred silent films. They thought it wasn't a night at the movies unless they could lean back in their seats and watch the flickering screen while they listened to Mrs. LeVaughn, who could play ragtime as well as Chopin. So Mr. Greer traded a movie ticket and a box of hot buttered popcorn for an hour of Mrs. LeVaughn's piano, before he turned off the house lights and turned on the projector.

Lizzy, Verna, and Myra May got popcorn and peanuts, then found their seats and settled in expectantly, listening to Mrs. LeVaughn play the "Maple Leaf Rag" and looking around to see which of their friends had come out for an evening's entertainment. The movie house wasn't quite full, but there was a respectable crowd and the audience wasn't disappointed in the film. *The Saturday Night Kid* was a romantic comedy about two lively young sisters—played by Clara Bow and Jean Arthur—who worked in a department store and were both in love with the same man, another store employee who was a compulsive gambler stealing company funds. After a half-dozen twists and turns, the characters got what was coming to them, and the audience went home smiling.

Back at the diner, Myra May turned on the gas burner under the coffee percolator. "I always thought that romantic comedies were silly," Myra May said. "But I've changed my mind. The world is pretty grim. People need something to smile about."

Lizzy leaned her elbows on the counter. The Closed sign was hung on the diner's front door and the only light was the one in the back, so the dining area was comfortably dim. They had the place to themselves, and Myra May had turned on the radio. A crooner was singing, "Let a Smile Be Your Umbrella."

"Heaven knows, there's enough heartache going around," Verna agreed. "People feel better if they can escape for a little while. Going to the movies on Saturday night gives them something to look forward to all week."

"Right," Myra May said, cutting generous slices of pecan pie. "The anticipation by itself is probably worth a quarter." She cocked her head, listening to the radio. "Let a smile be your umbrella, on a rainy, rainy day," she sang along with the music. "And if your sweetie cries, just tell her that a smile will always pay."

"I wish it were that simple," Lizzy said softly, taking the pie plates to the table. She was thinking of Violet and the situation in Memphis, and wondering how it was going to come out.

"I think what people need is to see the Nice and Naughty

Sisters doing their act in the talent show," Verna said with a wicked grin. "That would cheer them up pretty fast."

Myra May snickered. "You bet it would." The coffee was perking merrily, and she turned off the gas and picked up the pot. "But I thought you said that Miss LaMotte danced nearly naked, Verna. That kind of thing might be a big hit in New York, but this is Darling, for pity's sake. I can just imagine what the Baptist preacher would say about a naked woman doing the shimmy in front of God and everybody." She poured three cups of coffee and pushed them across the counter.

"Verna's just teasing." Lizzy said. "She knows Mildred Kilgore would never even consider inviting Miss LaMotte and her friend to do their act."

"Not the real vaudeville act," Verna protested. She picked up the coffee cups and carried them to the table. "They could do a cleaned-up version. I mean, there's all kinds of naughty, isn't there? The Clara Bow kind, for instance, which is funny and cute and clever, like what we saw tonight. I'll bet Miss LaMotte and Miss Lake could come up with something a lot less risqué than they did for Mr. Ziegfeld. Something that doesn't have any S-E-X in it."

"S-E-X." Myra May put her finger against her cheek and pretended a puzzled frown. "That spells *sex*, doesn't it?" She widened her eyes and lifted the pitch of her voice. "S-E-X. Why, of course it does!" She pulled three forks from a container of silverware and slid them across the counter. "Verna Tidwell, you wicked girl! Whatever can you mean, using that word in front of us ladies?"

All three of them laughed, but a little ruefully, because Miss Rogers, one of their Darling Dahlias, had said something very similar not very long ago. They all liked Miss Rogers but she was *very* old-fashioned.

"Well, it won't work at all if Nona Jean Jamison isn't

going to own up to being Lorelei LaMotte," Lizzy said in a matter-of-fact tone. "That's the first hurdle you'll have to get over, Verna. Let me know if that happens." She had her own reasons for wanting Verna to succeed, of course. If Miss Jamison could be persuaded to acknowledge that she was really Miss LaMotte, she might also be persuaded to agree to a newspaper feature story.

"You're right," Verna said thoughtfully. "I guess I'll have to work on that."

There was a loud, buzzy ring from the direction of the back room. "That's the long-distance line," Myra May said, wiping her hands on a towel. "You girls go ahead with your pie and coffee. I'll be back as soon as I can."

Lizzy and Verna sat down at the table. They were silent for a moment, eating their pie and drinking their coffee and listening to the radio. The band was now playing the first bars of "Life Is Just a Bowl of Cherries." The announcer said, "Ladies and gentlemen, give a warm welcome to a new singer with a fabulous voice—somebody you'll want to keep your eye on and tune your ears to. Here he is, Bing Crosby!"

The crooner came in on the beat. *"Don't take it serious,"* he sang. *"Life's too mysterious."*

In a thoughtful tone, Verna said, "Hey, Liz, how about if you and I have a talk with Bessie after the Dahlias' meeting tomorrow." She grinned. "Bessie loves to dig around in people's family history. She may know bushels about Lorelei LaMotte."

"Sounds like a good place to start," Lizzy agreed. "Sure. Let's do that." She hesitated, thinking that she ought to let Verna know what she had in mind. "Actually, I'm thinking of talking to Mr. Dickens about the possibility of writing a—"

But she didn't get to finish her sentence. Myra May had just come into the diner from the Exchange. Her face was somber and there was a dark look in her eyes.

Lizzy was startled—and concerned. The switchboard operator was always the first to know if there was a fire or an automobile accident or if somebody had died and the relatives were calling Mr. Noonan, who ran Darling's only funeral parlor. "Has something happened, Myra May? Who was that on the phone?"

Verna got up and pulled out a chair. "Here. Sit down and have some coffee. You look pale."

Myra May sat down with a thump. She took a sip of coffee and put down the cup. "What's happened," she said bleakly, "is that Violet's sister has died."

"Oh, dear," Lizzy exclaimed, horror-stricken. She knew how much Violet had loved her sister, how close they had been. "Oh, Myra May, that's too bad! I am so sorry!"

"The baby's going to be all right?" Verna asked.

"The baby's fine. It's the mother who's dead."

"*So keep repeating 'It's the berries,'*" Bing Crosby sang. "*And live and laugh at it all.*"

"Applesauce." Verna got up and switched off the radio.

Lizzy put her hand on Myra May's arm, glad that the song, with its forced, phony cheerfulness, was gone. Into the silence, she said softly, "What's Violet going to do?"

Myra May gave a heavy sigh. She looked down at her hands and Lizzy could see the worry gnawing away at her. "Bury her sister, I guess. Stay in Memphis and take care of the baby while the daddy is at work. There isn't much else she can do." Another sigh. "Trouble is, he's a drinker, and he didn't really want the kid in the first place. Plus, the apartment is a really small place. She's sleeping on the couch, with Dorothy in a dresser drawer." She dropped her head into her hands.

Lizzy shivered. A drinker. Prohibition—the Volstead Act had gone into effect nationally in 1920—was supposed to take care of that, wasn't it? But of course it hadn't. There seemed to be a lot more booze than there ever was before. In small towns everywhere, local moonshiners and bootleggers made sure that anybody who wanted a bottle could get one— even in the South, which, as Will Rogers joked, was dry and would continue to vote dry as long as people were sober enough to stagger to the polls. In big cities like Chicago, gangsters such as Al Capone and Bugs Moran were making millions out of the sale of bootleg alcohol, and black markets were flourishing everywhere.

"How about Violet's mother?" Verna asked. "Can't she help?"

"She died a couple of years ago," Myra May replied, her voice muffled. "There aren't any other relatives, on either side of the family." She raised her head and pushed her pie plate away. "Sorry, girls. I don't much feel like eating dessert. I'd just rather . . . rather be alone, I guess."

"We understand, Myra May." Verna stood and picked up the empty plates and cups. She glanced at the clock on the wall. "Come on, Liz. It's past ten. Time we were heading home."

Lizzy got up, too, then bent and dropped a quick kiss onto her friend's dark curls. Myra May always appeared tough and in control, and she never liked to show her feelings. It was as if she were a turtle, retreating inside its shell when something threatened. But she was far more vulnerable than she looked, and Lizzy knew she was hurting.

"We're here if you need us," she said quietly. "All you have to do is call."

As if that were a signal, the switchboard buzzed. Myra May stood and picked up her coffee cup. "Well, that's it," she said wearily. "Feelin' sorry time is over. Gotta go to work." She gave her friends a crooked grin. "Just a bowl of cherries, huh? Wonder whose life that idiot is singing about. Nobody I know."

As Myra May went in the direction of the switchboard,

Lizzy and Verna let themselves out the diner's front door, locking it behind them.

The streetlights around Darling's courthouse square, installed a couple of years before, were always turned off at nine thirty to save on electricity. Even on dark nights, this didn't much matter, since the movie was usually over by nine and everybody was home by the time the lights went out. But tonight there was a moon, nearly full, hanging like a huge silver coin in the eastern sky, turning the silent street into a moving tapestry of lights and shadows. There wasn't a sound except for the distant sputtering of an automobile and the sharp yap-yap-yapping of a small dog, somewhere a little closer.

Lizzy looked up at the moon swimming in a sky full of stars, and was glad that the streetlights were off. She took a deep breath, loving the warm dark and the fragrance of honeysuckle. She felt terribly sorry for Violet and for the new little baby, who would never know her mother. But she felt even sorrier for all the people, everywhere, who had to live and work in big cities like Memphis and Chicago, where there was crime and lawlessness and ugliness everywhere they looked. They would never know how it felt to live in a safe and beautiful place like Darling, where people cared about each other and about their little town.

Verna gave her a sharp look. "You okay about walking home alone, Lizzy?"

"Of course," Lizzy said. Home was just a couple of blocks away. Daffodil would be waiting for her, and her own sweet little house, and the companionable screech owl that lived in the live oak outside her bedroom window. "And this is Darling, you know."

"Yeah, it's Darling," Verna said. "But that doesn't mean we shouldn't be careful." She pushed her hands into the pockets of her skirt. "Wonder what Myra May will do if Violet decides to stay in Memphis to take care of that baby."

"I don't know," Lizzy said, shaking her head. "I've been wondering that, too. Times are tough. People have to make hard choices. But we have to look on the bright side. Whatever Violet does, it'll be the right thing. I hope."

"Yeah," Verna said again. "I hope so, too. But the right thing for some folks is sometimes the wrong thing for others." She let that hang in the air for a moment, then said, "Don't forget. We're talking to Bessie Bloodworth right after the meeting tomorrow. About Miss Jamison." She grinned. "Also known as Lorelei LaMotte."

"I won't forget," Lizzy said. "Good night, Verna." She turned and began to walk down the street.

Verna turned to go the other way, took a few steps, then stopped and flung out her arms. "Don't take it serious," she called. She did a little soft-shoe shuffle. "Life's too mysterious."

Lizzy laughed and waved, then headed home, feeling a little lighter. Life might not be a bowl of cherries, but you could always find something that would cheer you up—as long as you lived in Darling, anyway.

FIVE

The Roof Falls In

Lizzy's ample mother couldn't fit comfortably into the narrow dining nook and Lizzy's small house didn't boast a dining room, so they would be eating at the kitchen table. Lizzy dressed it up for their Sunday dinner, spreading an embroidered tablecloth and setting it with her favorite yellow china plates, rimmed in green and decorated with decals of flowers and fruits. Her napkins were green, and in the middle of the table, she added a vase filled with pretty asters and cosmos and a few sprigs of autumn honeysuckle.

Lizzy stood back and surveyed her work, feeling satisfied. She and her mother would have a pleasant dinner and talk over whatever it was that her mother wanted to discuss— probably something trivial, like that green straw hat. She just wanted some attention, that was all, and Lizzy thought guiltily that she probably hadn't visited her mother often enough the last few weeks. She would make it a point to drop in on her every few days. Then, when they had finished dinner, they would take their pie and coffee into the backyard, where they could enjoy the hollyhocks and morning glories still blooming along the fence and the marigolds and four o'clocks bordering the vegetable garden. And at one thirty, Lizzy would tell her mother that she had to leave for the Dahlias' meeting. She had given quite a lot of thought to the way she would handle that worrisome business about the door key, and had a little speech already planned.

"Please stay and finish your coffee," she would say, "but be sure and leave your key on the table when you go home. Otherwise, I'll have to change the locks." She would say it casually and sweetly but firmly, and then walk out the door and leave her mother to consider her options. Unlike her mother (by nature an argumentative person), Lizzy did not like disagreements. She always tried to think of a way to avoid unpleasant encounters.

But that wasn't exactly the way things happened, for Mrs. Lacy delivered her news the moment she set foot in the kitchen, even before she took off the black gloves and wide-brimmed black straw hat with fanciful fuchsia flowers that she had worn to church. When she heard her mother's announcement, Lizzy felt as if the roof had just fallen in on her, or the earth had opened up and swallowed her. In fact, she could think of nothing worse, unless it was cancer or tuberculosis, and even then there was sometimes a cure, and always hope, until the very end. But there was no cure for this, and no hope, either, as far as she could see.

Mr. Johnson, at the Darling Savings and Trust, was about to foreclose on her mother's house.

Lizzy put her hand to her mouth, scarcely able to get her breath. "Foreclose!" she gasped. "But—"

"The fifteenth of October!" Mrs. Lacy cried dramatically. She was a large woman with a pillowy softness that was belied by her habit of sharp, petulant speech, which not even her Southern drawl could soften. Between her physical size and the power of her vocal chords, Lizzy always felt small and squeezed, as if her mother took up all the space and sucked up all the air, leaving almost no space and no air at all for her.

"October! But that's just a few weeks away!" Lizzy protested, bewildered. "He can't do that! Why, how long have you known?"

Her mother looked away. "Only since April."

"April!" Lizzy exclaimed in disbelief. "But that's . . . that's over five months! Why didn't you tell me earlier, Mama? We might have been able to work something out."

"Work what out? There's no workin' out something like this where Mr. George E. Pickett Johnson is concerned. That man is just bound, bent, and determined to be as heartless as he can be." Mrs. Lacy whipped a lawn handkerchief out of the lace-trimmed bodice of her purple rayon chiffon dress. "He says I have to move all of my furniture and belongings out by the fifteenth. But where am I goin' to go?" She sniffled and dabbed at one eye. "Where, I ask you?"

It was a calculating question, and Lizzy refused to answer it. "But how . . . how could this be?" she asked wonderingly. "Daddy left the house to you free and clear, with a little annuity—enough money to make you comfortable for the rest of your life. What on earth could have happened?"

Mrs. Lacy dabbed at the other eye, then tucked her hankie back where it came from. "Yes, that's what your daddy did," she said in a defensive tone. "Your daddy was a good man. He took care of us. As for the annuity—" She lifted her broad shoulders and let them fall in a gesture of resignation, implying that it, too, was gone.

"But what could have—"

Mrs. Lacy lifted her chin. "The stock market was blazin' away like a house afire, and I couldn't stand to be left out. So I borrowed some money to invest and put the house up. Collateral, is what it's called."

"Oh, Mama, you didn't do anything so foolish!" Lizzy

exclaimed despairingly. "You didn't put the money into the stock market!"

Mrs. Lacy bristled. "Well, I don't know why not. Everybody was doing it. Every time I opened a newspaper or magazine I read about people makin' a fortune on Wall Street. So I asked Miss Rogers for the name of her broker and I invested—"

"You didn't *invest*, Mama," Lizzy cut in grimly. "You gambled. You gambled with your house and you lost."

Mrs. Lacy pulled out a chair, examined it to be sure there was no dust, and sat down. "Well, there's no point in givin' me one of your lectures, Elizabeth," she said in a huffy tone. "What's done is done, and that's all there is to it." She picked up her glass. "Are we goin' to have something to drink, or did you put the glasses out here just for show?"

Lizzy opened the refrigerator and took out a pitcher of cold water. "Have you talked to Mr. Johnson?" She poured water into her mother's glass, and then into her own.

Her mother picked up the glass and wrinkled her nose. "No lemonade?"

"I've stopped buying lemons," Lizzy said. "They've gotten expensive." She added pointedly, "And I've been saving my money. I'm hoping to buy a car."

"A car. I don't know what you'd want a car for. That fine Mr. Alexander would be glad to let you drive his whenever you want." Her mother put the glass down, hard. "Of course I've spoken to Mr. Johnson."

"Well, have you tried to negotiate some kind of settlement?" Lizzy knew that George E. Pickett Johnson (a descendant of a Confederate War general) was considered a hard man, but surely he would listen to reason. There had to be a way to solve this.

"A settlement?" her mother asked indignantly. "I have begged him. I have pleaded with him. I have pointed out that he and his bank won't look good at all if he snatches a God-fearin' widow's home away from her and puts her out on the street. But he won't budge. He is a terrible man. Everybody says so."

Lizzy turned away, not trusting herself to speak. She took the dish of potato salad out of the refrigerator and the meat loaf and green beans out of the gas oven, where they were keeping warm. The crust of her freshly baked peach pie, made from fruit she had picked from the tree in the backyard and canned right here in this kitchen, looked crisp and luscious, and there was almond-flavored whipped cream for the topping. But she had lost all appetite.

Still, she was not going to show her mother how hard she had been hit by news of the foreclosure. Smiling gamely, she put the food on the table and said, in as cheerful a voice as she could summon, "Let's enjoy our Sunday dinner, Mama. I'm sure that things will look brighter after we've eaten."

Her mother's appetite didn't seem diminished in any way by the awful prospect of her house being foreclosed in just a few weeks. She ate rapidly and with enthusiasm and helped herself to seconds. And when Lizzy poured coffee and served the peach pie (she had decided against going into the backyard), she asked for three large spoonfuls of almond whipped cream. The pie disappeared in no time.

Mrs. Lacy patted her lips with a folded napkin. "Well, now, Elizabeth, we need to discuss what we are goin' to do. We've had our differences over the years, as I'll be the first to admit. But I am sure that my only daughter—my only *child*—will not let her mother be put out on the street." She put her elbows on the table and went on, not giving Lizzy time to respond. "You know, I hated the idea of your movin' over here, but it looks like it's turned out to be just a real good thing. You have fixed this place up so it's neat as a pin and pretty as a dollhouse. I won't have to go on the street at all. I can just move in here with you."

"Oh, no, Mama," Lizzy said firmly. "That's not—"

"It might be a squeeze for a while," her mother went on, as if Lizzy had not spoken. "But I'm sure we can find room for everything." She regarded Lizzy's G.E. Monitor refrigerator, humming quietly against the wall. "Not all my furniture, of course. Your stove is new, and your electric fridge is much better than my old icebox, which leaks water all over the floor." She chuckled mirthlessly. "Mr. George E. Pickett Johnson can have the musty old thing, if he wants it."

"No, Mama." Lizzy pulled in her breath and let it out. "I won't let you be put onto the street. I'll help you find someplace to live. But you are *not* moving in with me, and that's all there is to it. Tomorrow I will go see Mr. Johnson myself and tell him that he needs to give you more time. He—"

"Absolutely not!" Mrs. Lacy snapped, throwing down her napkin. Her eyes were narrowed and her neck was blotched with red. "You will do no such thing, Elizabeth. I will not abide the humiliation of my daughter goin' crawlin' to that wretched bully. Sally-Lou will start bringin' my things over here tomorrow. Mrs. Oliver's colored man, Tiny, has promised to help with the heavy pieces. The parlor will be a little crowded, but we can manage. I'm sure you'll agree that my chintz drapes will look much better in there than your plain ones. I've never liked that awful burlap weave, anyway."

"But, Mama—"

Mrs. Lacy held up her hand. "Hush, Elizabeth, until I'm finished. I'll take the front bedroom upstairs. It will be a tight fit gettin' my bed up those narrow stairs, but I measured yesterday, and it'll go. We can put a cot in the storage room for Sally-Lou until you and dear Mr. Alexander are married, and then she can have your bedroom."

"Married!" Lizzy was incredulous. "What on God's green earth are you talking about? I have no intention of getting married anytime soon. In fact, I have no plan whatsoever to get married—to Grady Alexander or anybody else!"

As she spoke, she realized that this foreclosure business must have been the moving force behind her mother's puzzling reversal on the question of Grady Alexander. And all of a sudden, the whole scheme became crystal clear. Faced with the market crash, Mr. Johnson's foreclosure order, and the need to find somewhere to live, her mother had come up with a plan. She had started urging Lizzy to marry Grady so she could have Lizzy's house. She got the key copied so she could come over while Lizzy was at work and decide where to put her furniture. And she had put off all discussion of this awful business until the very last minute, when there was no time to have a reasonable conversation about alternatives.

At the thought of having her perfect little house invaded by her quarrelsome, outsize *mother,* Lizzy felt sick. But she felt even sicker at the thought that her mother was so carelessly, so cruelly manipulative that she would push her daughter into getting married just so she could take over her house!

"Oh, gracious me. Not gettin' married?" Mrs. Lacy heaved a dramatically disappointed sigh. "I am so sorry to hear that, Elizabeth. I think you and Mr. Alexander make the most marvelous couple. And of course I never raised my daughter to be an old maid." Another sigh, this one of long-suffering forbearance. "But there's no point in gettin' all upset about that part of it. Sally-Lou won't mind sleepin' on the cot. Of course, it would be nice if this house was just a teensy bit larger, but we can manage." She leaned over and patted Lizzy's hand. "Don't worry your pretty little head about it, dear. We'll be a tad crowded, but we'll make do. And maybe, in a few months, after you've had time to ponder, you'll see your way clear to marryin' that fine Mr. Alexander, who loves you so very much. As I do, of course. You know I do."

Lizzy stared at her for a long moment, and then the sick feeling suddenly turned into something else, a searing, volcanic anger at her mother's manipulations.

"Mama!" She stood up, clenching her hands. "Mama, you listen to me and you listen hard. I do not know the answer to your predicament, but I am telling you one thing for certain. You are *not* moving into my house, not now, not later, not under any circumstance. You are going to give me that key you had made, right now, or I will be changing the locks first thing in the morning. Furthermore, you will not step foot in my house again without my express invitation. Do you hear me, Mama? Do you *hear*?"

"Not moving in—" Mrs. Lacy turned pale and her eyes were wide, staring. Her hand went to her bosom. In a quivering voice, she cried, "You'd let me be put out on the street?"

"I have no idea what's going to happen about that," Lizzy replied stonily. She could feel herself shaking. She had never before spoken to her mother in this way. "But I do know that you are not moving in here. It is simply out of the question." She held out her hand. "Now, you give me that door key you had Mr. Musgrove copy for you at the hardware store."

Mrs. Lacy widened her eyes. "Key? What key?"

"The key that you used to come in here so you could measure for your furniture, Mama." Lizzy hardened her voice. "I want it. Now."

Her mother pushed out her lower lip like a pouting child. "I don't have it with me."

"Then I will go to the hardware store first thing tomorrow. I will tell Mr. Musgrove that my mother copied my door key without my permission and I can't trust her to stay out of my house. I will ask him to put new locks on the front and the back doors."

Mrs. Lacy looked aghast. "You wouldn't tell him that, Elizabeth! Why, Mrs. Musgrove is a terrible gossip. She'll tell everybody in town that I—" She swallowed. "That you—"

Lizzy folded her arms. "Try me," she said icily.

In the end, Mrs. Lacy surrendered the key.

SIX

The Dahlias in Full Bloom

The Dahlias met at their clubhouse at two in the afternoon on the second Sunday of every month. During nice weather, there were usually several absences, since moms and dads liked to pile the kids into their Fords or DeSotos or Chryslers on Sunday afternoons and drive out to visit their kinfolk. But when Lizzy called the meeting to order, she saw that everybody was present except Myra May, who was working Violet's shift on the switchboard. Lizzy suspected that the rest of the Dahlias might have shown up out of self-defense. They knew the club would be discussing the talent show. If they missed the meeting, they'd likely find themselves appointed in absentia to chair a committee.

Lizzy never handled angry encounters very well, and the scene with her mother had been so nerve-wracking that she was still shaking when she called the meeting to order. But she pushed the awfulness to the back of her mind and focused as intently as she could on the business at hand. After Ophelia's minutes and Verna's treasurer's report were approved, she called on Miss Rogers to present the program, then sat down next to Verna.

Miss Rogers, still wearing her Sunday-go-to-meeting navy faille dress and narrow-brimmed baku braid hat, read a paper she had submitted to the *Southern Regional Garden Club Newsletter*. It was all about late-season flowering shrubs that ought to do well in the Gulf Coast's hot, humid climate, especially the Holly tea olive (*Osmanthus heterophyllus*), senna (*Cassia corymbosa*), and sasanqua camellia (*Camellia sasanqua*). She spelled out the Latin names not just once but twice, so that people who were taking notes could get them right. The reading went on a little long and when she was finished, her audience rewarded the conclusion by clapping—those who were still awake, that is. The scattered applause woke the others up and they sat up straight in their chairs, pretending that they had just been resting their eyes.

The next item was a little livelier. Bessie Bloodworth reported on the garden jobs they could check off the club's to-do list and the things that still needed to be done before the first freeze. Bessie took names for the work days. Lizzy was happy to see that everybody volunteered—all but Mrs. Johnson, who regretted that she was expecting company from out of town.

Then Aunt Hetty Little (everybody called her Aunt Hetty because she was near kin to almost everybody in town) gave a report on the repair work on the clubhouse, paid for out of the Treasure Fund.

"Donny Lee Arnett charged us seventeen dollars and fifty-two cents to fix the leaks in the roof," she said, "and it cost us four dollars and seventy-five cents for Raby Ryan to repair the front and back steps so we don't all sprain our ankles."

"Money well spent," Miss Rogers observed. "Nobody can afford to see the doctor these days." Earlynne Biddle leaned over and gave Miss Rogers' hand a comforting pat. It was common knowledge that she had invested every cent of her money on Wall Street and lost it all on Black Tuesday, not quite a year ago. Now, she was living on the few dollars a week she earned as Darling's part-time librarian. Her salary barely covered her room and board at Bessie Bloodworth's Magnolia Manor, next door to the Dahlias' clubhouse. She lived in fear that the town council would decide that Darling couldn't afford to keep the library open and she'd be out of a job. But it wasn't just Miss Rogers, of course—almost everybody who had a job shared the very same worry.

Aunt Hetty cleared her throat. "We also need to get Mr. Kendrick to come over and clean the stovepipe before it's time to start building a fire in the stove here in the clubhouse," she went on. "And we need to pay Sam Westheimer to haul a load of coal for us. I guess we should have a motion. Liz?"

"Liz," Verna nudged her. "Liz, wake up."

Lizzy wasn't asleep. She had been thinking about her mother's predicament. She had no idea what the motion should be, but she got up anyway. "Do I hear a motion?"

Everybody turned to look at Mrs. George E. Pickett Johnson, because the Treasure Fund was in Mr. George E. Pickett Johnson's bank, the Darling Savings and Trust. "I so move," Mrs. Johnson said. "Both the stovepipe and the coal."

"I second it," Beulah Trivette spoke up briskly. "But be sure and tell Mr. Westheimer to bring us some *clean* coal," she added. "We don't want none of that dirty ol' smoky stuff he'll deliver if you don't especially tell him not to."

"I agree with Beulah," Alice Ann Walker said firmly. "More than once, I've had to sweep Sam Westheimer's black coal dust up off the floors before the kids and the dogs tracked it all over." Everybody (except for Mrs. Johnson, who had a gas furnace) agreed with Beulah because at one time or another most of them had been on the receiving end of one of those dirty coal deliveries and knew about the extra work it caused.

Then it was Mildred Kilgore's turn, so all the Dahlias took deep breaths and sat up straighter in their chairs. Mildred (who had that effect on people) was in charge of this year's talent show. She and her husband Roger lived near the Cypress Country Club, where Mildred grew Darling's most gorgeous camellias. Her garden was always scheduled as the last stop on the annual Garden Tour, because no self-respecting Dahlia wanted visitors to see *her* garden after they had been ooh-ing and ahh-ing at Mildred's camellias.

"The show is less than four weeks away," Mildred said, in her brisk, I've-got-everything-under-control voice, "so it's time to roll up our sleeves and get busy. I've been working on the program for the past month, and so far, I have nine acts lined up. You'll probably recognize most of them."

Mildred took out a typed list and began to read names. "I thought we would start with the Carsons' Comedy Caravan, then Sammy Durham's drum solo." Aunt Hetty groaned and everyone else smiled. Sammy Durham considered himself to be a jazz drummer. Most people thought he was just plain loud. "Then the Tumbling Tambourines—they're bringing their own mat this time—and after that, Mr. and Mrs. Akins will do their famous Spanish fandango."

Mrs. Johnson cleared her throat delicately. "I thought there was an objection to that dance at the last show. Something to do with Mrs. Akins' costume, wasn't it?"

"Mrs. Akins says she's adding more frills to lower the hem, and putting a ruffle at the neck," Mildred replied, and Mrs. Johnson gave a grudging nod. "After the dance, Mr. Trubar and Towser will do their trombone act, and then we have something brand-new. It's a family of jugglers from over near Monroeville. The Juggling Jinks."

"Oh, I've seen them!" Lucy Murphy exclaimed. "They juggled at the Methodist picnic in July. They're amazing!" Lucy was the club's newest member, bringing their number to thirteen. She had been nominated by Ophelia Snow, whose husband was Lucy's husband's cousin. Lucy and Ophelia had had an exciting little adventure the previous May, when a convict escaped from the prison farm and ended up in Lucy's kitchen. Ophelia beaned him with a jar of raspberry jam.

"I understand they're quite good," Mildred said, "but unfortunately, they're the only new act in the program. After them, our very own Miss Rogers will perform Tennyson's 'The Charge of the Light Brigade.'"

"No matter how many times I've heard it, I always love it," Earlynne Biddle said enthusiastically. "It's my favorite poem." Miss Rogers gave her a modest smile.

"The last number will be my own little Melody," Mildred said, looking up from her list. "She will tap dance to a recording of Nick Lucas singing 'Tiptoe Through the Tulips.'"

There was a scattering of applause, but Aunt Hetty Little piped up. "Mrs. Eiglehorn isn't going to recite 'Curfew Must Not Ring Tonight'? Why, she's practically an institution."

"She said she thought she wouldn't perform this year," Mildred replied diplomatically, and one or two people tittered. At the last talent show, a child in the front row had started to cry at the most theatrical moment in the poem, and poor old Mrs. Eiglehorn—eighty if she was a day and proud of her ability to memorize—had gotten so flustered that she forgot her lines. While the embarrassed mother carried out her screaming child, Mrs. Eiglehorn's husband (several years older than his wife) had to find the place in the book and prompt her.

"It's a pity you couldn't find another new act or two," Mrs. Johnson said in a negative tone. "The program is fine, but everyone has already seen and heard the whole thing."

"I could work up another poem, I suppose," Miss Rogers said doubtfully. "'The Rime of the Ancient Mariner,' for instance."

"You did that one at the library benefit last year," Verna reminded her.

"Well, then, perhaps 'The Raven.'" She deepened her voice. "'Once upon a midnight dreary, while I wandered, weak and weary—'"

"Pondered," Verna said helpfully.

"Excuse me?" Miss Rogers asked, blinking.

"Not wandered, pondered. 'While I pondered, weak and weary.'"

"I think 'The Raven' would be wonderful, Miss Rogers," Earlynne Biddle hurried to say. "It's my second favorite poem."

"We ought to have another new act or two," Mrs. Johnson insisted.

"I have done my best," Mildred replied defensively.

"I'm not suggesting you haven't, Mildred," Mrs. Johnson said. "I'm only saying that we need new blood."

Mildred frowned. "Then it's up to the rest of you to come up with a new act or two. Any volunteers?"

Beside Lizzy, Verna leaned forward, opening her mouth. But Lizzy, who had the feeling that Verna was about to suggest Lorelei LaMotte and Lily Lake, fastened a firm hand on Verna's knee and shook her head. Verna sighed and sat back, folding her arms.

"Well, if you don't want to show off your talents on stage," Mildred said, "there's still plenty of other work to be done. We need somebody to type the program onto mimeograph stencils and be responsible for running off copies on the Academy's mimeo machine. We also need someone to organize the refreshments we're selling at the intermission, and another couple of people for tickets sales. Who will volunteer?"

She looked around expectantly, and when nobody raised a hand, heaved a resigned sigh. "Well, then, ladies, I'll just have to start naming names. Mrs. Johnson, you and Lucy Murphy will be in charge of organizing the ticket sales. Myra May and

Ophelia, refreshments—yes, I know Myra May isn't here today, but she's logical because she owns the diner and Euphoria can bake up a couple of batches of those praline cookies she makes. Ophelia, if you would please tell her, I'd appreciate it."

"I'll bring some of my Southern Comfort cookies," Aunt Hetty Little offered.

"Southern Comfort cookies?" Miss Rogers asked, frowning. "But liquor is prohibited!"

A titter ran around the room. "Miss Rogers," Verna said, "where *have* you been?"

"I'm sure Aunt Hetty knows where to get whatever ingredients she needs for her cookies," Mildred said hurriedly. She looked down at her list. "Just two more things. Verna, you did a great job with the stage management last time. Please do it again. And to type and run off the program—"

Lizzy raised her hand. "I'll take care of it," she said, preferring to volunteer before her name was called. She was a good typist and she didn't mind typing the program. But she hated wrestling with the Academy's old mimeograph machine, which was known to eat stencils and couldn't be counted on to produce more than forty copies in a run. But unless they got some new acts for the show, they might not need more than forty copies.

Mildred gave her a grateful smile. "I think that takes care of it for now. Thanks, ladies."

Lizzy took over the meeting again, with a few reminders. Monday night was the usual Dahlias' card party. Bessie's Bible Study had been changed to Thursday nights, so she was hosting the party at the Magnolia Manor. Lizzy also reminded everyone to turn in their items for the gardening column in Friday's Darling *Dispatch*.

"Tuesday's the deadline," she said. "That'll just give me time to get it typed up before I have to hand it over to Mr.

Dickens on Wednesday. Oh, and if you've got any more housecleaning tips for the other column we wanted to run, let me have them, too. I only have about six or eight, and I was hoping for a dozen."

That wrapped up the meeting, and Liz asked for a motion to adjourn. Verna moved it and Alice Ann seconded it speedily, and the ladies descended on the refreshment table as fast as grasshoppers on a bean patch. It was a pretty table, too, spread with an orange cloth and decorated with a large wicker cornucopia spilling colorful autumn gourds and blossoms of asters, zinnias, marigolds, and sunflowers.

While the ladies were filling their plates and chatting noisily with one another, Ophelia Snow came over to Lizzy. Ophelia, a short person with a cherubic face, flyaway brown hair, and an irrepressibly optimistic outlook on life, was usually wreathed in smiles. But just now she wore a look that was halfway between impatient and cross.

"We need to find another member," she said shortly. "I was going to bring it up at the meeting but I thought it was something the officers ought to talk about first."

"Okay," Lizzy replied, and beckoned to Verna to join them. "Ophelia says we need to find another member," she said.

Verna frowned. "Why? Are we losing somebody?" The club had begun with fourteen members. Then Mrs. Ross had moved to Montgomery and Dahlia Blackstone, the founder, had died, leaving them with twelve. Lucy's membership had brought them to thirteen.

"No—at least nobody that I know of," Ophelia replied. She took a deep breath. "But some of the ladies are saying that thirteen is an unlucky number. And Beulah says she's heard several people whispering about a 'witches' coven' when they're waiting to get shampooed and set." Beulah Trivette owned and operated the Beauty Bower, which was gossip central for the Darling ladies. (The men, of course, preferred to get their gossip—which they liked to call "news"—from their buddies at the Darling Diner. And for shut-ins, there was always the party line.)

"Witches' coven!" Verna repeated incredulously.

"Oh, really, Ophelia!" Lizzy exploded. At a questioning look from Mildred Kilgore, who was standing nearby, she lowered her voice. "That is just utterly ridiculous! Who is spreading such nonsense? We ought to stop it at the source, or it'll get out of hand." There were plenty of superstitious people in Darling, and superstitions—even silly ones—could cause trouble.

"I know." Ophelia sighed. "I asked who it was, but Beulah didn't want to name names, and of course you can't blame her. They're paying customers, after all. She's probably afraid that if they found out she tattled, they might leave the Bower and go over to the Curling Corner." Julia Conrad ran Darling's other beauty parlor, and there was an intense competition between the two shops.

"Well, I suppose the problem is easily remedied," Verna replied with a shrug. "All we have to do is find another new member, which will get us back to fourteen."

"How about Violet Sims?" Ophelia asked. "She helps Myra May with that big vegetable garden, and we all know her. She'd be a great addition."

"She would," Lizzy replied, "but she's up in Memphis right now. Her sister died, and she's taking care of the new baby. Myra May doesn't know when she's likely to be back."

"Maybe Bettina Higgens?" Verna hazarded. Bettina worked for Beulah at the Beauty Bower and was intimately acquainted with all the Dahlias—with their hair, anyway.

Ophelia gave her head a decided shake. "Bettina can't even grow okra. Whenever the conversation gets around to gardening, she always says that she kills anything she puts in the ground. If Beulah nominates her, everybody'll know it's a desperation move on our part."

"Fannie Champaign, maybe," Lizzy suggested. Fannie owned Champaign's Darling Chapeaux, Darling's only millinery shop, on the west side of the courthouse square, next to the Savings and Trust. Fannie lived above the shop and had a small but lovely garden at the back. "She always says her garden is the inspiration for her hats. Want me to ask her?"

"Yes, do," Verna said. "We'd better come up with a couple of other possibilities, too, in case we get turned down."

"And we'd better hurry," Ophelia said in a warning tone. "Halloween will be here before long, and we certainly don't need people whispering that we're witches."

When the refreshments had disappeared and people were leaving, Lizzy stopped Bessie Bloodworth, who was on her way out the door. "Oh, Bessie, will you be at home for a few minutes? When we've finished the cleanup, Verna and I would like to come over for a little talk."

"Of course," Bessie replied. Short and stocky, in her fifties, she had thick, dark eyebrows and salt-and-pepper curls that always looked as if she'd combed them with her fingers, which she probably had. "I've been meaning to ask you to drop in, anyway. I wanted you to see my Angel Trumpet. It's absolutely gorgeous. It's a beautiful afternoon—we can sit out in the backyard and have some lemonade." She gave Lizzy a curious glance. "What did you want to talk about?"

"Oh, just a little family history," Lizzy said evasively. It was too difficult to explain.

"Goodie!" Bessie said with a broad smile. "There's nothing I like to talk about more than family history. Unless it's my own." Her smile faded slightly. "That's a different story."

As the other Dahlias took their empty dishes and left, Lizzy and Verna stayed behind to tidy up the clubhouse, put the chairs back, and sweep the floor.

"Would you check the windows, Verna?" Lizzy called over her shoulder as she wielded the broom. "Make sure they're all locked and the curtains are drawn."

Until the last few years, nobody in Darling had bothered to lock their houses. But since jobs had gotten so scarce, men and boys (and sometimes even girls) were riding the rails, looking for work and food and a place where they could sleep out of the weather. Darling wasn't on the main Louisville & Nashville rail line, but the hoboes often rode in on the freight cars that came to the sawmill. If a house looked vacant, they might try to break in. The residents of Darling weren't exactly afraid, but they were—well, uneasy. The town felt different, somehow, with strangers traipsing through it.

And even though the strangers might only be down on their luck and without a shred of malice in their hearts, they were also quite likely to be desperate. In Mobile, a string of local household robberies had been attributed to a pair of young vagrants picked up by the police when they were found sleeping in a nearby park. The boys, barely out of their teens, protested their innocence and the only evidence that connected them to the crimes was circumstantial.

At least, that's what Mr. Moseley had said to Lizzy, after he read about it in the Mobile *Register.* He called it scapegoating and had gotten quite angry, saying that it sounded to him like the police had simply collared the nearest hoboes, in order to make an object lesson of the poor fellows. But a jury had agreed with the police, and they were sent to jail.

As the district attorney said during his final summation to the court, "Desperate men will commit desperate acts. It is our duty to be watchful."

SEVEN

The Skeleton in Bessie Bloodworth's Closet

Bessie Bloodworth was a dedicated student of Darling's history and knew the family stories of almost all of the local residents. She could tell you anything you wanted to know about who was related to whom and where people's ancestors had come from. She had even written a little book, which was sold by the local history club. It was called *A Few Skeletons in Our Closets: A Peek at Darling History.*

Unfortunately, Bessie had recently been reminded that she had a few skeletons in her *own* family closet. She had climbed up to the attic to get the old green living room drapes that she was planning to donate to the Darling Quilting Club to make comforters for the needy. Under the drapes, shoved far back in a corner, she found a box of her father's business papers, left after his old office had been cleaned out. Today was both his birthday and the tenth anniversary of his death, so Bessie thought that maybe she should sit down and sort through everything. Or maybe tomorrow, or next week. There was really no hurry, she told herself. Bessie and her father hadn't been close for years. That was only one of her painful memories. There were others.

Bessie lived at Magnolia Manor, next door to the Dahlias' clubhouse. She had given this name to her family home after her father had died, when she turned it into a boardinghouse for older unmarried and widowed ladies. (Mrs. Brewster, over on West Plum, operated a boardinghouse for younger unmarried ladies. Her Rules for Proper Behavior were very strict, whereas Bessie had no rules at all, believing that if her boarders didn't understand proper behavior by now, they probably never would.)

Running a boardinghouse was the last thing Bessie had planned to do with her life. She had hoped to train as a nurse. But her mother had died when she was a girl—one of the painful parts of the Bloodworth family story—and her three older brothers had left Darling just as quickly as they could. They wanted to get away from their father, who had changed after their mother died. But Bessie didn't have the same freedom. She couldn't leave, even if she wanted to. As her father's only daughter, she was expected to live at home until she was married—to a local boy, of course. After that, she was expected to live close enough to be available to manage her father's household and take care of him whenever he needed her. There was nothing unusual about this. It was a duty that every Darling parent expected and an obligation that all Darling girls understood.

And that was what Bessie had expected, too. She fell in love with Harold, the boy across the street, and when she graduated high school, agreed to marry him. They planned to live with her father until they could afford their own home. Lots of young people in Darling did this, but it wasn't an ideal situation and they knew it. Mr. Bloodworth was a volatile man who was given to rash, temperamental outbursts, and he hadn't approved of his daughter's choice of a husband.

As Darling's only undertaker and a member of the City Council, he thought Bessie could have done much better if she'd taken the time to look around a little, instead of settling for Harold Hamer, whose prospects were not exactly bright. That's what her father *said*, anyway, although Bessie suspected that he would have felt the same way about anyone she chose. Nobody would ever be good enough to marry a Bloodworth.

But the young man's sister, who had raised him and with whom he lived, was equally temperamental and equally unimpressed by her brother's choice of a bride, and let Harold know about it in no uncertain terms. So to Bessie and Harold, living with Bessie's father (who was at least gone all day and quite a few evenings, tending to his funeral parlor and gravestone business) seemed the lesser of two evils.

But as it turned out, they didn't live there at all—and this was the most painful part of Bessie's story, the part she had tried so hard to forget. About a week before the wedding, her fiancé left Darling, abruptly and without a word of good-bye, and neither Bessie nor Harold's sister nor anyone else had ever heard another word from him. The wedding was at first postponed and then canceled, and all over town, people were saying that poor Bessie had been jilted. Everybody felt sorry for her. She could see the pity written on the face of every single person she encountered. The loss of Harold and the pity of the townspeople—taken together, it was almost too much to bear, and her heart had broken.

Surprisingly, Mr. Bloodworth had shown his daughter many small kindnesses in this terrible time, taking her wedding dress back to Mann's and canceling the arrangements she had made at the church. When she had cried out loud, "Why? Why?" he had answered gruffly but kindly, "Some things don't bear looking into, child." It was as good an answer as any, and at the time, she had felt her father was right. Harold was gone. That was all she had to know. The *why* could remain a mystery forever.

Bessie wept until she couldn't weep anymore, and then she pulled herself together and went on doing the things she was expected to do. To help her get through, she played a game with herself, pretending that Harold had just gone off on a trip to New Orleans or Memphis and would one day walk through the door and everything would be exactly the way they had always planned it. It wasn't pretending, she told herself: she believed to her soul that it was true.

But time passed, as time has a way of doing, and one morning Bessie woke up and discovered that Harold was only a dim memory, a distant melody, like a song sung so far away that it could scarcely be heard. She no longer wanted to pretend that he was coming home, and she found to her surprise that this was all right. "Time heals all wounds," she reminded herself, and felt that the hoary old proverb was true. She still loved Harold, she supposed, and she still longed to know what had happened to him and whether he was well and happy. But she was ready to stop living on the hope that he would come back.

There were other changes in Bessie's life, not all of them as healing as this one. Her father had become increasingly temperamental and hard to live with. He sold his funeral parlor to Mr. Noonan and the gravestone business to a man from Mobile and retired. Within a month, Doc Roberts diagnosed him as having cancer of the lungs. Bessie took care of him until at last he died and was buried next to her mother in the Bloodworth family plot in the Darling Cemetery on School-house Road—the cemetery that Mr. Darling had owned and where so many of his professional duties as Darling's only undertaker had been carried out. And there she was, all by herself in the big house, faced with the challenge of supporting herself and unexpectedly, surprisingly lonely.

But not for long. As soon as word of her father's death got around, two suitors—Mr. Hopper and Mr. Churchill, both recently widowed—appeared at her door with bouquets in their hands and hopeful grins on their faces. At first Bessie was flattered, even though she didn't care for either of them as much as she had cared for Harold. But it wasn't long before she began to suspect that Mr. Hopper was only looking for a place to live and Mr. Churchill chiefly wanted someone to cook and do his laundry, and if her domestic services were what they were after, she might as well open a boardinghouse and be done with it. And anyway, she needed the money, since Mr. Noonan's payments on the funeral home note were her only income, and they didn't amount to very much.

So she said shoo to both of her suitors, put a notice in the Darling *Dispatch* ("Room and board for older ladies of refinement"), and within a few weeks all of her bedrooms were full. Magnolia Manor was not a hugely profitable business—she cleared only five or six dollars a month on each of her boarders. But that was enough to pay the taxes and buy coal and electricity and food and household supplies, and her own living expenses were negligible. Lots of people, she told herself, were in much worse straits, and they had *jobs.*

At the present time, there were four boarders—the Magnolia Ladies, they called themselves, all of straitened means. Dorothy Rogers, the town's part-time librarian, had lost all her money on one awful day in the stock market. Leticia Wiggens was a retired teacher who lived on a very small pension. Mrs. Sedalius had a son who was a doctor in Mobile and sent her a check once a month, although he almost never came to see her. Maxine Bechdel was slightly better off than the others. She owned two rental houses whose tenants were able to pay their rent about half the time.

Bessie managed the place with the help of Roseanne, a live-in colored lady who cooked and did the laundry. But the

Magnolia Ladies did their part, too. Leticia and Maxine washed the dishes and cleaned the kitchen and dining room. Mrs. Sedalius swept and dusted upstairs, and Miss Rogers swept and dusted downstairs, and of course each boarder kept her room neat. In addition, they all worked in the Manor's flower beds and the impressive vegetable garden and tended the half-dozen hens that lived in the coop against the back fence and delivered three or four fresh-laid eggs every morning, just in time for breakfast.

And Bessie discovered, to her surprise, that managing the Magnolia Manor was decidedly preferable to managing her father's household, and that her new life was a great deal more interesting and livelier than the old—and a great deal livelier and less stressful than life with either Mr. Hopper or Mr. Churchill would have been. Her beloved fiancé was a long-ago dream, the Magnolia Ladies were the sisters she had never had, and her family history was by now just that: history.

When Bessie got home from the Dahlias' meeting, she went upstairs and changed into the gray cotton work dress and old shoes that she wore in the garden, then took a pair of clippers and went out to deadhead the roses. The peaches from the trees near the back fence were already in their jars in the cellar, pickled and spiced and canned, and the apples would soon be ripe. They had picked the last crop of green beans and would be digging the sweet potatoes in another few weeks, to wrap in newspaper and store in bushel baskets in the cellar. The Magnolia Ladies had a lot to show for their gardening efforts this year.

"Yoo hoo, Bessie!"

She looked up from her work to see Liz and Verna ducking through the hedge between the Manor and the Dahlias' clubhouse. She dropped the clippers into her basket and wiped her forehead with her sleeve, pushing her hair out of her eyes. It was a muggy afternoon. The way her shoulder was hurting, there'd be rain by supper time.

"Whew," she said. "Enough of that. Come and see my Angel Trumpet." She left her basket where it was and led them to a corner of the garden where a tall, sturdy-looking shrub was growing against the fence. It had large, coarse green leaves and was covered with huge, pendulous blossoms, a beautiful shade of creamy peach. They were tightly furled now, ready to open at twilight. "You can't believe the perfume," she said. "It's heavenly. We leave all the upstairs windows open when we go to bed, just so we can smell it."

"Gorgeous," Verna said, touching one of the blossoms with her finger. "Will you save us some seed?"

"Or a few cuttings," Liz said enviously. "I have the perfect site for it."

"Of course," Bessie said. "Oh, and you can mention it in your 'Garden Gate' column, Liz. Tell folks that they can come and get some cuttings. But you might also tell them it's poisonous. They need to be careful with it, especially if there are children around."

"Hard to believe that something so beautiful could be harmful," Liz said.

Bessie nodded. "My grandmother claimed she smoked it for her asthma, but it's a pretty powerful narcotic. Now, shall we sit down?" She led them toward a trio of white-painted chairs and a little table in the shade of a weeping willow, pausing at the kitchen door to ask Roseanne to bring out a pitcher of lemonade and some glasses.

"Where is everybody?" Verna asked as they sat down. "It's such a lovely afternoon, I figured they'd all be out here in the garden."

"Leticia and Maxine are playing canasta on the front porch," Bessie said. "Can't you hear them bickering? Dorothy went to her room to read, but five will get you ten that she's really having a nap. And Mrs. Sedalius' son is here for a visit. He's taken his mother for a ride in his car. First time in a year he's been to see her." She cocked her head at her guests. "So. What's this family history you wanted to talk about?"

"Liz and I were curious about Miss Hamer's niece," Verna said. "Nona Jean Jamison. We understand that she's moved in with her aunt, and we were . . . well, just wondering." She glanced at Liz. "We know that you're interested in family history, and that you've been friends with Miss Hamer for a long time."

"So we thought you might be able to tell us something about the Hamer family history," Liz added.

Bessie drew in a deep breath and leaned back in her chair. She knew Verna, and from the tone of her voice, thought that there was more here than simple curiosity. Verna was a suspicious person by nature, and in this case—

"The Hamer family history?" she asked. She rubbed a knuckle in her eye, trying not to show that the Hamer family was as disturbing a subject as the Bloodworths. At that moment, Roseanne appeared with the pitcher of lemonade—the pitcher was decorated with painted oranges and lemons—and matching glasses on a tray. "Thanks, Roseanne," she said, grateful for the interruption, and began to pour lemonade.

"I met Miss Jamison when she came to do some business with Mr. Moseley," Liz went on in an explanatory tone. "And Verna—" She took the glass Bessie handed her. "Verna had a little conversation with her at the drugstore. But maybe she'd better tell you about that part."

Verna leaned forward with an intent look. "The thing is, Bessie, I've met her before. Miss Jamison, I mean. About ten years ago."

"In Monroeville, maybe?" Bessie guessed, handing Verna a glass and setting the pitcher on the low table in front of them. "That's where Nona Jean grew up. Her mother—she's dead now—was Miss Hamer's younger sister. At least, that's what I understand. I met her for the first time last week, when she got into town." She settled back in her chair. This was all true, and easy. It was the part of the story that didn't harbor any ghosts.

"Not in Monroeville," Verna replied sharply. "And she wasn't Nona Jean, either. When I met her, she was in New York City, going by the name of Lorelei LaMotte."

"Lorelei—" Bessie blinked. "Who did you say?"

Bessie listened as Verna told her story. By the time it was finished, she was shaking her head in disbelief.

"A vaudeville act?" she exclaimed incredulously. "You're *sure?*" She paused, pursing her lips and thinking about her own first reaction to Miss Hamer's niece. "Although Nona Jean does rather look like . . ." She laughed a little. "I don't know why I should be surprised. She certainly has the figure for it. Still—"

"Go on, Verna," Liz urged. "Show her what you showed me earlier this afternoon, before the meeting."

Verna's black leather handbag was on the ground at her feet, and she picked it up and pulled out a creased piece of paper. "Lorelei LaMotte signed this playbill for me, Bessie, backstage at the New Amsterdam Theater after her act. That's her signature."

"My gracious." Bessie took the playbill and studied the picture for a moment, feeling her mouth drop open. Miss Hamer's niece, revealing all that bare skin? What would the old lady do if she saw *this?* She took a breath. "Well, I must say it does look like her, platinum hair and all—although she's certainly not showing so much of herself these days."

"It's her," Verna said flatly, "although for some reason or another, she doesn't want to admit it."

Bessie took one last look—really, those *breasts*! And all

that bare skin!—and handed the playbill back. "Well, Darling is a quiet little place. I don't suppose she wants people here in town—most especially her aunt—to know what she's been up to since she left Monroeville." She looked from Verna to Liz, trying to calculate just how much she should say. "And I don't doubt that she is Miss Hamer's niece, if that's what you're wondering. Miss Hamer really did ask her to come, although not very willingly, I have to say. In fact, I'm sure she wouldn't have done it if DessaRae's back hadn't gone bad. And if Doc Roberts hadn't insisted."

"That's actually what we wanted to ask you about," Liz said. "Since you know Miss Hamer so well, we thought you might be able to fill in the details. Forgive us for being nosy," she added. "Miss Jamison is . . . well, an unusual person. Here in Darling, anyway."

Bessie couldn't help herself. She gave a sarcastic chuckle. "What makes you think I know Miss Hamer? To tell God's honest truth, often as I've talked to that old lady, I don't really know her. Nobody does. She's a mystery," she added darkly. "And not a very pleasant one, in my considered opinion."

"But we thought you were helping her," Liz said, raising her eyebrows in surprise. "That you were a friend."

"Of course I'm helping her!" Bessie said indignantly. "That's what neighbors do, when a person lets them. But Miss Hamer has alienated everyone else on Camellia Street over the years. I'm not a friend, I'm just the only one left— aside from DessaRae, of course—who will have anything to do with her. And that's only because she and I go back a long, long way." She pressed her lips together and looked away. And then, quite unexpectedly and entirely without intending to, she added, "And because of her brother."

"Her brother?" Verna asked, looking puzzled.

A bright yellow butterfly lit on the clipped green grass at Bessie's feet, fluttered its delicate wings for a moment, then flew away, dancing on the light breeze. Wishing she hadn't spoken, Bessie straightened her shoulders and clasped her fingers in her lap.

"Anyway, the current situation is pretty straightforward," she said, not answering Verna's question. "Miss Hamer hasn't been able to manage without help since the beginning of summer. She's not bedridden yet, but nearly. DessaRae's back finally got so bad that she couldn't lift the old lady the way she used to, or get her into her chair or onto the chamber pot. So Doc Roberts finally put his foot down and said that Dessa Rae could do the cooking and light work, but that somebody else was going to have to do the heavy lifting. He suggested one or two ladies he knew were available, but they didn't want to live in—and they wanted to be paid." She chuckled drily. "And since Miss Hamer is so hard to get along with, they wanted to be paid quite a lot. One of them asked for twenty cents an hour."

"Ah," Verna said thoughtfully.

"Exactly," Bessie replied. "Miss Hamer has plenty of money—in fact, she's got more than all the rest of us put together. Some people say that she keeps it under her mattress, because she doesn't trust Mr. Johnson at the bank."

"I can understand that," Liz muttered.

"But however much she's got," Bessie went on, "she doesn't like to spend it. So that's why Nona Jean is here. A few weeks ago, out of the blue, she wrote to her aunt from Chicago. Said she was wanting to come back to Alabama and wondered whether Miss Hamer could help her get a job and find a place to live."

"Out of the blue," Verna repeated in a meaningful tone. "It sounds as if they hadn't been in contact over the years. Is that right?"

"I think that's right," Bessie replied. "Miss Jamison's mother—Miss Hamer's sister—has been dead going on twenty or twenty-five years. I don't remember Miss Hamer ever mentioning that she had a niece." Although of course it wasn't a subject they talked about. Like the other part of the Hamer family history, which neither of them had ever mentioned to the other, at least not in the past twenty years. The Hamer and Bloodworth history, two chapters of a single story.

Verna was frowning intently, as if she were mentally sorting through a series of filing cards. "Did Miss Hamer verify who she was?"

Bessie could see where this was going and wondered why she hadn't thought of it herself. "You mean, did the old lady get somebody to check her out? No, I don't reckon she did. Why are you asking?"

Verna cast an I-told-you-so look at Liz, who said, rather hurriedly, "I don't suppose Miss Jamison mentioned anything to her aunt about dancing. Or vaudeville or Broadway or Mr. Ziegfeld."

"You're certainly right about that," Bessie said caustically. "If she had, she'd still be in Chicago. Dancing is one of the things Miss Hamer can't abide. One of the *many* things."

"I suppose that's why Miss Jamison refuses to admit that she's Lorelei LaMotte," Verna said reflectively. She folded the playbill and put it back in her handbag, then gave Liz another look. "I guess there's no point in even thinking about the talent show, then."

"The talent show?" Bessie had to laugh at that. "You were planning to ask Nona Jean Jamison to put on an act for the Dahlias' talent show?"

Verna shrugged and gave her a half-embarrassed grin. "Well, yes, I was. Not a very good idea, huh?"

"Sure it's a good idea," Bessie agreed. "That is, if she really is Lorelei LaMotte. And if she could clean up the act enough to be decent. And if she weren't nursing her aunt. And if her aunt didn't hate dancing so much." She shook her head emphatically. "Miss Hamer finds out about the Naughty and Nice Sisters, and Nona Jean Jamison will be out on the street in the blink of an eye. She and Miss Lake both."

Verna chuckled. "It's a little hard to think of Lorelei LaMotte as a nurse."

Bessie lifted her shoulders and let them fall. "Well, these days lots of people are doing things they never thought they'd do. And she's not getting paid. Miss Jamison said on the phone that she'd do it just for the board and room, if her friend could come with her. That's what got her the job, most likely. Miss Hamer would probably die before she paid out any real money."

"On the phone?" Liz asked. "Was that when she called from Chicago? Myra May mentioned that there was a call."

Bessie nodded. "That's right. She wanted to find out about the living arrangements—simple questions she could've asked Miss Hamer, if the old lady had a phone, which she doesn't. Miss Jamison wanted a bedroom for herself and one for Miss Lake, and asked about DessaRae—whether she lives in. One odd question I remember: she especially wanted to know whether many people came to the house."

Far away to the south, purple clouds were piling high and thunder rumbled. Her shoulder had made the right call—they would get rain before dark. Which was good, Bessie thought. The shrubs could use a good watering.

Liz chuckled. "I suppose you told her that *nobody* ever goes to that house—except for you and Doc Roberts."

"Yes, I did," Bessie said. "To tell the truth, I thought that might change her mind. But it actually seemed to make her feel better." Another rumble of thunder, this one closer. "I got the idea that she and Miss Lake don't much want to see people."

Verna harrumphed. "Well, if that's her intention, she'd better change her style, because people will want to see *her*. In fact, Bailey Beauchamp made an extra trip around the courthouse square, just so he could get a better look at that red dress—and what was inside it." She paused. "You've met them?"

Bessie nodded. "I went over to say hello yesterday morning. I talked to Miss Jamison, but not to Miss Lake." She paused. "There's a bit of a mystery there."

The thunder seemed to have broken the quiet of the neighborhood. A screen door slapped shut somewhere close by, and the sound of a neighbor's lawnmower being pushed across the grass came through the hedge. Down the street, some boys called to one another, and a dog barked excitedly.

"A mystery?" Liz asked, looking puzzled. "You mean—"

"When they got here," Bessie said, "Miss Lake was wearing a big floppy hat and an old-fashioned black motoring veil that completely hid her face. She didn't take it off. She just went straight upstairs to her room and that's where she has stayed. She never comes out, DessaRae says, not even to eat. Miss Jamison takes her meals to her and brings back the empty plates."

"Ah," Liz said, nodding. "Sally-Lou told me about that."

Verna blinked. "Takes her meals to her? That's odd, don't you think?"

"No odder than anything that goes on in that house," Bessie said with a wry chuckle. "There's no such thing as 'normal' where Miss Hamer is concerned." She was silent for a long moment, feeling the words rising inside her, an irresistible force, like lava from some long-dormant volcano. She hadn't talked of this to anyone, not since it happened, all those years ago. And now—

She heard herself saying, as if the words were coming from someone else, "Did you know that I was once engaged to Miss Hamer's brother?"

"Really?" Liz was surprised. "I didn't know she had a brother."

"His name was . . . Harold," Bessie said. She said it again, testing it, almost tasting it. "Harold. If we had married, I would be Miss Hamer's sister-in-law. And Miss Jamison's aunt-by-marriage." Put that way, it seemed almost funny, and she smiled.

"But you didn't marry?" Verna asked gently.

"No." The sudden, painful sadness washed her smile away, and Bessie felt her mouth trembling. She should stop, she knew. She didn't want to say the words, or to hear them, either. But she couldn't. She swallowed and went on.

"It was a long time ago, when I was still in my early twenties. Back then, of course, it seemed like a terrible tragedy, the worst thing that had ever happened to anybody in this world. Which it wasn't, I know." She sighed heavily. "But still . . ." Her voice trailed off.

Verna put her glass down, obviously intrigued. "So what happened, Bessie? Did you quarrel?"

Bessie swallowed again. "I never knew what happened," she said matter-of-factly. "There wasn't any quarrel. The wedding arrangements were made, the church reserved and everything, and I even had my dress. Harold and I were planning to borrow Daddy's car and drive over to the jewelry store in Monroeville and pick out our wedding rings." Her mouth twisted around the bitter words. "But then he was just . . . gone, that's all. I never heard a word from him. No letter, no telegram, not one single word, from that day to this."

"I am so sorry, Bessie," Liz whispered. She opened her mouth, then closed it again, as if she couldn't think what else to say.

Bessie looked down at her fingers clasped in her lap. "I always suspected that Miss Hamer drove him away. I reckon he just couldn't take her bossing him around any longer, telling him what to do. She didn't like me one bit, of course. But then, she wouldn't have liked any girl Harold wanted to marry. She wanted to keep him all to herself, and she was determined to make life miserable for anybody he cared about. He knew that, I think. So he left."

Verna frowned. "He didn't get in touch with his parents, to tell them where he'd gone?"

"They were dead," Bessie replied. "They died in a railroad accident when Miss Hamer was in her twenties and Harold was just a tiny child, before he'd had his first birthday. She raised him all by herself—and pretty well smothered him, too." She sighed, remembering. "That's the way Harold saw it, anyway, although to be fair, I don't suppose anybody could blame her. She was doing her best to take care of a young boy who would've run wild, left to his druthers. So she kept him on a short rein, like a rebellious young horse. I used to think maybe he wanted to get married just to get out from under his sister's thumb."

"I can understand that," Liz said. "I got engaged to Reggie just to get away from my mother. Not that I didn't love him," she added hastily. "I think we would have been happy together, if he'd come home from France."

"Well, it wouldn't have worked for us," Bessie said, and heard herself saying a truth she had known but had never spoken out loud. "Getting married, I mean. I understand that now. There wasn't any way Harold could be free of his sister as long as he stayed here in Darling. She would have made both of us miserable, meddling in our marriage. He must have known that, too. So he left. He didn't ask me to go with him because he knew I couldn't leave my father. In a way, I suppose, it was a kindness. He didn't force me to make a choice. He did the choosing himself."

She stopped, startled. A kindness? Did she really think that? But after all these years, the real truth was that she still didn't know what to think.

"My gracious, Bessie," Verna said in surprise. "I never heard a word of any of this."

"No reason you should," Bessie replied with a short laugh, "either one of you. It's not something I wanted to talk about. And it happened a long time ago."

"But didn't you think it was really strange that he didn't try to get in touch with you?" Verna persisted. "Especially since you hadn't quarreled."

"Of course I thought it was strange, Verna. I was devastated." And now that she'd said this much, the rest just came tumbling out, as if the words were speaking themselves. "For once in his life, my father was kind to me, even though he could barely hide how glad he was that Harold had left. He'd never made any secret of the fact that he hated the idea of our getting married. But he was kind to me—canceled all the wedding arrangements himself, so I wouldn't have to do it. For months, I wouldn't talk to Miss Hamer, because I was convinced that she knew where her brother had gone and was refusing to tell me. And of course I just kept thinking there'd be something—a letter, or a postcard. But there was nothing. It was as if he had fallen right off the face of the earth."

"And Miss Hamer?" Verna asked, narrowing her eyes. "She didn't hear from him either?"

Bessie could feel her mouth trembling and she pressed her lips together. "If she did, she didn't tell me. I'd ask, and she'd just shake her head. But of course she wouldn't tell, since she was the very reason he left."

"So sad," Liz murmured. She looked stricken. "For both you and Miss Hamer. For Harold, too."

"Yes," Bessie said stoutly. "I survived, maybe because I knew I hadn't done anything to drive him away." She had always felt good about that, in the private corner of her mind where these memories were stored away—that they hadn't quarreled, that her last words to him had been soft and loving. "But I think she blamed herself, and the thought of what she did has been driving her crazy."

"You mean, really crazy?" Verna asked.

"Nutty as a fruitcake," Bessie said. "And she's gotten crazier and crazier every year. Ask the neighbors—they can hear her screeching like a madwoman, sometimes in the middle of the night. Or ask DessaRae, or Doc Roberts. They know."

"And Miss Jamison?" Verna asked, tilting her head. "What does she know?"

Bessie frowned. "I haven't heard Miss Hamer shrieking since the ladies got here, so Miss Jamison probably doesn't know about that yet. And there's no reason why she would know anything about Harold—unless Miss Hamer told her, which I'm sure she wouldn't." But now that she thought about it, she wondered whether she herself ought to tell Miss Jamison. It might help her to understand the situation she had moved into.

"What an incredible story," Liz said in a low voice.

"Yes, it is, isn't it?" Bessie replied. She pulled in a deep breath and let it out. "But as I said, it was a very long time ago." She closed her eyes, trying to conjure up Harold's face. "You know, I almost can't remember what he looked like—not really. I have a photograph of the two of us together, playing in the water at the swimming hole on Pine Mill Creek. When I think of him, that's how I picture him, smiling and happy, still just a boy. I never think of the way he must look now, gray-haired and wrinkled and maybe even bent and stooped." She sighed reminiscently. "Sometimes I think how different my life would have been if we'd married. We would've had children. And I wouldn't have—"

"Oh, there you are, Bessie, dear!" came a bright voice at the kitchen door. It was Leticia Wiggins, hobbling down the back steps. She was moving carefully, leaning on her cane with one hand, holding on to the banister with the other. Leticia had fallen the year before and broken her wrist. She didn't want to do it again. "Maxine and I have finished our canasta game. I won forty-two dollars!"

"Forty-two dollars!" Verna raised her eyebrows. "My goodness!"

"It's just pretend money," Bessie said in a low voice. "They started out gambling for pennies but now they've made up these colored paper bills. And they can never agree—"

"Forty-two?" Maxine Bechdel snapped, coming down the stairs behind Leticia, her white hair gleaming. "Don't be ridiculous, Leticia. It was only thirty-two. You added wrong, as usual." She peered nearsightedly at Bessie's guests. "Oh, it's Elizabeth and Verna! Hello, girls. We haven't seen you for a while. Mind if we join you?"

Liz put her glass down and stood up. "Somebody can have my chair," she said. "I'm afraid I have to go. It's thundering, and I need to get home and close my windows."

"I'd better be on my way, too," Verna said, standing up. She put her hand on Bessie's shoulder. "Thanks for sharing all that family history with us, Bessie."

"You're welcome," Bessie said, reaching up to clasp Verna's hand. She shook her head with a wicked grin. "I'll bet old Miss Hamer doesn't have an idea in her head that she's harboring a couple of vaudeville dancers. But that's what comes of letting those naked ladies bloom in her front yard."

"Who's a vaudeville dancer?" Leticia wanted to know, hobbling across the grass. "You'll have to speak up, Bessie, if you want people to hear you." She sat down in the chair that Liz had vacated and glanced at the partly emptied pitcher. "Maxine, darlin', you're still up. Bring us two more glasses, will you, and we'll have us some of this lemonade." She looked back at Bessie. "Now, do tell, Bessie. Who's a vaudeville dancer?"

"No, no," Bessie said hastily, raising her voice. "We were talking about the Dahlias' talent show. I said that it's going to be as good as watching a vaudeville review. Don't you think so, Verna?"

"Oh, definitely," Verna said, and Liz nodded, too. They said their good-byes, leaving Bessie and her friends to enjoy the fragrance of the Angel Trumpet drifting across the backyard.

EIGHT

Verna Has a Visitor

That was quite a story, wasn't it?" Verna said, as she and Liz walked down Camellia Street—hurrying a little. The growl of thunder was coming closer and neither of them had an umbrella.

"I wonder what happened to him," Liz said reflectively. "Bessie's fiancé, I mean. It's so sad." She shivered. "At least I knew what happened to Reggie—his mother got a letter from his commanding officer after he was killed, telling her where he was buried. Bessie never even knew what became of her fiancé. It must be hard to live with a mystery like that."

"There's another mystery," Verna replied darkly. The suspicion had been growing on her all afternoon, while she listened to Bessie tell her story. "Now that I know a little more about this situation, I'm beginning to wonder whether Lorelei LaMotte really *is* Miss Hamer's niece." She turned to her friend. "Honestly, now, Liz. Tell me what you think."

Liz was silent for a moment. "The other day, I read about an odd situation in Florida. These people's son was kidnapped years ago, and when he came home, all grown up, they were thrilled to death. It turned out, though, that he wasn't their son after all. Some smart police detective revealed his real identity and they were shocked at how they'd been duped."

Verna turned to stare at her. "You know, Liz, the same thing could be true here. Nona Jean's mother is dead. Her aunt doesn't know her—not really, I mean. *Nobody* here in Darling knows her, not a soul."

Liz frowned. "Didn't Walter's cousin tell you that he had known her when she was a girl back in Monroeville?" A streak of lightning raced across the southern sky, under a pile of threatening clouds.

"Yes," Verna conceded, "but he could have been wrong. Gerald has been wrong a lot, over the years." She thought back to their visit to New York, where Gerald had strutted around, the big-city hero lording it over his small-town cousins. "Or maybe he was saying it to make himself look important—the way men do, you know."

"I'm confused, Verna," Liz said. "Miss Jamison told you that she isn't Miss LaMotte, and now you're saying she might not be Miss Jamison, either."

"It is confusing," Verna replied. "But that's what makes it a mystery—and intriguing. All I'm saying is that we need to know more about her."

"More what, exactly?" Liz asked, over the roll of thunder.

"Just *more*," Verna said. She thought for a moment. "You said that Miss Jamison had some legal business with Mr. Moseley. What was it?"

"You know I can't talk about specifics," Liz said patiently. "Attorney-client privilege includes me, too. Mr. Moseley has drummed that into me from the day I went to work in his office." She hesitated. "But I guess maybe it won't hurt to tell you that it had to do with a house she's put up for sale. She's asked Mr. Moseley to handle it for her."

"In Chicago?"

"Not exactly, but close." She sighed. "If you must know, it's in a suburb on the west side of the city. Cicero."

Verna stared at her. "Cicero! Don't you read the newspapers, Liz? Cicero is all over the front pages. That's where Al Capone hangs out, so he can stay out of the clutches of the Chicago police. Haven't you heard the saying, 'If you smell gunpowder, you're in Cicero'? You don't suppose—"

"No, I don't suppose anything of the sort." Liz pulled down the corners of her mouth. "Verna, you would suspect your own grandmother—if you had one."

Verna chuckled wryly. "If my grandmother lived on Twenty-second Street in Cicero, I might suspect her. That's where Capone has his headquarters. In the Western Hotel on Twenty-second, according to *The Dime Detective*."

The Dime Detective was one of the tough-guy crime magazines that Verna read every chance she got. It often included snippets about real-world mobsters—and always lots of information about Al Capone and his gang. For instance, Al Capone had a violent temper and was known to take a bloody revenge against anybody he thought was disloyal. At the same time, he'd been the first to open soup kitchens right after the Crash and distribute clothes and food to the needy. Many people in Chicago saw him as a Robin Hood, a romantic hero who defied the law to give them what they wanted (alcohol) and what they needed (food, clothing, and employment). "Public service is my motto," Capone was quoted as saying. "Ninety percent of the people of Cook County drink and gamble and my offense has been to furnish them with those amusements." Lots of people seemed to agree with him.

Verna looked at Liz. "Well, Liz? Would you dig up the address of Miss Jamison's house for me?"

"Maybe," Liz said reluctantly. "I guess it would depend on whether it's really important. And I hope you're not trying to tell me that Miss Jamison has anything to do with Al Capone."

Verna was candid. "I don't know if it's important. And I have no idea whether Miss Jamison is connected with Al Capone or not. But somebody ought to try to find out who this woman really is and what exactly she's doing here in Darling, don't you think?" She gave her friend a closer look. "What's eating you, Liz? You've been quiet all afternoon. Not your usual bouncy self."

Liz sighed heavily. "You wouldn't believe it if I told you, Verna."

"Try me," Verna invited, and linked her arm in Liz's. "Come on, Lizzy, give," she said affectionately. "Something's up. Is it Grady?"

Liz rolled her eyes. "No. It's not Grady. I haven't even seen him all week."

"Well, then, it must be Mr. Moseley." Verna chuckled. "I know he's been pestering you to—"

"It's not Mr. Moseley," Liz said, so quickly that Verna suspected it actually was Mr. Moseley. Then she added, in a subdued voice, clearly worried, "It's my mother."

"Uh-oh." Verna frowned. "What about her? Is she sick? Is she—"

"She's not sick." Liz sighed. "Although what's happened makes *me* sick. She's lost her house."

Verna turned to stare. "Lost her *house*?" she said incredulously. "But I thought your father—"

"He did. He left it to her free and clear, along with enough money to keep her for the rest of her life. But she took out a mortgage a couple of years ago and put the money into the stock market, with Miss Rogers' broker. And we all know what happened to Miss Rogers."

"Oh, dear!" Verna exclaimed, feeling a deep sympathy. "There's nothing left, I suppose."

The same thing had happened all across America, Verna knew. The market had risen so fast and so far in the late 1920s that a great many ordinary people—housewives, truck drivers, retail clerks, teachers—had been infected by stock market fever. The newspapers and magazines and radio programs spilled over with tempting stories about taxi drivers making a fortune, or a school teacher from Peoria or a janitor from Poughkeepsie striking it rich. Even in Darling, far away from Wall Street, the stock market was all people talked about, from the farmers gathered around the stove in the back room at Snow's Farm Supply to the women buying dress goods at Mann's Mercantile. Everybody believed that the market was like an elevator in one of those New York skyscrapers. It was only going to go higher, all the way up to the very top, wherever that was. Everybody wanted to get in on the ground floor.

And you didn't need a lot of money to get on board. Fork over ten or twenty percent of whatever you wanted to buy, and any broker would happily loan you the rest. Of course, if there was a brief downturn, you might get a "margin call" and have to pony up some more money. But the next day, the stock would bounce up again and you'd be in the clear and on your way to a fortune, so nobody worried about the temporary dips. Up and up and up—until the Dow Jones Industrial Average reached the dizzying peak of 381. People in the know—bankers, brokers, big investors, even President Hoover himself—were saying that the Dow could go as high as 400 or 450, when it would likely reach a plateau before it took off again. Some of them were still saying this on the day the bottom dropped out and panic-stricken people began selling. Last week, Verna had read, the Dow had slipped to 180 and was still on its way down, no telling how far.

"Every last penny is gone," Liz replied wretchedly. "Mama has no income, and no way to repay the loan, and Mr. Johnson is foreclosing. He told her that she has to be out by October fifteenth."

"October fifteenth!" Verna exclaimed. "But he has to give her more time than that!"

"She's had time, Verna. She got the notice in April. You know my mother—she deliberately waited to spring this on me until the very last minute, when there was nothing more that could be done."

Verna shook her head despairingly. In the probate office where she worked, she heard hard-luck stories like this every day, a lot of them involving the Darling Savings and Trust. Once one of the most respected men in Darling, Mr. George E. Picket Johnson, was well on the way to becoming the most hated—especially since it had been revealed, just a few months before, that he had made unsecured loans to Mrs. Johnson's father and brother, prompting the bank examiner to put the Savings and Trust on the "troubled banks" list. The family loans had been repaid and the bank was back on solid footing, but people in town still suspected him of playing fast and loose with their money.

"What's your mother going to do?" Verna asked. To the south, over the trees, lightning flashed again.

"What do you think?" Liz asked helplessly. She was crying now, twin rivulets of tears streaking her cheeks. "She intends to move in with *me*, naturally! But just until I marry Grady, of course." She gulped back a sob and her voice became bitter. "After that, she has the idea that I will go live with him and she can stay in my beautiful little house forever—without paying any rent, of course, since she doesn't have any money. And where she's going to get the money for groceries and the doctor, I don't know. Or even to keep on paying Sally-Lou the pittance she pays her now."

Verna put her arm around her friend's shoulders. "I am so sorry, Liz," she said sympathetically, and then became practical. "But you and I both know that you can't live with your mother again. Not now. Not after you've had your own place."

She might well have added, "Not after you have declared your personal independence," but she didn't. Verna knew very well how much courage and hard-won maturity it had taken for Liz to escape from her domineering mother's control. And she also knew that Liz hadn't escaped very far. Not far enough, probably—just across the street. She thought fleetingly of Bessie's fiancé. Poor Bessie was probably right. He had fled Darling to escape from his sister.

"You're right," Liz said fiercely. "I can't live with her again. But I can't allow her to be put out onto the street, can I?" She wiped her eyes. "I'm going to talk to Mr. Johnson tomorrow. Maybe I can get him to put off the foreclosure until I can figure out what to do."

Verna was silent for a moment, thinking what to say and how to say it. She wasn't excited at the thought of having a roommate, even a temporary one. But she knew what a calamity it would be for Liz if she had to live with her mother again.

"Well, if worse comes to worst," she said at last, "and you feel that you have no alternative but to let your mother move into your house, you can come and stay with me. I have an extra bedroom, you know. I'll be glad to share."

"Thank you," Liz replied simply. Her brown eyes were swimming with tears and her delicate chin quivered. "I can't tell you how much I appreciate that."

"You're welcome," Verna said. She felt a splat of something warm and wet on her arm, and looked down. Liz's tears?

No. At that moment, the heavens opened and the rain began to pour.

The shower was brief but heavy, and by the time Verna had dashed the two blocks to her house, she was thoroughly soaked. She lived at the corner of Larkspur Lane and Robert E. Lee Street, in the same two-bedroom white frame house that she and Walter had bought after they were married. She had paid off the mortgage with Walter's insurance money, updated the plumbing and installed electric lights, and figured she would live there the rest of her life. She liked her privacy, but if Liz couldn't work things out with her mother and needed a place to stay, she'd make room. Times were hard right now, and lots of people had to make unexpected— and sometimes unwelcome—compromises. Not that having Liz staying with her was unwelcome, exactly. It would take some getting used to, though.

Verna was met at the front door by her feisty black Scottie, Clyde, who let her know in no uncertain terms that he was glad she was home and hoped that she wouldn't be going out again anytime soon. She knelt down and ruffled his shiny black fur.

"What would you say if Liz's orange tabby moved in with us?" she asked. It was a serious question, because Clyde was decidedly territorial. If Liz came to live with her, he might have a hard time compromising with Daffy.

Clyde declined to comment on the possibility of a cat but felt strongly about the prospect of dinner, which according to his reckoning was already a half-hour late. So Verna hurried to her bedroom, where she stripped off and hung up her wet things, toweled her hair, and pulled on a green print housedress. Her next stop was the kitchen, where she took an open can of Ken-L Ration out of the icebox and mixed it with some leftover mashed potatoes and a little hamburger from last night's dinner. As usual, Clyde made short work of it.

She let the dog into the fenced backyard and glanced at the clock. It was time for her own supper, so she opened the icebox and took out a couple of eggs, a small tomato, an onion, some parsley, and a package of Velveeta cheese. She beat the eggs with a couple of spoonfuls of cream and cooked them in a skillet on her gas range. She added chopped tomato, onion, and parsley and some thin slices of Velveeta, then folded the omelet in half and slipped it onto a plate. She poured herself a glass of milk from the bottle in the icebox, took off her apron, and sat down to eat at the kitchen table, her current reading propped up on the green glass butter dish in front of her.

Usually, this was a mystery from the library, but tonight she was reading a story in the crime fiction magazine *The Black Mask*, one of the pulps that she enjoyed. The story involved a Chicago gangster who was trying his best to go straight, but kept getting hooked back into a life of crime. It was the same issue of the magazine (September 1929) that had carried the first installment of an exciting novel—*The Maltese Falcon*—by a new writer, Dashiell Hammett. Verna had copies of the third and fourth installments (in the November and December issues of the magazine) but she was still looking for the other two issues, so she could read the whole story from start to finish. She had heard that the book would be out soon, but she doubted that Miss Rogers would get it for the Darling library. Miss Rogers was not a fan of hard-boiled detectives. She wouldn't like Sam Spade. And anyway, there might not be any money for new library books. The town budget was getting awfully tight.

Verna was deep in her story when she heard Clyde— always a reliable watchdog—barking at the side fence and then a sharp rapping at the front door. She turned the magazine over to mark her place and went to the door. Standing on the porch was a complete stranger, a man she had never seen before. He was heavy-bodied, with a round, jovial face, small eyes, and a fleshy-lipped smile that showed off a gold tooth. He looked like a dandy in a gray woolen double-breasted suit, vest, blue silk tie, hat, and polished black shoes. When he raised his hat, she could see that he was completely bald.

"Good evenin', ma'am," he said in a flat, expressionless voice that carried a slight lisp and was colored by a definite Yankee accent. "Sorry to bother you, but I'm lookin' for a lady friend who's visitin' in your fine little town." He reached into the breast pocket of his suit and produced a small black-and-white snapshot with a white, wavy-edged border. "A real looker, she is. A blonde. I been askin' around, tryin' to find somebody who knows where she's stayin'."

It was Miss Jamison. She was turned half away from the camera, smiling coyly over her shoulder, her chin buried in the luxurious fur stole that was thrown over the shoulder of her elegant wool coat. Her pale hair, marcelled, could be seen beneath a stylish, narrow-brimmed dark felt hat with a single pheasant feather. She looked confident, sure of herself, and slyly flirtatious. In the background of the photograph was a redbrick building. It bore the street number 4823.

Verna felt a cold shiver across her shoulder blades, but something told her that it wouldn't be smart to let on that she recognized the woman in the photograph or the street number on the building. "Pretty," she said, pretending to study it. "Nice fur, too. What did you say her name is?"

The man's hard gray eyes were as flat and expressionless as his voice. "Well, sometimes it's one name, sometimes another. Could be she's usin' the name LaMotte. Lorelei LaMotte."

With a shake of her head, Verna handed the photo back to the man. "Haven't seen her. I'm sure I'd remember if I had. You say she's a friend?"

He nodded curtly and pocketed the photograph. "I'd appreciate it if you'd keep an eye out. I've got something to give her—a repayment on a loan. She'd sure as shootin' hate to miss out on that, so you'll be doing her a big favor to help me find her."

"Sure thing," Verna replied in a careless tone. "If I see her, I'll let you know. Where are you staying?"

"Where else?" His harsh laugh turned into a harsher cough. "The only hotel in town. If I ain't around, leave a message for Mr. Gold—that's me. I'll be here through tomorrow, at least. Maybe longer. Good evenin', ma'am."

He tipped his hat politely and went down the path to the street. As she watched from behind the lace curtain on the door, Verna saw a bulge under his suit coat. She had never seen one, but she had read enough descriptions of such a thing to know exactly what she was looking at. A shoulder holster.

She shivered again, watching Mr. Gold cross Larkspur Lane and walk up Robert E. Lee in the direction of the hotel. But he turned in at the first house up the block. Clearly, he was canvassing the neighborhood. Sooner or later, he was bound to run into someone who had seen the woman he was looking for. Miss LaMotte's platinum hair was a dead give-away, and his claim that he had money for her would encourage someone to tell him where she was staying.

Frowning, Verna dropped the curtain, turned away from the door, and crossed the living room to the bookshelf where she kept her collection of true crime magazines. She picked up one and leafed through it, then another. In the third, she found what she was looking for. She had remembered correctly, and her breath came quicker.

She went straight to the telephone on the wall, gave a short crank, and when the operator answered (it was Olive, sounding very froggy with her cold), gave Liz's number. In a moment, Liz herself was on the line.

Mindful that someone else was probably listening—like most people in town, both she and Liz had a party line— Verna measured her words.

"You remember what I asked you this afternoon, Liz, about looking for that address in the file? Well, it turns out to be important, after all. The lady we were talking about—she definitely has a connection with that man who's been in the news recently. The man in Cicero."

"You're kidding."

"I wish," Verna replied.

There was an astonished silence as Liz processed this. "How do you know?" she asked cautiously.

"A gentleman came to my door just now. Said his name was Gold, and that he's looking for her and her friend. He showed me a photo of her standing in front of a building with a street number on it." Verna couldn't keep the excitement out of her voice. "Liz, it was the very same number as the hotel I mentioned to you!" According to the *Dime Detective,* 4823—the number on the wall of the building in the photo—was the address of the Western Hotel, on Twenty-second Street in Cicero. The place where Al Capone hung out.

A longer silence. "You've *got* to be kidding," Liz said at last, with a little whoosh of her breath.

"On my honor," Verna replied grimly. "It's true, every word of it. I just double checked the street number in the magazine where I read about it." She took a deep, shivery breath. "And what's more, I have the feeling that the gentleman who came to my door is an associate of that fellow we're talking about."

Liz gulped. "Gee whiz," she said incredulously. "You mean—"

"That's right," Verna said quickly. "That's exactly who I mean. And now I really do need your help, Liz. The address of that house you mentioned—do you think you could get it to me tomorrow morning?"

"I . . . I can't promise," Liz said slowly. "I'm not sure I ought to do it. And anyway, what makes you think that an address will be any help?"

"I know it's a long shot. But given the situation, don't you think somebody ought to . . . investigate?"

"Well, I'll think about it," Liz said at last.

"Thank you." Verna knew that Liz took her work—and its confidentiality—seriously. A promise to think about it was the best she was going to get.

She said good-bye and hung up, but she didn't go back to her book. She was remembering the bulge of the shoulder holster under Mr. Gold's coat and the hard look in his eyes when he said Lorelei LaMotte's name. Fictional detectives—not even those tough-talking tough guys she liked to read about—no longer seemed terribly exciting, not when she suspected that she had just been talking to one of Al Capone's henchmen, in person!

But while Verna was sure that she could trust her instincts on this, she knew that suspicion wasn't enough. She needed to find out whether this man was really connected to Capone—some sort of positive identification. But what?

She went back to the kitchen table and sat down to think for a few minutes. She picked up a pencil and doodled on a piece of paper, pushing her lips in and out, in and out, still thinking. Outside in the yard, Clyde was barking excitedly again—this time, to announce the arrival of their next-door neighbor, Buddy Norris. At the sound, Verna got up and went to the window that looked out on the grassy side yard between her house and the Norris place, where Buddy—a Cypress County deputy sheriff—lived with his elderly father.

Actually, Verna didn't need Clyde's barking to know that Buddy had arrived. The racket of Buddy's motorcycle took care of that. He rode a 1927 red Indian Ace, which, if truth be told, was probably the reason Roy Burns had picked him to be his deputy. Sheriff Burns had read that the New York Police Department's crack motorcycle squad rode nothing but Indian Aces, so when Buddy applied for the position vacated by the retiring deputy, the sheriff hired him without hesitation. Buddy's Indian Ace gave Sheriff Burns the right to brag that Cypress County had the only mounted deputy in all of southern Alabama.

Frowning speculatively, Verna watched as Buddy—who everybody said looked so much like Charles Lindbergh that he could be his brother—cut the engine on his motorcycle. He swung a leg over, got off, and pushed it toward the back of the house. He was favoring his arm, which he had broken some months before when he rode his motorcycle through Jed Snow's cousin's corncrib. Buddy had always been a reckless sort.

Verna tilted her head, watching him. She didn't think much of Sheriff Burns, who kept his job by staying on the good side of the local heavyweights. Of course, Darling wasn't Cicero or Chicago, and its law enforcement officers didn't have to deal with any serious lawlessness, except for bootlegging, of course. Even so, when it came to investigations, Sheriff Burns didn't display a lot of initiative. And when it came to fighting crime, he wasn't inclined to step out swinging.

But Buddy was a different matter. If push came to shove, he might—just might—be useful in dealing with Mr. Gold. For one thing, he was enterprising, and even ambitious, always looking for a way to stand out from the crowd. He was smart: he had bought a mail-order how-to book on scientific crime detection from the Institute of Applied Sciences in Chicago and taught himself how to take fingerprints, identify firearms, and take "crime scene" photographs. He had taught himself to shoot, too. Verna knew this for a fact, because he'd rigged up a shooting range in the pasture behind the Norris house and spent a couple of hours a week (and way too much expensive ammunition) practicing with his service revolver, much to the consternation of Mr. Norris' old horse Racer, who lived in that pasture and hated loud noises. And because he had only recently celebrated his twenty-fifth birthday, Buddy was inclined to believe that he was immortal, which made him brave, as well as reckless. If there was trouble, Deputy Norris might be a good man to have around.

But there wasn't any trouble just yet, Verna thought. And there was no point involving Buddy until she had some idea what kind of situation she'd be asking him to get involved in. Still staring out the window, she thought for several moments, then turned and went to the telephone again.

She rang up Coretta Cole, her part-time assistant in the probate clerk's office, to see if she could come in the next morning, instead of her usual Tuesday. When Coretta agreed, Verna thanked her, hung up, and stood for a moment, debating whether to telephone Myra May or walk up the street to the diner and have a conversation with her in person.

She decided on the conversation, since the favor she had to ask was a little complicated and might require that Myra May bend a few rules. She would rather ask the favor face-to-face. And she certainly didn't want to risk anybody listening in.

She pulled on a cardigan over her housedress and went out into the quiet Sunday evening twilight.

NINE

Beulah's New Customer

When Beulah Trivette woke up on Monday morning and began to think about the week ahead, she counted herself as the luckiest woman in Darling—and with good reason. She herself was beautiful, a fact that she recognized every time she looked into the mirror and saw her blond curls, her dimples, her generous mouth, and those cornflower blue eyes. What's more, she had a deep-seated artistic appreciation for true beauty. And even better, she had the privilege of spending all day, every day (except Sunday, of course), making ordinary women pretty and pretty women beautiful. Which as she saw it, was one of the worthiest occupations any woman could be lucky enough to choose.

Beulah's natural sense of beauty had been enhanced by a degree (the certificate was framed and hung on the wall at her haircutting station) from the Montgomery College of Cosmetology. She saw herself as a true artist, especially where hair was concerned. She could cut the latest bob, manage a marcel iron, work miracles with a curling iron, and color hair in all shades. In fact, Beulah sometimes worried (just a little) that her training and talents were wasted in Darling, for most of the ladies who came to her Beauty Bower merely wanted a quickie shampoo and set, or a trim and shampoo, and sometimes a permanent wave. They plucked their own eyebrows, used lemon to bleach the age spots on their hands, and even made their own dry skin lotions, rather than purchasing the products she displayed on glass shelves beside the door. Still, Beulah was for the most part happy and fulfilled in her work, even though she occasionally wished for a greater artistic challenge.

Of course, a big chunk of the reason for Beulah's happiness was the fact that she owned her very own Beauty Bower, which was a beautiful place to work. The first thing she did when she and her husband Hank bought the house on Dauphin Street was to paint a beautiful sign for the front of the house and decorate it with a basket of lush pink roses. BEULAH'S BEAUTY BOWER BLOOMING SOON!! (In addition to her other talents, Beulah could paint beautiful pictures of flowers.)

While she was doing this, Hank enclosed the screened porch across the back of the house so it would be comfortable during cold weather and installed two shampoo sinks and haircutting chairs and two big wall mirrors in front of the chairs. He also wired the place for electricity so that Beulah could have the latest beauty equipment. The new Kenmore handheld hair dryer she coveted, for instance, and the electric permanent-wave machine with amazing drop-down curlers that heated the hair to create a long-lasting curl, not to mention the electric hot water heater, which meant that there'd be no more pouring hot water out of teakettles and pitchers, with the danger of scalding somebody. Beulah added the finishing touches, painting the wainscoting peppermint pink (her favorite color), wallpapering the walls with fat pink roses, and spatter-painting the pink floor with gray, blue, and yellow.

Then she painted out the BLOOMING SOON on the sign and replaced it with BY APPOINTMENT & WALK-INS WELCOME and she was in business.

After a few months, the Beauty Bower was such a runaway success that Beulah advertised for a helper, which resulted in Bettina Higgens. Bettina was not what you might call pretty (her brown hair was stringy and thin and she was as skinny as a bean pole) and she had never been to beauty school. But Beulah saw an innate talent in Bettina's nimble fingers and knew that she had what it took to make women beautiful. Within a couple of weeks, the two were wearing twin pink ruffled aprons embroidered with *Beulah's Beauty Bower* and working elbow-to-elbow at the shampoo sinks.

One of the things that Beulah and Bettina liked best about their workplace was its conviviality, for each day of the week brought its regulars who looked forward to seeing their friends, saved up their tidbits of gossip to share, and even brought cookies and cupcakes to go with the hot coffee and iced tea that Beulah always kept ready, depending on the season. Beulah was careful not to schedule the day's appointments so tightly that they couldn't accommodate somebody with a hair emergency, though. She hated to turn away a potential customer. Why, the person might get in over at Conrad's Curling Corner and be lost to the Bower forever!

Fridays and Saturdays were always the Bower's busiest days, with people getting prettied up for Saturday night parties and Sunday morning church. Monday mornings were usually fairly quiet, with Myra May Mosswell and Miss Dorothy Rogers coming in at nine and Bessie Bloodworth and Leona Ruth Adcock at nine thirty.

But on this particular Monday morning, both nine o'clocks had already canceled, Myra May because she was shorthanded at the diner and the telephone exchange (Violet Sims was still out of town), Miss Rogers ostensibly because she was coming down with a head cold and didn't want to sit around with wet hair. Beulah suspected that it was because Miss Rogers was short of funds again, and the thirty-five cents she spent on a shampoo and set had a better use elsewhere. But of course Miss Rogers couldn't be blamed for she, like so many others, was in a very difficult predicament. Beulah was just grateful for every customer who could still afford the luxury of becoming beautiful.

So this morning, when the clock said nine and there was still a half-hour before the regular nine-thirties arrived, Bettina sat down with a tray of metal Kurley Kew curlers in her lap and began to sort them by size, while Beulah went out to her backyard garden to pick an armload of chrysanthemums, gerbera daisies, and zinnias, along with some ferns for greenery. Flowers, she always thought, gave the Bower the "salon look." She had brought them in and was arranging them in a big glass bowl when the door opened and a stranger walked in.

Beulah knew right away, however, that this woman was no stranger. She was a kindred soul who obviously cared deeply about beauty. Her platinum blond hair (Beulah always saw hair first, before she saw anything else) was styled in loose, soft curls like Jean Harlow's, although the roots were in definite need of some attention and the curls were a trifle untidy. She was stylishly dressed in a bright blue dress with a bolero jacket trimmed in blue velvet (which did nothing to hide her generous bosom), a blue pillbox hat with a veil, blue gloves, and shiny patent shoes with tasteful rhinestone-trimmed buckles on the straps, just as if she had stepped off the streets of New York or out of the pages of *Vogue*. She had a pretty face, with pencil-thin plucked eyebrows, a delicate nose, a rosebud mouth, and a dark beauty mark just above her lip. Beulah, whose experienced eye could catch the flaws and imperfections in even the most expert makeup job, noticed that there were a few crow's-feet wrinkles around the

woman's eyes, and if you looked close, you might see a sprin-
kling of largish pores on either side of her nose. But as Beulah
often put it to her customers, what did a few wrinkles and
pores really matter? A beautiful woman was beautiful at any
age. And in Beulah's expert opinion, this stranger was a
beautiful woman who was simply in need of a few touch-ups
here and there.

Beulah's feeling of kinship was reinforced when the
stranger lifted her hands, gasped at the flowers, and cried,
"Oh, how stunning! What a lovely thing to see on a Monday
morning. Flowers do get the week started out just right, don't
they?" She sounded like a Yankee, but as far as Beulah was
concerned, anybody who loved flowers was a true sister.

"They purely do," Beulah said happily. She turned to Bettina, who was staring, openmouthed, at this platinum-haired
vision of feminine loveliness. "Bettina, honey, would you fill
this bowl with water, please?"

"Oh, yes, ma'am," Bettina said, and jumped up, scattering
Kurley Kews all over the floor.

Beulah left Bettina scrambling to pick up the curlers and
turned back to her customer. "Now, dear, how can we help
you on this beautiful mornin'?"

The woman's face became serious, and she looked around,
as if she were making sure she had come to the right place. "I
hope you do coloring," she said hesitantly. "Not just sham-
poos and sets."

"'Course we do colorin'," Beulah said, in her most comforting voice. "We do tints, dyes, and color rinses, in all shades.
And it sure looks like you could use some fresh color, honey, if
you don't mind me sayin' so. Those roots are gettin' just a
teensy bit dark. And you're way too pretty to let that happen,
Miz—" She paused, letting the word hang delicately in the air.

"Jamison," the woman said, holding out her gloved hand.
"I'm Nona Jean Jamison. I've come from Chicago to stay with

my aunt, Miss Hamer, over on Camellia Street. She needs a little taking care of, and I'm between . . . projects."

"So nice to meet you, Miz Jamison," Beulah said cordially, taking her hand. Chicago. She wasn't surprised. She knew that bright blue bolero dress hadn't come from Darling, or even from Mobile or Montgomery. Carson Pirie Scot and Company, on the Loop, maybe. Beulah had never been to Chicago but she had read that Carson's on the Loop was *the* place to shop for women's fashions. "I am Mrs. Beulah Trivette, owner of the Beauty Bower. And that's Bettina down there on the floor, pickin' up the Kurley Kews." Bettina lifted a hand, waved, and smiled nervously. "Welcome to Darlin', Miz Jamison. We're a real friendly little town, and we'll do our best to help you feel at home for just as long as you're here. Now, if you'll just let me have your hat, we'll get started on those roots."

Miss Jamison took off her hat and handed it to Beulah, who put it carefully on a shelf. "Actually," she said, putting a hand to her hair and fluffing it up, "I don't want the roots retouched. I want you to dye my hair dark. And bob it."

Beulah blinked. "Dark?" she asked incredulously. This was the last thing in the world she would have expected. "You mean—"

"Dark brown." Miss Jamison's voice held a mournful quiver. "Black always looks so dead, I think. A rich, dark brown is what I have in mind. Like dark brown chocolate."

Beulah paused, frowning doubtfully. She always said that her customers knew best, but when it came to beauty, she considered herself an expert.

"Are you real sure 'bout this, Miz Jamison?" She put her head on one side, studying the woman. "That platinum color is just right for you—with your skin tone and all, I mean. It looks so light and stylish. Dark is goin' to muddy you up and make you look . . . well, older. And a bob—" She pressed her lips together. "Don't you think it would be a shame to lose those pretty waves?"

She didn't want to come right out and say so, but she hated to see all that beauty going out the window. Bob that beautiful hair, dye it dark, and Miss Jamison wouldn't look anything like the extraordinarily stylish woman she was at this moment. She'd look like . . . well, she'd look ordinary. She'd look just like everybody else. That's how she'd look.

"I know all that." Miss Jamison sighed heavily and began to strip off her gloves. "I hate it, too, Mrs. Trivette. But I have my reasons. Believe me, this is not something I *want* to do. But when I think—" Her chin was quivering and she looked as if she were about to cry. She turned away, but not before Beulah (who was an empathetic person) glimpsed something like fright in her eyes.

Fright? Now, that was strange. Sadness, maybe, at losing all that beauty. Or even regret. But fright? Something else was going on here under the surface and Beulah knew it. But she had worked with women's hair for a long time and understood that big changes were always scary, whether you were going dark to blond or blond to dark again, or getting bobbed after you'd had your hair long for your whole, entire life. When it came to that, getting bobbed could be a whole lot scarier than getting dyed.

Sympathetically, she patted Miss Jamison's arm. "Well, hon, whatever your reasons are, I'm sure they gotta be good ones, to push you into takin' such an important step." She almost added "toward ugliness," but thought better of it.

"Oh, they are good reasons." Miss Jamison sighed. "But before we get started, there's something else I need to ask. Do you happen to have a wig catalog I could order from?"

"Well, I do," Beulah said, now more than a little confused. "But I thought you were wantin' to color your—"

"Oh, yes," Miss Jamison said hastily. "Yes, I have to go

brown. But I was thinking about an auburn wig, maybe even really red? Not short, but not long, either. Doesn't have to be real special."

Beulah frowned a little. "As it happens, I might have what you're lookin' for right here in the shop. It's a copper-red wig I used to practice on when I was at the beauty college up in Montgomery. I've loaned it out a time or two so it might not be in the very best condition. But it's clean, and if you don't care about a bare spot here and there—"

"Copper-red would be wonderful and a few bare spots wouldn't matter one bit," Miss Jamison said eagerly. "Could I see it?" And when Beulah found it in the closet and brought it out, she was delighted. "It's perfect," she exclaimed. "And better yet, I can take it with me. How much do you want for it?"

Beulah looked at the wig, thinking that it wasn't as frayed as she remembered. It had cost three dollars, she recollected, and she'd already gotten as much good out of it as she was going to get. "How does a dollar fifty sound?" To her, that sounded a little high, so she brought it down. "Let's make it a dollar."

"A dollar fifty sounds good to me, considering that I won't have to order and wait and wait," Miss Jamison said generously, and watched while Beulah put it in a box. "I can't tell you how glad I am to get that."

Beulah couldn't imagine why a platinum blonde who wanted her hair dyed brown would also want to pay a dollar fifty for a red wig, but that was none of her business. "Well, now," she said, taking a pink cape off the rack, "you just come over here and sit down in the shampoo chair and we'll get you started." She raised her voice. "Bettina, darlin', before Miz Bloodworth gets here, would you go into the kitchen, please, and fetch Miz Jamison a cup of coffee. One for me, too. Black."

She had the feeling she was going to need it.

TEN

Bessie Bloodworth
Learns a Thing or Two

The story Bessie had told Liz and Verna on Sunday afternoon had awakened memories in her heart and a painful longing that she thought she had put away long ago, and for good. A longing for Harold? No, that wasn't quite it, she told herself. Not a longing for *him,* for the man himself. Too much time had passed for that, and Bessie had already lived too much of her life on her own terms to wish it otherwise. No, what she felt was more of a longing to know why Harold had left and what had happened to him, and why he had never gotten in touch. She sighed. Maybe it was time to finally sit down and talk to Miss Hamer. Harold's sister surely had to know more than she had let on.

At the thought of Miss Hamer, Bessie frowned. What exactly was going on at the house across the street?

This question had become even more interesting after Bessie and the Magnolia Ladies had heard Miss Hamer shrieking on Sunday evening, so loudly that she could be heard over the vocal acrobatics of the operatic soprano they were listening to. Miss Rogers enjoyed classical music, and it had been her turn to choose. So they were sitting out on the front porch after supper, with the Victrola volume turned up and the parlor window open so they could hear it. Rosa Ponselle, the Metropolitan's soprano sensation, was singing one of her famous arias from the opera *Norma* when the shouting began.

By itself, this was not unusual, for Miss Hamer shrieked whenever she felt like it—and apparently for the fun of it—as often as once or twice a week. Miss Rogers said she thought it was entertaining, because the yelling seemed to go with Miss Ponselle's music. Mrs. Sedalius supposed that Miss Hamer might be singing along (although it didn't sound all that melodic) and maybe they should turn down the volume, which they did. But still, as the shrieking went on and on and got so loud that it could be heard over Rosa Ponselle, Bessie wondered. What was going on behind that closed front door, those curtained windows?

She wondered about Miss Jamison, too. If Miss Hamer's niece was also Lorelei LaMotte, the dancer, why had she come to Darling? There was no place around here to perform—and certainly not in the kind of costume she was wearing in the photo on Verna's playbill. The Dance Barn occasionally featured burlesque, but even there, she couldn't dance half-naked. She'd have to wear a lot more clothes.

And—the essential question, now that Bessie had had a chance to think about it—was this woman *really* Miss Hamer's niece? If she was, could she prove it? If she wasn't, how would they know?

These intriguing questions were at the top of Bessie's mind the next morning when she put on her third-best mauve cambric dress (the one with the purple buttons and the Peter Pan lace collar), set her black felt hat on her salt-and-pepper curls, and started out for Beulah's Beauty Bower to keep her nine-thirty appointment for her weekly shampoo and set. She was still puzzling over the question of Miss Jamison's real identity as she walked up the steps to the Bower. And when she opened the screen door and saw who was sitting in Beulah's haircutting chair in front of the mirror, big as life and twice as natural, she had to blink to make sure she hadn't conjured up the vision.

But beyond a doubt, the woman sitting in that chair truly was Miss Nona Jean Jamison. Or Miss Lorelei LaMotte. Or both. Caped in pink, she was holding a cup of coffee in one hand and a cigarette in the other and watching in the mirror as Beulah smoothed her damp platinum locks with a comb and snipped them with a pair of barber scissors. She was getting her hair cut.

Bessie covered her surprise with a pleasant smile. "Good morning, Beulah," she said cheerfully, taking off her hat. "Good morning, Bettina. I'm afraid I'm a teensy bit early. If you-all aren't ready for me, I can wait." She looked into the mirror and met Miss Jamison's startled eyes. "And good morning to you, too, Miss Jamison. You probably don't remember me. I'm your neighbor across the street—Bessie Bloodworth. I met you and Miss Lake the day you arrived at Miss Hamer's."

Miss Jamison flushed and dropped her glance, and Bessie thought she saw a glimpse of something like apprehension. But she took a drag on her cigarette and managed a slight smile.

"Why, hello, Miss Bloodworth." Her voice was thin. "Such a surprise."

"No surprise," Beulah chirped. "Miz Bloodworth is one of our regulars. Never misses a Monday mornin'—her and Leona Ruth Adcock. Good to see you, Bessie." She glanced up at the clock. "Leona Ruth will be along here d'rectly. Bettina, you can go ahead and get started on Miz Bloodworth right now."

Bessie put a hand to her hair. "I was thinking I'd ask Bettina to trim me this morning." She put a hand to her hair. "Feel like I'm getting a mite shaggy."

Strictly speaking, she knew she didn't need a trim for another week or two. But a haircut would put her side-by-side with Nona Jean Jamison in front of their twin mirrors, where she could maybe get an answer to some of her questions. And there was nobody else in the Bower. It was too good an opportunity to pass up.

But it was a little while before Bessie could sit beside Nona Jean. By the time Bettina got her shampooed and in the chair for her trim, Miss Jamison was stretched out on her back with her head in the shampoo sink and Beulah, gloved, was working brown dye into her platinum hair. Bessie knew it was brown because she could hear Beulah telling Miss Jamison that, when she asked what shade it was.

"'Mocha brown' is what it says on the package," Beulah said. "Exactly what you want."

Mocha brown! Bessie had to blink again. Why in the world was Miss Jamison having that beautiful platinum hair dyed mocha brown—especially when she must have invested a ton of money into getting it platinum in the first place? It made no sense at all. Bessie was itching to know why she was doing it.

But by the time Bettina got Bessie pin-curled and finger-waved and ready to go under the dryer, Miss Jamison was sitting on the other side of the room, her head in a wrap, a magazine on her lap, and a cigarette in her hand, waiting for the mocha brown color to set. And when Bessie was dry and ready to be combed out, Miss Jamison was back with her head in the shampoo sink, and Beulah was rinsing and conditioning her mocha brown hair.

But at last they were sitting side by side in the chairs. Bessie met Miss Jamison's eyes in the mirror and gave her head a wondering shake.

"Mercy me," she said. "What a difference a little color makes."

"Don't it just?" Beulah replied cheerfully, snipping a bit off the left side of Miss Jamison's bob and shaping it with her hands. "I said to Miz Jamison, I was afraid the brown might make her look just a teensy bit older. But it don't at all, do you think, Bessie?"

"Not a bit of it," Bessie lied, as Bettina pulled the last curler out of her hair. "I think brown is a perfect color for you, Miss Jamison. But if you'll forgive a bit of neighborly nosiness, why would you—"

Miss Jamison cut her off. "Because I felt like it," she replied, in a curt, mind-your-own-damn-business tone clearly designed to deter other questions. She reached for the pack of Marlboros and the gold cigarette lighter on the counter, and lit one.

"Just wanted a change, I'll bet," Bessie said, and wondered who it was that Miss Jamison was trying to hide from. It was the only reason she could think of for dyeing that pretty platinum hair a muddy brown. "By the way, how's your aunt this morning?" In explanation, she added, "I heard that little commotion over there yesterday evening."

"She's better, thank you." Miss Jamison blew out a stream of smoke, glancing warily at Bessie in the mirror as if she were wondering just how much she had heard.

"Miss Hamer gets like that every so often," Bessie said in a comforting tone. "Of course, the folks who live on her block are used to it, but I wondered if maybe it bothered you, you being new and all. Next time she starts screaming up a storm, I'll run across the street and give you a hand."

Miss Jamison began, "We don't want—" She bit her lip. "Thank you, but I think we can manage."

Bessie went on. "And how's Miss Lake? Is she feeling some better, too?" To Beulah, who was still wielding the comb, she said, in an explanatory tone, "Miss Lake is Miss Jamison's friend, who came with her from Chicago."

"Oh, really?" Beulah said. She smiled. "Why, how nice, Miz Jamison. You tell your friend that we're here to help, whenever she needs a trim or a set. All she has to do is ring us up. Or just come on over. We can almost always fit her in."

"Actually, DessaRae is kind of worried about her," Bessie went on. "Says she keeps to her room and won't come out, even for meals." She looked back at Miss Jamison. "Is there something we can do to make her feel more at home? Or if she's sick and needs a doctor, I'm sure Doc Roberts would be glad to—"

"Oh, for heaven's sake!" cried Miss Jamison piteously. "This is none of your beeswax! Why is everybody in this one-horse burg so damned nosy?"

Beulah leaned forward and put her hand on Miss Jamison's shoulder. "We don't mean a thing on God's little green earth by it, Miz Jamison, really we don't. We're just friendly, is all."

Bettina, who had said nothing all this while, added, "This is the South, y'know, Miz Jamison. Down here, we may not have much to share, but we *do* care 'bout one another." She grinned. "That's partly 'cause we're all related. Turns out I'm Beulah's second cousin twice removed, and we didn't even know it."

That was the cue Bessie had been waiting for. "Which reminds me," she said brightly. "I was thinking last night, Miss Jamison—I met your mother when she visited Miss Hamer, years ago. I was trying to remember her name, but my memory isn't as good as it used to be. I'm sure I have it somewhere in my genealogical records, though. I've got family trees for every family in town." This wasn't exactly true (she was missing three or four), but she thought it might give Miss Jamison—if that's who she really was—something to think about.

"My mother?" Miss Jamison said hesitantly, looking startled. "You met her?"

"Oh, I'm sure I did. What was her name?"

Miss Jamison frowned, pulling on her cigarette and blowing out a cloud of smoke. But if she was stalling for time, she was saved by the slam of the screen door. Leona Ruth Adcock burst in, her sweater flapping around her thin hips.

"Sorry I'm late," she cried in her usual excitable tone. "Miz Jergins came over to tell me that her oldest daughter Jolina is goin' to have a baby. She's just thrilled to death. It's early days yet, though, and she said not to tell anybody. But I'm sure she wouldn't mind me lettin' you-all know about it."

Bessie suppressed a smile. Mrs. Jergins would not have mentioned Jolina's baby to Leona Ruth if she hadn't wanted the whole town to know. Everybody in Darling knew that Leona Ruth was constitutionally unable to keep a secret.

Bettina looked up from her work on the back of Bessie's head. "Jolina's havin' a baby!" she exclaimed. "Oh my goodness, that's just so nice. They've been wantin' one for the longest time. She told me that Doc Rogers said it was likely her husband who couldn't." She frowned a little "Guess Doc must've been wrong, huh? Either that or—"

"Bettina," Beulah said briskly, "it's time you got Bessie finished up. I'm sure she's got better things to do this mornin' than sit there waitin' for you to finish combin' her out."

"Yes'm," Bettina said, and busied herself with the comb.

"There's coffee in the kitchen, Leona Ruth," Beulah said. "Help yourself."

"I just had half a pot, with Mrs. Jergins," Leona Ruth replied, parking herself in a chair where she could see everybody. She straightened the skirt of her green plaid cotton dress. "I'll sit down here and take a load off. Mornin', Bessie."

"Good morning, Leona Ruth," Bessie said, and waited to see what would happen next. She didn't have to wait long.

"Why, I don't think I know you," Leona Ruth said, craning her neck to get a better look at Miss Jamison, whose brown bob was by this time nearly finished. "Do I?"

Bessie thought Miss Jamison must be getting very tired of questions, but she managed a halfway civil tone. "I don't believe we've met." She tapped her cigarette ash in the ashtray on the counter. "I'm Miss Hamer's niece, over on Camellia Street." She met Bessie's eyes in the mirror, almost as if she were challenging.

"Well, ain't that nice!" Leona Ruth said enthusiastically. "Miss Hamer is a dear soul." She looked down her long, sharp nose and her tone turned mournful. "Although Miz Jergins— she lives a couple houses down from your aunt—said the pore ol' thing had a terr'ble bad spell again last night. Said she hollered for the better part of an hour. Sounded like she was bein' murdered."

Miss Jamison started to reply, but Bessie beat her to it.

"It wasn't anything like an hour," she said, coming to Miss Jamison's rescue. "Wasn't more than ten minutes. The ladies and I were sitting out on the front porch and heard the whole thing, start to finish." But she knew Leona Ruth. By the time she got through telling the story, Miss Hamer would be yelling bloody murder from noon to way past midnight.

Beulah took off Miss Jamison's pink cape and brushed the back of her neck. "Well, Miz Jamison, what d'you think of your new look?" She handed her a mirror so she could see the back of her hair. "Turned you into a completely different person, don't you think? Your friends up there in Chicago will never in the world recognize you."

Bessie suddenly put two and two together. Why, the reason Miss Jamison had changed her hair color was staring her right in the face. The woman didn't want to be recognized by somebody who knew her as a blonde! Maybe she was running away from her career as a dancer. Maybe she was trying to escape from a jealous lover, or—

"Doesn't look like me at all, that's for sure," Miss Jamison said in a resigned tone, inspecting her image from all angles.

She glanced up at Beulah. "I'm sorry, Mrs. Trivette. You did a swell job on short notice, and I don't mean to sound ungrateful. It's just that . . ." She put the mirror down and got out of the chair. "It's such a change, that's all."

Bettina looked up from her combing. "It's the cat's meow," she said in an admiring tone. "Why, if somebody hadn't seen you before you walked in that door this mornin', they'd never in the world guess that you were platinum."

Leona Ruth looked startled. "You were platinum?"

"She sure was," Beulah said, sounding proud. "As silver and sassy as a new-minted dime. Never know it to look at her now, would you? A totally new woman."

"Well, my word," Leona Ruth said, in a wondering tone. "Platinum. Why, you must be the person that man was lookin' for."

"Man? What man?" Miss Jamison asked sharply.

"Oh, some fella," Leona Ruth said, screwing up her face. "It was yesterday afternoon, maybe five o'clock. Right after it rained, anyway. I heard a knock at my front door. When I went to see who, it was some man I'd never seen before. All dressed up an' dapper in a three-piece suit and tie and hat, an' not one of those Monkey Ward suits, neither. Shoes shined so bright, they looked like they'd been polished with a cold buttered biscuit. Said he was a visitor in town, which I already knew, o' course, since I'd never seen him before, and I could tell he was a Yankee from the way he talked. Said he was looking for a couple of friends of his. One was a platinum blonde, he said. Had to be you!"

Bessie looked at Miss Jamison. Her eyes were growing large and the color was draining out of her face.

"What did he . . . What did he look like?" she whispered.

"Look like?" Leona Ruth pulled her brows together. "Well, that's easy. He was wearin' one of those snappy brim hats, but he took it off when he was speakin' to me, real polite, an' he was bald. Bald and shiny as a billiard ball. Kind of man, you see him once, you cain't never forget him."

"No," Miss Jamison moaned. "Oh, no." She was so pale that Bessie was sure she was about to pitch face forward in a dead faint. Her knees began to wobble and she put out her hand in a helpless appeal.

"Come on, honey, you gotta sit down before you fall down." Beulah put her arm around Miss Jamison's waist. Bessie, still wearing her pink cape, jumped up to help. Together, they got her to a chair and she sank into it. Beulah turned to Bettina.

"Bettina, honey, go and get Hank's whiskey bottle. He hides it in the hall cupboard, second shelf, back corner, where he thinks I never look. And bring a glass of water, too. Hurry!"

"I don't want any whiskey," Miss Jamison whispered. "I'm all right." But she wasn't all right, Bessie saw. Her face was white and her fingers were trembling. She clasped her hands together tightly and looked at Leona Ruth. "Did he . . . Did the man say who he was?"

Leona Ruth was watching avidly, and Bessie knew that this story was going to be all over town before dinnertime. "Yes, he did. Gold is what he said. Mr. Gold."

"Gold." Miss Jamison gave a half-hysterical laugh. "Gold. That's rich. Oh, that's *rich*."

"Why?" Bessie asked.

"Because his name is Diamond," Miss Jamison said miserably. "Frankie Diamond." She closed her eyes. "Oh, god," she moaned. "What am I going to do?"

Bessie turned back to Leona. "What exactly did this fella say, Leona Ruth?"

"Well, like I said, he was lookin' for a platinum blonde and a woman with short black hair. Said he knew they'd come to Darling, but he didn't have any idea where they were stayin', so he was knockin' on doors and askin' around." She swallowed, looking anxious. "He was real polite and soft-spoken. Nice as pie, he was, but he had a cold look in his eye. I wouldn't want to tangle with that one."

"Oh, he's polite, all right," Miss Jamison said bitterly. "He's a charmer, he is. A real *snake*."

Bettina was back with a glass with water in it and the whiskey bottle—the local bootleg whiskey. Beulah uncorked the bottle and poured a healthy slug into the glass. "Here. Drink this, honey. You'll feel better."

Miss Jamison took a sip, coughed, and took another. The color began to come back into her face.

Leona Ruth peered at Miss Jamison. "This Yankee fella— I reckon he's not a friend of yours, huh?"

"No," Miss Jamison said, and took another sip. "He's defi-nitely no friend." The fear in her voice was so plain that every-body heard it. In a pleading tone, she added, "If he comes back, Mrs. Adcock, I beg you not to tell him that you've seen me." She looked at the others. "Everybody. Please don't tell him about me!"

"Well, of course we won't tell him," Beulah said heartily. She looked at Bettina, who nodded.

"No platinum blondes whatsoever in this town," Bettina added. She put an imaginary key in her lips and turned it.

Bessie scowled at Leona Ruth. "Did you hear that, Leona? This is *not* something you can go around telling people about, the way you usually do." She hardened her voice. "And if I hear one word of this outside this room, I'll know it was you who told." She looked from Beulah to Bettina. "We'll *all* know, won't we, girls?"

Beulah and Bettina nodded solemnly.

"I won't say a word." Leona Ruth held up her hand, palm out. "I promise. But he said he was goin' around askin' peo-ple, so I'm not the only one he's talked to."

"Did this Mr. Gold say where he was staying, Leona?" Bessie asked. "Or how long he was going to be in town?"

"Said he'd be at the hotel through Monday afternoon or maybe later, and if I happened to run across his friends, I should be sure to stop and leave a message for him at the front desk." Leona Ruth was eyeing Miss Jamison with an avid curiosity. "If he's not a friend of yours, then why is he lookin' for you?"

"Leona Ruth," Bessie said sharply, "it is none of our business why that man is looking for *anybody*."

"You're a hundred percent right, Bessie," Beulah said. "Bettina, you can get started on Miz Adcock's shampoo now. I'll finish up with Miz Bloodworth." To Miss Jamison, she said, "You just sit there for a few minutes and sip on that whiskey."

"No," Miss Jamison said. She put down the glass and pushed herself out of the chair. "I have to get back to Miss Hamer's right away." Her pocketbook was on a nearby chair, and she picked it up. "What do I owe you for everything?"

"Well, let's see," Beulah said. "We agreed to a dollar fifty on that wig, and your cut and color was two dollars. Call it three fifty." She went to a shelf and took down a blue hat and gloves and a cardboard hatbox tied with a string.

Miss Jamison took out four dollar bills. She gave it to Beulah and took the box. "Keep the change."

"Why, thank you," Beulah said, surprised. The Bower ladies didn't often tip.

"Are you sure you're going to be able to get back to Miss Hamer's house all right?" Bessie asked worriedly. "If you'll hold up until I'm finished, I'll walk with you."

"No, no, I'll be fine," Miss Jamison said. "But I'm wondering—is there a back alley I could take?"

"Sure is, hon," Beulah said. "Just go through the fence by the hollyhocks, turn right, and keep on goin' for a couple blocks. You should end up right smack behind your aunt's house." She glanced down at Miss Jamison's high heels. "Better stay with the street, though. Won't do those pretty shoes any good to walk on cinders. The alley is where people dump their coal clinkers."

"I'll chance it," Miss Jamison said grimly. "Thank you." She went to the door and peeked out apprehensively, as though she was afraid that the baldheaded man might be lurking in Beulah's rose garden. The coast must have been clear, for she turned and waved and then went down the stairs. She was wobbly, Bessie saw, but she'd probably be all right, once she got out in the air.

"A wig?" Leona Ruth asked with a short laugh, as the screen door closed behind Miss Jamison. "Did you sell her that ratty old redhead wig of yours, Beulah? Shame on you!"

Bessie got back in the chair and Beulah picked up a comb. "Bettina," she said, "get started on that shampoo, will you?"

When Bettina had the water running, Bessie asked, in a low voice, "Did she really buy your old beauty school wig, Beulah? The one you loaned to the Ledbetter girl for the Academy's senior play?"

Beulah nodded. "She was thinkin' to order one, but when I showed her mine, she said it would do just fine, especially since she wouldn't have to wait for it to come in the mail." Beulah's eyes met Bessie's in the mirror. "You want to know what I think, Bessie? I think Miz Jamison bought my old red wig for that friend you mentioned, Miss Lake. The one Dessa-Rae says is hidin' out in her room. And she dyed her hair brown 'cause she's hidin' out from that baldheaded Yankee, who means her no good, whoever he is. Those two ladies don't want that man to know they're here in Darlin'."

"I agree," Bessie said. "I don't know who he is, but Miss Jamison is obviously afraid of him." She thought of telling Beulah about Lorelei LaMotte and the Naughty and Nice Sisters and decided against it. The fewer people who knew about

Miss Jamison's previous career as a dancer in Mr. Ziegfeld's Frolics, the better. She chuckled to herself. She always learned something when she came to get her regular shampoo and set. But today took the cake. She had learned so many different things, she hardly knew which to believe.

"That fella." Beulah leaned forward, her cornflower blue eyes large and dark. "Do you reckon he might be a policeman from Chicago, Bessie?" She considered this. "Or maybe Mr. J. Edgar Hoover sent him from Washington. Do you think those two women could be wanted by the Bureau of Investigation? Do you suppose they're on the *lam*?" Her voice was hushed and eager—but not quite hushed enough, and Leona Ruth had good ears.

"The Bureau of Investigation?" she cried, from her place at the shampoo sink. "Why, Beulah, I'll bet dollars to dumplings you're right. That man at my front door—that Mr. Gold or Frankie Diamond or whoever he is—he looked for all the world like one of Mr. Hoover's special agents, with that snap-brim hat and those shiny shoes. I wonder how come I didn't think of that."

"Oh, pooh, Leona Ruth," Bessie said, making her voice light and teasing. If she didn't put a stop to this, things were going to get out of hand. "There you go, jumping to conclusions. If Mr. Gold was a special agent, he would've shown you his badge. That's what they're supposed to do."

"Not if he was undercover, he wouldn't," Leona Ruth retorted darkly. "Don't you read the papers? Government agents go undercover all the time, especially revenuers. Makes me wonder what that woman is wanted for. Don't it you, Bessie? D'you reckon she stole some money? Helped her gangster boyfriend rob a bank and kill somebody? She looks like a gun moll on the lam, don't you think?"

"A gun moll?" Bettina asked incredulously. "Right here in Darling?"

Leona Ruth bolted straight up, a look of horror on her face, shampoo lather dripping onto her shoulders, so that Bettina had to make a grab for a towel. "Mercy me, Bessie," she cried. "Do you s'pose that woman might've had a gun in that pretty blue handbag of hers?"

"Pretty please with sugar on it, Miz Adcock," Bettina beseeched. "Lay back down and lemme rinse those suds outta your hair." Leona Ruth, protesting, allowed herself to be rinsed.

Bessie's heart sank. By the time Leona Ruth finished telling all her friends what she thought she'd seen, everybody in town would believe that Mr. J. Edgar Hoover himself had sent an undercover special agent from the Bureau of Investigation to round up Miss Hamer's niece and her friend and take them back to Chicago or Washington or New York, where they would be charged with robbing a bank and shooting three or four innocent bank tellers.

"My goodness gracious sakes alive." Beulah let out her breath in a rush. She leaned closer and whispered into Bessie's ear. "I hate to say it, Bessie, but Leona Ruth could be right. I kinda liked Miss Jamison, but there's really no tellin' who she is or what she's doin' here. Do you reckon Miss Hamer is in any danger?"

"I don't have any idea," Bessie replied. She was about to add, "And I'm not sure I want to know, either," when Beulah cut her off.

"Well, I think you oughtta find out," she said in a tone of rebuke. "After all, you live right across the street, don't you? And aren't you just about the only person in this town— except for DessaRae and Doc Roberts—who'll have anything to do with that crazy old lady? You may be one of the only friends she has in this whole entire town."

Bessie sighed. It was not a distinction she coveted. But she had to admit that Beulah had a point. And she had been thinking that perhaps she should have a talk with Miss Hamer about Harold—after all these years, surely they could discuss the matter civilly.

And if they couldn't, who cared? Miss Hamer might as well yell at her as shriek at nothing at all.

ELEVEN

Lizzy Goes to Work

Lizzy was always wakened at sunrise by the lusty crowing of Mrs. Freeman's rooster, who lived in a backyard coop two doors down and celebrated the morning with an extravagant delight. But this Monday morning, not even the cheerful rooster could prod Lizzy out of her bed. She had lain awake until after midnight, trying to come up with a solution to her mother's plight. When she finally fell asleep, exhausted, her dreams were filled with a grotesque cartoon caricature of her mother, blown up to the size of a huge balloon, like the ones they sold at the carnival at the County Fair, bouncing from room to room of Lizzy's beautiful little house, knocking things off the shelves and making a wreck of the place. Lizzy herself, reduced to the size of a helpless mouse, could do nothing but run in circles, squeaking her protests, while Verna, wearing an Al Capone mask and brandishing a tommy gun, cheered her on from the sidelines.

It was Daffy who finally forced Lizzy to get up, rubbing his face against her cheek and purring loudly, eager for his breakfast. When she dragged herself out of bed and glanced in the mirror over her dresser, she was horrified by the dark shadows under her eyes and the harsh lines around her mouth. She looked positively awful, and no amount of red lipstick and pancake makeup, applied with a damp sponge and dusted with face powder, made her look any better.

Then, with the idea that a little color might brighten her outlook, she put on a cheerful yellow-checked cotton dress with puffy angel sleeves, a white piqué sailor collar, and a white straw belt. The hat she chose was one of her mother's more whimsical millinery creations: a wide-brimmed yellow straw with yellow silk jonquils and a small yellow chenille bird. But neither the color nor the whimsy helped very much. She felt like a wispy gray cloud on an otherwise sunshiny day.

The law offices of Moseley & Moseley were located on Franklin Street, directly across from the Cypress County Courthouse and upstairs over the Darling *Dispatch.* Mr. Matthew Moseley (the elder Mr. Moseley) had been dead for a dozen years and the eldest Mr. Moseley (Matthew Moseley's father) dead for twenty years more. But their white-whiskered, stern-faced photographs still hung at the top of the stairs, their commanding presences were still felt all across Cypress County, and the law office was still the same sober, lawyerly place that it was when the eldest Moseley opened it before the War.

Another secretary might have wished for an updated look to the place where she spent her days, but Lizzy rather liked the fact that Mr. Benton Moseley (Bent, to his friends) hadn't changed much of anything, except for hanging his own certificates and diplomas beside his father's and grandfather's. She felt that the dusty old rooms had a great deal of dignity, with their creaky floors and wood-paneled walls lined with glass-fronted bookshelves and the sepia prints of maps and old documents. The rooms and the books and the documents seemed to her to symbolize all that was established and stable and unchanging and trustworthy about the law. The office implied a much greater security and reliability than the color print of blindfolded Justice that hung beside Mr. Moseley's desk. Her twin scales and her sword and her blindfold always made Lizzy shiver. If Justice was blind, how in the world could she ever be fair? Didn't Justice have to peek out from under that blindfold and see who was in trouble and who needed help before she used that sword?

This morning, Lizzy was especially grateful for Moseley and Moseley's comforting security and stability—and as always, grateful for her job. So many people were out of work these days that steady employment of any kind was simply a blessing. She opened the venetian blinds and raised the windows in the reception room and in Mr. Moseley's office, letting the cool morning air freshen the rooms and the bright sunshine flood the polished wood floors. She ran the carpet sweeper quickly over the faded oriental-style rug, dusted the old-fashioned wooden furniture, and made a fresh pot of coffee on the gas hot plate.

Then she checked the court calendar and Mr. Moseley's appointment book and stacked the files he would need in the upper right hand corner of his green desk blotter. He was working on a property matter this morning but leaving around eleven thirty to drive to Montgomery, where he was meeting with the Alabama attorney general to discuss a hush-hush criminal matter. He hadn't told her what it was, except to say that it involved an income tax case and that if everything worked out, a very important arrest would be made shortly. He seemed to be quite pleased with himself about it.

But all the while Lizzy was doing these housekeeping chores, she was thinking about what Verna had told her—about the stranger who had knocked on her door and the need to get more background on Miss Jamison (if that's who she really was). Lizzy was the kind of person who normally respected the rules, and under ordinary circumstances, she wouldn't even consider breaking the office code or violating a client's confidence. It was tantamount to a betrayal of Mr. Moseley and everything he stood for.

But she didn't like the idea that Miss Jamison might be someone other than the person she was pretending to be. What if Verna was right and the woman was somehow connected to the most notorious gangster in America? And what if someone from the Capone gang was here in Darling, looking for her? While Mr. Moseley would be upset if he knew she'd given away a client's address, he certainly would not want to risk something bad happening in Darling. A repeat of that horrible massacre that had taken place on Valentine's Day the year before, for example, when Capone's gang, two of them wearing police uniforms, had gunned down seven members of Bugs Moran's gang in a garage on Chicago's north side. Lizzy had felt sick when she saw the gruesome photograph of the seven dead men on the front page of Mr. Moseley's *New York Times.*

So she put her feelings of apprehension aside, took the key to Mr. Moseley's desk out of the empty ink bottle where it was hidden, and opened the bottom right-hand drawer, where the confidential case folders were kept. She bent over it for a moment, hesitating. She would only get the information that Verna had asked for—she wouldn't snoop through the rest of the folder.

But on the card that contained the address—1235 S. 58th—there was a telephone number, too, jotted down in Mr. Moseley's neat handwriting. *UNderwood 3-4555.* The number was followed by a name and note: *Mrs. Molly O'Malley, housekeeper, still on premises.* Lizzy had to smile. Mr. Moseley was always thorough: if he had to call about the house Miss Jamison wanted to sell, he'd want to talk to someone who was familiar with what was going on there. She copied the information, closed and locked the drawer, and telephoned the information to Verna, at the probate office.

"Thanks, Liz," Verna said. "This is really swell. I owe you."

"What are you going to do?" Lizzy asked.

"I have a plan," Verna said, and lowered her voice. "Two plans, in fact. I can't talk about them right now, but when I find something out, you'll be the first to know. I promise." She raised her voice to someone in the office. "I'll be right with you." To Lizzy, she added, "See you later. And thanks again!"

Lizzy returned to her desk, took the cover off her Underwood typewriter, and settled down to transcribing some of the shorthand notes she had taken on Friday afternoon. It was slow going. Mr. Moseley had dictated faster than usual, and she was having trouble reading her Gregg. She was having trouble concentrating, too. Her thoughts kept slipping away from the task at hand to her mother's terrible problem. What in the world were they going to do?

Mr. Moseley usually came in late on Mondays. This morning, it was a little after ten when he tramped up the stairs, tossed his gray felt hat onto the hat tree next to Lizzy's, and smoothed his shiny brown hair, parted in the middle, with his hands.

"G'morning, Liz," he said cheerfully. "My, you look pretty and bright today in that yellow dress. A ray of sunshine. A treat for the eyes."

Lizzy looked up from her typewriter and tried to smile. "I'm afraid I don't feel very bright," she replied ruefully. She was always a little bothered by Mr. Moseley's compliments. She knew he didn't mean to be condescending, but that's what it sounded like to her.

Mr. Moseley frowned and came toward her. He leaned both hands on her desk, peering down at her. "Mmm. Now that you mention it, I have to say that you do look a mite tired." He chuckled. "You and Grady Alexander do a little too much partyin' over the weekend, huh?"

Lizzy sighed. More condescension. And worse, after he had come into the office one day last spring and caught Grady kissing her, Mr. Moseley never missed a chance to tease her about the relationship. That had happened just about the time that Mr. Moseley's wife Adabelle—a willowy debutant from a wealthy Birmingham family with important political connections around the state—announced that she was going home to Mama and Daddy and taking the two Moseley daughters with her. A month or two after that, Mr. Moseley had asked Lizzy to go with him to the tent theater over in Frisco City. A few weeks later, he tried again. They had been working late, getting ready for a trial on a civil matter, and he asked her to go to supper at the Old Alabama.

Both times, she had said no. For one thing, his divorce from Mrs. Moseley wouldn't be final for some time yet, and Lizzy had made up her mind a long time ago that she would never date a married man. For another, she thought that going out with her boss would unnecessarily complicate things in the office. Carrying a torch for him had been okay, because she had known that nothing would ever come of it. She was proud of the fact that she had successfully extinguished those unruly feelings several years before, and she had no intention of reigniting them. Anyway, there was Grady. She wasn't going to go out with Mr. Moseley as long as she was going out with Grady, and that was that.

She frowned. "No, Grady and I did *not* do too much partying this weekend," she retorted, nettled. "He's out of town. I didn't even see him."

"Ah-ha! No Grady?" He quirked one eyebrow in that annoyingly superior way of his. "You mean, there's hope for me, after all?" He straightened and held up his hand, forestalling whatever she had been about to say. "Seriously, Liz, what is it? What's wrong? You look like you didn't get much sleep last night."

"Nothing's wrong," Lizzy lied. She lifted her chin. "I'm fine." While she had been tossing and turning and trying to come up with a way to deal with her mother's foreclosure, she had thought of talking it over with Mr. Moseley. He dealt with property matters all the time, and he might be able to come up with a simple solution to the problem. But she had decided that he would have to be a last resort. If he helped her out, she would be deeply in his debt. Mr. Moseley was a gentleman and would never use that to pressure her in any way, but still—

She pushed back her chair and stood. "Today's files are on your desk, Mr. Moseley. I'll get your coffee."

Mr. Moseley looked at her for a moment. "Tell you what," he said. "I'll be leaving for Montgomery before lunch. Why don't you treat yourself? Take the afternoon off. You've worked late several times lately. You've got it coming."

"Oh, I couldn't!" Lizzy said quickly. "There's so much to—"

"No, there isn't," he said. He smiled at her. "Boss's orders. No argument, now. You're taking the afternoon off." Then he turned and went into his office.

Lizzy stared after him. An afternoon off? Well, she could certainly use the time, couldn't she? She could walk over to the bank and talk to Mr. Johnson about her mother's foreclosure. Surely she could persuade him to put off the eviction for a few weeks—maybe even until after the holidays. It would be cruel to throw somebody out now, with Thanksgiving and Christmas on the way. And even though her mother's house was nice and well maintained, it wasn't likely that anybody would be interested in buying during the holidays. In fact, with so many empty houses for sale, it might not sell at all.

Feeling grateful to Mr. Moseley for letting her take some time off, Lizzy sat back down at her desk and pulled out the big leather-bound account ledger. Between the long drought and the low cotton prices, the farmers had had a difficult time of it in the past few years. Some of Mr. Moseley's clients had begun paying their legal bills in kind, bringing eggs, boxes of figs, and lard pails full of fresh robbed honeycomb to the office, not to mention a few live chickens. Mr. Moseley always accepted these payments, told Liz how much to credit against what was owing, and then carted everything over to the Presbyterian Church for its Food for the Darling Needy program. This morning, she caught up the accounting quickly, finished typing the notes, then typed two legal documents that would be needed later in the week—with carbons, which she hated, since she had to erase every mistake and retype the correction carefully, to avoid smudging. Typing carbons slowed her down.

The bookkeeping and typing finished, Lizzy got up and went to the stack of case files that were waiting for filing in the gray metal cabinets on either side of the front windows. She was just getting started when she heard hasty footsteps on the stairs, the door opened, and Bessie Bloodworth burst in. She was wearing a lace-colored mauve cambric dress and what looked like a freshly done shampoo and set, her springy, precise salt-and-pepper curls peeking out from under her straw sailor hat.

"Why, hello, Bessie," Lizzy said. She was surprised, since Bessie didn't come to the office very often—but then she remembered that she had asked the Dahlias to turn in items for her garden column, which she had to finish by tomorrow. Now that she had the afternoon off, she'd have plenty of time. "Have you brought me a piece for the column?"

"No," Bessie said. "To tell the truth, I forgot all about that." She glanced in the direction of Mr. Moseley's closed door and lowered her voice. "I don't want to interrupt while you're working, but do you have a minute, Liz?" Her face was pink with the exertion of climbing the stairs and she sounded excited. "I need to ask you something."

"Sure," Lizzy said, and pointed to one of the reception room chairs. "Why don't you sit down there and catch your breath, Bessie? I can listen and file at the same time." She picked up the first file, opened a drawer, and dropped it in place. "What's on your mind?"

"It's not a what, it's a who," Bessie said. She pulled the chair around so she could see Liz and sat down, crossing her thick ankles. "It's Miss Jamison."

Lizzy flushed guiltily, thinking of the information she had given to Verna. "What about her?"

"I've just come from the Beauty Bower. Beulah was already working on her when I got there. On Miss Jamison, I mean." Bessie puffed out her breath and fanned herself with a hankie. "She was dyeing her brown. Transforming her from platinum to brown, right there in front of my eyes."

"Brown!" Lizzy exclaimed. "Gracious sakes! Why in the world would Miss Jamison want—"

Bessie held up her hand. "Wait, there's more, Liz. Lots more. In fact, you might as well hear the whole thing, start to finish."

It took a little while for Bessie to tell the whole story, which she did in one long sentence, from Miss Jamison's purchase of Beulah Trivette's red wig and the blond-to-brown coloring job she got on her hair to Leona Ruth Adcock's tale about the baldheaded man with shiny leather shoes (who might or might not have been a special agent for Mr. J. Edgar Hoover), who had shown up at Leona Ruth's front door the afternoon before, introducing himself as Mr. Gold (although Miss Jamison said he was really Mr. Diamond, Frankie Diamond) and asking if she had seen a platinum blonde and a girl with short dark hair.

"I haven't actually laid eyes on Miss Lake myself," Bessie

added breathlessly. "She had already hidden herself away in her bedroom when I went over to say hello after they arrived. But I'll bet a nickel that she's the one with short dark hair—except that by this time, she's probably wearing Beulah's old red wig. She's in disguise. Both women are hiding out."

Lizzy stared at Bessie. Why, this was the very same story that Verna had told her on the phone the afternoon before, although Verna hadn't said anything about her caller looking like a special agent. Quite the contrary, in fact.

"Do you think Mrs. Adcock is right?" she asked tentatively. "That this fellow is a *policeman?*" She looked down at the folder in her hand, realized that she'd gotten so caught up in Bessie's story that she hadn't filed it, and opened a drawer.

"I have no idea," Bessie said. "But whoever the man is, Mr. Gold or Mr. Diamond or whoever, I'm here to tell you that he scared the stuffing out of Miss Jamison. She almost fainted when Leona Ruth described him. And it wasn't any stunt, either. She got white as a sheet and Beulah and I had to make her sit down. She is scared to death of him." She narrowed her eyes and leaned forward. "There is something truly fishy going on over at Miss Hamer's house, Liz. I think we ought to find out what it is. How much time do you take at noon?"

"An hour, usually. But Mr. Moseley is driving to Montgomery and he's given me the afternoon off."

"That's good," Bessie said with satisfaction. "But an hour ought to be way more than enough time for us to do it."

"Do what?"

"To walk on over to the Old Alabama Hotel and get a quick bite. I know it's more expensive than the diner, but if we just got a sandwich and split it between us, it shouldn't be any more than a quarter apiece. I would've asked Verna, too," Bessie added, "but she wasn't in the office when I stopped. Mrs. Cole said she was out running an errand."

Lizzy frowned. "Why do you want to go to the hotel?"

"Because Mr. Gold told Leona Ruth that he's staying there," Bessie replied. "If that's true, then he ought to be taking his meals there, wouldn't you reckon? I thought, if we could get a good look at him, we might be able to tell whether he's a special agent or—" She stopped.

"Or what?" Lizzy asked, thinking of Verna's guess that he was one of Al Capone's henchmen. Both seemed equally improbable to her.

Bessie sighed plaintively. "I don't know. Maybe it's not a good idea. I just have this feeling that somebody ought to be doing something to find out who this man really is and why Miss Jamison is so deathly afraid of him. I can't think of any other way to do it—and I certainly can't go to the hotel by myself."

Lizzy understood why. Nobody thought twice of a woman eating by herself at the diner, where she could sit at the counter and talk to Myra May or Violet or Euphoria while she enjoyed her meal. But it would be odd for a woman to eat in the Old Alabama dining room unless she was traveling or with someone. Still—

"I'm not sure why we should care who he is," Lizzy said, stalling for time. "What business is it of ours?" She dropped another folder into the drawer. Then she realized that she'd put an "E" folder into the "L–R" drawer, and took it out.

Bessie leaned forward, her lined face intent. "Well, for starters, if *he* is a policeman or a special agent looking for those two women, it stands to reason that *they* are criminals, doesn't it? Leona Ruth said that Miss Jamison looks like a gun moll to her—and she is no doubt spreading that very same thing all over town, right this minute." She leaned back and folded her plump arms. "You know Leona Ruth. When she gets through with Miss Jamison and her friend, nobody in Darling will have a blessed thing to do with them, regardless of who they are."

Lizzy understood this, too. In Darling, there were the facts, and then there were the facts according to whoever was telling them, which might or might not be the same thing and usually wasn't. If Leona Ruth was telling folks that these women were gun molls, that's exactly what people would believe. Even if they were totally innocent, their reputations would be completely destroyed.

She opened the "E–K" drawer and put the file into the right place. "I wonder how Mrs. Adcock knows what a gun moll looks like," she said thoughtfully.

"Maybe from the movies?" Bessie hazarded. "To me, Miss Jamison didn't look much like a criminal, but of course you can't always tell. Anyway, there's Miss Hamer to consider. If those two women are criminals, she could be in danger." Bessie turned down her mouth. "I was even thinking that we might ought to have a talk with Sheriff Burns about the situation."

Lizzy didn't think much of Roy Burns. She'd had a few dealings with him when Bunny Scott was killed, and it was her impression that he liked to wear the badge but wasn't much of a crime fighter. He had taken over the job of Darling police chief when Chief Henny Poe had retired and the Darling town council decided they couldn't afford to replace him. But Sheriff Burns and his deputy, Buddy Norris, could usually handle what crime there was in Cypress County, which was mostly tempers getting out of hand at the Watering Hole or the Dance Barn, and cow and chicken rustling (there was more of that, now that so many were short of money), and moonshiners out in the piney woods. Most people didn't really consider moonshining a crime, though. Somebody had to do it, or nobody would have anything to drink. The preachers liked it, too, for it gave them something to preach against besides lying, stealing, skipping Wednesday night prayer meeting, and committing adultery.

Lizzy thought about Verna's theory. "And if the man isn't a policeman or a special agent? What if he is—" She let the sentence dangle.

"That makes it easy," Bessie replied cheerfully. "If he's not a policeman, we can stop fretting about Miss Jamison and her friend being criminals. We don't have a thing to worry about."

Lizzy didn't point out that this wasn't exactly logical. But she had the feeling that, if the baldheaded man was a gangster instead of a special agent, they had something *else* to worry about. Anyway, now she was curious. She wanted to see him for herself. And Bessie was a Dahlia, after all. Dahlias stuck together.

She glanced up at the Seth Thomas clock on the wall over the Chamber of Commerce certificate, its copper-colored pendulum swinging back and forth. It was almost eleven thirty, and Mr. Moseley would be leaving for Montgomery at any moment.

"I'll finish this filing," she told Bessie. "After Mr. Moseley leaves, we can go."

A little later, Lizzy put on her yellow straw hat and locked the office. Then she and Bessie went down the stairs and out onto Franklin Street, which ran east and west along one side of the courthouse square. The dusty streets (the Darling Women's Club were still lobbying for pavement but with tax revenues falling, it looked like a lost cause again this year) were busy on this midday Monday, and loud with the noise of people going here and there and doing this and that. From the opposite side of the square, on Dauphin, an ooga-ooga horn blurted, several automobiles chugged loudly, and a hammer pounded sharply and irregularly—Mr. Dunlap repairing the sagging awning of his five-and-dime. A train whistle sounded from the rail yard several blocks to the east, where in years past, great stacks of cotton bales had waited for shipment to the textile mills. Now, between the drought and the growing recession (some newspapers were even beginning to call it a depression), there were far fewer bales and almost no corn, and the rail cars mostly hauled lumber from the Bear Creek sawmill north of town. Still, some people had plenty of money, as Lizzy recalled, as she saw Bailey Beauchamp's lemon yellow Cadillac cruising west on Franklin. It turned the corner and bumped to a stop in front of the Darling Savings and Trust, where Lizzy intended to go, just as soon as she and Bessie had finished their little chore.

But not everybody drove a late-model auto. Next door on the west, tied to the wooden rail in front of Hancock's Groceries, stood a brown mule hitched to an Old Hickory farm wagon, patiently flicking flies with its tail. Many of the farmers drove horses and wagons when they brought their butter and eggs and honey to Mr. Hancock to trade for tea and coffee and flour and salt. Next to the mule was an old black Model T Ford that had been made into a truck by pulling out the back seat and the window and adding a big wooden box. And next to that was the old green Packard that belonged to Mr. Howard, who was leaning against the fender with a cud of tobacco in his cheek, waiting for Mrs. Howard to do her week's grocery shopping. On the backseat of the Packard was a crate of live chickens and a small goat.

Lizzy and Bessie turned left on Franklin in front of the *Dispatch* office. Looking through the window, Lizzy could see Charlie Dickens hunched over his typewriter, his green celluloid eyeshade pulled down over his eyes. She was uncomfortably reminded that she needed to get her column finished tonight, if she intended to meet tomorrow's deadline. She was thinking of this when Bessie grasped her arm.

"Liz, that must be him!" she exclaimed in a half whisper, pointing. "Mr. Gold! Or Mr. Diamond—depending on who you believe."

The man who had just crossed Franklin Street paused in front of the diner, took off his hat, and mopped his bald head with a handkerchief. He was of medium height and wore a light gray three-piece suit and gray hat. He put his hat back on, pocketed his handkerchief, and glanced back over his shoulder with an air of caution, as if to make sure he was not being followed.

Lizzy pulled in her breath and peered, trying to get a good look. This was the man Verna suspected of being a member of the Capone gang—or was he a government agent? "It looks like he's going into the diner," she said.

Bessie's grip tightened and she pulled Lizzy forward. "No. He's heading for the telephone booth. He's going to make a phone call!"

The booth was a new feature in town, and the only one of its kind. It was said of Mr. Whitey Whitworth, half owner of the Darling Telephone Exchange (Myra May and Violet owned the other half), that he had more money than sense, and that the phone booth was a good example.

The year before, Mr. Whitworth had taken a trip to Atlanta, where he had seen his very first telephone booth on the sidewalk in front of the National Bank of Georgia. All you had to do was plug enough nickels, dimes, and quarters into the three slots at the top of the phone and you could call anybody, anywhere in the country, maybe even the world, if the person you were calling in France or Italy or wherever had a telephone and you knew the number. He had been so fascinated by the way the pay telephone worked and the cheerful clink-clink-clink of the coins dropping into the coin box that he had spent all of three dollars making long-distance calls to his whole family.

And when somebody told him that big-city folks had been using outdoor telephone booths since before Theodore Roosevelt built the Panama Canal, he had decided that it was high time Darling had one, so that people who came to town and discovered that they needed to telephone their homes or businesses wouldn't have to pester the merchants on the square to use their phones. And if a citizen of Darling didn't have a phone at home, by golly, he or she could walk the few blocks to the square and use the pay phone. Mr. Whitworth thought it was bound to be a paying proposition.

At first, people thought it was a joke. They said that the phone booth looked like a privy and they wouldn't be caught dead going into it right out there in front of God and everybody on the town square. But it wasn't long before they got used to the convenience, and sometimes you'd see two or three folks lined up, waiting for their turns. To make a call, you simply picked up the receiver, cranked the handle for the operator (who was on the other side of the wall, in the Exchange office behind the diner), and gave her the number you wanted to call. She connected you and told you how many coins to drop into the slots so you could start talking. She listened for the sounds of the coins you put in, and told you to go ahead with your call. When you were finished, you hung up and waited for the operator to call you back and tell you how much more money you owed. (Nobody ever tried to leave the booth without paying the rest, because there was a note on the wall that said that the switchboard operator would send somebody out from the diner to collar the cheap-skate.) The new arrangement had proved to be so popular that Mr. Whitworth was planning to install a pay telephone in the lobby of the Old Alabama Hotel, so that hotel patrons would have access to a private phone, since there were no phones in the rooms.

By now, Lizzy and Bessie were close enough to get a good

view of their quarry—a little too close for Lizzy's comfort, actually, especially if Verna was right and he was one of Al Capone's boys. But Mr. Gold paid no attention to them at all. He paused in front of the phone booth's folding glass door, put his hand into his pocket, and took out a leather coin purse. He dumped his change into his palm, counted it, and then—apparently deciding that he didn't have enough coins to make his call—turned and went into the diner.

Lizzy and Bessie followed as Mr. Gold stepped up to the counter and took out his wallet. "Gimme some change for the pay phone," he said to Myra May, and put down two dollar bills.

"You won't need all that if it's a local call," Myra May said pleasantly, as she rang up a no-sale on the cash register. She was wearing khaki-colored trousers, a green knit polo shirt, and a bleached cotton apron. Violet had embroidered the words *The Darling Diner* across the apron's bib in purple and red embroidery floss.

"It's long distance," Mr. Gold said. He frowned, cocking his head. "I can make a long distance call from that phone out there, can't I?"

"Sure thing," Myra May said, and slid eight quarters across the counter. She grinned as he took the change and paused, glancing up at the chalkboard that displayed the noon menu. "You look like a hungry fella," she added. "The dinner special today is fried chicken. Mashed potatoes, gravy, green beans, a biscuit, and your choice of pie. Thirty-five cents, includes coffee. That phone call can wait till you have yourself something to eat, can't it?"

Mr. Gold took a large pocket watch out and consulted it. "Don't have to make it until noon," he said. "Yeah, why not? Fix me up with the special, baby." He slid onto one of the red leather–topped stools, took off his hat, and put it on the counter beside his elbow. His bald head glinted.

Lizzy leaned over to Bessie. "Why don't you get a table for us," she suggested. "And keep an eye on that man. I'm going to visit the washroom."

But instead of turning right when she got to the back of the diner, Lizzy turned to the left, pushed open the door, and stepped into the Darling Telephone Exchange. She didn't have a very clear idea of what she was going to do. But she knew that there must be a way to find out who the man was calling. Since Myra May was working the counter and Violet was still in Memphis, one of the other girls—Olive or Lenore—had to be on the switchboard. Lizzy knew the rules, but she was hoping that maybe she could talk the operator into not flipping the switch so she could eavesdrop on—

She didn't get to finish the thought. She stopped inside the doorway and stared at the operator's back.

"Verna!" she exclaimed, in great surprise. "Verna Tidwell, is that you? What in the world are *you* doing here?"

TWELVE

Verna Makes a Phone Call

Verna had learned to be a telephone operator a few years before, when Mrs. Hooper needed extra help and she needed extra money, but she didn't usually spend her lunch hour—or any hours—at the Darling Telephone Exchange. But being on the switchboard at noon was part of the plan she had mentioned to Liz, a plan that she had sold to Myra May the evening before.

At eight o'clock on Monday morning, as usual, Verna opened the probate office. Located on the second floor of the courthouse and to the right at the head of the stairs, the office had a reception room divided by a long wooden counter, with the public area on one side and three wooden desks and chairs on the other: one for Verna, one for Coretta Cole, and the third, behind a low partition, for Mr. Earle Scroggins, the elected probate clerk, just in case he should happen to drop in, which he didn't, usually.

Mr. Scroggins was a fat, jovial man with a bulbous red nose and twin white mustaches that curled up on the ends.

He wore red suspenders and a bow tie and owed his reelection for three consecutive six-year terms as probate clerk to the goodwill of the friends who, in their turn, called on him for important favors, usually (but not always) legal. Mr. Scroggins owned a cotton gin on the south side of town and a cottonseed oil mill over by the river, and (although he was always careful not to miss the monthly meetings of the county commissioners) did not see much point in spending a lot of time in the office, especially since Verna took such good care of everything.

Whenever he dropped in, Verna would hand him a pen and a bottle of ink and a few papers requiring his signature (she had already signed the rest), bring him up to date on anything that might present a major problem, and ask his opinion about one or two minor matters. He would smile and pat her on the shoulder and say, "Don't reckon I could do without you, Miz Tidwell," and go back to his cronies and his cotton gin.

To some people, Verna's job might have seemed boring, but she enjoyed being responsible for the multitude of property transactions, tax liens, wills, probate orders, and election details that kept the machinery of Cypress County moving. She also liked her work because it gave her an inside look at what was going on at the moment. She always knew who was buying and selling property, because the office managed the property records. She knew who died or was born or got married, because the probate clerk issued marriage licenses and birth and death certificates, as well as filing wills and probate documents. The office also collected property tax payments, so Verna knew who had gotten so far behind on their taxes that the county was planning to put the property up for auction. When that happened, she was the one who recorded the sale. In fact, Verna often said that nothing of any consequence could happen in Cypress County without leaving a paper trail across her desk.

Until a few months ago, there had been two women full-time in the office, Verna and Coretta Cole. But tax revenues were down, and Mr. Scroggins had decided to save money by cutting staff hours. Now, Coretta worked only two days a week, usually Tuesdays and Thursdays. But Coretta had agreed to come in on Monday, instead. So Monday morning, when Liz Lacy phoned the probate office to give Verna the address she had found in Miss Jamison's file, and (to Verna's pleased surprise) a telephone number and a name as well, Verna could ask Coretta to take over for her. She could turn her attention to the plan she had concocted the evening before—the plan to deal with Mr. Gold.

It was not a plan that Verna could carry out for herself, however, which was why (after she had called Coretta on Sunday evening) she had put on a sweater and walked to the diner for a talk with Myra May. She told the whole story, from start to finish, laying all her cards on the table. But while Myra May had been intrigued by Verna's suspicions (she read the newspapers and listened to the radio and was as interested as the next person in what those gangsters were doing up there in Chicago), she had at first said a firm "no" to Verna's proposal, which appeared to violate certain important rules of the Darling Telephone Exchange.

But after Verna have finished explaining her plan and why she felt it was necessary, and especially after she had offered to work on the switchboard during the next day's noon dinner hour (the diner's busiest time), Myra May had agreed. With Lenore gone to Mobile for a few days and Violet still up in Memphis taking care of her dead sister's new baby, Myra May was stretched as thin as a rubber band and just about as ready to snap. Most times of the day, she could handle both the diner and the switchboard if she had to, but not during the noon dinner rush, so Verna's offer was welcome. Anyway, both Myra May and Verna were Dahlias, and Myra May knew that another Dahlia wouldn't ask for that kind of help unless she really needed it.

Verna's plan—she thought of it as Phase One—had two parts. The first part involved a phony telegram, which she wrote on one of the blank Western Union forms she got at the Exchange. There were three short sentences: MR C WANTS YOU CALL NOON MONDAY STOP USE PHONE BOOTH STOP NOT HOTEL PHONE STOP. It was not signed. She paid Mr. Musgrove's boy to deliver this fake telegram to the hotel on Sunday night.

To Verna's analytic mind, the telegram was a very simple test, with two—and only two—possible outcomes. If Mr. Gold passed the test by making the call, it was because he was a member of the Capone gang and knew who Mr. C was and how to reach him. If he didn't make the call and therefore failed the test, it was because he had no idea who he was supposed to call, at what number. Of course, failing the test didn't mean that the man wasn't up to some nefarious purpose. It just meant that he wasn't connected to those gangsters in Cicero.

The second part of Verna's plan required Miss Jamison's address. That's why she was thrilled and delighted when Liz called the office on Monday morning and gave her not only an address but a telephone number and a name—two more items than she had expected. Of course, she reminded herself, as she went behind the partition and sat down at Mr. Scruggs' desk and reached for the black candlestick telephone, this was only a fishing expedition and probably wouldn't net much of a catch. Realistically speaking (and Verna was almost always realistic), the most she could hope for was a tiny tidbit of information that might tell her whether Miss Jamison was somehow connected to the Capone gang. She could just as easily come up empty-handed.

The circuits were busy and it took a little while for Verna to get through to UNderwood 3-4555. But when she did, she hit the jackpot, for Mrs. O'Malley proved to be an older woman with an Irish accent who had apparently been waiting on pins and needles for any word from Miss LaMotte and Miss Lake.

"Oh, dearie me, I'm so glad to know the ladies arrived safely!" she exclaimed excitedly. "I was beginnin' to fret that something might've gone wrong somehow. O' course, I know there's no phone in her auntie's house, but still—" She paused for breath. "Anyway, dear, it's verra sweet of you to call for them! Was there somethin' special they was wantin'?"

Verna, inventing on the spot, said that Miss LaMotte had asked her to telephone Mrs. O'Malley and ask if she had left her ivory-backed hairbrush and mirror set behind. Mrs. O'Malley didn't hesitate to offer to run and look. She came back in a moment (and a bit short of breath) to say that she didn't see it anywhere, but she would be sure to keep on looking and hoped that Miss LaMotte was getting settled and Miss Lake was feeling better.

"I've been worried to death about Miss Lake," she added anxiously. "Those dreadful knife cuts on her face—so slow to heal. All the way to the verra bone, y'know." She pulled in her breath. "Why, one of them awful slashes just missed her right eye!"

Knife cuts? Verna thought swiftly, cataloging the possibilities. "Miss Lake is better," she said, cautiously feeling her way, "but of course she's still suffering dreadfully. Takes her meals in her room and doesn't come downstairs and of course you can't blame her. Such a pretty woman, and in show business, too. I saw them once in New York, when they had their Naughty and Nice Sisters act."

"Oh, you did?" Mrs. O'Malley exclaimed. "Miss LaMotte and Miss Lake had the lead act at the Star and Garter for the longest time, y'know. 'The Naughty, Naughty Sisters,' they called themselves. Real classy burlesque. That's where Mr. Capone ran into 'em, o' course."

"Is that right?" Verna said in a marveling tone. "Well, gracious sakes." The Naughty, Naughty Sisters? They had obviously changed the act.

"Yes, and after that, they was all as thick as thieves for a year or more, Mr. Capone and his friends and Miss LaMotte and Miss Lake. Which is what makes it so hard. They was friends! And then he sent one of his thugs over here to cut both of 'em up. And poor Miss Lake—" She gulped back a sniffle, then broke into sobs. "Poor Miss Lake!"

"But she's lucky it wasn't worse, don't you think?" Verna said in a comforting tone. "Why, she might have been killed!"

Noisily, Mrs. O'Malley blew her nose. "Oh, aye! And her such a brave little dear, too. Why, after it happened—and after Miss LaMotte pulled out her gun and shot that brute, y' know—she wouldn't for the longest time let me call a doctor. All we could do was try and stop the bleeding until she finally gave in. And when he came and told her she ought to be in the hospital, she refused, o' course, because the doctors in the hospital, just like everybody else in this town, are all in cahoots wi' the Capone gang."

Shot that brute? Verna was taken aback. She tried to get a word in edgewise but without success as Mrs. O'Malley took a deep breath and hurried on.

"I know those stitches all over her pretty cheeks are big and clumsy and I'm sure there'll be terrible scars, which o' course means that her dancin' career is over. But I canna blame the doctor, poor young man. Miss Lake was screamin' her lungs out and all we had to give her was whiskey, and he was in a hurry to get it over with because we all thought the thug might come back and try to finish the job while he was there, sewin' her up, and Miss LaMotte, standin' over 'em both with her gun, just in case." One more breath. "Still, I think I could've done better with that needle m'self. Everybody says they ain't nivver seen quilting stitches as pretty as mine."

Finally, Verna got a chance to break in. "That was very brave of Miss LaMotte," she said. "To shoot the fellow, I mean. It's a good thing she had the gun handy." What kind of gun, she wondered. Where was it now? But she couldn't think of a way to ask those indelicate questions. Instead, she said, "Was he badly wounded, do you know?"

"Badly wounded!" Mrs. O'Malley exclaimed incredulously. "Why, gracious sakes alive, dear, dinna she tell you? That Remington pistol o' hers ain't verra big but it packs a wallop, it does. Sal Raggio—they call him 'the Blade,' he's the man she shot—got as far as the Western Hotel. That's where they found 'im, dead as a doornail, propped up against the brick wall out front. The papers was full of it the next mornin'."

The Blade, dead in front of the Western Hotel. Verna was beginning to piece the details of the story together, but she needed more. "I don't suppose the police knew that Miss LaMotte was the one who pulled the trigger," she hazarded.

"Police?" Mrs. O'Malley cried, with a bitter gale of Irish laughter. "Police! Why, sure and begorrah, o' course they knew who pulled that trigger! Sal Raggio was a friend of Mr. Capone, and Mr. C himself ordered 'em to come and haul Miss LaMotte off to jail. And that's exactly what they would've done, too, if she'd've been here."

"So Miss LaMotte is a fugitive from justice," Verna said, half to herself.

Mrs. O'Malley gave an indignant sniff. "Well, I s'pose you could call her that—except that it ain't 'justice' she'd likely get in this town. More like 'revenge,' is what I'd call it. But then, I guess you folks down there in Alabama dinna know that the police up here in Cicero are hand-in-glove with Mr. Capone and his mob. Not to mention the prosecutors and the judges and the juries and all the rest. If Mr. Capone's cops get their hands on her, she'll nivver see the light o' day again. Nivver."

"Of course," Verna murmured, as the last piece fell into place. "Of course."

"And that's why they had to leave town so quick," Mrs. O'Malley continued mournfully. "I miss 'em with all my heart, truly I do, but I'm glad they had a place to go, and I'll be gladder yet when the house is sold and I can go, too. 'Twas the dear Lord's blessin' that Miss LaMotte was already makin' arrangements with that old lady down there, Miss what's-her-name. All they had to do was pack and run."

"Miss Hamer," Verna supplied. "Her aunt?" She let the question mark hang in the air.

"That's right—Hamer, that's the auntie," Mrs. O'Malley replied. "An' you tell Miss LaMotte that I'm verra glad that they hurried up and got on that train when they did, even though 'twas pourin' down rain, 'cause Mr. Capone's police-men showed up not thirty minutes after the door closed behind 'em."

"Well, my goodness," Verna murmured.

"Aye, indeed! If they'd waited to leave when they planned, they'd be in jail right now. Or dead."

"Dead?"

"Dead." Mrs. O'Malley's voice became tremulous. "You tell Miss LaMotte that the verra same day, after the police came and went, that baldheaded man come lookin' for her. Diamond, Frankie Diamond—she'll know the one. He's another friend of the Blade's. He was mad as a stuck bull, he was, and he's mean and dang'rous. Said when he caught sight of either of 'em, he'd shoot 'em." She made a shivery sound. "Just the thought of it gives me the cold chills. I'm glad Miss LaMotte knows how to use that Remington—and that she took it with her. You tell her what I said, now. Don't forget."

"I sure will," Verna said. So the baldheaded Mr. Gold was really Mr. Diamond, Frankie Diamond—and he was out to kill! It was all the confirmation she needed, and time to wind up the conversation. She looked down at the notes she had made after Liz's call. "It's good for them that they have you to look after the house until it's sold."

"I do my best," Mrs. O'Malley said, with a note of quiet pride. "If I do say it myself, I'm a good manager, I am. When this house is sold and after Miss LaMotte's aunt is dead and gone, she's asked me to come and live down there, which I will cert'nly be pleased to do, and the sooner the better. Dinna know that I'll like small-town livin', but these northern winters are hard on my old bones. And I just hate all this gangster stuff. Why, a body canna walk safe on the streets these days!"

Verna knitted her brows together. "Dead and gone? Her aunt?"

"Oh, aye." Mrs. O'Malley's voice became mournful again. "Miss Hamer's not expected to live much longer, poor old thing. The Lord could take her any day now, I reckon. The house is a nice big one, Miss LaMotte said—at least, that's what she heard from the neighbor across the street, when she talked to her on the phone. Big enough for all three of us." She paused and added curiously, "What did you say your name was again, dear?"

Verna shivered. *Not expected to live much longer.* It sounded ominous. Was Miss LaMotte expecting Miss Hamer's speedy demise? She suddenly thought of the prescription for Veronal that Miss LaMotte had tried to get Mr. Lima to fill at the drugstore. Mr. Lima had said that it was a dangerous barbiturate. Had Miss LaMotte planned to use it to kill Miss Hamer? What Verna had learned about Miss LaMotte's shooting of Sal Raggio made this seem altogether too plausible. A woman who had killed once could kill again. And maybe Raggio wasn't her first victim.

Out of a sense of caution, Verna decided not to give her real name. "I'm Bessie Bloodworth," she lied quickly. "I'm the neighbor Miss LaMotte telephoned, across the street from Miss Hamer's.' "

"Well, it's been verra good talkin' to you, Miz Blood-worth," Mrs. O'Malley said cheerfully. "You give both the ladies my best love, now, will ye? And tell 'em from me to be careful. I'm sure they're where it's safe, but they need to keep a sharp eye out." She sighed. "Oh, and tell Miss LaMotte that there's been nobody looking at the house. Seems like people don't have the money to buy property right now. Things is pretty grim here. People out of work, with nowhere to go." She sighed. "People sleeping in the parks, even."

"I'll do that," Verna said. "And if you find that hairbrush and mirror, please do send them along. Miss LaMotte is so anxious to have them."

"Aye, I will," Mrs. O'Malley promised. "G'bye now!"

Verna hung the earpiece on the phone and sat for a moment, thinking. The conversation with Mrs. O'Malley had given her more information than she had dared to hope for. She now knew why Miss Lake had hidden herself away in her room and wouldn't let anybody look at her; why Miss Jamison was so frightened; and why she refused to acknowledge that she was Lorelei LaMotte. She knew that Miss LaMotte and Miss Lake had been starring in a burlesque show at the Star and Garter, where one or both of them had attracted the attention of Al Capone; that Miss LaMotte was packing a Remington pistol; and that she had been brave enough—or foolish enough—to use it on one of Capone's friends. She also knew that the baldheaded man was another friend of her victim, a member of the Capone gang, and a very danger-ous man.

But there were big gaps in her knowledge, and they made Verna nervous. She still didn't know whether Miss LaMotte was really Miss Hamer's niece or a clever imposter who was looking for a hideout where she and her friend could cool off while the heat was on, as *The Dime Detective* might put it. What's more, she didn't know whether Miss Hamer herself might be in danger, as Mrs. O'Malley had seemed to suggest. Filling these gaps would require an entirely different investigative strategy—exactly what that would be, she wasn't sure.

Troubled, Verna pressed her lips together. This part of her plan had unexpectedly given her almost all the information she needed, and she was sorry now (*verra* sorry, as Mrs. O'Malley would say) that she had set the other part into motion. When the baldheaded man—Frankie Diamond, that is—followed the instruction contained in the telegram and telephoned Mr. Capone, he would learn that nobody there knew anything about the telegram, and figure out that it had to have come from someone in Darling. He would be on his guard. And then it would be more difficult to—

Abruptly, Verna pushed the chair back and stood up from the desk. More difficult to what? Now that she knew who Frankie Diamond was and why he was here in Darling, she ought to be getting ready to move to Phase Two of her plan. She should be shifting from speculation, investigation, and analysis to operation. To action.

But what kind of action? To tell the truth, Verna didn't have a clue.

She sighed and looked down at her wristwatch. It was eleven, time for her shift at the Darling Telephone Exchange. And only an hour before Frankie Diamond telephoned Mr. Capone and learned that the telegram he had received was a hoax.

according to a simple system, and all you had to do was keep your mind on what you were doing.

The operator (in this case, Verna) sat in front of a vertical board that displayed rows and rows of empty sockets, one socket for every telephone in town, and a horizontal panel with a dozen pairs of cords with phone jacks on the ends. Say that Ophelia Snow was at home and decided to call her husband Jed at Snow's Farm Supply to tell him to stop at Hancock's Groceries and pick up five pounds of sugar. When Ophelia rang the switchboard, a little bulb would light above her socket—or rather, the socket for her party line, which connected several different houses. Verna would pull one of the cords out, plug the jack into Ophelia's socket, and say "Number, please," into her headset microphone. When Ophelia gave Jed's number (or just said, "Verna, connect me to the Farm Supply, please."), Verna would plug the second cord of the pair into the socket for the Farm Supply. Then she would send a signal down the line that rang the Farm Supply phone. When Jed answered, she would flip the switch that cut off her headset so that Ophelia and Jed could talk in private. (That was the theory, anyway, although everybody in town knew that the operators didn't always bother to turn off their headsets, especially when they didn't have any other calls to tend to.) When Ophelia and Jed hung up, Verna would unplug the cords from the sockets and that was that.

Long-distance phone calls were a little more complicated. The switchboard had a couple of lines that connected to the long-distance office in Mobile. If Ophelia wanted to talk to her cousin in New Orleans, she would give the number to Verna, who would connect with the Mobile long-distance office, tell the operator she had a call for New Orleans, and would eventually be able to give the New Orleans operator the number for Ophelia's cousin. When the cousin was on the line, Verna would connect Ophelia, and the two could talk.

The process often took fifteen minutes or more, especially if the call had to go through several long-distance offices before it finally reached its destination. Circuits were often busy, and callers were sometimes told to hang up and try again later.

Verna was just getting into the swing of things—plugging in a call from Mrs. Sedalius at Magnolia Manor to Beulah's Beauty Bower—when she heard a familiar voice behind her.

"Verna!" Liz Lacy exclaimed, sounding surprised. "Verna Tidwell, is that you? What in the world are you doing here?"

Verna turned around. "I'm working the switchboard," she replied, somewhat nettled. "What are *you* doing here?"

Liz, looking like a ray of sunshine in her yellow dress and bright yellow straw hat, closed the door behind her and leaned against it. "I'm here because of that baldheaded man you told me about—the one who came to your house yesterday afternoon. Bessie says that Miss Jamison is scared to death of him, and he—"

"Bessie?" Verna asked sharply. "How does Bessie know about him?"

"Because she was at the Beauty Bower this morning when Miss Jamison was getting her hair dyed brown," Liz replied. "Leona Ruth Adcock came in for her appointment and was telling everybody about this baldheaded man—she thinks he's one of Mr. J. Edgar Hoover's government agents—who came to her house looking for a platinum blonde. Bessie said Miss Jamison almost fainted. She also bought a red wig for Miss Lake." She added, "Bessie's out there in the diner now, waiting for me."

"Wait a minute, Liz," Verna said, holding up her hand. "What's this about Miss Jamison getting dyed brown? And J. Edgar Hoover? How does he fit into this?"

Liz shook her head. "That's all beside the point," she said hurriedly. "I'll fill you in later. The point is that your baldheaded man is out there at the counter getting a plate of Euphoria's special right this very minute, and as soon as he's done, he's going to make a long-distance call from the booth, so he got two dollars' worth of quarters from Myra May. I thought maybe I should try and find out who he was calling, so I came in here to the switchboard to see if I could listen in and—"

But Liz was interrupted as the door opened and Myra May came into the room. "Verna, that man you're looking for, the one you sent the telegram to—he's out there at the counter. He—" She stopped and frowned at Liz. "What're you doing here, Liz?"

"It's okay, Myra May," Verna said. "Liz knows." To Liz, she said in an urgent tone, "What's that you were telling me about a wig, Liz? And Miss Jamison dyeing her hair brown?"

"They must want to disguise themselves," Liz replied. "That's what Bessie thinks, anyway. She thinks they're trying to hide from—"

The switchboard buzzed and Verna turned around to connect Mr. Dickens at the *Dispatch* to Mr. Whitman at the Darling Academy, and disconnect Mrs. Sedalius from the Beauty Bower.

"Anyway," Myra May said to Verna's back, "what I was saying is that your man is getting Euphoria's fried chicken and mashed potatoes with gravy, which might slow him down a little. He may not get out to the phone booth right at noon to make that call. Don't worry if he's a little late." There was the clatter of a plate being dropped and she rolled her eyes. "That'll teach me," she muttered. "Step away from the counter for a second and everything goes to hell." She slipped out the door.

Liz leaned forward, frowning. "What do I know?" she challenged. "You told Myra May that I know something, but I don't know *anything*, Verna. I'm completely and totally in the dark."

"You know who he is," Verna replied, and plugged in another cord. "Number, please." She connected Mildred Kilgore, who had a private line, to her husband at Kilgore Motors, and unplugged Mr. Dickens, who had finished talking to Mr. Whitman. While she was doing this, she made a mental note to call Mildred back and ask her to give Myra May a hand behind the counter.

"No, I don't know who he is," Liz said crossly, when Verna turned back to her. "Bessie says that Mrs. Adcock says that he's a government agent."

"What would Leona Ruth Adcock know about government agents?" Verna scoffed. "Quite the contrary. He's a member of the Capone gang."

Liz's eyes got round. "You're sure? How do you know?"

"I'm sure. His name is Diamond, Frankie Diamond. Mrs. O'Malley says that he's a friend of the man who slashed Miss Lake's face."

"Slashed——!" Liz's hand went to her mouth.

"What's more," Verna went on, "Miss LaMotte shot the slasher—some gangster named Sal Raggio."

Liz's eyes were like saucers. "Shot him!" she whispered.

"With her Remington pistol. He died on the street in front of the Western Hotel. The hotel where Al Capone conducts his business. Where Miss LaMotte was standing in that photo the baldheaded man showed me yesterday. Mrs. O'Malley says that Frankie Diamond wants to kill Miss LaMotte, to pay her back for killing his friend."

"I just can't believe this is happening in Darling," Liz muttered, biting her lip. "It sounds like one of those awful gangster movies!"

"I know, Liz. But it's true, at least according to Mrs. O'Malley, and I don't think she'd lie about something like this. She said they called a doctor, who came and stitched up the cuts on Miss Lake's face. Miss LaMotte and Miss Lake caught a train the next morning—just before the Cicero police, under the direction of Al Capone, showed up to arrest Miss LaMotte for shooting the slasher."

"So that's why that business with the disguises that Bessie told me about," Liz said thoughtfully. "The wig and the hair dye. The women thought they'd be safe with Miss Hamer, but something must've happened to make them afraid. Maybe they were somehow tipped off that this man—this Frankie Diamond—might show up here in Darling, looking for them."

"They might even have looked out the window and seen him walking past," Verna said. "My house isn't that far from Miss Hamer's."

"Or maybe he even knocked at Miss Hamer's door, and DessaRae sent him away." Liz rolled her eyes. "And to think that I wanted to write a charming story about Miss Jamison—a hometown girl who made good in the big city. Some story! It belongs in a true-crime magazine, not in a family newspaper."

"I'm afraid you're right." Verna sighed. "I'm also afraid I've outfoxed myself, Liz. And I'm not happy about it." She told Liz about the telegram she had faked, with its instruction to call "Mr. C" at noon from the phone booth.

"I was thinking of it as a kind of test," she added. "I thought if that fellow made the call, it would prove definitively that he was connected to the Capone gang. But Mrs. O'Malley has already given us all the evidence we need. And now Diamond is going to call that number and find out that it wasn't his pals up there in Cicero who sent him that telegram. He'll know that somebody here in Darling has figured out who he is. I wish I hadn't done it."

"Well, for pity's sake, Verna," Liz said, with a wave of her hand. "That's an easy problem to solve. Just don't connect him."

Verna frowned. "Excuse me?"

"Think about it, Verna," Liz replied patiently. "You're the telephone operator. You can pretend to be putting him through all the long-distance offices, but you really won't. You can make him wait for fifteen or twenty minutes and then tell him that all the circuits are busy and he needs to try again later." She grinned crookedly. "Happens to me about half the time when I want to make a long-distance call. Doesn't it happen to you?"

Verna rolled her eyes, wondering why she hadn't thought of this splendid subterfuge. "Oh, you bet. What a grand idea, Liz. That's exactly what I'll do."

"Swell," Liz said. She hesitated, frowning. "You know, Verna, if this guy really is dangerous, somebody ought to keep an eye on him."

"Shadow him, you mean?" Verna suggested helpfully. "Maybe that's something you could do, Liz. If you don't have to get back to the office right away." Liz was right that somebody ought to watch the fellow.

"I'm available," Liz said. "Mr. Moseley left for Montgomery and gave me the afternoon off. I was planning to go over to the Savings and Trust and talk to Mr. Johnson about Mama's situation, but that can wait. How about you? Can you help to . . ." She frowned. "To *shadow* him?"

"I promised Myra May I'd work on the switchboard until one or one thirty," Verna replied. "But if you and Bessie could keep an eye on him for an hour, I could relieve you after that."

"How will you know where to find us?" Liz asked.

Verna frowned. "He's not likely to go very far, I wouldn't think. He might just walk around the square, stopping in businesses, flashing that photograph, and asking for information. All you have to do is hang around behind him. Don't let him see you, of course. And in an hour, grab the nearest phone and call me here at the board and let me know where you are."

"We'll try," Liz said. She turned to go. "Say, Euphoria's fried chicken looks really good. Want me to have her make up a plate for you?"

"Sure thing," Verna said. The light blinked over Doc Roberts' socket. She turned back to the switchboard, plugged in a jack, and chirped, "Number, please." When she noticed that Mildred Kilgore was finished talking to Kilgore Motors, she rang up Mildred and asked her if she wouldn't mind volunteering to help Myra May out behind the counter on Tuesday. And when Mildred said yes, she asked if Mildred would be willing to round up three or four other Dahlias to help on Wednesday and Thursday and Friday and Saturday—just until Violet got back from Memphis. Mildred said she would do her best, and they hung up.

Fifteen minutes later, as Verna dawdled over a plateful of Euphoria's delicious fried chicken, mashed potatoes and gravy, and green beans, she was doing exactly what Liz had suggested. On the other side of the diner wall, in the phone booth, Mr. Frankie Diamond (aka Mr. Gold) was waiting—and waiting, and waiting, and waiting—to be connected to the number he had given her, which should be taking the usual long-distance route from Darling through Montgomery, Nashville, Memphis, and Chicago to its final destination, but was of course going nowhere at all.

Finally, Verna finished eating a leisurely meal, wiped her fingers and her mouth, and set her plate aside. Then she opened the line to the telephone booth and said, in a pleasantly lilting voice, "I'm sorry, sir. All the circuits are busy now. Please try your call again later."

She pulled the plug before she could hear her victim's sputtered curse. She waited five minutes, then put through the call to the number Frankie Diamond had given her. It zipped right through, smooth as silk and without a single delay, to Montgomery, Nashville, Memphis, Chicago, and Cicero.

"Western Hotel," said a brusque male voice on the other end of the line. "Who're you callin'?"

"Is Mr. Capone available?" Verna asked.

"Who is it wants to talk to him?" the man demanded roughly.

Quietly, Verna broke the connection.

FOURTEEN

Buddy Norris Collars a Crook

Outside on Franklin Street, Bessie and Liz stood in the shade of the faded green canvas awning of Musgrove's Hardware, next door to the diner on the east. They were looking in the hardware store window, engrossed in a discussion of the merits of the new ten-gallon cast-aluminum National pressure canner that Mr. Musgrove had put on display.

The canner was a hefty contraption with a lid that strapped down and gauges and valves and various other doohickeys, made of heavy-duty aluminum to contain the steam pressure. In the window with the pressure canner were several of the more usual blue enamel canning kettles with wire racks, a pyramid of glass Mason and Kerr canning jars, a basket of lids and rubber rings for older jars fitted with wire bales and the newer screw-on metal rings and flat self-sealing disks, a jar lifter, canning tongs, and a large metal canning funnel— every up-to-the-minute device that a modern housewife would need to outfit her canning kitchen.

Bessie tilted her head to one side, thinking that she and Roseanne could certainly put that pressure canner to use in the kitchen at Magnolia Manor. "You know, Liz," she said, "if everybody had one of those things, nobody would ever go hungry. They could can all the garden vegetables they could grow—beans, corn, okra, tomatoes, lots of things." Her own mother and grandmother had always canned most of the family's food, and she herself put up peaches and tomatoes and green beans and the like, using her mother's canning kettle. But Mrs. Hancock stocked a variety of canned goods on her grocery shelves, and most women had decided that it was silly to put a lot of time and work into home canning. Using a can opener was very convenient, and if you put plenty of seasoning on the vegetables, most husbands couldn't tell the difference.

"I'm sure people could can their own food," Liz said thoughtfully. "But I wonder—" She craned her neck to peer at the price tag. "Why, it costs fourteen dollars and ninety-nine cents, Bessie!" she exclaimed. "Around here, who can afford that? And it looks a little daunting, don't you think? You'd have to learn how to use all those dials and valves and things."

Bessie shrugged. "Well, at that price, it's out of the question. I guess we'll just have to keep on using the old canning kettle—although it isn't always safe for things like beans and corn. And it takes hours and hours in the hot kitchen." But she couldn't resist a last longing look at the canner. "If we had that at the Magnolia Manor, I'll bet we wouldn't have to throw out so many jars of spoiled food."

"That's one of the problems with the canning kettle," Liz agreed. "Tomatoes are okay, but if the food isn't acid enough, it doesn't always keep. And no matter how long you boil the jars, they don't always seal just right. When you bring a quart of green beans from the fruit cellar, it might be moldy, or worse." She made a face.

Bessie cast a quick look over her shoulder. She and Liz were not standing in front of Mr. Musgrove's hardware store window for the purpose of discussing what could be done with that pressure canner, interesting as it was. They were waiting for Mr. Frankie Diamond to emerge from the telephone booth on the other side of the diner.

When Liz had come back to the table from her visit to the Exchange, she had told Bessie that Verna was back there, working the switchboard. And that earlier that morning, Verna had had a long telephone conversation with Miss LaMotte's housekeeper in Cicero. She had learned—among other things—that an attacker had slashed Miss Lake's face and that Miss LaMotte had shot him.

Bessie stared at Liz across the table. "Shot the slasher?" she gasped incredulously. "Mercy me! Did she . . . Did she kill him?"

"Dead as a doornail," Liz replied, picking up her glass of iced tea. "And if you ask me, he deserved it."

Myra May had come up with their dinner plates and was standing behind them, listening. "Who shot a slasher?" she asked anxiously. "When? Where?"

"Shhh," Liz hissed, shooting a meaningful glance at the baldheaded man at the counter. "Don't talk so loud. We'll tell you all about it later."

But Bessie was sure the man hadn't heard a word of what they'd said. The volume was turned up on the noon agricultural price reports on the radio, and the man was bent over his plate, shoveling in his mashed potatoes and gravy as fast as he could. He was obviously in a hurry to finish his dinner so that he could get back to the booth and make that telephone call.

Over their meal, Liz related to Bessie the rest of the details Verna had gotten from Mrs. O'Malley, including the fact that the man sitting over there at the counter, enjoying Euphoria's fried chicken, was a member of the Capone gang named

Diamond. Frankie Diamond. Verna had set it up so he was supposed to use the phone in the phone booth to make a call to Mr. Capone, but she wasn't going to put the call through. When he came out of the booth, she wanted them to shadow him.

Bessie listened to all of this with increasing astonishment. A member of the Capone gang, here in Darling? Miss Jamison's friend, her face slashed? Miss Hamer's niece, a killer? And she and Liz were supposed to do *what*?

"Shadow him?" She sneaked a look at the man out of the corner of her eye. There was a bulge in the back of his coat. Was it a gun?

"Follow him," Liz explained. "Keep an eye on him. Find out where he goes. It's something Verna got from reading those true-crime magazines of hers. But we have to keep out of sight. He's not supposed to see us."

"Oh," Bessie said, understanding. She picked up her biscuit and slathered it with butter. "Well, as for keeping out of sight, you know as well as I do that we're just a pair of small-town women. You're too pretty and wholesome-looking to be any kind of a threat to him, and I'm almost old enough to be his mother. We might as well be invisible. He will never in this natural world suspect that we're 'shadowing' him."

And this seemed to be the case. As Bessie and Liz watched from their vantage point in front of the hardware store window, Mr. Diamond came out of the phone booth. His thick-featured face was a mottled red, his eyes were narrowed to slits, and his expression was surly. Bessie suppressed a giggle. He looked exactly like a man who had been cooped up for twenty minutes in a hot, stuffy telephone booth, only to learn that his critically important long-distance call could not be connected because all the circuits were busy.

Mr. Diamond jammed his snap-brim hat down on his bald head and strode angrily past Lizzy and Bessie. Without wasting so much as a look in their direction, he stalked across Robert E. Lee, dodging a pair of mangy dogs and a cart pulled by a mule. He was heading in the direction of Mann's Mercantile. Taking their time, the two women strolled casually behind him, chatting as they went.

In front of Mann's, Diamond paused, took out a cigarette, and lit it with a match. He was about to go into the store when a woman, coming out, bumped him. It was Leona Ruth Adcock, carrying a shopping bag full of purchases. She stopped, looked at Mr. Diamond in some surprise, smiled, and opened her mouth.

"Uh-oh," Liz said, under her breath. "Didn't you tell me that Leona Ruth has got it into her head that this man is a government agent?"

"I sure did," Bessie said grimly. "She might be going to tell him how to find Miss Jamison. We ought to try to stop her." She stepped forward. But she was too late.

"Oh, Mr. Gold!" Leona Ruth exclaimed in a tittery voice. "How nice to see you again." Her black hat was tipped forward over her freshly done curls, a red rose bobbing in a nest of red ribbons over one ear. "It's such a coincidence, runnin' into one another like this."

"You got me mixed up with somebody else," Mr. Diamond growled impatiently, clearly in no mood to chat with a woman wearing a red rose over her ear. He made as if to dodge around Leona Ruth and into the mercantile, but she sidestepped adroitly, planting herself right in front of him.

"Why, don't you recall?" She pouted, as if she were put out at him for not remembering. "You stopped at my house just yesterday afternoon, askin' about a platinum blonde. I was just on my way over to the hotel to leave you a message."

Mr. Diamond pulled his eyebrows together in a dark scowl, not even attempting to be polite. "I been stoppin' at a lot of houses in this stinkin' little burg, sister," he snarled around his cigarette. "You got something juicy for me, spill it fast, before I lose what's left of my temper. I been hangin' out in a phone booth for twenty minutes and I ain't in no mood to stand here and listen to some dumb dame bash her gums."

Bessie saw that Leona Ruth was clearly taken aback by this out-and-out rudeness, but she pulled herself together and persevered.

"The lady you were inquirin' about yesterday. I just might be able to tell you something about her." She leaned forward and lowered her voice, darting a coy look at him. "That is, if you'll tell me why you're lookin' for her. It's a trade, y'see. You give me something, I give you something back." She smiled, pleased with herself. "Tit for tat."

"Tit for—" Mr. Diamond laughed harshly. He pulled on his cigarette, frowning, and began processing what Leona Ruth had said. "That blonde—you're tellin' me that you know where she is?"

"I'm tellin' you that I *might* know," Leona Ruth said demurely. "And I *might* be willin' to tell you what I know. But you have to tell me something first." She paused for emphasis. "What's she wanted for?"

"Wanted for?" Mr. Diamond repeated. If he understood, Bessie thought, he was pretending not to. Or maybe he wasn't quite as smart as he wanted people to think. Maybe he was the kind of man who relied on brawn instead of brains. She looked again, and saw the bulge under the back of his coat. She shivered. It had to be a gun.

Leona Ruth, however, couldn't see the bulge. She wasn't fazed by the man's response, either. She arched her eyebrows, tilted her chin, and giggled like a gaga schoolgirl with a crush.

"Well, o' course, Mr. Gold, I understand that you cain't tell me everything, since you're carryin' out this investigation incognito and undercover, which is just naturally right. But I ain't askin' for much, really." She held up her gloved thumb and forefinger, measuring a small amount. "Just one teensy-weensy little hint about—"

"Undercover?" Mr. Diamond's eyes narrowed. He threw his cigarette on the dirt and ground it out with the toe of his shoe. "Lady, are you tryin' to pull a fast one? You tryin' to muscle in on—"

"Perfect!" Leona Ruth trilled happily and clapped her hands. "Why, you sound exactly like one of those Chicago gangsters—Bugs Moran and Al Capone and all those other thugs! Y'see, Mr. Gold, we're not as *rural* down here in South Alabama as you might think. There has been a radio in my house since right after the Great War, when the late Mr. Adcock insisted on buyin' one so we could be informed about what was goin' on. 'Miz Adcock,' he said, 'we need to know what's happenin' out there in the world, so we are buyin' a radio,' which was exactly what he did, an RCA batt'ry-powered receiver in a mahogany case, and it has worked perfectly ever since." She pulled herself up importantly, looking down her nose. "And in addition to the radio, we have a first-class weekly newspaper—it comes out on Fridays—and Mr. Greer at the Palace Theater shows a newsreel before every movie feature. We may live in a small town, but we keep up with the times."

Mr. Diamond was staring at her, shaking his head as if he did not quite believe what he was hearing. Bessie understood his confusion. Leona Ruth often had that effect on people.

"Lady," he growled, now almost plaintively, "will you *pu-leez* just get to the point? Where is that blonde?"

"Not so fast, Mr. Gold." Leona Ruth became brisk. "The point is that I know who you are, and I am eager to do my patriotic duty as a citizen to help you capture the criminal you are lookin' for. All I ask in return is a tidbit of inside information. I am sure that Mr. Hoover wouldn't mind in the slightest if one of his government agents gave just a teeny tiny hint to a valuable informant." She smiled meaningfully and repeated the phrase, with emphasis. "A *valuable* informant."

"Mr. . . . Hoover?"

"Mr. J. Edgar Hoover, of course." Leona Ruth tittered. "You didn't think I was talkin' about the *president* of the United States, did you? Just a tidbit of information," she cajoled. "What's she done? What's she wanted for?"

There was a moment's silence while Mr. Diamond, knitting his brows, worked through all of this. Bessie had just come to the conclusion that the man really was a thickheaded dimwit when he smiled, snatched off his hat, and took Leona Ruth's gloved hand in one pudgy paw.

"Okay. Okay. Now I gotcha. Yes, ma'am. Sure thing. Now I unnerstand." He dropped Leona Ruth's hand. "You wanna deal. Well, I don't think Mr. J. Edgar Hoover back in Washington, D.C., would be too mad at me if I told you that the broad in question—the blonde—is wanted by the police in Cicero, Illinois. She shot Salvatorio Raggio."

"Shot!" Leona Ruth's eyes widened and she fell back a step, her nostrils quivering. "You mean, she's a . . . a *murderess*? I was at the Beauty Bower, gettin' shampooed and set in the comp'ny of a *murderess?*"

Mr. Diamond said through his teeth, "You got it, ma'am. What's more, she shot Sal Raggio with a Remington 51 that was give to her by one of Al Capone's gang members."

Leona Ruth's hand went to her mouth. "Al Capone!" she squeaked. "Did you say Al . . . Capone, Mr. Gold?"

"Yes, ma'am, that's who I said. The gentleman who give her the gun—Diamond, his name is, Frankie Diamond—was convicted twice, once for runnin' numbers and once for sellin' illegal booze, for which he was sent up two years. It was an unfair trial and a rotten conviction, but that's the kinda criminal associates this broad has got. I hafta tell you, lady, she ain't got no decency. She don't play fair with nobody, neither her friends or the local flat-feet."

Liz elbowed Bessie in the ribs. "*He* gave Miss LaMotte the gun himself!" she whispered excitedly, and Bessie nodded. "They must have been involved," she whispered back. "Romantically, I mean."

Leona Ruth put her tongue between her teeth, shaking her head, big-eyed.

"You don't believe me on this," Mr. Diamond went on, "you just go to the phone and call up Captain Ricardo at the Cicero police department and ask him who he's lookin' for in the murder of Mr. Salvatorio Raggio. He'll put you wise—if you can get through to him, that is. I didn't have no luck callin' Cicero just now myself." His voice hardened. "Okay, lady? Now it's your turn. Cough it up. Where is this broad? Where can I find her?"

"W-where?" Leona Ruth stuttered. Her face was white, and Bessie could see that she was genuinely frightened. Whatever she may have imagined Miss Jamison's offense to be—tax evasion? petty theft? littering?—murder obviously wasn't on the list.

"All right, sister, let's cut the comedy." Diamond leaned forward so that his face was only inches from Leona Ruth's. In a threatening voice, he growled, "I ain't got time to fool around. This here is a dangerous woman we're talkin' about. She carries that gun of hers around in her pocketbook, ready to shoot anybody who looks at her crosswise. You said you know where to find her. So tell me, or so help me I'll—" He lifted his hand.

Leona Ruth looked cornered. "She's stayin' with her aunt," she began in a halting voice. "The old lady lives on Camellia Street, right across from the—"

Bessie couldn't let Leona Ruth spill the beans on Miss Jamison. Knowing it was now or never, she abruptly charged forward, brushed past Mr. Diamond, and seized Leona Ruth by the arm, knocking her hat askew.

"Why, Leona Ruth Adcock!" she cried. "I have been looking all over this town for you, and here you are, standing on Robert E. Lee, right here in front of Mann's! Your sister sent me to tell you that you're wanted at home, this very minute! It's an emergency."

"My . . . my sister?" Leona Ruth faltered. "But I don't have a—"

"Oh, swell, Miss Bloodworth! You've found her!" Liz rushed around Diamond and took Leona Ruth's other arm. "Your sister says it's a case of life and death, Mrs. Adcock. We hate to interrupt your conversation with this gentleman, but you've got to come with us. Right now! There's not a second to lose." And both Bessie and Liz began to pull Mrs. Adcock away.

Diamond was suddenly jarred into action. "Hey!" he exclaimed indignantly. He reached out and grabbed Bessie's arm. "What's with yous dames? I'm talkin' to this lady. She's about to give me some very valuable information." To Leona Ruth, he said, "Across Camellia Street from what?"

Leona Ruth replied, "Across from the Magnolia—"

"Help!" Bessie cried, trying to wrench her arm free from Diamond's grip. She let go of Leona Ruth and whapped the man with her handbag. "Get your hands off me!" she screeched. "Help, police!"

Hanging on to Leona Ruth, Liz stepped forward. "Let her go!" she yelled at Mr. Diamond. "You let Miss Bloodworth go, you big thug!" She turned back to Leona Ruth and began to pull. "Hurry, Mrs. Adcock! It's an emergency. There's not a minute to lose!"

"Wait! You can't go!" Diamond protested loudly. Still holding Bessie's arm, he grabbed for Leona Ruth's sleeve, pulling her jacket half off and tilting her hat across one eye. Leona Ruth screamed and dropped her shopping bag, and an assortment of nuts, candies, and raisins spilled out and rolled across the ground. "Across Camellia from the Magnolia what?" he demanded.

"Help!" Bessie shrieked frantically, and hit the man with her handbag again. "Get your hands off me! Help!"

Leona Ruth was staring at Diamond as if she were mesmerized. She began, "Across from the Magnolia Man—" But she didn't get to finish. Liz clapped her hand over her mouth.

At that moment, the glass door to the store slammed wide open and Mr. Mann, the proprietor, strode out, wearing a white shirt with red sleeve garters, a black bow tie, his usual red suspenders, and a white apron. He was a burly man with powerful shoulders, at least two heads taller than Diamond.

"What's goin' on out here?" he demanded. "Ladies, is this fella botherin' you?" He peered through his gold-rimmed bifocals at Bessie. "Why, Miz Bloodworth, for heaven's sake! And Miz Adcock!" He turned to Diamond. "Get your big fat hands off these ladies," he barked, pushing him backward, forcing him to release his hold on both Bessie and Mrs. Adcock. "You oughtta be ashamed of yourself!"

"Oh, Mr. Mann, I am so glad to see you!" Bessie cried, straightening the sleeve of her dress and righting her hat. "Mrs. Adcock has an emergency and has to go home, right this minute, but this gentleman is attempting to detain her. Could you talk some sense into him for us?"

"Oh, you bet, Miz Bloodworth," Mr. Mann replied. He was scowling furiously, his face as red as a turkey's wattle. "I don't know who the Sam Hill you are or what you think you're doin', stranger," he bellowed, "but I'll thank you to keep your hands to yourself. It ain't polite to molest a Southern lady."

"Keep yer shirt on," Mr. Diamond said, taking a step backward and raising his hands as if to defend himself. "I ain't molestin' nobody. I am only tryin' to get the information I was promised by this lady right here."

"Well, I advise you to give up tryin'," Mr. Mann snapped. He thrust a thick forefinger into Diamond's nose. "Whoever the hell you are, I want you off my proppity, right now. You hear?"

"But it ain't what you think, Mr. Mann!" Leona Ruth was struggling to free herself from Bessie and Liz. "His name is Mr. Gold. He's a gov'ment agent! He's here in Darling to arrest—"

"A gov'ment agent?" Mr. Mann shouted, and his face got so red that it looked as if he were about to explode. "A gov'ment agent, huh? Well, I don't give a good gol-durn who he's here to arrest, Miz Adcock. And I don't know why in tarnation you're actin' like it's your duty to defend him."

"Of course I'm defendin' him," Leona Ruth shrilled. "He's doin' important business for Mr. Hoover. He—"

"And I am tellin' you for your very own personal good that he's got no bidness layin' his dirty hands on Miz Bloodworth, or on Miz Lacy, or on you. And I am surprised right down to my toe bones that you are tryin' to make excuses for him. Gov'ment agent—ptui!" And he spit contemptuously on one of Diamond's shiny shoes.

Bessie knew exactly why Mr. Mann was so furious. Deep in the wooded hills to the west of Darling, between the town and the Alabama River, Mr. Mann's second cousin, Mickey LeDoux, ran the biggest moonshine operation in all of South Alabama. Mickey supplied an excellent corn liquor not only to the residents of Darling, but to Monroeville, Frisco, and all the little villages roundabout. What's more, everybody in town—including Sheriff Roy Burns—knew for a certain fact that Mr. Mann had a secret shelf behind the horse harness and saddles in the back room at the Mercantile, where he would be glad to sell you a bottle or two of Mickey's best. Hearing the words *government agent*, Mr. Mann had quite naturally assumed that Mr. Diamond was a revenue agent—a revenooer, as the locals called them—and that he was planning to arrest Mickey Mann and anybody who was associated with him.

Afterward, Bessie wondered what might have happened next, but as things turned out, whatever it was didn't get a chance to happen. Whether it was blind luck or Divine Providence or maybe even the work of the devil, at that very moment, Deputy Buddy Norris came roaring up Robert E. Lee on his red Indian Ace motorcycle, a cloud of dust spinning along behind him like a miniature tornado. He was wearing his khaki deputy's uniform and jacket, his leather motorcycle helmet and goggles, and his gun. Bessie didn't know whether he was on duty or not, because Buddy loved his work so much and was so diligent about it that he wore his uniform constantly. Some folks guessed that he even slept in it, with his gun under his pillow.

Seeing Buddy coming, Mr. Mann stepped into the dusty street, windmilling both arms. "Hey, Buddy, stop!" he yelled. "We got us a problem here."

Buddy Norris skidded to a stop, kicked down his motorcycle stand, and lifted his leg gracefully over the machine. He was a tall, lean, well-built young man with a shock of brown hair across his forehead and a straggly growth of beard on his chin. He was known to be somewhat reckless and accident prone, but he was a good deputy and a better law enforcement officer, in most people's estimations, than Sheriff Roy Burns. Bessie agreed, for she knew Buddy Norris well. He had mowed her grass twice a month every summer from the time he was ten until the sheriff had picked him to take Deputy Duane Hadley's place. A decent young man, willing to help, if sometimes a rapscallion.

"A problem, you say, Mr. Mann?" Buddy asked pleasantly, hooking his thumbs into his belt and pushing his jacket aside so that his holstered weapon was clearly visible. His deputy's badge, polished to a fare-thee-well, was prominently displayed on the lapel of his brown jacket. He smiled his Lucky Lindy smile at Bessie and gave her a little salute.

"Afternoon, Miz Bloodworth." His glance went to Liz, approving her yellow hat. "Miz Lacy. That's a right purty hat."

He didn't look at Mrs. Adcock. Bessie knew that he had once hit a baseball through Leona Ruth's front window and she had made him pay for the broken glass by spading up her spring garden, which at the time was about the size of the baseball field out behind the Academy.

"A real serious problem," Mr. Mann said sternly. "This fella here has been annoyin' these ladies. He—"

"He's not annoyin', he's a gov'ment agent!" Leona Ruth cried. "He's here to—"

"I'm afraid that Mrs. Adcock is very high-strung," Bessie said sweetly. "If you want to know the truth, Buddy, you go right on over to the Exchange and have a little talk with Verna Tidwell. She's on the switchboard this afternoon. She'll tell you who this man really is. He is from—"

"I don't give a good goose turd who he is or where he's from," Mr. Mann said heatedly, "although it is purty obvious from the way he talks that he's a damn Yankee from up north."

"He's also armed," Bessie said.

"Armed?" Liz repeated in surprise.

"Under his jacket, left side," Bessie explained. "My father had one of those shoulder holsters. He was attacked by a crazy man at his funeral parlor once when he was laying out the man's wife, and after that, he wore it every time he worked on a corpse or did a funeral. I could always tell when he had it on by the bulge in his coat."

"Armed, is he?" Buddy drawled. His glance sharpened and he took a step closer.

"Armed? Well, o' *course* he's armed," Leona Ruth protested. "I tell you, he's a gov'ment agent, sent here by Mr. J. Edgar Hoover to—"

"Lemme see your badge, Mr. Gov'ment Agent, *sir*," Buddy said. Like Mr. Mann, he was taller than Diamond, and younger and fitter. And unlike Mr. Mann, Buddy had a gun.

Diamond cleared his throat and looked nervously away. "I ain't carrying no badge right now."

"Because he's incognito," shrilled Leona Ruth. "He's undercover! He is on the trail of a—"

"Miz Adcock," Mr. Mann said with exaggerated politeness, "I reckon you don't know what you're talkin' about, so I'll ask you to jes' keep still and let us menfolks get this sorted out."

"No badge." Buddy made a tsk-tsk noise. His voice hardened. "Then lemme see your gun. Slowly, now, Mr. Gov'ment Agent. No fast moves."

Diamond looked from Buddy to Mr. Mann, assessing the possibilities of escape. Seeing none, he opened his jacket and withdrew a wicked-looking snub-nose revolver. Sullenly, he handed it to Buddy.

"Well, sir." Buddy stuck the gun in his jacket pocket. "An armed undercover gov'ment agent with no badge who is botherin' our womenfolks is something we just cain't tolerate here in Darling." His eyes narrowed. "Ain't it about time for your train, do you reckon?"

Diamond shook his head quickly. "Not until tomorrow morning."

"No, sir," Buddy said. He cocked his head. "I can hear that train whistlin' now, on its way in from over at Monroeville. Which means it'll be goin' out again in just about twenty minutes. You got a suitcase?"

"At the hotel," Diamond said sullenly. "But I'm not—"

"Well, good," Buddy said, and clamped a hand on Diamond's collar. "Let's go and get that ol' suitcase, Mr. Gov'ment

Agent, and I'll make sure you get to the depot in time to catch your train."

"You ain't gettin' rid of me so easy!" Diamond shouted, dancing on his toes, trying to wrestle free of Buddy's grip. "I'll be back! You can't keep me away."

"Better not try," Mr. Mann muttered darkly. "We'll be waitin' for you." He raised his voice. "In Darlin', we tar and feather revenooers."

"But he's an undercover agent!" Leona Ruth cried, as Buddy marched Mr. Diamond across the street to the Old Alabama Hotel. She was weeping now, big tears running down her face. "And that woman is a murderess! She is right here in our little town, walkin' to and fro amongst us Christians like the devil in the Book of Job, figurin' on who she's goin' to kill next. We're none of us safe! Nobody!"

"Hysterical," Bessie said in a pitying tone, shaking her head sadly. "This whole affair has been too much for the dear old thing. Come on, Miss Lacy. Let's take Mrs. Adcock home, where she can go to bed with a wet washrag on her forehead."

She took one arm and Liz took the other and they led Leona Ruth, weeping and sniffling, down Robert E. Lee Street.

FIFTEEN

Lizzy Faces the Lion
in His Den

Lizzy and Bessie got Mrs. Adcock—who had worked herself into a satisfying case of hysterics—back to her house and put her to bed. Leaving Bessie to cope, Lizzy used the crank telephone on the kitchen wall to call Verna at the Exchange.

"Do you think the man has really left town?" Verna asked worriedly. Lizzy had told the story in very general terms, leaving out all of the exciting details. She had counted the clicks and knew that there were at least three people listening on Mrs. Adcock's line. One of them had a cuckoo clock.

"Buddy Norris said he was going to put him on the train," Lizzy replied guardedly. "I have to stop at the Savings and Trust for a few minutes, Verna. How much longer are you going to be on the switchboard?"

"Olive just phoned and says she's stopped coughing but she'll be late," Verna replied. "I'll be here another hour, anyway. Come over to the diner when you're finished at the bank and we can talk about what we're going to do next."

"I will," Lizzy said, and went back to the bedroom to tell Bessie good-bye.

"You're coming to the Dahlias' card party tonight, I hope," Bessie said. "Ophelia said she'd be there, and Verna, too. You?"

"Wouldn't miss it," Lizzy said. "See you at seven thirty."

She walked back up Rosemont in the direction of the Darling Savings and Trust, on the west side of the courthouse square. She was still mulling over the many misunderstandings and the surprising twists and turns that the encounter with Frankie Diamond had taken. She was glad that Buddy Norris had appeared and was willing to escort the fellow off to the train depot. But she had ridden that spur line between Darling and Monroeville herself, when she went to Monroeville to go shopping. The train moved so slowly that it was easy for people to jump off and on—and plenty did, to avoid paying the twenty-cent fare that the station masters collected at either end. Frankie Diamond was no patsy, like several of the revenue agents that Mr. Mann had mistaken him for, easily bribed or intimidated and all too eager to leave town before somebody built a fire under a tar barrel and the chicken feathers started flying. Diamond had most likely been in tougher spots than this, Lizzy thought nervously. He had a job to do and he was here to do it. He wouldn't be easily deterred.

But there was nothing she could do about Diamond at the moment, so there was no point in worrying about him. She squared her shoulders, straightened her yellow straw hat, and looked straight ahead. She had a task ahead of her, an altogether unpleasant one, and she wasn't sure exactly what she was going to say or do. All she knew was that she was about to face a lion in his den. A formidable lion. And she was going to do it before the afternoon got a single hour older.

*　*　*

The Darling Savings and Trust was an imposing red brick building. It was fronted with twin white pillars and two marble slabs that stepped up to a pair of polished oak front doors with large panes of sparkling plate glass and big brass handles. Inside, the floor was polished marble tiles; the ceiling was embossed tin, painted ivory; and gilt-framed oil portraits of several generations of Johnsons hung on the walls. In the center of the floor stood a mahogany table that always featured a vase of Mrs. George E. Pickett Johnson's flowers, usually white ones or the palest pink, provided daily from her garden. To the left was a paneled wall behind which the tellers worked, the brass bars of the teller windows gleaming. Alice Ann Walker, a fellow Dahlia, was waiting on a customer at her window. She looked up and caught sight of Liz and waved and smiled, and Lizzy waved back. After a ruckus a few months before, when Alice Ann had been falsely accused of embezzling from customers' accounts, she had been promoted to head cashier, much to the satisfaction of Lizzy and her fellow Dahlias.

Lizzy continued past the teller windows, past the bookkeeping office and the door that led to the stairs down to the big bank vault in the basement. She was heading for an office with curliqued, ornate gold lettering on the glass door: *Mr. George E. Pickett Johnson, President.* Lizzy opened the door and went in. Mr. Johnson's secretary, Martha Tate, a tiny woman with mouse brown hair and a prissy, thin-lipped mouth, looked up from a ledger and recognized Lizzy, who had frequent dealings with the bank on behalf of Mr. Moseley.

"Good afternoon, Miss Lacy," she said, in her precise voice. "How may I be of service to you?"

"I'd like to see Mr. Johnson," Lizzy announced, in a tone that sounded braver than she felt.

Mrs. Tate made a show of looking at the appointment calendar. "I'm so sorry," she said, not sounding sorry at all. "He's extremely busy this afternoon. Would you like to make an appointment for—"

"Tell him I'm here about my mother's house," Lizzy said, trying to keep her voice from quivering.

"Oh." Mrs. Tate got up with alacrity. "I'll see if he's free." A moment later, she was holding open the door to Mr. Johnson's wood-paneled office with its rich Oriental rug and book-lined walls, and Lizzy was ushered in. Mrs. Tate closed the door firmly behind her. If this was the lion's den, Lizzy was trapped in it.

Back in the old days, when the soil was still rich, the plantations still flourished along the river, and cotton was still king, the Johnsons had gloried in their position as one of Darling's premier aristocratic families. The only son of his father, who was the only son of *his* father, young George E. Pickett Johnson—named for a Confederate general who fought under General Lee at Gettysburg—had been expected to do great things. And so he had, or at least he had gotten off to a strong start. He had graduated from Tulane University in New Orleans, returned to take up his father's scepter as the president of the Darling Savings and Trust, and married (as expected) his childhood sweetheart, Miss Voleen Pearl Butler of the aristocratic Butler clan and a graduate of Sophie Newcomb College, the premier Southern college for young ladies, also in New Orleans.

But down the decades, the glory of the old days had been dulled by a series of debilitating disasters: the War Between the States, the Depression of the 1890s, the Panic of 1907, the advent of the boll weevil. If there had been any glory left for the local aristocracy, it was tarnished by the long, bitter drought of the late 1920s and the catastrophic Crash of '29.

While many of the old Darling families had fallen apart

under the weight of these difficulties, the Johnsons, however, had flourished. They and their bank had become the most admired and respected members of the community. Oh, there had been that fracas of a few months before, when it looked as if the bank might be in serious straits and people had waited in line outside the front door to withdraw their money so they could hurry home and hide it under their mattresses. But that little problem had been smoothed over and Darling was assured that the bank and their deposits were safe. In fact, Mr. Johnson had taken out a full-page ad in the Darling *Dispatch* to let everyone know that whatever minor concerns there might have been, all was well. The Darling Savings and Trust was as solid as a rock.

But things had changed. People could look around and see that Mr. Johnson's bank now owned many of the houses and businesses in town and almost all of the plantations that had once belonged to the other aristocrats. The bank was the community's most profitable business, and George E. Pickett Johnson, almost the last aristocrat left standing, was the richest man in Darling. These extraordinary financial successes had had a certain inevitable result, however, for the more properties that were acquired by Mr. Johnson, the less respected and admired he and his bank became. The Darling Savings and Trust was regarded as an adversary, rather than an ally, and Mr. Johnson was even more hated than he was feared—although of course there was quite a bit of envy mixed in, too.

But that was neither here nor there today, for Lizzy was on a mission. She had to save her mother's house—from the lions, as she saw it. From Mr. Johnson and his bank.

"Ah, Miss Lacy," Mr. Johnson said, and looked up from a tidy stack of papers—foreclosure documents, no doubt—on the desk in front of him. "You wanted to speak to me about your mother's house, I believe you said? Please. Sit down."

Lizzy was trying hard not to be afraid, but it was difficult.

Mr. Johnson was a thick-bodied, broad-shouldered man with a jutting jaw and pointed chin; a thin dark mustache over thin, colorless lips; and black, oiled hair that was parted precisely down the middle of his scalp. Behind gold-rimmed glasses, his eyes were hard and glittery, like chunks of black coal, and his black eyebrows rose to a peak. He had a satanic look about him, folks in Darling said. And he had a satanic manner of dealing, too. He was not, people said, a man to be crossed.

"Thank you," Lizzy said, seating herself. She folded her hands in her lap and tried to keep her fingers from trembling. "Mother has told me that you are about to foreclose on her house."

Mr. Johnson scowled, rocked back in his leather-upholstered swivel chair, and twirled his pencil between his fingers like a drum major. "Let us be clear," he said, in a voice that was like a fingernail scraped across a blackboard. It sent shivers up Lizzy's spine. "*I* am not about to foreclose on her house. The bank is. The papers are being prepared as we speak."

Lizzy swallowed. "I've come to ask you for a little more time, Mr. Johnson," she said. "The holidays will soon be here and—"

Mr. Johnson cast his glance heavenward. "Time?" he asked rhetorically. "Your mother has known of her difficulties for almost a full year, Miss Lacy, ever since the Crash. The foreclosure has been pending since April. And since she herself has told me that she is quite willing to turn her house over to the bank—"

"Quite willing?" Lizzy asked blankly.

"Why, yes, of course. She has explained that she plans to live with you until you and Mr. Alexander are married, at which point you will of course go to live in the house he recently purchased." Mr. Johnson's smile did not quite reach his eyes. "Please accept my congratulations, by the way. I am acquainted with Mr. Alexander and find him to be an engaging—"

"But I am *not* being married!" Lizzy exclaimed fiercely. "I am not leaving my house. And I have no intention of allowing my mother to move in with me." This last, she knew, was an awful heresy, for every decent daughter ought to be glad to provide her impoverished mother a home.

Mr. Johnson's black eyebrows went up. "Well, then," he said after a moment. "Mrs. Lacy will have to find another place to live, I suppose. I am sorry." It was not clear whether he meant that he was sorry Lizzy was not going to marry, or sorry that she refused to take in her mother.

Lizzy leaned forward. She had been taught that a lady could always catch more flies with sugar than with vinegar, but at this moment, she was in no mood to be sweet, or to be a lady, either. She was angry. She spoke with as much reasonableness as she could summon.

"Mr. Johnson, my mother did a very foolish thing, and she is paying a high price. I cannot excuse what she has done. But there is nothing to be gained by evicting her from that house. If it is occupied and maintained, the property will someday be of value to the bank. It can be sold when the real estate market turns up again, for a much better price than it could command now. If it's empty, it will be the target of vagrants and vandals. I think you ought to allow my mother to live there and maintain your house—the bank's house—and pay a rent. A modest rent, I'm afraid, because that's all she can afford." Actually, she couldn't afford any rent, but Lizzy hadn't thought quite that far.

Impatiently, Mr. Johnson tapped his pencil on his desk. "And why should I do this?" he asked in an arch tone.

"Because it's the right thing to do!" Lizzy exclaimed heatedly. "And it's the smart thing. You—the bank, that is—

should be doing it with every single house you've foreclosed on. Empty, they are a disgrace. You should let people stay in their houses and take care of them, at least until they can be sold."

"Come, come, Miss Lacy." Mr. Johnson pulled down the corners of his mouth. "That's not the way the system works. People need to learn that credit isn't cheap. They must be obliged to take responsibility for their foolish choices. They must learn that their actions have very real consequences. *That* is how the system works."

"But not everyone who has lost a house was foolish," Lizzy burst out. "Some people have had accidents or gotten sick and some have lost jobs through no fault of their own. Don't you see? That mean, cold-hearted, calculating attitude is exactly what makes people despise the bank and hate—" She stopped. It was true, but she couldn't bring herself to say it.

Mr. Johnson said it for her. "Hate *me?*" He leaned forward on his elbows, his brows pulled together in a deep scowl. Lizzy quailed, thinking that he looked exactly like Satan. "Miss Lacy, I am quite aware of the . . . esteem, shall we say, in which I am held in this town. Given the situation, that is unavoidable. People need a villain. They need someone to blame for their sad plight, and I—and the bank—will do as well as any. Better, in fact, than most. I cannot blame them, either, for they are not privileged to see the many, many instances in which the bank—and I—have given extensions and made accommodations. That is only as it should be, of course, since we must respect our clients' privacy."

Lucy was about to speak when Mr. Johnson held up his hand and continued.

"In your mother's case, she was offered the opportunity to remain in the house and pay a rent—a modest rent. She declined."

Lizzy felt as if she had been punched in the stomach. "She . . . declined?"

"Yes. She said that she preferred to live in a house where she didn't have to pay any rent at all." Mr. Johnson was looking at her with what seemed to be a genuine sympathy. "She also said that your house has recently been modernized and she likes it better." He sighed. "There was something about an electric refrigerator, if I remember correctly. She prefers it to her icebox. Her *musty* icebox."

Lizzy was staring at him, struck speechless. By now, there was no mistaking the compassion in his voice.

"I am deeply sorry to have to tell you this, Miss Lacy. The bank is not in the least anxious to find itself in possession of all these empty houses. We have tried to work out arrangements with the defaulting owners, and in some cases, we've been successful. Not, I'm afraid, in your mother's case. The mortgage payments, principal and interest, were twenty-five dollars and ninety-seven cents a month, on a balance of—" He shuffled through his papers and came up with one. "A balance of nineteen hundred dollars, at four percent interest, on a note to be repaid in seven years. She has been delinquent since the beginning of this year. In January."

Lizzy pressed her lips together. *The bank had tried to make an arrangement? But her mother had said*—She took a deep breath.

"Is . . . Is it too late?"

Mr. Johnson put down the paper, frowning. "If you mean to ask whether the bank is still willing to come to an agreement with your mother, the answer is yes, of course. However, she maintained that she had no source of income and that the payment of any sum at all—not even the fifteen dollars a month I proposed to her—was an impossibility. I pointed out that I was aware that she does indeed have a source of income, an annuity that is deposited every month in her account here at the bank. That, at least, was not compromised by her stock market losses."

The annuity? Her mother had given her the distinct impression that the annuity was gone, and claimed that the bank had refused to negotiate. She had lied on both scores!

Lizzy pulled her attention back to Mr. Johnson. "It is also in my power," he was saying, "to debit your mother's annuity for the amount of her mortgage payments. I have declined to do this, since it appears to be her only source of income." He sighed. "Therefore, since the payments are in serious arrears, foreclosure is the only—"

"Don't foreclose," Lizzy heard herself saying. "Sell the house to me. I'll assume the existing loan."

The words came out of her mouth without her even thinking of them, and she almost bit them back. *Buy her mother's house? Twenty-six dollars a month?* Could she pay that much?

Well, she supposed she could. She earned eighteen dollars a week at Moseley and Moseley and was managing to save five dollars a week for the car she hoped to buy. That was twenty dollars a month, right there. She lived frugally, her own house was paid for, and her mother's house was certainly worth more than the nineteen hundred dollars she had borrowed against it, or would be, when property values picked up again.

Yes, she could manage it. But *should* she? What would her mother say when she found out that Lizzy had bought her house?

"Are you sure you are able to do this?" Mr. Johnson asked gently. "I know that you have had steady employment with Mr. Moseley, but I don't want you to take on a financial burden that you can't manage."

"I'm sure," Lizzy said. She took a deep breath and made herself unclench her fists.

"Very well, then." Mr. Johnson put his pencil down and

spoke with alacrity. "Under the circumstances, I think the bank will be willing to extend the mortgage period to ten years and reduce the payment to—say, twenty dollars a month, principle and interest. We can also waive the delinquent payments and closing costs, as a gesture of goodwill. Will that be satisfactory?"

Twenty dollars. Lizzy let her breath out. "Yes. Very satisfactory. Thank you."

"Excellent. I'll have Mrs. Tate draw up the papers for you. If you would like to have Mr. Moseley look them over before you sign, that would certainly be agreeable." Mr. Johnson paused, regarding her thoughtfully. "I don't mind telling you, Miss Lacy, that in my estimation, this is an elegant solution to your mother's dilemma. She is allowed to remain in her home, while you are making an investment that will appreciate in value."

He didn't add, "And the bank will get at least some money out of this mess," although he might well have. Lizzy had just saved him quite a bit of trouble, not to mention money—and the dead weight of another empty house.

Lizzy nodded numbly. It wasn't elegance she was after. It was her privacy. Her sanity. If she had to live with her mother again— She didn't finish the thought. She couldn't.

Papers in hand, Mr. Johnson stood. "Perhaps it's not my place to say so," he added diffidently. "But I did think that, with a little encouragement, your mother might be able to market her skills and earn enough to help with the monthly payment. I am not making a recommendation, mind you. Just an observation."

Lizzy looked at him, not quite understanding. "Her . . . skills?"

"Why, yes." He smiled. "That is an extremely attractive yellow hat you're wearing. It's one of your mother's creations, isn't it? And I happen to know that Mrs. Johnson—who has an eye for the latest fashions in hats—regularly admires the hats your mother wears to church. She has often said that she wished she could ask Mrs. Lacy to make one for her. I would have mentioned this to your mother, but I was afraid that it would seem—" He cleared his throat gruffly. "A little patronizing. Or worse. She might think I was telling her that she should go out and get a job in order make her mortgage payments."

Lizzy regarded him, thinking how different he was from what she had expected, and from what the townspeople said about him. "Thank you," she said, and meant it. "I'm glad to have the suggestion."

As she left the bank a little later, Lizzy was turning Mr. Johnson's observation around in her mind. She had planned to go straight to the diner to talk with Verna. Instead, she turned right on Rosemont and walked up the steps to the neighboring frame building, which had a decorated sign over the door: CHAMPAIGN'S DARLING CHAPEAUX. Lizzy had two reasons for making this call. One of them was to invite Fannie Champaign to become a member of the Darling Dahlias, something she had promised Verna and Ophelia she would do.

The other had to do with her mother.

Ten minutes later, Lizzy came out again with a new spring in her step and a new hope in her heart. Fannie Champaign, the only milliner in Darling, had taken a careful look—inside and out and from all angles—at the yellow straw hat she was wearing and said that she would be glad to accept Mrs. Lacy's millinery creations on consignment.

"To be frank, Miss Lacy," Miss Champaign said, "I don't sell many hats here in Darling—the ladies don't have much money and several of them enjoy making their own hats. But my sister has a shop in Miami, and my cousin has another in

SIXTEEN

"The Game Is Afoot!"

When Lizzy got to the diner, the noon rush was over, the place was almost empty, and a happy celebration was going on. Al Jolson was singing "Back in Your Own Backyard," Myra May was dancing behind the counter, Verna was looking elated, and Euphoria, brandishing a big spoon, was beaming from ear to ear.

"Violet's coming home on Thursday!" Myra May shrieked when Lizzy walked through the door. "We just got a call from Memphis." She spun around in a circle, hugging herself, nearly sending the coffeepot flying. "'Oh, you can go to the East, Go to the West,'" she sang along with Al Jolson. "'But someday you'll come, weary at heart, back where you started from! Back in your own backyard.'"

"That's grand, Myra May," Lizzy said happily. "What's Violet done about the baby?"

"She didn't say," Myra May replied, and turned down the radio a bit. "You know Violet—she is so soft-hearted, I'm sure she's found a good home for the poor little thing. Maybe the baby's father has some family that's willing to take her in." She picked up a cloth and began to wipe the counter. "I am just so happy that she's coming home!"

"We are, too," Verna said emphatically. "But until she actually gets here, several of the Dahlias are happy to make themselves available to help out behind the counter, so you can be free to manage the switchboard." She pulled a list out of the pocket of her dress and handed it to Myra May. "Mildred Kilgore organized the Dahlias. Here are the names. They said to call them and let them know when you'd like them to come in."

Myra May scanned the list, then looked up, her eyes misting. "Verna, I don't know how to thank you. What swell help!"

Verna shrugged. "Don't thank me. Thank Mildred—and the Dahlias. They're the ones with all the spare time on their hands." She turned to Lizzy. "Say, Liz, how about if we sit down over there in the corner with a cup of coffee. I want to hear everything you couldn't tell me over that party line. And we have to come up with some kind of plan." She glanced at Myra May. "You want to join us? Since a lot of what happened went through your switchboard, seems to me you ought to be in on it."

"I have to work the board," Myra May said. "But there are still a few pieces of sweet potato cake left. Let me treat you-all."

"That'll be wonderful," Lizzy said gratefully, taking off her hat. "I am ready for a break." She ran her hands through her hair. "And to think that Mr. Moseley thought he was giving me the afternoon *off.*"

The switchboard buzzed. "Cut the girls some cake and pour 'em some coffee, Euphoria," Myra May said over her shoulder. "Duty calls."

"Don't forget about the card game tonight, Myra May," Verna said. "At Bessie's. Seven thirty."

"Doesn't look like I'll be able to be there," Myra May said, and sighed. "I'll be on the switchboard."

"Oh, boo," Lizzy said.

"Next week," Myra May promised. "When Violet is back." The switchboard buzzed again and she disappeared.

Lizzy and Verna took their coffee and cake—luscious and crumbly, with nuts and a brown-sugar frosting—to the table in the corner. Behind the counter, the radio was playing Ruth Etting, singing "More Than You Know," and Lizzy hummed along. "Whether you're right, whether you're wrong, man of my heart, I'll string along—"

She stopped. She liked Ruth Etting, but the song was silly. She wouldn't string along with a man when she knew he was wrong, even if he was the man of her heart.

Verna sat down. "I hope your talk with Mr. Johnson went okay," she said sympathetically. "Were you able to come to an understanding?"

"I guess so." Lizzy rolled her eyes. "I've just bought my mother's house."

"Oh, for cryin' out loud!" Verna exclaimed. "You don't mean—"

"Yes, I do mean," Lizzy replied, picking up her fork. "Maybe it's a huge mistake, but maybe not. Maybe it'll be okay. I may even have found a new job for her, making hats for Fannie Champaign's shop." She leaned forward. "But that can wait, Verna. I really need to tell you what happened with Frankie Diamond."

Lizzy had just finished the story when the bell over the front door tinkled and the hero of her story came in, walking with his usual Lindy swagger, pulling off his motorcycle cap and goggles. Without it, Buddy looked as if he were barely out of his teens. He glanced around and spotted Lizzy and Verna.

"Afternoon, Miz Tidwell. Hey, I been lookin' for you, Miz Lacy. Wanted to tell you that your man left town on the train. He wasn't too anxious to go, but I gave 'im the old bum's rush. He's long gone by now, so you can breathe easy." He gave Lizzy a curious look. "Say, I would sure like to get the straight scoop on that fella, if you know it. He didn't look like no rev'nue agent I ever seen. I tried to get 'im to talk but he clammed up on me. Shut up tight as an oyster. Wouldn't say a single word."

Verna leaned over and whispered to Lizzy, "I think it'd be a good idea to let Buddy in on what's been going on, don't you? If Diamond comes back, we might need some firepower. What's more, Buddy is the law—at least, he's wearing a badge. I'd certainly trust him a lot further than Sheriff Burns."

Lizzy, who had been wondering what in the world would happen if Frankie Diamond jumped off that slow-moving train and doubled back to Darling, agreed with Verna. Aloud, she said, "Yes, we've got the straight scoop, Deputy Norris. Sit down and have some sweet potato cake and coffee, and we'll tell you who he is."

"But you're going to be surprised," Verna put in. "It's not what you think."

"Cake sounds swell," Buddy said, pulling out a chair. "But if it's all the same to you, I'll have a bottle of Nehi, instead of coffee."

Verna suppressed a shudder. "Euphoria," she called. "How about a bottle of Nehi for Deputy Norris here? And a piece of that sweet potato cake."

"Sho' thing, Miz Verna," Euphoria returned. "Whut color soda pop he wantin'?"

"Reach me an orange if you got it, Euphoria," Buddy said over his shoulder. "Cherry'll do, if you cain't."

"Orange comin' up," Euphoria replied.

Fifteen minutes later, Lizzy and Verna had told the whole story, beginning with the arrival of Miss Jamison and Miss Lake: "The Naughty and Nice Sisters," Verna said, watching

Buddy's eyebrows go up. She reported what she had learned about the slashing and the shooting in Cicero, from her conversation with Mrs. O'Malley. Lizzy filled in the rest, including a description of the mix-up in front of Mann's, where Leona Ruth Adcock had claimed that Mr. Diamond was one of Mr. Hoover's special agents and Mr. Mann had got the notion that he was a revenue agent.

Buddy pushed his empty plate away. "You-all are sure you ain't just feedin' me a bunch of baloney?" He looked from Verna to Lizzy, his freckled face pale, his Adam's apple jumping. "You-all are tellin' me that there is a dame right here in this town who bumped off a hood who was cuttin' on her friend?" He scowled. "You-all are sayin' that the fella I put on the train is one of Al Capone's goons, and he was here in Darlin' to polish off the bird who rubbed out his buddy?"

Lizzy blinked, but Verna (who understood every word) smiled. "Exactly," she said. "That's it in a nutshell, Deputy Norris."

"Jeepers," Buddy whispered. "And I gave 'im back his gun."

"That is really too bad," Verna said, "because you know as well as we do that there is nothing to keep that goon from hopping off that train and hoofing it back to Darling. He's probably on his way right now."

"What's more," Lizzy put in, "I'm afraid that he knows where Miss Jamison and her friend are staying. Before I could get a hand over Mrs. Adcock's mouth, she managed to tell him that they're on Camellia Street, across from the Magnolia Manor. She didn't get the whole word out but he could probably figure out what she was trying to say. I wouldn't be one bit surprised if he didn't try something." She dropped her voice. "*Tonight*. He's going to do it tonight."

"Uh-oh," Buddy said, very low. "You reckon?"

"Of course," Verna replied grimly. "That man can't afford to hang around this town any longer than it's absolutely necessary—especially after Mr. Mann threatened to tar and feather him." She leaned forward and put her hand on Buddy's arm. "These women are guests in Darling, Deputy Norris, and they are in desperate need of protection. They need the strong arm of the law." She squeezed. "They need *you*."

Buddy tried not to look pleased. "You're sayin' a true thing there." He leaned back in his chair, reached into his shirt pocket, and took out a packet of Camels. "We cain't have no gangsters from Chicago comin' down here and tryin' to kill womenfolk, no matter what they done." He pulled out a cigarette, struck a match on the sole of his boot, and lit it, the way he had seen Hoot Gibson do in one of his silent Westerns.

Verna straightened. "I am so glad you see the situation that way," she said sweetly. "Perhaps you'd even be willing to help us." She hesitated. "Although I'm not sure that Sheriff Burns would approve. You know how he is."

"I sure do. An old stick-in-the-mud is what he is." Buddy pulled on his cigarette and squinted against the smoke, trying to look as if he were ten years older. "So what do you-all have in mind?"

"Here's what we've been thinking," Verna said, and began to outline a strategy. Lizzy contributed a suggestion or two, Buddy added another, and it wasn't long before the details of their plot were mostly worked out. There was a lot they didn't know, so they couldn't be too specific, but at least they had a plan.

Lizzy could tell that the more Buddy heard, the more he liked the idea of being the "strong arm of the law," especially because he was being called upon to protect a pair of damsels who were obviously in distress. He swigged the last of his Nehi and put his motorcycle cap back on. He pushed his goggles to the top of his head and stood, hooking his thumbs in his belt and cocking his head at an angle, like Tom Mix.

"Okey dokey, ladies," he said, drawling it out. "Look for me along about dark. Where'll you be?"

"At the Magnolia Manor, right across the street," Verna told him.

"It's Monday night," Lizzy added, "and the Dahlias always get together on Mondays to play cards. You just rap on the door."

"I'll do it," Buddy said. "Three raps, so's you'll know it's me." He looked down at Lizzy, his eyes light. His voice became shy. "Say, I hope you won't mind if I happen to mention that you look awful purty in that yellow dress, Miz Lacy."

Lizzy could feel herself blushing. When he had gone, Verna chuckled. "Got yourself another admirer, Liz? A mite young for you, maybe."

"Maybe," Lizzy said, and couldn't help a giggle. "But he's cute, don't you think?"

"Not as good-looking as Grady Alexander," Verna said firmly. "And not as mature as Mr. Moseley."

"I wish you'd stop with that Mr. Moseley business," Lizzy said sharply. "I have absolutely no interest in that man."

"Oh, right." Verna gave a skeptical chuckle. She glanced up at the clock over the counter. "I'd better get on back to the probate office and see what kind of a mess Coretta's managed to make of things. Where are you headed?"

"Back to the office. I'm almost finished with the 'Garden Gate' column. I just have to add a couple of items and retype it. Mr. Dickens doesn't need it until late tomorrow, but Mr. Moseley will be back by then and things are likely to be busy. It's nice to have the rest of the afternoon to spend on it."

"Where did Mr. Moseley go today?" Verna asked, as they carried their plates and cups and Buddy's empty Nehi bottle back to the counter.

"Montgomery. He had some sort of hush-hush meeting with the Alabama attorney general. Something about a tax case. He sounded excited about it."

"Taxes." Verna wrinkled her nose. "Lawyers get excited

about the durndest things." She gave Lizzy a conspiratorial grin. "Come, Liz, the game is afoot."

"Afoot?" Lizzy asked, puzzled. She looked down at her shoes. "What game? What are you talking about?"

Verna sighed. "It's just something a detective said once, in a book. Well, I'll see you tonight, at Bessie's. Maybe Buddy will do something brave."

"See you tonight," Lizzy said, and picked up her handbag with a sigh. She would finish her garden column, turn it in, and then go home and tell her mother about the house. She wasn't looking forward to it.

SEVENTEEN

THE GARDEN GATE

By Miss Elizabeth Lacy

❧ On Sunday, the Darling Dahlias held their planning meeting for the annual talent show that's coming up on October 24 in the gymnasium at the Darling Academy. The program, under the direction of Mrs. Roger Kilgore, includes the Carsons' Comedy Caravan, the Tumbling Tambourines, the Akins' Spanish fandango, the Juggling Jinks, and many other unique and exciting acts. We're still looking for another act or two, so if you sing, dance, play the accordion, or recite poetry, please give Mrs. Kilgore a call. Admission to the program is only twenty cents, children a nickel. We hope you will come and bring the whole family. (Mrs. Kilgore says to tell you that there has been a costume modification in the Spanish fandango.)

❧ Miss Bessie Bloodworth's Angel Trumpet (*Brugmansia*) is blooming now. I saw it this weekend, and it's beautiful. It smells heavenly, too, especially when the big peach-colored trumpets open in the evening. Miss Bloodworth says to tell you that she'll be glad to show it to you and give you some cuttings, as well. But you have to remember that this is a poisonous plant, so if you have children, you might want to think twice before you fall in love with it.

  ❧ Mrs. Kilgore has some lovely summer phlox in her garden just now, along with zinnias and marigolds, cosmos, asters, and roses. She'll be glad to share some of those blossoms for a beautiful bouquet on your dining room table, but she hopes you'll come prepared to help dead-head. (She's got an extra pair of clippers she'll let you use.) If you don't know what dead-heading is, Mrs. Kilgore explains it this way: "The plant's main purpose in life is to flower, set seed, and make baby plants. So if you clip off the flowers, you frustrate the plant, and a frustrated plant just sends out more blooms to try to frustrate *you*." Thank you, Mrs. Kilgore, for that explanation.

  ❧ The summer rains came at just the right time and it's been a bountiful year for Darling's vegetable gardens, as you can probably see by the stands along the roadsides, where people are making a little extra money by selling part of their bountiful harvest. Between now and frost, you'll be able to find tomatoes, cucumbers, eggplant, okra, beans, squash (summer and winter), sweet potatoes, pumpkins, southern peas, maybe even some late corn. If you've got some extra jars and lids, why not get out that canning kettle and get to work? Come January or February, when you start bringing up those gleaming jars from the fruit cellar, you'll be glad you did!

❧ Speaking of pumpkins, looks like there'll be plenty this year and you're certain to want one or two for your front porch when Halloween rolls around. But if you'd like to keep some over the winter, you'll want to know how to keep them from spoiling. Pick only the deep orange, solid pumpkins, and leave a three-inch stem. Try not to scratch or poke a hole in the rind. Dip the pumpkins in a bucket of water and chlorine bleach (4 teaspoons per gallon). Cure them at room temperature for a week to harden the rind, then store in a cool place. Rinse before using. Your pumpkins will keep at least through Christmas, by which time you will have turned them all into holiday pies.

❧ It's planting time again! Lots of people think that gardeners do all of their work in the spring. But every gardener knows that fall is another good time for planting. Here are some of the things the Dahlias will be putting into their gardens through the end of October: shrubs; spring-flowering bulbs (hyacinths, daffodils, crocuses); hardy winter vegetables (turnips, mustard, kale, spinach, onion sets); and hardy annuals, such as pansies, poppies, and sweet peas. Oh, and strawberries, of course. You don't want to miss out on strawberry shortcake next spring!

❧ Aunt Hetty Little wants to remind you that as you clean up your garden, you should burn or bury any plant debris that has insects in it. These little pests like nothing better than to snuggle up for the winter inside a curled-up leaf or a dead stem and jump out and surprise you in the spring. Right now, she says, you need to be on the lookout for cabbage loopers. If your cabbage leaves have turned to lace, you definitely have a problem. The best cure: hand-picking. (Use

gloves if you're squeamish.) Aunt Hetty says: "To con-
vince these little boogers that they don't want to mess
with your garden, you can mash up a couple of cups of
hot peppers and some garlic, stir into a pint of water,
and spray. Some people also like to smoosh up a few of
the little boogers themselves, and dump them in the
mix, on the theory that this will scare all their friends
and relations. Next year, be sure to move your brassi-
cas (cabbage, broccoli, cauliflower, Brussels sprouts,
and the like) to a different corner of the garden, so the
bugs will at least have to go looking. Replanting in the
same place makes it just a little too easy for them."

◈ Alice Ann Walker reports that she has been remodel-
ing her garden this month, now that it's a little cooler.
Her husband, Arnold, is disabled, but he doesn't let
that stop him. He is a talented whittler and has made
several large wooden animals and birds for her, including bunnies, chipmunks, ducks, and pink-painted fla-
mingoes. He has also made a flock of wooden geese
with wings that go around and around like a wind-
mill, painted in all different colors. Arnold is willing
to sell a few of these for just thirty cents each, so if
you'd like to buy one, stop out front and honk and
somebody will come out and help you pick the color
that's just right for your garden. (Arnold says the fla-
mingoes are for sale, too.)

◈ While I'm mentioning colors, I should like to say that
I have some beautiful lilies in my garden just now.
There are the usual daylilies, but also spider lilies,
ox-blood lilies, and some naked ladies (not as pretty as
those in Miss Hamer's front yard, on Camellia Street).
I also have some truly gorgeous torch lilies. (Miss Rogers will remind me that I should use a proper name:

Kniphofia Pfitzeri.) A reader from Florida sent me a delightful ginger lily (*Hedychium coronarium*, Miss Rogers), which has two other pretty names: butterfly lily and garland flower. The ginger lily is four feet tall, a strong, robust plant, with leaves like cannas, sprays of fragrant white flowers, and showy pods full of bright red seeds. It likes partial shade to full sun; a hard frost will kill it to the ground, but it'll come back again. It's easy to propagate: just dig it up, slice the root into six- or eight-inch pieces, and replant. If you want some, let me know. I'll be digging next week and will be glad to save some for you.

❧ And don't forget to turn to the back page and read the Dahlias' "Dirty Dozen" tips for cleaning house without spending a lot of money. You're bound to learn something you didn't already know! If you have tips to share, they're welcome. Just write them down and leave them for Elizabeth Lacy at the *Dispatch* office.

EIGHTEEN

Bessie Bloodworth Pays a Call

After Leona Ruth was safely asleep—and snoring—Bessie started for home, only a few blocks away. As she walked, she was thinking about what had happened, and was glad that Frankie Diamond was on his way back to Chicago and that nobody in Darling needed to be afraid of him.

But she was also troubled, once again, with the questions that had been swirling in her mind and heart since yesterday, when she had told Liz and Verna about Harold. Now, she was sorry she had spoken of him. Those old sad times were behind her, and there was no point in reawakening the memories or in wondering what had happened to him. She should just forget it. But Bessie knew herself well enough to know that she wasn't going to be satisfied with this easy, just-let-it-alone answer. Now that the questions were all stirred up again, she couldn't let them go.

So, in her characteristic way, Bessie took action. Instead of going home to get ready for the Dahlias' card party that evening, she went to the front door of Miss Hamer's house and knocked. After a few moments, she knocked again, and at last, DessaRae opened the door. She was a thin-faced, narrow-boned woman, slightly stooped and very black, with graying hair clipped close to her head, and dressed in a black maid's uniform and white apron.

"Hello, DessaRae," Bessie said. "Is Miss Hamer in?" It was a silly question. Miss Hamer was always in. She hadn't been out of the house for ten years, so far as Bessie knew.

"Who is it, DessaRae?" called an anxious voice. It was Miss Jamison, standing at the top of the stairs. She sounded afraid, and Bessie thought she knew why. She also thought she would like to tell her that Frankie Diamond was safely on the train and headed back up north, but she wasn't sure she should. She found herself wondering, as well, whether she should tell Miss Hamer that Miss Jamison, aka Lorelei LaMotte, was wanted for shooting the man who had slashed Miss Lake's face. But she wasn't going to do that, either. That wasn't what she was here for.

"It's Miz Bloodworth, from across the street," DessaRae called over her shoulder. "She here to see Miz Hamer."

"That's fine, then," Miss Jamison said, sounding relieved, and disappeared.

DessaRae turned back. "Miz Hamer a bit wandery today, Miz Bloodworth. More'n usual, maybe. You sure you want to see her?"

"Thanks for the warning," Bessie said. "Yes, I'd like to see her."

DessaRae nodded and stepped back. "Well, then, come on in."

Bessie followed DessaRae into the parlor on the right-hand side of the hall, where Miss Hamer spent her days. Endless days, Bessie thought, at least, they must seem endless. The old lady—she must be nearly eighty—was slumped in a wooden, cane-back wheelchair with pillows at her back and sides, a book on her lap. But she wasn't reading, Bessie saw. Her spectacles hung around her neck on a black ribbon, and the watery blue eyes in her lined face, as leathery and wrinkled as a dried fig, held a vacant look. Her cheeks were hollowed and empty. Her arms were so thin Bessie could see her bones, fragile, like the bones of a bird. Her white hair, under an old-fashioned ruffled cap, was dry and wispy.

DessaRae bent over her chair. "Miz Bloodworth's here to see you, Miz Hamer," she said loudly.

"Tell her I'm busy," Miss Hamer said, as petulant as a small child. She picked up her book and held it in shaking hands. "I'm reading. I don't have time for visitors."

"How nice to see you, Miss Hamer," Bessie said, unperturbed. It had always been this way. Harold's sister always said she never had time for visitors. Bessie usually took no for an answer and left, since there was nothing to be gained from trying to talk to somebody who wouldn't talk to you. But today she was determined. She pulled up a chair and sat down.

"I get you some iced tea and cookies," DessaRae said.

"Don't bother," Miss Hamer said sharply. "She's not stayin'. She'll be gone before you get back in here with the tray."

"Yes'm." DessaRae disappeared, closing the door behind her.

Bessie folded her hands in her lap. "I hope your niece and her friend are settling in," she said loudly.

Miss Hamer made a scornful noise.

"I hope Miss Jamison is some help to you," Bessie persisted.

"Help to DessaRae, not to me," Miss Hamer said. Her voice was cracked and brittle. "Her old back won't let her lift me and I can't lift myself. Doc Roberts said I had to get somebody in to help or he'd take DessaRae away from me. Said he wasn't going to let one old invalid wait on another."

She gave a self-pitying sigh. "Even made me find another home for Robert E. Lee."

Robert E. Lee was Mrs. Hamer's dog. Bessie was a little surprised to hear all this, since Mrs. Hamer usually didn't talk. "Well, it's nice," she said in a comforting tone. "That your niece is a help, I mean. Must be good to have family with you."

Miss Hamer looked at her sideways and said nothing.

"Speaking of family," Bessie said, "I was thinking of Harold the other day."

"Who?" Miss Hamer leaned forward and put her hand behind her ear. "Who?"

"Harold." Bessie raised her voice. "Your brother."

Miss Hamer gave a dismissive gesture. "Why are you thinkin' of him? Don't be a fool, Bessie. You're too old for romantic thoughts. Anyway, it's all in the past. It's done."

Bessie leaned forward, speaking distinctly. "Not romantic thoughts. I got over that a good many years ago. More like wanting to get unfinished business out of the way." She paused. "You never heard from him, over the years?"

"Wouldn't I have told you if I did?"

Bessie chuckled. "I doubt it."

There was a silence. "Why are you bringin' him up now?" the old lady asked.

Why? Bessie asked herself, and answered her own question. "Because I found a box of my father's papers in the attic, and it was his birthday, and I got to thinking about him. And thinking about my father got me thinking of Harold. And then a couple of ladies from the garden club came over and I started telling them that we'd been engaged once. And wondering—"

Miss Hamer turned to look her full in the face. Her eyes were no longer vacant, but sharp, piercing. "Wonderin' what?"

Bessie lifted her shoulders and let them fall. "Just . . .

wondering, is all. Where he went and why. But mostly wondering why he never got in touch." She met Miss Hamer's eyes. "That wasn't like Harold."

Miss Hamer turned away. There was a long silence. Finally, she said, "No. It wasn't like Harold." She looked Bessie in the face again. "Why don't you ask your daddy why he left?"

"Ask my daddy?" Bessie said, in some surprise. "Why, Miss Hamer, my father has been dead for over ten years. And anyway, why would he know about Harold?"

"Dead? Ten years?" Miss Hamer shut her eyes, then opened them. "Why didn't I know he died?" she asked pitiably. "How come DessaRae never told me?" Her voice became thinner, wilder. "How come *you* didn't tell me, Bessie Bloodworth?"

"I'm sure I did," Bessie said, trying to soothe her. "Or maybe I just thought you knew." Or maybe you forgot, you silly old thing, she thought to herself. "He died over at Monroeville, in the hospital. He had lung cancer. We buried him in his very own cemetery, beside Mama." Putting him there had been like taking him home.

"Ten years," Miss Hamer muttered, shaking her head in disbelief. "Your daddy's been gone from this green earth for ten whole years. And all this time, I've been sitting here in this chair, hating him, wanting him dead." She broke off with a crackling laugh, like dry paper ripping. "Ten years!"

"You've been hating him?" Bessie frowned. "Why? And why are we talking about my father, anyway? Why did you tell me to ask him about Harold? He had no idea why you sent your brother away. He didn't want us to get married any more than you did, but—"

"*I* sent Harold away?" Miss Hamer's laugh had a ragged edge. "*I* did?"

"Yes, you." Bessie paused and softened her tone, wanting

to keep the bitterness out of her voice. After all these years, being bitter didn't help anybody. "You aimed to keep your little brother all to yourself. You were bound and determined to make life miserable for any girl he cared about. He knew that. So he left. Maybe you didn't actually send him away, but it amounts to the same thing."

"Huh!" Miss Hamer said sarcastically. "I reckon that means you don't know."

"Don't know what?"

"It was your daddy who sent Harold off. Offered him money to just up and leave town. Just disappear."

Bessie felt suddenly cold. "Offered him . . . money?" she whispered. "How do you know?"

"Because he told me, your daddy did," the old lady said triumphantly. "Told me his very own self, right here in this room. Bragged that he was goin' to offer money to Harold to jilt you, and that he knew Harold would take it."

"But Harold would never—"

"That's what I said. I told him that Harold was a prideful, stubborn boy, and he had his whole heart set on you. And your daddy laughed and said, well, we'll just see who is prideful and stubborn—when it comes to money."

Bessie sucked in her breath. "I don't believe—"

Miss Hamer pounded her fist on the arm of her wheel-chair. "So I told Harold what your daddy had said and he swore up and down to me—yes, right in this room, sittin' right in that chair you're sittin' in now—that he wasn't going to take the money. He was going to meet your daddy that night and tell him to go to hell. Told me to go to hell, too, when I said to him that he ought to take whatever was offered and leave." She laughed again, then fell into a coughing spell that went on for a very long time. When she had recovered her breath, she produced a white lawn hankie and wiped her mouth. She said, in a weak, thin voice, "That was wrong of me. I admit it. And I've suffered for it all these years. It's been like a worm gnawin' at my innards evermore."

"You told him—" Bessie swallowed and tried again. "You told him to take it?"

"I did. I am not proud of it now, but I did." Miss Hamer gave a long, trembling sigh and her thin fingers fluttered. "And I reckon he decided to do like I said. He went off to see your daddy that night and never came home, not even to get his clothes. I reckon he was ashamed of lettin' himself be bought off, which is why he didn't say good-bye or write to either of us. He was ashamed. Ashamed of takin' your daddy's money to jilt your daddy's daughter."

"I don't believe it," Bessie said fiercely, balling up her fists. "I can believe that my father might've offered . . . something. But I can't believe Harold took it! He couldn't. He wouldn't!"

"Dead," Miss Hamer muttered. "Your daddy dead ten years, and I never knew." She licked her lips. "All that hatin', all that time. Wasted." She dropped her head into her hands and began to weep. After a moment, she lifted her head and began to beat her balled hands against her breasts, and then to shriek. Long, agonized shrieks that made Bessie want to cover her ears.

The old black woman hurried in. "Best you go now, Miz Bloodworth." She bent over and put her arms around the shaking woman. "There, there, now, honey," she crooned, rocking her. "I'll git you some o' dat ol' Miles Nervine Miss Nona Jean bought for you. It'll be all right. It'll be jes' fine."

Bessie was about to step off the front porch when the front door opened behind her.

"Miss Bloodworth, please."

Bessie turned, startled. At first she didn't quite believe her eyes, but she knew it had to be true. It was Miss Jamison, a print scarf tied around her brown hair. She was wearing a shapeless gray cotton housedress that must have once belonged to Miss Hamer, felt bedroom slippers, and not a trace of makeup. She looked, Bessie thought, like a sharecropper's wife.

"What happened at the beauty parlor today—" Miss Jamison raised her voice, to be heard over Miss Hamer's anguished cries. "I hope it won't go any further, Miss Bloodworth. I don't want the whole town gossiping about me. Or about Miss Lake, either. As it is, the poor thing is so distraught that she can't sleep. I tried to get her some of her Veronal, but the druggist refused to fill her prescription."

Bessie hadn't meant to tell this, but maybe it would relieve Miss Jamison's mind. "If you're worrying about Frankie Diamond, you can stop right now. Deputy Norris put him on the train back to Chicago earlier this afternoon."

"He—what?" Miss Jamison's hand went to her mouth. "Are you *sure*? How do you know?"

"I saw him collared myself," Bessie replied. "On the square, in front of Mann's Mercantile. We—" She was about to mention about what Verna had found out in her telephone conversation with the talkative Mrs. O'Malley, but she was interrupted by the sound of an automobile. She turned.

Mr. Bailey Beauchamp's lemon yellow Cadillac Phaeton was purring along Camellia Street. The canvas top was folded back, Lightning was at the wheel, and Mr. Beauchamp was sitting in the back seat. As they approached Miss Hamer's house, Mr. Beauchamp leaned forward and tapped Lightning on the shoulder with his cane. The car slowed and Mr. Beauchamp slid over in the seat, peering at the street numbers. He saw the house and the two women on the porch, smiled broadly, and began to raise his hat. Then he got a good look at Miss Jamison. He stared, frowned, jammed his hat back on his head, and spoke curtly to Lightning. The Cadillac sped up.

Miss Jamison's disguise was a success.

NINETEEN

Lizzy Lays Down the Law

Lizzy took her column—neatly typed, double-spaced, the pages numbered—to the *Dispatch* office downstairs, which smelled of ink and cigarette smoke. Charlie Dickens was sitting at his battered wooden desk, typing fast with two fingers on an old black Royal typewriter, a cigarette stuck crookedly in one corner of his mouth. He wore his usual green celluloid eyeshade, a rumpled white shirt with the sleeves rolled up and tie askew, and a gray vest. Rolls of newsprint were stacked along one wall, and behind him, at the back of the large room, loomed the silent newspaper press. Mr. Dickens and his helper, Boomer Craig, would crank it up and start printing the paper on Thursday evening, after Lizzy and Mr. Moseley had gone home for the day. The press rattled the building and made as much noise as a locomotive.

Lizzy put her column on Mr. Dickens' desk. She hesitated, remembering that, just a couple of days ago, she had planned to talk to him about writing a feature story about Miss

Jamison (aka Lorelei LaMotte) and her stay in Darling. That was out of the question now, of course—as was Verna's notion of getting the two ladies to put on an act for the talent show. But depending on what happened tonight, there might be a different story to tell. Of course, it would take a while to get all the facts and write it up.

She cleared her throat. "What's the deadline for news this week, Mr. Dickens?"

"Thursday morning," Charlie said, without looking up. He was balding and fleshy, a large man pushing fifty, with sharp, hard eyes that seemed out of place in his round face. He ripped the paper out of his typewriter. "Here's a very important piece of news, don't you think? Think I'll run it on Page One, right next to the story about construction beginning on Boulder Dam." He read it out loud in a mocking, sarcastic voice. "On Wednesday morning Mrs. Campbell Young entertained very delightfully at her charming home on Rosemont Avenue. The affair was a morning bridge party given on the vine-covered porch. At noon a luncheon of garden salad, cold cucumber soup, and tiny ham sandwiches was served to the appreciative guests. Prizes were awarded to the winning players."

"Well," Lizzy began politely, "I'm sure that Mrs. Young's friends—"

"Wait, there's something else. This goes on Page Two." He picked up another piece of paper, which Lizzy could see was an ad. "Ironing Board and Electric Iron, $3.95. A convenience no modern housewife can afford to be without." He snorted. "And a rattan porch rocker for three dollars and fifty cents, so the housewife can take her leisure when she's finished ironing. Both of these swell bargains are courtesy of Mann's Mercantile. Ain't that just the bee's knees?"

Lizzy might have said that an electric iron was a great improvement over the heavy flatirons that had to be heated on the cook stove, which Charlie would know if he had to iron his own white shirts, especially in the summertime. But of course she didn't. There wasn't any point in saying anything at all, really. Charlie Dickens was given to fits of depression, often brought on by what he thought of as the inconsequentiality of the things he had to put into the newspaper. It sounded as if he was at one of his low points today.

He raised one finger. "But don't give up yet, Liz. Here's something else for your edification, from one of the feature services." He read:

"Benito Mussolini of Italy professes principles of government which are bitterly hated by the American farmers, stout defenders of democracy—but just the same, he has solved the farm relief problem. While the American Congress has passed laws which are of doubtful help to the troubled tillers of the soil, and while Ramsay MacDonald's government in Great Britain is still talking about helping the sadly crippled British farmer, Mussolini is doing something. He intends to make Italy almost, or entirely, self-supporting in the matter of food, so the country can spend more money on raw materials, increase the prosperity of its factories, and cut down the adverse balance of trade. Not incidentally, this will also increase the well-being of the Italian farmer."

He put down the paper and looked up at her. "This opinion piece ran a couple of weeks ago in the Anniston *Star*, right here in Alabama. And to my knowledge, nobody has burned the newspaper office or lynched the editor." He squinted at her. "Do you think I ought to run it, Liz?"

"Well, I don't know," Lizzy said hesitantly. "Lots of Darling folks might not be too anxious to hear about what Mussolini is doing. Jed Snow says that he's a Fascist dictator.

He's taken over the government. He's outlawed political parties. He—"

"Yes to all that, Liz." Charlie heaved a heavy sigh. "Jed's right, of course. Mussolini is a dictator. But he gets things done, damn it. He gets things done." He threw the paper down on the desk, pulled off his eyeshade, and dropped his head in his hands. "Why can't we have a government that gets things done?"

Lizzy didn't have an answer to that question. Instead, she said, "If I have a piece of news—important news—that I can't turn in until Thursday noon, will there still be room for it?"

"Depends on how long it is and how urgent." Charlie shrugged heavily. "I could cut Mrs. Campbell Young's bridge party, I guess. Or I could move the Mercantile ad to the back page. Or—"

"Thanks," Lizzy said, and fled.

When she got to her block on Jeff Davis, Lizzy could see her mother sitting out on the front porch. Not wanting to confront her just yet, she cut through Mrs. Hoffman's side yard, walked up the alley, and entered her mother's kitchen, letting the screen door slap shut behind her.

"Don' slam that screen." Sally-Lou didn't look up from the piecrust she was rolling out on the pine-topped table. "How many times I gots to tell you, Miz Lizzy? You know yo' mama don' like it." She was wearing her usual gray uniform dress, neatly pressed, and a white apron. On the table beside her was a metal pie tin, the bottom crust heaped with sliced peaches and topped with dots of butter and a sprinkle of cinnamon.

"Sorry," Lizzy said automatically, reflecting that one of the pleasures of being grown-up and having her own house was being able to slam the screen whenever she felt like it.

Sally-Lou gave a final push to the rolling pin. "Yo' mama out on the front porch, where it's cool. She makin' a list of all the things that's gots to be done afore we move 'cross the street to yo' house."

Oh, dear, Lizzy thought, and her stomach clenched. There was going to be another big argument, and she hated arguments. But there was something else that had to be taken care of before she could tell her mother that there would be no move.

"Sally-Lou," she said, "I wonder if you could go over to Miss Hamer's house this evening and have a little visit with DessaRae."

There was a silence. "Might could." Sally-Lou rolled the piecrust around the rolling pin and then neatly unrolled it over the top of the peaches in the pie tin, something that Lizzy had tried to do a hundred times and failed every time. "Why fo' would I be visitin' with Aunt Dessy?"

Lizzy had learned a long time ago that there was no point in trying to fool Sally-Lou, but the situation was complicated, and she didn't want to go into it now. "Just something I need you to do." She hesitated. "It's important, or I wouldn't ask."

"Like maybe spyin' on those two ladies livin' there, huh?" Sally-Lou asked. She pulled the pie tin toward her, picked up a knife, and slashed a vent across the top so juices and steam could escape.

"Sort of," Lizzy said, and felt compelled to add, "It might be a little dangerous." She didn't really think so, but felt she should warn Sally-Lou anyway. They needed an insider in the house. An insider who had instructions on what to do, in case something should happen. Sally-Lou was smart, resourceful, and dependable. They could count on her.

"Dang'rous?" Sally-Lou chuckled. She began to crimp the pastry between her fingers, sealing the top and bottom crusts together. "Well, reckon I could," she said judiciously. "Seein's how it's you that's askin', Miss Lizzy. And seein's how I jes' loves to do dang'rous things. Does 'em ever chance I gets."

"Oh, good." Sally-Lou loved drama, so Lizzy had been pretty sure she'd do it. But she had a mind of her own, and she was stubborn as all get-out, so you could never tell. "I have to go to the Magnolia Manor, so I'll walk over with you and tell you all about it on the way." Lizzy squeezed Sally-Lou's arm. "Thanks. I'll let Mama know, so she won't fuss."

Sally-Lou rolled her eyes. "Yo' mama gone fuss anyhow. But I be used to it. Don' you worry none."

Mrs. Lacy was sitting in her white wicker rocking chair on the front porch, a tablet on her lap and a pencil in her hand. She looked up. "Oh, there you are, Elizabeth," she said cheerfully. "I will be wantin' that key again tomorrow. I'd like to take another look at the dining room. I think we can fit—"

"There will be no key, Mama." Lizzy pulled a porch chair around so that she could face her mother, and sat down. It was time to lay down the law, in the only terms her mother would understand. "And no dining room, and no electric refrigerator. I had a frank discussion with Mr. Johnson this afternoon. About this house, and his efforts to come to some kind of accommodation with you, and your refusal. He told me—"

"You . . . you had no right to talk to that man, Elizabeth!" Mrs. Lacy cried. "This house is my business! You—"

"I had every right, Mama," Lizzy broke in, feeling the hot anger boiling up inside her like a teakettle steaming on a hot stove. "You *lied* to me. You said that Mr. Johnson refused to negotiate on the mortgage. You let me think that Daddy's annuity was ended and that you were destitute." She pulled herself up. "Anyway, this house is *my* business now, not yours. I have bought it."

Her mother stared at her. The loose skin under her neck was quivering. "You have . . . *bought* it?"

"Yes. I am assuming your mortgage." The heat of her

boiling anger suddenly evaporated, and in its place Lizzy discovered a cool, crisp determination. "You are not moving after all, Mama. You and Sally-Lou are staying here. I will be making the monthly mortgage payments. To support yourself, you will continue to have the annuity Daddy left you, and there may be some income from your millinery work."

"My . . . millinery work?" her mother asked blankly.

"Yes. Mr. Johnson told me how much his wife admires your hats, and I went next door and spoke to Fannie Champaign. She is willing to take your work on consignment—not just here, but in Miami and Birmingham, where her work is shown at other shops."

Mrs. Lacy's hand had gone to her heart. Her eyes were huge and horrified. "Elizabeth, you know I could not possibly consider going to *work*. Your father would turn over in his grave if he—"

"I don't know anything of the sort, Mama." Surprisingly, Lizzy found herself feeling sorry for her mother, and she spoke gently. "The times are different now than when Daddy was alive. Lots of people are doing things they might not otherwise do. I can't force you to earn money. But I can tell you that you and I are *not* going to live together. I am all grown-up now, and I won't go back to being your little girl, fighting with you over every square inch of space." She cleared her throat. "I will be glad to accept whatever rent for this house that you think is fair. I will leave the amount to your conscience."

Her mother shook her head violently. "Elizabeth, this is utter nonsense. I am not going to listen to another word of such wild talk."

"You don't have to." Lizzy took a deep breath and stood up. "It's all been said. There's nothing more to say." She dropped a quick kiss on her mother's head and went to the porch steps. "Oh, by the way, I'm taking Sally-Lou out with me after supper."

"Elizabeth!" Mrs. Lacy shrilled angrily. "You come back here this instant! I won't have you talkin' to me in that tone of—"

"Thank you, Mother. Have a good evening." And with that, Lizzy went down the steps and across the street, and home, to her own dear little house, where Daffy was waiting on the porch railing, his ears glinting golden in the afternoon sunlight.

She picked him up and buried her face in his soft fur, feeling the low rumble of his purr vibrating against her cheek.

All grown-up. Was she?

She hoped so.

TWENTY

The Dahlias Score

Bessie left Miss Jamison on the front porch and went across the street to Magnolia Manor. She had several things to do to get ready for tonight's card party. But she was still shaken by what Miss Hamer had told her, and she couldn't get it out of her mind. Her own father had paid Harold to go away? He had told Harold's sister what he was going to do, had even bragged about it?

At first she refused to believe it. It was just another of the old woman's crazy stories, an explanation that satisfied her because it absolved her of responsibility. But after a little while—after Bessie had mixed up a batch of her mother's favorite lemon chess squares for tonight's card party and put the crust in the oven, then poured herself some cold tea and taken it outside to the shade of the willow tree—she began to think that it was possible. And after a little while longer, that it was probable. And then that it was likely.

The part that she didn't understand, though, was the business about her father actually *paying* Harold. For as long as

Bessie had known him, her father had been a miserly skin-flint who paid his employees not one penny more than he had to and doled out the housekeeping allowance as if it were the crown jewels. She just couldn't imagine that he would offer a large amount of money to anybody, for any purpose, under any conditions. And how much would it have taken to tempt Harold to leave Darling and go into what amounted to a lifelong exile? Fifty dollars? A hundred? Five hundred? A thousand?

The late afternoon breeze lifted the willow leaves over her head and Bessie sighed, remembering Harold's gentle smile, his beckoning glance, his young man's eager hunger for her young woman's willing body. She shook her head in disbelief. Miss Hamer was right. Harold had been proud and stubborn—and passionate. Bessie couldn't imagine that he would willingly abandon her—the girl she had been then—for anything less than a king's ransom. And she certainly couldn't imagine her scrooge of a father forking over more than a few dollars for what was at bottom an uncertainty. There wouldn't have been anything to keep Harold from taking the money, leaving for a few days, and then coming back.

A blue dragonfly, its transparent wings quivering, dropped onto a blade of grass at Bessie's feet and she sat very still, watching it. Her father had been a volatile, temperamental man who was given to explosive outbursts. If Harold had refused his offer, had stood up to him and announced that he and Bessie were getting their rings and meant to be married whether he wanted to or not, he might have—

"Bessie!" It was Maxine, shouting from the back screen door. "What have you got in the oven? Smells like it might be scorching!"

Bessie jumped up and flew into the kitchen. After she rescued her crust and added the lemon filling, Leticia and Rose-anne came in to start supper. They planned to eat early, because Leticia, Maxine, and Mrs. Sedalius were all going to a baby shower for Maxine's granddaughter. Then Miss Rogers came in, asking Bessie's advice on a dress pattern she was sewing. There was so much commotion that she could not pursue the unbearably ugly thought she had broken off when the cookies began to scorch.

It was just as well.

She didn't want to think it. She didn't dare.

The Dahlias' Monday evening card party—they almost always played hearts—was open to all the club members, but only seven or eight usually came. Voleen Johnson, Miss Rogers, and several others never played cards, while Aunt Hetty Little played only poker. Mildred Kilgore often played hearts, but she had phoned to say that she and Mr. Kilgore had been asked out to supper at the country club. Alice Ann Walker and Lucy Murphy, also regulars at the card party, had gone to a meeting of the quilting club. Myra May had to work the switchboard. So it would be just one table of four: Bessie, Verna, Lizzy, and Ophelia. And since the Magnolia Ladies were all otherwise occupied tonight, they could set up their game in the parlor.

It was beginning to get dark and Bessie—still resolutely refusing to think that dreadful thought about her father and Harold—turned on the porch light. Then she put a pitcher of iced tea and a china plate filled with lemon chess squares, along with glasses, dessert plates, forks, and napkins, on the cherry sideboard. She was getting out the deck of cards and paper and pencil for scoring when she heard a knock at the door and opened it to Liz and Verna. The three of them were just sitting down at the card table when the telephone rang. It was Ophelia, regretting that she couldn't come because her daughter had a fever and her husband had to go to a town council meeting.

"So it will be just us three," Bessie said, and took out the two of diamonds, so that the deck had just fifty-one cards. "I always think it's more fun to play with four, but——"

"Actually," Verna said, with a glance at Liz, "it's just as well that Ophelia isn't here. I don't know how much playing we're going to get done tonight."

"Oh?" Bessie asked, shuffling the cards. The hostess always dealt the first hand. "Let's see, now. Since it's just the three of us, we each get seventeen cards. Isn't that right? And pass three instead of four?" She started to deal, then paused and looked at Verna. "Why aren't we going to get much playing done tonight?"

"Because there might be a ruckus across the street," Liz said. "Along about dark, maybe." She glanced at Bessie. "Would it be okay if I opened the parlor window? We want to be able to hear."

"Maybe we'd better tell Bessie what this is all about," Verna said. "So she won't be surprised."

Bessie put down the cards. "Okay," she said expectantly. "What's it about?"

"Frankie Diamond," Liz and Verna said, practically in unison.

Bessie raised her eyebrows. "What about him? He's on the train back to Chicago, isn't he?"

"Maybe, maybe not," Verna said. "We think maybe not."

"We figure he's not like the government revenue agents who let themselves be pushed around," Liz said.

"He's tough," Verna said grimly. "He's used to slugging it out with those Chicagoland gangsters. We think he might've jumped the train and come back. And if he was listening to Leona Ruth, he may know where to find the women. But it's likely to be tonight. He won't want to hang around here and risk getting collared again."

"Oh, dear! And I told Miss Jamison that she didn't need to

worry!" Bessie reported what she had said, lamenting, "Now she'll let her guard down!"

"No, she won't," Liz comforted her. "Sally-Lou is over there, paying a little visit to her auntie DessaRae. She'll—"

"Hush," Verna said, tilting her head and narrowing her eyes. "I think I hear something. Bessie, let's turn out the lights and go out on the porch. But we need to be quiet. It might not be happening just yet."

"*What* might not be happening?" Bessie asked.

"You'll see," Liz said.

Bessie flicked the light switch and, moving silently, the three of them went out onto the porch. The night air, still warm from the heat of the day, was rich with the sound of cicadas and tree frogs. The moon had not yet risen and the sky was nearly full dark, the street darker yet under the overhanging trees. There were lights in the neighbors' parlors and kitchens, and one house had a porch light. Across the street, Miss Hamer's house spilled a block of light from the kitchen window, and there was a dimmer light upstairs.

They all stood quietly for a little while, for three minutes, maybe four. Bessie was just about to suggest that they go back inside and play a hand or two while they waited, when she saw a hunched-over shadow, heavy and bulky, moving slowly, creeping along the side of the house near the kitchen window. The shadow wore a hat.

She gasped and grabbed Verna's arm. "Look there!" she squeaked. "It's . . . it's—him!"

"Bessie's right, Verna," Liz said excitedly. "Shouldn't we go over there? What if Miss Jamison is in the kitchen, and he manages to get a shot through the window before—"

"Hang on a sec," Verna said in a low voice. "Leave it to—"

Suddenly there was a shrill whistle. "Drop the gun, Diamond!" Buddy Norris shouted from behind the oak tree in Miss Hamer's yard. "Hands against the wall! Now!" A glaring light spotlighted the shadowed figure and it froze, arm extended. Bessie could see that Frankie Diamond was holding a gun.

"Drop it, I said!" Buddy Norris shouted, but the figure didn't move.

And then from inside the house came a sudden loud clanging, somebody banging on a big metal pot with a metal spoon—several somebodies, several pots, louder and faster, faster and louder, strangely syncopated. Then to this accompaniment they heard a wild, weird, wordless, otherworldly wailing that Bessie recognized from old African slave songs, passionate reverberations at the gates of the underworld. And then Miss Hamer's shrill screeches split the air in a bloodcurdling, bone-shivering, banshee crescendo. It was, unmistakably, a Rebel yell.

It was the Rebel yell that toppled Frankie Diamond—and no wonder, for it was the same yell that had scared the pants off every Union soldier when he heard it through the trees or over a stone wall. Diamond dropped the gun and fell to his knees, covering his head with his arms, cowering.

"Lots of good old-fashioned Alabama yellin' goin' on over there," Liz remarked cheerfully, as Buddy Norris ran up, kicked the gun away, and jerked Diamond to his feet.

"That damn Yankee must think all the hounds of hell are after him," Verna observed with satisfaction. In one swift move, Buddy pulled the man's hands behind his back and handcuffed him. Then he went to the kitchen window and rapped on it, and the pot-clanging and African wailing stopped. The Rebel yell continued for a moment, then it stopped, too. The night was quiet once again, as front doors all along the street popped open and people spilled out onto their porches to see what was going on.

Mr. Butler, two doors down, called, "Dep'ty Norris, you need a hand over there?"

"I reckon if you've got ten minutes, you can help me march this Yankee off to the hoosegow," Buddy replied. "I'm gonna book 'im on a charge of attempted assault with a deadly weapon, attempted burglary, trespassin', and disturbin' the peace. And maybe by the time I get him there, I'll think of something else to pin on him."

"Lemme get my shoes on," Mr. Butler replied. "Be with you in a shake."

So that was why the neighbors along Camellia Street were treated to the satisfying sight of Deputy Buddy Norris, accompanied by Mr. Butler in his undershirt, trousers, and suspenders, escorting one of Al Capone's most dangerous gangsters to the Cypress County jail, upstairs over Snow's Farm Supply. It wasn't a comfortable jail, just two small cells, one of which was probably already occupied by a drunk or a vagrant.

"Well, my goodness," Bessie said limply to Verna and Lizzy. "How in the world did you girls manage all that?"

"We didn't do anything much," Verna said in a modest tone. "Buddy wanted to be a hero, so we asked him to hang around in the dark and see if Diamond showed up. And Liz put Sally-Lou up to organizing a little noisemaking with those clanging pots and pans. We thought that maybe some racket from inside would confuse Diamond and make it easier for Buddy to nab him."

"And that Rebel yell?" Bessie asked.

"That," Liz said with a chuckle, "was Miss Hamer's own idea."

Verna let out her breath. "Well, now that Buddy's got his man, what say we play some hearts?" She rubbed her hands. "I'm ready for a game!"

"Maybe we could have refreshments first," Liz said. "All this excitement has made me thirsty. And didn't I see some lemon chess bars on a platter on your sideboard, Bessie?" She grinned. "You must've known that they're my favorite."

*   *   *

The three of them polished off the refreshments, then played a couple of games. The Magnolia Ladies came home from the baby shower and Liz and Verna said good night and went home. Bessie put away the card table and straightened the parlor, then climbed the stairs to her bedroom.

All in all, it had been a memorable day, from its inauspicious and rather ordinary beginning at Beulah's Beauty Bower to its extraordinary conclusion with Miss Hamer's Rebel yell and the arrest of a Chicagoland gangster right across the street—not to mention Miss Hamer's claim that her father had paid Harold to jilt her and leave Darling. Who would have thought that all those amazing things could happen on just one day? She rather hoped that things would go back to being ordinary again tomorrow. She'd had just about all the excitement she could handle.

In her room, Bessie turned on the light beside her bed. She was tired, but her mind was still racing and she knew she wouldn't be able to sleep. Her glance went to the box of her father's papers that she had carried down from the attic, sitting on her dresser. She hadn't had an urgent reason for going through them—until now. Of course, it wasn't likely that she'd find anything to confirm or refute Miss Hamer's assertion. But still, she ought to make the effort. When she didn't find anything, she would at least know that there wasn't anything to find.

Mr. Noonan had brought the box over from the funeral home one day not long after her father had sold the business. He was already too sick to be able to go through the papers, so Bessie had carried the box to the attic without bothering to take a look. Mr. Noonan told her that he'd kept the business items he had found in the files—burial records, grave marker and grave location information, invoices, employee records, and the like—and was returning items that looked to be of a more personal nature: newspaper clippings, notes from grateful clients, complaints, and so on. There was a note inside the box from Mrs. Noonan, saying that she had put everything into folders, a folder for each year. Now, Bessie was grateful. Her father had been in the funeral and gravestone business for decades and had accumulated a great many papers. At least she didn't have to sort through dozens of scraps.

The file folders were neatly labeled and arranged in chronological order. Not all the years were represented, and the files were variously thick and thin. Bessie flipped through the folders, found the year she was looking for—the year Harold disappeared—and opened the file. There were only five or six items in it. A clipping about a death in neighboring Monroeville; a plaintive letter from a mother in North Carolina, asking for information about the burial of her son, with a carbon copy of the typed letter her father had written back; and several dated notes in her father's cribbed and almost illegible handwriting, scribbled on the backs of funeral cards. She was about to close the file when she noticed another piece of paper, the familiar plat of all the graves in the Darling Cemetery, neatly numbered.

Bessie had seen similar copies many times before, at the funeral home and on her father's desk at home. The plat was necessary, he had once told her, because sometimes people came in from out of town and needed to know where their father's cousin or their mother's great-aunt Clara were buried. But this one caught her eye because it was dated in the top corner: the day of Harold's disappearance, a date she would never forget.

Curious now, she studied it. There was the road and the gate and the lane that meandered around to the back, where an old stone wall marked the graveyard's farthest boundary.

And in the far right corner of her father's cemetery, there was a tiny penciled square and two letters. *HH.*

Her heart beating fast against her ribs, Bessie stared at the sketch map, remembering that awful week, the week of Harold's disappearance. Her father's unaccustomed kindnesses, his tender gestures, his gruff words: "Some things don't bear looking into, child." Her breath caught in her throat, and she put her finger on the penciled square. *HH.* What had he done? What had her father *done?*

Outside the open window, a night bird called from the willow tree and the fragrance of the Angel's Trumpet, its pale blossoms unfurled in the darkness, hung heavy on the air, like the stifling scent of funeral flowers.

TWENTY-ONE

Mr. Moseley Clears Up
a Mystery

Lizzy was always the first to arrive in the law office, but when she opened the door at her usual early hour the next morning, she found Mr. Moseley already at his desk, a steaming cup of coffee at his elbow, his suit jacket draped over the back of his chair. He glanced up when she stood in his doorway and his eyes lightened.

"New dress, Liz?"

It wasn't. She had worn the same dress—a flared-skirt, rose-print silk crepe with lace ruffles at the V-neckline— several times before, but she only smiled and nodded. She had been looking forward with great excitement to telling him about the extraordinary events of the day before. But before she could open her mouth, he was speaking.

"Swell news, Liz!" He wore a broad smile and sounded extremely pleased with himself. "Looks like this tax case is going to go forward. It's not wrapped up—there are still depositions to be taken, more evidence, that kind of thing.

But it's looking solid. And I've just worked a deal that takes our client off the hook."

"The tax case?" she asked, not sure which client he was talking about. "The case you were working on in Montgomery?"

"Yep. The tax *evasion* case. Which—happily for our client—has turned into a deal between the local gendarmerie and the Feds." He leaned back in his chair and clasped his hands behind his head. There were circles of perspiration around his armpits, and judging from the scatter of papers across the desk, Lizzy guessed that he had been working for several hours already. There was a half-smoked cigar in the ashtray and the office reeked of stale cigar smoke. She crossed to a window and opened it, letting in a cooler morning breeze.

"Will it result in an indictment, do you think?" she asked, hoping for a clue to whatever in the world Mr. Moseley was talking about.

"I sincerely hope so," Mr. Moseley replied. "He is a slippery sonovabitch, and I hope they nail him. But in the last analysis, it's up to the boys at Treasury. All I did was the witness work at this end. It was the special agents out of Chicago who deserve all the credit. They combed through four years' worth of bank remittance sheets and deposit records, they tapped telephones, they raided bookie parlors and confiscated business records. My hat's off to those guys, Liz. They did a helluva lot of work—dangerous work. They were actually risking their lives. And by damn, when this is over, they're going to have Capone right where they want him. I know it."

"Capone?" Lizzy blinked, startled. *"Al Capone?"*

"You bet." Mr. Moseley leaned forward, propping his elbows on the desk. "You're not to talk about this outside the office, Liz—not to Verna, not to anybody. I especially don't want Charlie Dickens to get his paws on the story. There's a strong local angle, but our client doesn't want the exposure."

"A local angle?" Lizzy asked urgently. The picture was beginning to emerge, like a partially finished puzzle. But she still lacked a few pieces. "What local angle? Which client?"

But Mr. Moseley was just getting warmed up. "The Feds have been working this case for over five years, Lizzy. They managed to get Capone's brother Ralph, and they sent him to Leavenworth. They've put Jack and Sam Guzik and Frank Nitti behind bars. Louis Lipschultz is waiting trial." Excitedly, he hit the desk with his fist. "Al Capone is next, by damn. And we've got the witness who's going to nail him, right here in Darling, Liz! Our client!"

Lizzy sat down in the chair on the other side of the desk. "Our client" was the last piece in the puzzle. "You're talking about Miss Jamison," she said. "Lorelei LaMotte."

"Exactly. She's a burlesque dancer from Chicago—" He stopped, frowning. "Hey. How did you know that? And how in hell did you know her stage name?"

"I'll tell you in a minute." Lizzy waved her hand. "Go on."

"Huh." He regarded her, still frowning. "Well, I guess there's no reason not to tell you the rest of it, as long as you keep it under your hat. Miss Jamison is a former associate— no, make that a former *girlfriend* of Al Capone. She had an inside track with that guy for at least two years. But they had a serious falling-out, and she decided to get even. She is now cooperating with the Feds to help them fill in his financial picture." He chuckled drily. "That creep has never paid one penny of taxes. Never had a bank account, never signed a check, never let his name appear on any business records. And all the while the money has been coming in like Noah's flood." He shuffled the papers on his desk, fished one out and held it up. "Here's an example. For years, Capone has owned a bookie joint in the Smoke Shop at what is now the Western

Hotel, on Twenty-second Street in Cicero—although of course he's not listed as the owner."

The Western Hotel, Lizzie thought. That was the clue that had first alerted Verna to the connection between Miss Jamison and the Capone gang. And if Verna hadn't made the connection, Frankie Diamond might have gotten away with murder.

"Just listen to this, Liz," Mr. Moseley was going on. "In 1924 alone, that one joint raked in some three hundred thousand dollars in profits. And there are other joints like that one, all over Chicago and Cicero. Every penny of profit went into Capone's pockets, of course, *after* it was thoroughly laundered. Tax-free income—or so he thinks. But he's got another think coming, believe you me. He may be able to skip out on a murder charge, although he's behind God-only-knows how many murders. But Treasury has got him dead to rights on tax evasion."

Lizzy sat forward. "What is Miss Jamison's role in all this? Why is she here in Darling?"

"She's hiding out. You see, she is Treasury's star witness. They've scratched together a lot of circumstantial evidence, but they had to find somebody on the inside to give them the lowdown. When she showed up in their office, mad as hell at Capone and offering to spill everything she knew about his finances, the T-boys knew they had a winner. In fact, they thought they had it all wrapped up. They were getting ready to move in when Capone somehow got wind that she was blowing the whistle on him. So he sent one of his men to have a little heart-to-heart with her. The talk turned ugly and the man—the Blade, he was called—ended up cutting Miss Lake's face pretty badly. Miss Jamison shot him. Killed him." He paused, cleared his throat, and looked at Lizzy, as if he expected her to be shocked.

She wasn't, of course, since she already knew this part of the story. "Go on," she said impatiently. "Go on, please."

He gave her a questioning look. "Well, anyway," he continued, "the shooting meant that the two of them, Miss Jamison and Miss Lake, had to get out of town fast. The Cicero police are in the pockets of the Capone syndicate, and Treasury couldn't risk letting the boys in blue get their hands on Miss Jamison. Luckily, she had already made arrangements to come here. She needed a safe refuge while she and the Feds—and I—worked out the details of her testimony on the Capone tax evasion case. When it looked as if she would be charged with murder, Treasury asked me to negotiate some sort of deal with the Illinois authorities. And meanwhile, to make sure that she stayed safely under wraps."

"She didn't," Lizzy said. "And she wasn't."

Mr. Moseley's eyebrows went up. "Didn't what?"

"Didn't stay under wraps. And she wasn't safe. She—"

"What?" Mr. Moseley jumped out of his chair. He put both hands flat, palms down, on his desk, and leaned on them. "What did you say?"

"They found her," Lizzy replied. "That is, Frankie Diamond found her."

"Frankie Diamond?" Mr. Moseley asked. "He didn't hurt her, did he? Don't tell me he managed to—"

"No, he didn't—but he tried. He showed up day before yesterday at Verna's door, looking for information about Lorelei LaMotte. He even had a photo of her, which was taken in front of the Western Hotel. That was a tip-off for Verna, because she had read in one of her crime magazines that the Western was Capone's headquarters. She suspected that he was up to no good and called Miss Jamison's place in Cicero. Mrs. O'Malley told her that Diamond was a friend of the Blade. So—"

"Mrs. O'Malley?" he interrupted, pulling his brows together in a frown. "Then you gave Verna—"

"Yes," Lizzy said staunchly. "I gave Verna the name and

phone number out of the file. And it's a darn good thing I did, too," she added. "Otherwise, Miss Jamison would likely be dead right now."

"*Dead?*" Mr. Moseley's eyebrows flew up. "You mean, Frankie Diamond tried—"

"Exactly. To kill Miss Jamison." Lizzy took a deep breath and pushed ahead. "Verna asked Bessie Bloodworth and me to shadow him, and there was an argument outside of Mann's and Diamond started pushing me and Bessie Bloodworth around and Mr. Mann came out and threatened to tar and feather him because he suspected him of being a revenue agent. But Buddy—"

Mr. Moseley interrupted again. "Archie Mann suspects every stranger of being a revenue agent, Liz. He's only right fifty percent of the time."

Lizzy nodded and went on, hurrying to get it all out before she was interrupted again. "Buddy Norris rode up on his motorcycle and collared Diamond and put him on the train. But before he did that, Leona Ruth Adcock spilled the beans on where Miss Jamison was staying. So Diamond jumped off the train and came back to town and went to Miss Hamer's house to try and shoot her through the kitchen window after it got dark. But Sally-Lou and DessaRae banged on pots and sang and Miss Hamer gave him the Rebel yell, which finished him off. Buddy Norris nabbed him and put him in jail, which is where he is right now." Lizzy stopped, concerned that she might have mixed things up a bit or left out something important. "But of course," she added, "Verna and Bessie and I had no idea about the tax case against Al Capone, or that Miss Jamison was a witness."

"My god." Mr. Moseley was staring at her. "You're telling me that all this happened yesterday, while I was in Montgomery arranging Miss Jamison's plea bargain? And that *you* were involved? You and the other . . . Dahlias?"

"Well, yes, I guess you'd have to say we were involved. You don't have to worry, though. Miss Jamison is safe. Only she's not a platinum blonde anymore. Beulah dyed her brown, and Miss Lake is wearing Beulah's old red wig. Nobody will ever recognize either of them. And Frankie Diamond is in jail."

Mr. Moseley was reaching for his jacket, thrusting his arms into it. "Diamond's been booked? On what charge?"

"Attempted assault with a deadly weapon, attempted burglary, and trespassing. Oh, and disturbing the peace. And anything else that Deputy Norris was able to think of."

Mr. Moseley was already on his way to the door. Liz got up and followed him.

"I'm going over to the jail, Liz. Telephone Sheriff Burns and tell him to meet me there, pronto." He grabbed his hat from the coat tree and jammed it on his head. "I want to see that deputy, too. The kid deserves a medal. And there may be a reward, as well. Diamond is wanted on suspicion in a pair of murders last month in a Chicago whorehouse."

"My goodness," Lizzy breathed. "And to think that Bessie and Verna and Myra May and I were as close to him as—" Her breath caught.

In two strides, Mr. Moseley was standing in front of her. "I don't know how you and your buddies do it, Liz," he said, "but you've done it again." And then, to Lizzy's astonishment, he bent forward and kissed her, full and hard, on the mouth.

Then he turned and headed for the door again. "Call the sheriff," he commanded over his shoulder. "Now!"

TWENTY–TWO

Bessie Solves a Mystery, Myra May's Car Breaks Down, and Violet Sims Offers a Lift

A few hours later, Lizzy was straightening her desk and getting ready to go to lunch when the door opened. She turned to see Bessie step in and greeted her, surprised: it was the second time in two days that she had come to the office. But when Lizzy looked closer, she saw that Bessie's eyes were red and puffy. She had been crying.

"Why, what's the matter, Bessie?" Lizzy asked, putting an arm around the older woman's shoulders.

Bessie sniffled and held out a key ring. "Would you drive me out to the cemetery, Liz? Myra May said we can take her car. I asked her to drive, but Violet isn't back yet and she can't leave the diner during the dinner rush. I could walk—it's only a couple of miles, but I'd rather not do this alone. And I don't feel as though I can wait until late afternoon, when Myra May will be free."

With one more look at Bessie's face, Lizzy decided that lunch could wait. She reached for the car key. "I've never driven Big Bertha before, but if you're game, I'll give it a try."

Big Bertha, Myra May's 1920 green Chevrolet touring car, was parked in the ramshackle garage behind the diner. Bertha was ten years old and on her fifth set of tires and her second carburetor, but she still had a good many miles left in her. Lizzy climbed in feeling doubtful, but the car looked enough like Grady's Ford that she thought she could manage it. Bravely, she inserted the key and pushed the starter button, and (after a little coaxing) the engine started. Gingerly, she backed it out, shifted into low gear, and swung the car out onto Robert E. Lee, startling a fat white hen that clucked frantically and scurried to get out of the way. "Where are we going?" she asked, over the rattle and cough of the motor.

"Schoolhouse Road," Bessie said, holding on to her hat as they bounced along. "The Darling Cemetery."

The morning had been sunny, but gray clouds were beginning to gather to the south. The air felt heavy with moisture and the trees drooped, their limbs too languid to support the weight of their summer foliage. But driving was pleasant because the canvas-topped touring car, which had no side curtains, admitted a breeze.

Lizzy held her questions until they turned off Schoolhouse Road and drove through the black-painted ironwork gates and into the cemetery. The rolling, wooded grounds were crowded with gravesites dating back to Darling's founding, marked by simple headstones as well as elaborate stone urns, stone Confederate soldiers with stone rifles, and stone angels blowing silent stone trumpets to summon the dead to their eternal reward.

Lizzy felt an immense curiosity. What were they doing here? Why had they come? Why had Bessie been crying? But all she asked was, "Where to now, Bessie?"

Bessie's voice was shaky. "To the left. Follow the lane all the way around to the far right corner." A few minutes later, she put her hand on Lizzy's arm. "Stop, Liz. We're here."

Here, Lizzy saw, was the unoccupied back corner of the cemetery, where a barbed wire side fence right-angled into an old stone wall that was covered in kudzu vines. The rest of the graveyard was neatly mowed and trimmed, and there were bouquets of flowers tucked into Mason jars at the foot of many of the headstones. There was even a recent grave, a heap of wilted flowers from mourners' gardens blanketing the freshly turned soil—Mrs. Turner's grave, Lizzy guessed. The old woman had died the week before. But there were no headstones in the back corner, hidden behind a clump of trees. The area had been allowed to grow up in Johnson grass and weeds, and in contrast to the tended graveyard, it wore an air of unkempt neglect.

Lizzy and Bessie got out of the car. The sky overhead was darker now, and a moist breeze that smelled of rain lifted the kudzu leaves on the vines along the stone wall. Lizzy shivered, feeling somehow apprehensive, but not knowing why. She clasped her arms around herself and stood for a moment, glancing around.

"Okay, so we're here. What are we looking for?"

"I don't have any idea," Bessie said bleakly. "Maybe a grave marker, or maybe a metal stake. Or maybe nothing at all." She pointed toward the corner. "Let's just walk around and look. Back there, along the wall."

Lizzy followed her friend through the tall grass, the foliage catching at the hem of her dress. Not having any idea what they were looking for, she felt doubtful and hesitant. But following Bessie's lead, she kept her eyes on the ground— or rather, on what she could see of it through the thick grass. The light seemed to be dimming as the clouds thickened over the noon sun, and in a nearby tree a crow squawked, protesting their intrusion.

A moment later, she stubbed her toe against something and looked down. At first she thought it was a rock, perhaps fallen from the wall. But when she reached down to push the grass aside, she saw that it was a small, irregularly shaped piece of rough-cut granite, sunk crookedly into the ground and almost covered with earth. There was only a corner sticking up an inch or so—the corner she had stumbled against. In the center, there were two crooked letters, shallowly and inexpertly cut with a chisel. *HH.*

"Bessie," she called urgently. "Come and see."

Bessie hurried over and looked where Lizzy was pointing. With a little moan, she dropped to her knees and touched the stone, then began to pull the grass away from it. As she did, Lizzy thought she could trace out the larger outline of a grave, its surface sunken a little.

Lizzy put her hand on Bessie's shoulder. "It's Harold, isn't it," she said quietly.

"It's Harold," Bessie replied, no longer trying to hold back the tears. "We've found him. He's been here, right here, all these years. So close, so close!"

She bent over, her shoulders heaving, and gave way to sobs. Lizzy knelt beside her and took her in her arms, leaning her cheek against Bessie's gray hair. She did not try to speak. There was nothing to say.

The rain began a little later, a gentle rain, like a warm mist enveloping the grasses and flowers. Lizzy and Bessie left the gravesite and went to sit in the car.

"How did you know where to look?" Lizzy asked, taking a clean handkerchief out of her handbag and handing it to Bessie.

"It was Miss Hamer," Bessie said, wiping her eyes. "She told me yesterday that my father had bragged to her that he was going to pay Harold money to jilt me and leave Darling. But Harold wasn't the kind of man who would let somebody bribe him into doing something like that. In fact, he was likely to be pretty angry about it."

"I certainly hope so!" Lizzy exclaimed hotly.

Bessie was going on. "Anyway, I found a box of Daddy's papers in the attic, and last night, after you and Verna left, I looked through them. That's where I found this little map that my father had drawn. The date on it is the same week that Harold disappeared." She opened her handbag and took it out. "When I saw it, I had an inkling of what could have happened." She lifted her head and glanced around them at the softened outlines of the granite monuments, just visible through the mist. Her voice trembled and she drew in her breath to steady it. "I must've been here for buryings a dozen times since Daddy put him here, and I never knew. Never had the slightest idea."

Startled, Lizzy asked, "Do you think your father . . . *killed* him? Because he wouldn't take the money?"

Bessie gave a long, weary sigh, as if she were breathing out a century of sadness. "My father had a hair-trigger temper, Liz. He could explode at the littlest thing. Maybe he offered Harold some money—it wouldn't have been very much, because he was such a skinflint. Harold probably laughed at him and told him what he could do with it. Daddy got mad and shot him."

"He had a gun? Your father had a gun?"

Bessie's hands were clenched tight. "He had a little revolver that he kept with him when he was at work. He said people sometimes do crazy things when their nearest and dearest died." She opened her hands and flexed her fingers. "Or maybe he didn't shoot him. Maybe they got into a fight and Daddy hit him with a stick of stove wood or something. Maybe . . ." Her voice trailed off.

"But how could your father bury him here without anybody finding out?" Lizzy asked.

Bessie sighed. "I don't suppose it would've been very hard. There were always a couple of coffins in the back room at the funeral home, and Daddy was out here at the cemetery several times a week. He could have paid one of his gravediggers to dig the grave and given him a bottle of whiskey to keep it quiet." She chuckled sadly. "By the time the whiskey was gone, the gravedigger would have forgotten where he dug it. Daddy could easily have brought the coffin out here and buried Harold himself, maybe at night. Or maybe he thought he was safe, screened by those trees, so he did it in the daytime. People saw him out here so often that I doubt that anyone would ask him what he was doing."

"And the grave marker?" Liz asked.

"It's nothing but a scrap of granite. Daddy owned the gravestone business, Liz. It could have been just something he had around. It looks like he cut the initials himself." Another sad chuckle. "He was never much of a hand when it came to stonecutting."

"Oh, Bessie," Lizzy said. "I am so sorry. What . . . are you going to do?"

Bessie dried her eyes again and handed Lizzy's handkerchief back. "Do you mean, am I going to tell anybody? Like—the sheriff?"

Lizzy nodded. "Or have the body exhumed and autopsied, so you know for sure how he . . . how it happened?"

Bessie was silent for a moment. "I doubt if I have a legal right to ask that, Liz. And I really don't think Miss Hamer is strong enough to go through all that ugliness. She's convinced that Harold took Daddy's money and left and was too ashamed to ever get back in touch." She swallowed a little hiccup. "As for telling the sheriff— Well, Harold's been dead for nearly thirty years now, and nobody remembers him except for his sister and me. Miss Jamison is a cousin, but I doubt if she ever met him."

"And your father's been dead for a decade," Lizzy said. "A dead man can't be prosecuted."

Bessie nodded sadly. "So I'm not sure there's any point in telling anyone. I'm the only one who really cares." She looked back in the direction of the grave. "But the mystery is finally solved. And I know where he is—at last. Maybe I'll get a proper headstone. And have the area cleaned up and mowed."

"Yes, you could do that," Lizzy said gently. "I'll be glad to help, if you want."

"Thank you, Liz," Bessie said, reaching for her hand. "What would I do without you?" She sniffed. "Without you and Verna and Myra May and—" She shook her head, unable to go on.

"I know," Lizzy said, and put her arms around Bessie. "We all depend on one another. And that's good. That's the way it should be."

They sat together for a while, and then Lizzy glanced at her watch. "I'm sorry, but I need to get back to the office. Are you okay?"

"I'm fine," Bessie said. She swiped at her eyes with the back of her hand. "I hope I haven't kept you too long."

"Not at all," Lizzy said warmly, and pushed Big Bertha's starter button.

But nothing happened. She pushed it again. Still nothing. She pumped the accelerator pedal, but she knew that wasn't the problem. She tried again. "The battery, maybe?" she hazarded. "I'm not sure how often Myra May drives this car."

"Oh, dear," Bessie moaned. "Don't tell me we're *stranded*!"

"Looks like maybe we are," Lizzy said with a sigh. "At least it's stopped raining, and it's a little cooler." She picked up her handbag, opened the door, and got out. "We're no more than a couple of miles from town. I can walk back and send someone to pick you up."

"To heck with that," Bessie said smartly. "I'm not too old to walk."

But as it turned out, Lizzy and Bessie didn't have to walk all the way to town. They had gone about halfway, walking along the side of the dirt road, when Lizzy heard a vehicle chugging up behind them. She turned to look.

It was Mr. Clinton's old red Ford two-seater taxi, from Monroeville. Many people preferred to pay him to drive them home to Darling, instead of waiting all afternoon for the train. Sometimes, he brought more than one passenger, dropping them off along the way. Often, people flagged him down from the road and he took them where they needed to go, either to Darling or Monroeville, depending on which way he was headed. Most of the time, he charged only fifteen cents for a one-way trip (a nickel less than the twenty-cent train ticket).

This afternoon, he had just one passenger. In the backseat of the taxi sat Violet Sims, her red felt cloche askew, her taffy-colored curls slightly bedraggled. Her face was drawn and tired.

When she saw Lizzy and Bessie, she sat up straight and leaned forward to tap Mr. Clinton on the shoulder. "Stop!" she cried. "We need to pick these ladies up!"

Mr. Clinton, a cigarette hanging out of one corner of his mouth, braked the Ford. "You gals goin' into Darlin'?" he asked in his cracked voice. "Well, come on. Hop in. One up here in front with me, one in the back with the little mother."

Bessie climbed into the front seat. Lizzy opened the back door and got in beside Violet—and saw, to her surprise, that Violet was holding something in her arms, tightly wrapped in a pink flannel receiving blanket.

"Oh, my!" she whispered, leaning closer. Violet pulled the blanket back so Lizzy could see. The little face was round and pink, the mouth like a rosebud. "Why, it's a baby!" Lizzy exclaimed. "A beautiful baby!"

Bessie turned around in the front seat as Mr. Clinton put the Ford in gear and they chugged off. "A baby!" she asked. "Why, Violet, wherever did you—"

"She's my sister's baby," Violet said. Her delicate heart-shaped face was pale and the freckles stood out on her nose. "Baby Dorothy." She traced the baby's cheek with the tip of her finger. "My sister died last week."

"We know," Lizzy said, and touched her arm gently. "Myra May told us. But she didn't tell us you were bringing—"

"That's because she doesn't know," Violet said, her voice breaking. "I couldn't bring myself to tell her over the telephone—I was afraid she might say she didn't want us. But I couldn't just come home and leave Dorothy behind. Her father can't take care of her, and there's no family on either side. I'm all the family she has. And she's all I have left of my sister." The tears were streaming down her cheeks now, and she pulled the baby tighter against her, as if she were shielding her against harm. "Dorothy's father wanted to give her to an orphanage."

"An orphanage?" Bessie asked in a horrified tone. "That precious baby? How could he do such a terrible thing?"

"It's terrible, yes, but I can't blame him," Violet replied. "He's nearly desperate, you know—losing his wife and having to go to work every day, with no one to take care of the baby. So he had a talk with the social worker and told her to come and get her this morning. He said he never wanted to see her again."

"Oh, dear," Lizzy said.

"But I couldn't let them have her!" Violet exclaimed almost wildly, clutching the baby. "I packed her diapers and the little things I'd bought for her and sneaked out of the apartment before dawn. I walked to the station and caught the first train heading south. That's why I'm here today, instead of Thursday, which is what I told Myra May. Oh, I do hope she'll let me keep her!" The words tumbled out almost incoherently, and Lizzy could see that Violet was nearly exhausted.

"Well, of course you couldn't let them have her!" Lizzy exclaimed indignantly. "How could you? You're Dorothy's aunt, for pity's sake. You *had* to take her!" Lizzy didn't want to think about the possible legal problems that lay ahead.

But surely a court would agree that Baby Dorothy was better off with her aunt than with a strange family. And these days, so many families had had to place their children in orphanages that they were full. Maybe there wouldn't be any legal action.

"And you shouldn't go second-guessing Myra May, either," Bessie said in a practical tone. "You know as well as we do that she's got a big heart, and she cares about you. Why, you're her best friend! I'm sure that what's best for you and Dorothy is going to be just fine with her."

"I agree," Lizzy said. She grinned. "And I hope she's going to be so glad to see you—and so surprised and delighted to meet little Dorothy—that she doesn't notice that Bessie and I came back without Big Bertha."

Which is of course exactly what happened. Mr. Clinton dropped them all off in front of the diner. Bessie held the door for Violet, who was carrying the pink-wrapped bundle, and Lizzy brought up the rear, toting Violet's suitcase and the bag of Dorothy's diapers. Most of the dinner customers had finished and gone, and there were only a few to see Myra May give a loud whoop and rush to fling her arms around Violet, and then step back and give another whoop when she saw the baby. And if Violet had had any lingering worries about whether Myra May would welcome Baby Dorothy into their home, she must have been comforted when she saw Myra May's face soften and a smile quiver on her lips.

"Oh, my goodness," she breathed. "What a beautiful baby. What a *beautiful* little baby!"

It was a while before Lizzy could get Myra May's attention long enough to hand her Big Bertha's key and tell her that she'd have to send somebody from the filling station out to the cemetery with a battery, to see if they could get Bertha started and drive her home.

Myra May didn't seem to mind at all.

TWENTY-THREE

Showtime!

The Darling Dahlias' annual talent show was held a few weeks after Violet came home from Memphis with Baby Dorothy and Frankie Diamond was extradited to Illinois on murder charges and Miss Jamison's plea deal was successfully worked out between the Treasury (who needed Lorelei LaMotte as a witness against Capone and an honest Illinois judge, who was just as happy that the Blade was no longer roaming the streets). And as Mr. Moseley told Lizzy, the T-boys' case against Al Capone was moving right along. They expected to be able to indict him early in the next year on charges of tax evasion. As for Miss Jamison's safety, it was clear that the Chicago gangsters had no intention of sending another of their pals to Darling, where he might be subjected to an African slave song, a Rebel yell, and indefinite imprisonment in the Darling jail.

But of course, very few people in Darling knew anything about Frankie Diamond or Lorelei LaMotte or Al Capone's unpaid taxes. Most Darlingians had met Baby Dorothy, though, and agreed with Doc Roberts, who gave her a good going-over and pronounced her the sturdiest, sweetest little cupcake he had ever seen. In fact, business at the diner was up by nearly ten percent over the past few weeks, since lots of folks wanted to come in and meet Cupcake, the enchanting little blue-eyed creature with (as it turned out) the most beautiful strawberry curls in all of Southern Alabama.

But if Darlingians knew very little about the momentous events of national significance that had transpired in their own small town, most of them thought they knew exactly what was coming when they settled into their wooden folding chairs in the Darling gymnasium, where the basketball floor had been covered with canvas to keep it from getting scratched. All the acts were listed in their programs, produced during several frustrating hours with the Academy's old mimeograph machine, which had (predictably) eaten Lizzy's carefully typed stencils. The audience had already seen almost all of the acts, anyway, because they were old favorites that appeared every year.

The program started off with Carsons' Comedy Caravan, featuring the Carson brothers, Billy and Willy, two old men who had been on the vaudeville circuit back in the Gay Nineties. Their jokes were long out of date, but still the audience laughed, so as not to hurt their feelings. Next came Sammy Durham, who made a big hit with his drum solo, especially with the younger folks who appreciated his syncopated style. The quartet of Tumbling Tambourines flipped and flopped across the stage, astonishing all with their daredevil acrobatics, performed to the accompaniment of rattling tambourines, which they tossed from one to another. Mr. and Mrs. Akins followed with their famous Spanish fandango—but this time, the audience was in for a real treat, because they danced to a recording (played on the Academy's Victrola) of part of Maurice Ravel's stirring new piece, *Boléro*. However, some in the audience were disappointed, because the Akins' fandango wasn't nearly as *infamous* as it had once been. Mrs. Akins had added quite a bit more cloth coverage in crucial areas of her costume.

After the Akins danced off the stage, old Mr. Trubar and his dog Towser came on to do their trombone act, which was always fun, even if everybody had seen it five or six times. Trubar and Towser were followed by an act that most hadn't seen before, and the excitement brought the entire audience to the edges of their chairs. This was the Juggling Jinks, two boys who juggled balls, wooden clubs, apples and oranges, pineapples, knives, and even flaming torches—all the while making jokes and dancing and taunting one another. Their prowess and their glib patter so thoroughly amazed and entertained the crowd that they were called back for an encore.

After the Jinks, Miss Rogers' slow, sepulchral reading of Edgar Allen Poe's "The Raven" gave everyone a chance to settle back in their seats, catch their breaths, and calm down. But this politely applauded performance was not the finale of the program, oh, not at all! There was one more act to come. On the program, it was simply listed as "Tiptoe Through the Tulips with Melody Kilgore and Friend." It started with a tap dance by little Melody (Mildred and Roger Kilgore's daughter), dressed in a pink satin costume with a big pink tulip on her head. She tap danced to Nick Lucas' recording of "Tiptoe Through the Tulips," played on the Victrola, in front of a row of painted wooden tulips.

But that wasn't the end of it. When Melody finished her dance and scampered offstage, Miss Nona Jean Jamison stepped through the curtains and sang her own version of the song to the accompaniment of a mandolin, played backstage by her friend Miss Lake. The brown-haired Miss Jamison was *not* nearly naked, as the platinum-haired Lorelei LaMotte would have been, of course. Instead, she was dressed in a white, frilled, full-skirted Southern belle costume, with a lacy, flower-trimmed white parasol. Then Melody danced back onstage and joined Miss Jamison. Holding hands, the two tap-danced together, the little pink tulip and the big Broadway star, although of course only a very few people knew about Miss Jamison's previous career as one of the nearly naked dancers in Mr. Ziegfeld's Frolics—and they weren't telling.

The act brought down the house. For a long time afterward, nothing else was talked of but that adorable, demure, *darling* Miss Nona Jean Jamison.

The Dahlias'
"Dirty Dozen"
Housecleaning Tips

Terms that may be unfamiliar to modern readers are starred. You'll find a glossary at the end of this article. None of these cleansers contain any petroleum products and all are "natural."

- A good wood cleaner may be made of 1 quart hot water, 3 tablespoons boiled linseed oil*, and 1 tablespoon turpentine*. Mix together. Use while warm on wood floors or woodwork. (Mildred Kilgore)

- To clean silver without lots of polishing, bring 1 quart of water to a boil in an aluminum pan large enough to contain your silver. Remove from heat and add 1 teaspoon salt and 1 teaspoon baking soda. When fizzing stops, add silver. Soak, then wash. Double the mixture if necessary to completely cover your silver. (Bessie Bloodworth)

- To make your own wax (for hardwood baseboards, banisters, wood floors), melt ¼ pound beeswax in a double boiler. Remove from heat, add 1 pint turpentine*. Stir until it looks like a thick batter. Pour into a jar, cover, and use as needed. Outing flannel makes a good polishing rag. The more rubbing, the better. You can never rub too much! (Ophelia Snow)

- To make a good laundry soap, grate 1 bar of castile soap* and mix with ⅓ cup washing soda*. In a 3-gallon bucket, dissolve both in about 2 cups of boiling water. Fill the bucket with hot water. This will set to a soft gel. Use 2 to 3 cups for each load of wash. (Beulah Trivette)

- To clean your kitchen and bathroom floors, add 1 cup ammonia, ½ cup white vinegar, and ¼ cup washing soda* to 1 gallon of hot water. You can also use this on painted walls and woodwork. (Verna Tidwell)

- For cleaning windows, nothing beats plain old newspaper, crumpled up, and a spray made of 1 cup water, 1 cup rubbing alcohol, and 1 tablespoon of white vinegar. (Aunt Hetty Little)

- To wash the inside of your icebox, use a mixture of ¼ cup lemon juice in 1 gallon hot water. If you don't have a lemon, use vinegar. (Earlynne Biddle)

- To remove the lime deposit from my teakettle, I mix up 1½ cups vinegar, 1½ cups water, and 3 tablespoons salt. I pour it into my teakettle and boil it for fifteen minutes. I leave it overnight, then rinse it out in the morning before I make Arnold's tea. (Alice Ann Walker)

- When you're laundering your nice lace collars, cuffs, and scarves, add ½ cup of vinegar (the word can be traced to the French word for "sharp wine," or *vinaigre*) to the final rinse. Lay flat to dry in the sun. (Miss Dorothy Rogers)

- For a drain cleaner, mix 2 cups of salt, 2 cups of baking soda, and ⅛ cup of cream of tartar*. Store in a lidded container. To use, pour a little over one cup of this mixture down the drain. Let stand for about 20 minutes, and flush with cold water. For a stronger flush, dissolve 2 tablespoons of washing soda* in a quart of boiling water. Let stand for 15 minutes and repeat. Flush with hot water. (Verna Tidwell)

- To clean starch residue from the bottom of your flatirons (or your new electric iron), sprinkle a spoonful of salt on a cloth dampened with vinegar and rub the warm iron. (Elizabeth Lacy)

- If you need to remove mildew from clothing, furniture, or bathroom fixtures, use vinegar at full strength or mixed with water. Or if your dog smells like dog, rinse him with fresh water, then with a mixture of 1 cup white vinegar in 2 gallons of water. Dry without rinsing. (Myra May Mosswell)

Glossary

Borax is a naturally occurring mineral salt that is often used as a home cleaner, a stain remover on surfaces and clothes, a fabric and water softener, and a soap booster. You'll find it with the laundry products at the grocery.

Castile soap is a type of soap made from vegetable oil rather than animal fat or synthetic substances. You can find it in drugstores.

Cream of tartar (potassium bitartrate) is a by-product of winemaking that is used in food and as a cleansing agent. Small amounts may be purchased at a grocery; buy in bulk from a wine-making supplier.

Linseed oil (cold pressed from the seeds of flax, sometimes called flaxseed oil). Used as a wood treatment, it protects the surface. Available from paint stores.

Turpentine is distilled from pine resin, which is obtained by tapping trees of the genus *Pinus*. It is used as a solvent. Available from paint stores.

Washing soda (sodium carbonate, also known as soda ash) is a highly alkaline chemical compound which can be used to remove stubborn stains from laundry and for other cleaning purposes. Don't confuse washing soda with washing powder (powdered detergent) or with baking soda. Arm & Hammer washing soda is usually stocked with the bleach in the laundry aisle. If you don't find it in the national chains, try a local chain store, or ask a local grocer to order it for you.

Recipes

Several of these recipes list buttermilk as an ingredient. You can substitute milk (low-fat is fine) mixed with 1 tablespoon white vinegar or lemon juice per cup of liquid.

Euphoria's Saturday Night Special: Southern Fried Catfish and Hush Puppies

Southern Fried Catfish

Fish has long been a mainstay of Southern cooking, and every cook has her own special recipe. Traditionally, Southerners preferred white cornmeal, but you can substitute yellow. The paprika helps to brown the fish. Euphoria says to tell you that a cast-iron skillet is not absolutely required, but she certainly recommends it. (You might need two, actually. One for the catfish and the other for the hush puppies.)

8 catfish fillets (about 2 pounds)
1 cup buttermilk
2 teaspoons salt
1 teaspoon pepper
2 cups white or yellow cornmeal
1 cup all-purpose flour
1 teaspoon garlic powder
1 tablespoon paprika
Lard or corn or peanut oil for frying

Place fish in flat dish. Combine buttermilk, salt, and pepper, and pour over fish. Refrigerate at least four hours. Combine cornmeal, flour, garlic powder, and paprika in a pie plate or other similar dish. Remove fish from buttermilk mixture and dredge in the cornmeal mixture, one at a time, coating completely. (Really pat it on—and don't worry if the cornmeal mixture gets lumpy. If you need to, add more flour.) Melt lard or pour oil to depth of 2–3 inches in a cast-iron skillet; heat to 375°F. Fry fillets, a few at a time, about 4 minutes on each side or until golden brown. Drain on paper towels. Serve immediately.

Yield: 8 servings.

Hush Puppies

Hush puppies are thumb-sized deep-fried dumplings of corn-meal, traditionally served with fried catfish. Most of the explanations for the origin of the name have to do with keeping the dogs quiet. The most picturesque version involves Confederate soldiers preparing their meals over a campfire. If Yankee soldiers approached, the Rebs would silence the camp

dogs by tossing them some of their cornmeal cakes with "Hush,
puppies!" If you have a dog, you can experiment.

2 cups white or yellow cornmeal
1 cup all-purpose flour
¾ teaspoon salt
1 teaspoon baking powder
½ teaspoon baking soda
2 eggs, beaten
2 cups buttermilk
1 cup water
2 tablespoons melted bacon grease or other oil
Lard or oil for frying

In a large mixing bowl, combine cornmeal, flour, salt, baking powder, and baking soda. In a separate bowl, beat eggs, then stir in buttermilk, water, and bacon grease. (You can use another oil if you have to, although Euphoria says that would be a shame.) Make a well in the dry ingredients. Pour in the liquid ingredients and mix until batter is smooth and free of any lumps. It ought to be stiff. If it's too dry, add milk or water; too thin, add cornmeal. Experience is a great teacher.

In a cast-iron skillet (yes!) or a large, heavy fry pan over medium-high heat, heat lard or oil to 350° F or until a small amount of batter dropped into the hot oil sizzles and floats. (If the oil gets too hot, your hushpuppies will be doughy in the center.) Using two spoons, push a thumb-sized dollop of batter into the hot oil. Fry in small batches of 4 to 6 for approximately 5 minutes or until golden brown, turning to brown all sides. Remove from oil and drain on paper towels. You can keep these in a warm oven for about 30 minutes, until you've finished frying your catfish. Serve hot.

Makes 2 dozen hush puppies.

Aunt Hetty Little's Southern Comfort Cookies

1¼ cups flour
1½ teaspoons baking powder
⅛ teaspoon salt
½ cup pecan pieces
¾ cup golden raisins
½ cup sugar
¼ cup butter
2 eggs
¼ cup Southern Comfort whiskey
confectioners' sugar, for dusting

Combine flour, baking powder, salt, nuts, and raisins. In a separate bowl cream sugar and butter until light and fluffy. Beat in eggs, one at a time. To the egg mixture, alternately add whiskey and the flour mixture. Chill the batter at least 1 hour and then roll it into 1¼-inch-diameter logs. Wrap in wax paper and chill 4 hours. Slice ½-inch thick and place 1 inch apart on a baking sheet. Bake 8 minutes in a preheated 350°F oven. Cool and sprinkle with confectioners' sugar.

Makes about 3 dozen.

Aunt Hetty's Homemade Southern Comforter

Southern Comfort was first produced by Irish bartender Martin Wilkes Heron sometime in the 1880s in New Orleans' French Quarter. Heron moved to Memphis, Tennessee, in 1889, patented

*his booze, and began selling it in sealed bottles (to keep it from
being adulterated or diluted) with the labels "None Genuine
But Mine" and "Two per customer. No Gentleman would ask
for more." According to Master Distiller Chris Morris, the
original recipe for Southern Comfort began with bourbon and
included vanilla bean, lemon, cinnamon, cloves, cherries,
oranges, and honey. Aunt Hetty learned how to make her
"Southern Comforter" from her father, who claimed to have
misspent a portion of his youth in the French Quarter.*

1½ pounds fresh peaches
1 cup sugar
4 strips fresh lemon peel, about 2 inches long (don't include
    the bitter white pith)
4 whole cloves
1 cinnamon stick, about 2 inches long
2 cups bourbon or brandy

Peel, pit, and slice peaches. Place in a saucepan, add sugar,
and stir well. Warm over low heat until sugar is dissolved
and peaches are juicy. Place mixture into a large jar, add
lemon peel, cloves, cinnamon stick, and alcohol. Stir to combine. Cover and keep in a cool, dark place for 1 week, stirring
occasionally. Strain and filter, pressing out the liquid from
the peaches. Strain again. Homemade Southern Comforter is
ready for cooking after a week, for drinking after a month.

Elizabeth Lacy's Peach Pie

*Every Southern cook has a recipe for peach pie. Sally-Lou
taught Lizzy how to make this one. The almond-flavored
whipping cream topping is a perfect complement.*

Dough for 9-inch 2-crust pie
5 generous cups sliced peaches (5 to 7 large peaches)
Juice of ½ lemon
1 teaspoon almond flavoring
⅔ cup sugar
¼ cup flour
½ teaspoon cinnamon
⅛ teaspoon nutmeg
3 tablespoons butter, cut into bits

Lightly grease a 9-inch pie plate and line with half the pastry. Reserve remainder for top crust. Preheat oven to 425°F. (If you're using a glass pie pan, reduce heat by 25 degrees.) Peel peaches and slice into large bowl. Add lemon juice and almond flavoring and toss gently. In a separate bowl, mix together sugar, flour, cinnamon, and nutmeg. Add to peaches and mix well. Spoon into pastry and dot with butter. Roll out remaining dough. Moisten rim of bottom crust with water and put top crust in place. Trim overhanging pastry within 1 inch of edge, and fold top edge under bottom edge, pressing together to seal. Cut a few slits in top crust to allow steam to escape. Bake 45 to 50 minutes. Serve warm.

Almond Whipped Cream Topping

1 pint heavy whipping cream
½ teaspoon vanilla extract
1 teaspoon almond extract
¼ cup powdered sugar

Stir all the ingredients together in a mixing bowl, then whip the mixture with an egg beater until raised peaks form and hold their shape. (Modern cooks will want to use an electric beater.) Aunt Hetty says if you want to add a spoonful of her Southern Comforter to this, that would be fine.

Myra May's Mother's Sweet Potato Cake

Native Americans were already growing sweet potatoes (Ipomoea batatas) when Columbus arrived in 1492. Because they grow readily in warm regions, sweet potatoes became a staple food for Southern colonists and supplemented diets from late summer until spring. Most large plantations had a fenced sweet potato lot where low mounds of potatoes were grown, then dug and covered with straw and soil to protect them from the cold and frost of winter. During the War Between the States, when there were many shortages, the sweet potato—thinly sliced, dried, parched, ground, and brewed—became a substitute for coffee.

This recipe for sweet potato cake, perhaps descended from the many traditional recipes for sweet potato pudding, was handed down in Myra May's family for several generations. It is now a favorite at the Darling Diner.

½ cup butter or shortening
1 cup granulated sugar
1 cup packed brown sugar
2 eggs, beaten
1 cup cooked, peeled, and mashed sweet potatoes
3 cups all-purpose flour
4 teaspoons baking powder
¼ teaspoon baking soda
¼ teaspoon ginger

¼ teaspoon cinnamon
¼ teaspoon cloves
½ cup milk
1 cup chopped pecans
1 teaspoon maple or vanilla flavoring

Grease and flour 3 8-inch-round cake pans. Preheat oven to 350°F. Cream butter and sugars until light and fluffy. Beat in the eggs and sweet potatoes. In a separate bowl, mix together flour, baking powder, baking soda, and spices. Add dry ingredients alternately with milk to sweet potato mixture. (If batter seems too stiff, add 1 or 2 more tablespoons of milk.) Fold in nuts and flavoring. Spoon batter into cake pans. Bake for 30 minutes. Turn out on racks. Cool and frost with brown sugar icing.

Icing

1 cup confectioners' sugar
¾ cup (packed) dark brown sugar
½ cup whipping cream
¼ cup (½ stick) unsalted butter
¼ teaspoon vanilla flavoring

Sift confectioners' sugar into medium bowl. In a medium saucepan over medium-low heat, stir brown sugar, whipping cream, and butter until butter melts and sugar dissolves. Increase heat to medium-high and bring to boil. Boil 3 minutes, stirring occasionally. Remove from heat and stir in vanilla. Pour brown sugar mixture over confectioners' sugar, whisking. Whisk until smooth and lightened in color, about 1 minute. Cool icing until lukewarm and icing falls in heavy ribbon from spoon, whisking often, about 15 minutes. Stack layers, thinly icing between. Spoon icing thickly over top, allowing it to drip down sides of cake. Serve after icing is firm, at least 1 hour.

Bessie Bloodworth's Lemon Chess Squares

Chess pies and pastries are a traditional Southern dessert made with a filling of eggs, sugar, and butter, cooked in (or on) a pastry crust, with some sort of topping—basically, a cheeseless cheesecake. Some recipes include cornmeal, others are made with vinegar, and flavorings (vanilla, lemon juice, chocolate) are sometimes added. Some food historians believe that the word chess *is derived from the word* cheese. *Others believe that it is a dialect form of the word* chest, *referring to a pie safe or chest, where pies were often kept. And then there is the tale of the cook who, when asked the name of her pie, replied, "Oh, it's jes' pie." Whatever the derivation and whatever its form, chess pastries are a treat.*

2 cups flour
½ cup confectioners' sugar
¼ teaspoon salt
1 cup butter or shortening
4 eggs
2 cups sugar
2 tablespoons flour
2 tablespoons white or yellow cornmeal
½ cup melted butter
4 tablespoons lemon juice
confectioners' sugar for dusting

Preheat oven to 350°F. To make the crust, sift together the flour, sugar, and salt. Cut in the butter, using two knives or a pastry blender. Mix well and pat into a 10- x 15-inch cookie sheet. Bake for 15 minutes.

Beat remaining ingredients and pour over baked crust. Return to oven and bake for another 15 minutes. Sprinkle with confectioners' sugar when done. Cut into squares when cool.

Reading List

Here are a few of the many documents I found useful as background reading for this book in the Darling Dahlias series and a very brief explanation of the reasons for their inclusion.

Books

Daily Life in the United States 1920–1940: How Americans Lived Through the Roaring Twenties and the Great Depression, by David E. Kyvig. Helpful period background.

Dry Goods, Butler Brothers 1934 general merchandise catalog. What people were wearing and using during the early thirties.

Everyday Fashions of the Thirties as Pictured in Sears Catalogs, edited by Stella Blum. Helpful period descriptions of clothing styles, fabrics, materials.

Get Capone: The Secret Plot That Captured America's Most Famous Gangster, by Jonathan Eig. The real story of how the Feds nabbed Al Capone. Detailed, highly evocative of the life and times of gangland Chicago.

Happenings in Old Monroeville, Vol. 2, by George Thomas Jones. Monroeville local history from the thirties.

Mae West: It Ain't No Sin, by Simon Louvish. Life as a vaudeville burlesque queen (before becoming a movie star) wasn't easy, even for Mae West.

Month-by-Month Gardening in Alabama, by Bob Polomski. What Alabama gardeners might be doing at different seasons of the year.

The Ponder Heart, by Eudora Welty. Wonderful Southern voice.

To Kill a Mockingbird, by Harper Lee. Harper Lee grew up in Monroeville (the source for her descriptions of Maycomb, where *TKM* is set). Monroeville is only fifteen miles from Darling.

Websites

Ziegfeld 101, Biography Part III, by John Kenrick: http://www.musicals101.com/ziegbio3.htm. Last accessed 6.27.2010. The story of Ziegfeld's Frolics (yes, the overhead glass walkway is real!).

Historical Documents Relating to Al Capone: http://www.irs.gov/foia/article/0,,id=179352,00.html. Background documents (letters, reports) written by the investigators who dug up the dirt on Al Capone, released and published online by the IRS in 2008.

Newspaper Archives: http://www.newspaperarchive.com/. A subscription website that allows you to search, read, clip, and save newspapers from the United States and around the world.